ISABEL'S RUN

by

M.D. GRAYSON

 cedar coast press

Published by Cedar Coast Press LLC
www.cedarcoastpress.com

This book is a work of fiction. Names, characters, places, and incidents are either the product of the author's imagination or are used fictitiously. Any resemblance to actual persons, living or dead, or to actual events or locales is entirely coincidental.

ISABEL'S RUN

Cover designed by M.D. Grayson

Cover art:
Copyright © iStockPhoto #10519930_Woman Walking in Street by Burak Pekakcan

Visit the author website:
www.mdgrayson.com.

ISBN-978-0-9849518-3-3 (eBook)
ISBN-978-0-9849518-6-4 (Paperback)

Library of Congress Control Number: 2012949644
Version 2012.09.24

Printed in the United States of America

10 9 8 7 6 5 4 3 2 1

*This novel is dedicated
to the 100,000+ children
caught in the web of child
prostitution in America today
with the hope and a prayer that
their dark nightmares will end
and their tomorrows will rise up
to greet them with with all the
joy and happiness to which
they are entitled.*

Prologue

Tuesday, May 8, 2012
4:45 p.m.

ISABEL DELGADO WAS in trouble. She sneaked a glance out of the corner of her eye as the uniformed security guard approached. She was seated on an iron bench outside the Terraces food court, pretending to be absorbed in a directory brochure of the Alderwood Mall in Lynnwood, Washington. The guard drew closer. *Not again*, Isabel thought. She fought to remain calm. She'd already been run off earlier in the day by a different guard when she'd been unable to come up with a quick answer as to why she was hanging around in the same area all morning long. That guard threatened to call the police and have her arrested for loitering if he saw her again. Isabel had left in a hurry. She'd completely circled the mall, figuring that the guard wouldn't wait that long to catch her again. But in the end she had nowhere to go, so now, three hours later, she was back, and another guard was approaching.

Isabel had no desire to push her luck, but she was out of ideas, and she was out of prospects. She'd tried to lay low since the earlier episode while she waited for something to happen, and she'd been pretty successful—no one had even talked to her except for a cute girl with red hair a couple of hours ago who'd said that she, too, was running. But then the girl suddenly left ten minutes later, and Isabel was alone again. Since then: nobody. Which was fine with her. She knew she needed to do something—but she didn't want to make a mistake. Above all, she didn't want to be sent back home—couldn't be sent back home. She'd decided that if she were arrested, she'd lie about who she was so that they couldn't send her back. Meanwhile, she waited—waited for something to happen.

She used her peripheral vision and concentrated on the new guard. He was younger. If he stopped, maybe he'd be nicer. From twenty-five feet away, she could hear his footsteps as he approached, keys jangling quietly at his side. He whistled softly to himself, the same quiet, absent-minded way her father used to whistle when he came up the walkway to the house at the end of the day. Suddenly, the guard's radio crackled and came to life, causing him to stop before he reached her. Isabel was startled, but she caught herself—she didn't look up.

The guard listened and then keyed his microphone. "Unit Two, roger," he said. "I'll be there in five." At least his voice sounded kind.

He resumed his approach. Isabel suppressed a shudder as the man paused when he reached her. She felt him looking at her. *Steady, now.* She looked up. The guard was tall and nice looking. Isabel thought he had kind eyes.

The guard looked at her for a moment. Finally, he smiled. "Hey there. What's going on?"

Isabel fought back the urge to panic. She was a quick learner and, after the last encounter, she'd prepared a story. "I'm waiting for my mom." She trembled inside but she worked hard to keep her voice even as she used the words she'd rehearsed in her mind. "She's picking me up."

"That right?" The guard considered this. "If she's picking you up, how come you're not waiting down at the benches by the curb?" He paused and looked at her. "Say," he added. "Aren't you the girl who we ran off earlier this morning?"

Isabel tensed up and started to panic. She hadn't expected that particular follow-up question, and she was unprepared. She felt a quick surge of adrenaline. All she could manage for an answer was a quick shake of her head.

The guard studied her for a second—an eternity for Isabel. He pursed his lips, saying nothing, as if weighing whether or not to buy her story. Then, apparently coming to a decision, he reached for his radio. Just as he was about to key his microphone, though, he was interrupted.

"There you are!" Isabel jumped. She turned and saw an attractive young woman in her early twenties walking up the sidewalk, talking to her. Isabel had no idea who she was.

"I got mixed up," the woman said, smiling brightly as she reached the two. "I thought we were supposed to meet at the front of the mall." She turned to the guard, who'd frozen for a moment. "It's okay, officer. She's with me." She turned back to Isabel, "C'mon, sweetie. Let's go inside and grab a drink before we take off."

Isabel looked at the woman for a moment. She was dressed in a loose, shimmering green knit sweater over a white blouse. She wore tight black slacks and black shoes with heels so tall that Isabel wondered how she could stand up. Her dark brown hair cascaded over her shoulders in loose curls. Even her perfume smelled wondeful. She was one of the most beautiful women Isabel had ever seen. The woman made a small, urgent gesture with her head as if to say "C'mon."

Isabel felt the guard staring at her, so she made up her mind quickly. "Sure," she said, standing. "Let's go."

The woman smiled and took Isabel's arm. Together, they left the guard standing on the sidewalk, watching them. They turned and walked through the double doors into the food court. Once inside, the woman said, "C'mon. Let's sit over here for a minute and talk." She led Isabel to a nearby table.

The food court at the mall is a large open area of dining tables surrounded by restaurants. There were few shoppers there—the lunchtime crowd had left, and the evening shoppers had yet to arrive. The smells of the food from the different shops instantly reminded Isabel that she was hungry.

"Whew, that was a close one, huh?" the woman said as she scanned the area around their table. She turned back to face Isabel. "I'm Crystal. What's your name?"

"Isabel." To say that Isabel was confused would be a big understatement.

Crystal looked around again and then back at Isabel. "I couldn't help but overhear you talking to the guard, Isabel. It sounded like you might need rescuing. Are you really waiting for your mom?"

Isabel shuttered. "Yes," she lied. She didn't know this woman. "She's coming to pick me up."

Crystal smiled. "Good." She studied Isabel intently for several seconds. "Have you been waiting long?"

Isabel couldn't very well tell Crystal the real story—that she'd spent last night under the cedar tree by the trash bins, remaining out of sight of the roving security guards. Yet, despite her need to be guarded, she thought there was something about this woman that offered an invitation—a glimmer of hope. Something in her eyes and her tone of voice made Isabel think that Crystal might be someone who could help her. She certainly didn't want to relive the frightening experience of spending the night under the cedar tree again.

Isabel nodded. "A little while."

Crystal nodded slowly. "Can I buy you a Coke or something? While you wait?"

Isabel figured in the worst case, at least she'd be safe from the security guards for a while. "Okay," she said. Crystal bought them a couple of drinks from one of the vendors and returned to their table.

The two chatted about nothing in particular—food choices, the way this or that person was dressed, movies. After a few minutes had passed, though, Crystal's tone suddenly changed, and she became serious. "Can I ask you a real question, Isabel?" she said.

"Yeah."

Crystal continued to study her. "You're not really waiting for your mom, are you."

Isabel tensed up. Crystal had phrased it in the form of a statement, not a question. "Yes, I am," she protested. "Why do you say that?"

Crystal shrugged. Her eyes bored into Isabel. "Because we've been sitting here for oh—twenty minutes or so, and you haven't looked back at the door even once the whole time. You forgot your story."

Oh, hell. Isabel was mortified to realize that Crystal was right. She'd been so relieved to have someone to talk to that she'd completely forgotten she'd said she was waiting to be picked up. She tensed up and then started to push away from the table.

"It's alright," Crystal said, reaching across and putting her hand on Isabel's arm. "No need to leave. Don't worry about it. I'm not the police or security or anything like that."

Isabel stayed seated but kept her chair pushed back.

Crystal looked at Isabel intently for several moments. "You're running, aren't you, sweetheart?"

Isabel fought hard, but in the end, the weight of the last few days got to her, and she couldn't keep tears from forming in her eyes. She hesitated, and then she nodded.

Crystal produced a tissue and handed it to Isabel. Isabel wiped her eyes and said, "Thanks."

"It's nothing to be ashamed of, you know—running," Crystal said. "Sometimes, you've got to do what you've got to do, know what I mean?"

Isabel nodded.

"Did someone hurt you?"

Isabel studied the table without answering.

Crystal looked at Isabel. It was silent for a minute, and then she said, "I was just like you, you know."

"What do you mean?"

"I mean I ran. I had to leave—probably about your age. What are you sixteen? Seventeen?"

"Sixteen," Isabel said. "Yesterday was my birthday."

Crystal smiled brightly. "Happy birthday!" Then, just as quick, her smile vanished. "Did you leave on your birthday?"

Isabel nodded, tears starting again.

"That's dope. That takes guts," Crystal said. "You should be proud."

Isabel stared at her, then she looked down. "I had to leave," she said quietly.

Crystal leaned forward. "Isabel," she said, "look at me."

Isabel looked up.

"It's like I said—I know what you mean. I had two stepbrothers who took turns raping me for six years starting when I was ten years old," Crystal said. "When you say 'I had to leave,' I know exactly what you mean. *I* had to leave, too."

Isabel stared at her. "Really?"

"Really. I couldn't stay another day." Crystal rolled up the sleeve on her left arm and revealed a series of scars. "See these? I used to cut myself to make the pain go away." Isabel cringed at the thought. Crystal noticed. "You don't cut yourself, do you?"

Isabel shook her head. "No."

"Good girl. A lot of girls do, you know. But it doesn't work. The little pain's supposed to make the big pain go away. But it only works for a little while. Then you find out that the big pain's still there. And to top it off, you're left with these fucking scars." She rolled her sleeve back down. She looked at Isabel. "I understand where you're coming from, Isabel. I was right where you were five years ago."

It was quiet for a few moments. Then Isabel said, "It's my stepfather."

Crystal nodded.

"For more than four years now."

"Bastard. I'm so sorry, sweetie."

Isabel nodded.

"I hate how these fuckers think they can do this to us and get away with it."

Isabel nodded. "You really went through the same thing?" She could hardly believe that this beautiful woman had once experienced a horror similar to her own.

Crystal nodded. "Really. I showed you the scars, didn't I?" She paused.

"At least the scars that show. Most of 'em don't, you know."

Isabel looked at her for a second and then said, "What about now? What do you do now?"

Crystal smiled and flipped her long hair back over her shoulder. "I got lucky," she said. "I met a really great guy. Now, I work with him in his company; we do entertainment scheduling."

"You are lucky. You're really beautiful."

Crystal smiled. "Thank you. But you should know—you're as pretty as I am, sweetie. Maybe even prettier."

"Me?" Isabel said. She found this hard to believe.

Crystal laughed as she pretended to look around; then she returned her focus to Isabel. "Who else is here, girl? Yeah, you. A little makeup, some nice clothes," she waved her hand at Isabel, "you'd have guys falling all over you. And I mean good guys. Guys who have lots of money and who'll treat you right." Crystal seemed absolutely bubbly.

Isabel rolled her eyes. Given her situation at home, she didn't think about boys very often. This was more than she could even imagine.

"Isabel," Crystal said, leaning forward again and speaking softly. "Listen to me. You seem like a sweet girl. And I know where you're coming from because I was in the exact same boat."

Isabel nodded.

Crystal continued. "Donnie—he's my boyfriend—Donnie and I have a spare bedroom. If you want, I can ask him if it'd be okay if you stay with us for a little while—until you're on your feet, I mean. You'd have a safe place to stay, plenty to eat. I'll even take you shopping for some nice clothes."

Isabel hesitated. "Why would you do that?" she asked. It had been a long time since anyone other than her friend Kelli had been nice to her. She couldn't help being suspicious.

Crystal smiled. "Because I guess I see a little bit of me in you, that's why. And I sure wish someone would have helped me out when I was in your situation."

This resonated with Isabel. Things were moving fast, but at least they seemed to be moving in the right direction. Still, she hadn't planned things out this far, and she was struggling to keep up.

"By the way," Crystal said, "if you left yesterday, where'd you stay last night?"

Isabel looked down. "Under a tree," she said.

"Oh, sweetie," Crystal said, smiling, "you gotta stay with us. You don't want to do that again, do you?"

That reminder, plus the realization that she had no other real options, pushed Isabel over the edge. "I don't suppose it would hurt to stay with you guys for a while," she said. "I don't have any money to pay you, though."

Crystal smiled. "I didn't ask you for any money, did I?"

Isabel shook her head.

Crystal reached for her purse. "Let me call Donnie and ask him, alright?"

Isabel nodded. "Okay. Thanks."

* * * *

Twenty minutes later, Isabel and Crystal stood at the curb near the valet parking stand. Isabel wore her backpack and carried her purse. Soon, a white BMW 750i pulled up. All of the windows were darkened, so it was impossible to see inside. "Here he is," Crystal said.

Isabel didn't know much about cars, but she recognized the BMW logo and was impressed. The car was very shiny—even the wheels were sparkling chrome. The driver parked the car alongside the curb and got out. He was a tall, very good-looking, young black man with his hair cut short. He wore black slacks and a tight-fitting, short-sleeved black Under Armour shirt, covered with a loose-fitting burgundy linen jacket. A large, expensive-looking gold watch was just visible on his left wrist, peeking out from under the sleeve of his jacket.

As the driver walked around the front of the car to the curb, the passenger door opened, and another young man stepped out. He was shorter—average height and his skin was paler than the driver's.. His hair was straightened, gelled, and brushed back. He, too, was nicely dressed—a sharp young man. Both men made an impression on Isabel. They were as good-looking in their own right as Crystal was in hers. To Isabel, they all looked like wealthy fashion models.

"Hey, baby," the driver said as he walked up to Crystal and hugged her. "You all done?"

"Think so," Crystal said.

"Good," the man said. "We are, too." After a few moments, he glanced over at Isabel. He let Crystal go and said, "Is this your friend?"

"Uh-huh," Crystal said. "Donnie Martin—this is Isabel—" she turned and looked at Isabel, "—Isabel, I don't know your last name."

"Delgado," Isabel said.

"Isabel Delgado," Crystal said.

Donnie walked over to her. He towered above her by more than a foot. "Isabel," he said, reaching for her small hand. "What a beautiful name." His voice was smooth and deep.

Isabel blushed. "Thanks," she said. "It's good to meet you."

"The pleasure is all mine," Donnie said. His smile revealed a gleaming set of perfectly capped white teeth. He nodded toward the other man. "This ugly dude over here is my homeboy DeMichael. His friends—we— all call him Mikey."

DeMichael stepped over and shook Isabel's hand. Isabel thought his hands were very soft—softer even than hers. "I'm very pleased to meet you, Isabel," he said. "Does everyone call you Isabel, or do you have a nickname? Something like Belle or Bella—like that girl in *Twilight?*"

Isabel blushed slightly. "Some of my friends call me Izzy," she said.

"Izzy," he said. "That's even better. I like that. If you're straight with it, I'm gonna call you Izzy."

Isabel smiled. "Okay," she said, nodding.

DeMichael gazed admiringly at Isabel's hair. "Girl, you have beautiful hair," he said. "Long and thick and pure black." He paused and then added, "Like mine!"

Crystal laughed. "Yeah, you wish. Except Izzy doesn't have to spend a hundred dollars and two hours getting hers straightened every two weeks."

DeMichael reached for Isabel's hair then stopped. "Do you mind?" he asked.

"No," Isabel said.

DeMichael ran his hand slowly through Isabel's hair. "That's dope," he said, seemingly in awe. "And you don't have to do anything to get this?"

"No," Isabel said. "That's just how it is."

"Damn," he said.

"Imagine if we hooked her up with Janeka," Crystal said. "She can throw some conditioner on that, and Isabel's hair will shine like a black diamond."

"Say, look," Donnie interrupted from the sidewalk at the front of the car. "Y'all can share hair-styling secrets later. Right now, I need to talk to Isabel for a second, and then we got to scoot." He turned to Isabel. "Crystal tells me you having some problems on the home front."

Isabel looked him in the eye. "I don't have a home," she said. "Not anymore."

"That's what I'm talkin' about," Donnie said. "Bottom line—you're temporarily out on the streets. Right?"

"I guess."

Donnie smiled. "Don't have to be that way, baby—this is your lucky day. Crystal told you we got a spare bedroom."

Isabel nodded.

"Good. You're welcome to come stay with us for a while. Till you get yourself established. That sound okay?"

"It does," Isabel said. "Thank you."

Donnie smiled again. "Good. We gonna do some great things." He looked at her backpack. "That all your stuff?"

Isabel nodded. "That's it."

"Y'all travelin' light."

"I know."

He shrugged. "That'll change. Crystal'll probably hook you up with some of her stuff for now. Use it as an excuse to go shoppin'."

"Hell with that," Crystal said. "I don't need no excuse. Me and my homey Izzy—we're going shoppin' anyway. Tomorrow. Right, Iz?"

Isabel hesitated, then started to speak, but Crystal interrupted her. "I know," she said. "You don't have any money for shopping." She smiled. "Good thing for you, I do. You can owe me. We're going to get you all done up. Your hair, too. You'll be so dope, people'll have to wear sunglasses around you just to knock back the shine!"

Isabel smiled as DeMichael opened the back door.

"I'm riding shotgun," Crystal suddenly called out.

DeMichael looked at Isabel. "Guess that means me and you in the back. After you, my dear," he said gallantly. Isabel crawled into the back seat. She could hardly believe her luck. Less than twenty-four hours ago, she'd been shivering the night away hiding under a cedar tree to avoid the guards and to keep from getting rained on. An hour ago, she'd been sitting on a bench with no idea how to proceed. Now, she was sitting in a BMW, surrounded by nice people who wanted to help her out. She smiled as the car pulled away from the curb.

PART 1

Chapter 1

"CEASE FIRE! CEASE fire!" The Range Safety Officer's voice thundered down the line just as the last shooter fired his final round of the stage. The electronic noise-canceling features in my headset were designed to muffle the sharp reports of gunshots while still allowing voice commands to come through loud and clear—not that Gunny Doug Owens needed any help getting his point across. Twenty-one years in the Marine Corps prior to joining the Seattle Police Department as head firearms instructor gave him a "command voice" that left no confusion, no ambiguity as to the meaning of his message. Like many of the tough old sergeants I'd known in the army, Gunny Owens didn't so much speak when he was on the range; he barked. It reminded me of basic training at Fort Benning.

I lowered my Les Baer Thunder Ranch Model 1911 .45-caliber semiauto to a forty-five degree angle, finger indexed along the barrel. Keeping it pointed downrange, I turned my head quickly in each direction, automatically scanning the area around me for new threats, just as Gunny barked out, "Weapons to low ready!"

He followed this up a second later with, "Unload and make safe!" The slide on my weapon had automatically locked open when I'd fired the last round. I pressed the magazine release button, and the empty magazine dropped out and fell to the ground.

"After inspection by a Range Safety Officer, holster your safe weapon."

The RSO on my side of the line worked his way from shooter to shooter, checking their weapons as he went and tapping them on the shoulders when he was satisfied their weapons were completely empty, signifying it was okay to holster their weapon. I waited my turn as the gentle breeze cleared the smoke from the range.

When Gunny saw that the assistant RSOs on either side of the line had completed their inspections, he barked out "Line clear on the left?" The assistant RSO on my side of the line held up his hand in acknowledgment. "Line clear on the right?" The officer on the opposite end of the line did the same.

"Good," Gunny said. "Ladies and gentlemen, the line is clear! You may remove your hearing protection. Retrieve your magazines, and let's check targets."

It was a beautiful morning on June 5, 2012. The temperature was in the high sixties, and the sky was partly cloudy. My partner, Antoinette "Toni" Blair, and I had just fired the last sequence in the Washington State Basic Law Enforcement Firearm Training course at the Seattle Police Athletic Association range in Tukwila, just south of Seattle. This is the same test issued to retired law enforcement officers annually and, other than Toni and me, the thirteen guys on the line were all retired police officers. Thanks to the Law Enforcement Officers Safety Act that Congress passed in 2004, successfully passing this test gave these retired officers the right to carry concealed weapons almost anywhere in the nation. Can you say instant extended police force? At no additional cost? Clearly, this was one of Congress's smarter moves, if you ask me. Of course, Toni and I were not law enforcement officers, so passing the test wouldn't give us the same privileges. But the practice kept us sharp, and it helped keep our insurance premiums low. And if, God forbid, we ever had to shoot anyone, regular documented training would probably help us legally. We were fortunate that my friends at Seattle PD allowed us to train with them and use the range.

I reached down and picked up my empty magazine, dusted it off, and put it in my pocket. Toni was two shooters to my left; I saw her do the same thing. At twenty-seven years old, she'd just had a birthday two weeks ago. She was dressed in camouflage-print fatigue-style pants that had no business looking as good as they did on her, green tactical boots, and a beige long-sleeved T-shirt that had an American flag and *Made in the U.S.A.* printed on it in big, bold red letters across the chest—just in case you were having trouble noticing the way she filled out the shirt (which, I suppose, would have been pretty good proof that you were legally blind). The other guys didn't know it, but I knew that the long sleeves covered a full-sleeve tattoo on her left arm and a delicate little Celtic-weave tat on her right. Her thick, dark hair was covered with a backward-facing baseball cap, itself covered with her ear-protection headset. She wore yellow-tinted shooter's glasses. She looked like a Victoria's Secret model at a gun show—she was distracting as hell, and I was glad there was space between us. When we straightened up, she caught me looking and she smiled.

Oops. This wasn't one of her "I love you" smiles or even one of her playful ones, for that matter. We've been friends for a long time—I've known her for more than five years. I've seen her use about twenty different smiles—she's got one for every occasion. I know most of them pretty well, but as for this one, her meaning was quite clear. She was giving me the nasty, evil little grin that usually comes when we're locked in competition. We both hate to lose, and shooting qualifications bring out our competitive natures. She looked pretty smug—must have fired another clean stage. I turned away and started walking downrange to inspect my target.

"Holy crap, Nichols!" Gunny yelled as he inspected the first shooter's target. "You do know you're supposed to be shooting target number one, right? You fired five rounds, but I only see three damn holes!" He turned and looked at the next target on the line. "You got any extra holes on your target?" he said to that target's shooter. "Nope?" He turned back to the first unlucky guy. "Nichols, you had two rounds off the whole damn target! That's pathetic. Ten points each—it's going to cost you a twenty-point penalty." He shook his head with disgust. "What's worse, if this were real life, that means you'd be the proud owner of two .40-caliber projectiles flying through the air at 1,100 feet per second looking for something solid to hit besides their intended target." He looked at the sheepish shooter. "You understand that's bad, right?"

The man nodded. "Sorry, Gunny."

"Yeah, you are," Gunny nodded in agreement. "Looks like we'll be seeing you back here this afternoon."

Gunny moved down the line, examining each shooter's target. His comments were usually short and to the point. "You pushed this one," or "You flinched before you pulled the trigger here, see? Caused you to jerk low left." The shooters—all experienced police officers with years and years of training—listened carefully. Gunny Owens was held in universal high esteem. He'd forgotten more about shooting than most of us would ever know.

He reached Toni's target and stared at it for a second. "Holy hell, she's doing it again!" he called out. The other shooters turned to look at Toni's target. "This young lady," he said, "—a civilian, I might add—qualifies on this very course every ninety days without fail. And I have never—I repeat never—seen her put a round outside the ten ring. Look at this shooting here. Y'all should do so well. Excellent! Well done, young lady." Toni smiled demurely. "A solid 250," Gunny said. "Perfect score."

Gunny continued down the line until he reached my target. He examined it carefully, counting the number of holes. When he was finished, he turned to me. "Staff Sergeant Logan, did you yank one off the target?" Gunny liked to call me by my former military rank.

"Hell no, Gunny," I said. "Look here." I pointed to one of the bullet holes in the center of the target that was a bit more oblong than the others.

Gunny leaned forward and inspected the hole. "Oh, yeah," he said, smiling. "I see. Same damn hole." He stood up. "Folks, listen up! Another perfect score from the other civilian in the group." He paused for a moment, and then he continued. "Although technically, I ain't sure you can call him a civilian—he's former U.S. Army 101st Airborne. It don't happen often, but from time to time, the army turns out a damn fine shooter. Right, son?" That was about as high a compliment as an army grunt's likely to get out of a marine (MARINE: "Muscle are Required—Intelligence Not Essential").

"Hooah, Gunny!" I yelled out. You better believe it.

"Damn right," he said, nodding his head sharply. He turned and continued his inspection.

After he finished with the last shooter, he returned to the center of the line. "Gentlemen, and Ms. Blair," he said, "Y'all gather round." When we'd formed in a group around him, he said, "One of y'all's coming back this afternoon." He turned to the offender. "That's you, Nichols. I want you to practice with Officer Mendez here," he pointed at one of his assistant RSOs, "right after lunch: 1300 hours. If you're ready, you'll get another shot at qualifying at 1400. We'll see if you can keep all your rounds on your own target this time." He looked at the rest of us. "As for the rest of you—you've all officially qualified. Congratulations." The men nodded their heads quietly. They'd done this before and most were good—if not very good—shooters.

"Before you leave, though, we do have a dilemma," Gunny continued. "We have a tie for top honors—two perfect scores." *Here we go*, I thought. *Same as last time.* "And as some of you may know, I don't like to end things with a tie. No closure that way. So what say we have ourselves a quick little tiebreaker shoot-out?"

"Yeah!" the men agreed enthusiastically.

"Good. Randy—do me a favor and throw a couple of clean targets on lanes three and four, would you? The rest of you, follow me."

Gunny walked us back past the fifteen-yard marker where we'd fired the last sequence. He kept walking, past the twenty-five yard marker until he reached a marker that said thirty-five yards. "We'll do it from here," he said. "Make it interesting. A little over one hundred feet—a *real* test. Ms. Blair—you're on number three. Staff Sergeant Logan—you're on lane four. Everybody else: behind the line." I looked downrange at the small targets. One hundred feet is a long pistol shot if you have something solid to brace against. Without a brace, it was *really* long.

He waited until the targets were set and everybody was behind us. "Okay, you two," he said. "I want you to load one round—and one round only—into a magazine. This will be a one shot, do-or-die competition. We'll run you through one at a time. Who wants to go first?"

"I will," Toni said quickly. I looked at her, and we locked eyes. She no doubt was trying to psych me out. *Good luck with that.*

"Ladies first, then," Gunny said. "Oh, I forgot. We'll use the electronic timer. You'll start from the low ready position, two hand grip—or one hand if you want. Your choice of stances. When the timer beeps, you're to raise your weapon and fire. You'll have two seconds to get your shot off before the timer beeps again. If you go over, the timer will tell us, and you'll be DQ'd. So don't go over time."

Two seconds! Two seconds was very fast from thirty-five yards. I glanced at Toni. If she was concerned, she didn't show it. She was already concentrating on the target.

"You two ready?" We nodded.

"Okay, everyone. Hearing protection on!" Gunny reverted to command voice.

"Shooter number one, at this time, load and make ready!" Toni slapped a magazine into her Glock 23 and cycled the slide.

"Shooter, assume a low ready position!"

Toni crouched down, her weapon held before her pointed toward the ground at a forty-five degree angle.

"Shooter, watch your target!"

BEEP! The electronic timer sounded. Toni instantly raised her weapon, sighted, and one second later, fired. *BOOM!*, followed nearly instantly by *BEEP!* as the timer sounded again. Toni had beaten the clock by a fraction of a second.

Everyone looked downrange and strained to see the bullet hole in the target. "One point eight seven seconds, and she's in the bottle," Gunny called out, "chin level, just a hair right of center. Seven points. That's fine shooting from thirty-five yards, young lady. Especially in under two seconds." The "bottle" is the broad, bottle-shaped area of the target that includes the upper torso and the neck up to the center of the head. Toni's shot was very nearly right on the centerline in the "neck" of the bottle, but it fell midway between the four-inch diameter "ten" ring centered around the top of the target's nose and the six-inch diameter "ten" ring centered around the target's heart—in other words, just under the chin. It was an outstanding shot, but looking at Toni, I could tell right away she was not happy. She felt me staring, turned to me, and stuck her tongue out.

"The bad guy is definitely down," Gunny said. "Probably for good, I'd say. But—with a score of seven," he smiled with a nasty grin, "the door got left open for the staff sergeant just a hair. Ms. Blair, go ahead and unload and make safe." Toni released her empty magazine and held her pistol up for inspection by one of the assistant RSOs. He patted her on the shoulder, and she holstered her weapon. The RSO turned to Gunny and raised his hand.

"The line is clear," Gunny said. "Let's see if shooter number two can take advantage."

As I stepped up to the line, Toni said, "Check your fly, dude." I smiled. Psych!

I was in a tough spot. This was going to be a difficult shot. I like to win as much as she does. Lord knows she would've liked nothing better than to beat me on the firing range. In four years, it had never happened before. If she won one, she'd be delighted. This could be a good thing. Maybe it was her time. Thinking about it made me consider maybe giving her one—pulling the shot on purpose. But if I did that, I still needed to make it close. She knows I'm a good shot, and if she suspected I'd thrown the round, she'd have my ass. I made my decision.

"Shooter number two, load and make ready!" I slapped the magazine with the single round into my sidearm, released the slide, and lowered the weapon to the low ready position.

"Shooter, watch your target!" I crouched and tightened my grip.

BEEP! All at once, the outside world seemed to recede. Everything switched to slow motion and all my training kicked in. As my arms came up to target, my right thumb pushed the safety lever to the off position. During the same motion, I took one deep breath, then held it. My arms steadied on the target. My eyes instantly found the front sight, and the front sight centered on the target's head. With all my concentration, I focused on the front sight. Steady. Squeeze. *BOOM!* The round fired. *BEEP!* The timer sounded. I didn't need to look.

* * * *

We said our good-byes to Gunny Owens at 11:00 and jumped in my red Jeep for the drive back to our office. Our company is Logan Private Investigations—or Logan PI, as we like to call it. We have a small office on Westlake Avenue on Lake Union, right in the middle of Seattle, less than a mile from I-5. Unfortunately, the south end of Lake Union where we're located was currently wrecked by construction. Microsoft cofounder Paul Allen had decided to single-handedly rebuild Seattle, and he was starting with the South Lake Union area. As a result, traffic was stop-and-go. Actually, more stop than go—it was going to take a while. I hit the play button on the MP3 player, and the sound of a very sweet piano started to flow from the speakers.

Toni listened carefully when the singer started. "Is that—is that Brandi Carlile?" she asked.

"Yep."

"I've never heard this before."

"I know. That's because it's brand-new. It's called *Bear Creek*. Just released today. This song is called 'That Wasn't Me.'"

She listened for a minute, tapping her foot to the beat. Then she said, "Awesome. I love it. She sounds like Adele."

I considered this. "Yeah a little, maybe. On this song, anyway. Maybe a bit more country."

We listened to the new music for a minute while we waited for the traffic to move. Toni's cell phone rang, and I turned the music down.

"Okay," she said into the phone. "Tell her to wait. We're down by the park—only about a half mile away. As soon as traffic moves, we'll be there."

She hung up and turned to me. "That was Kenny. He says Kelli's at the office."

Kelli—Racquel Genevieve Blair—is Toni's eighteen-year-old little sister. I hadn't seen Kelli in a couple of months, although we'd been planning to go to her high school graduation the following week.

"He say what she wants?" I asked.

"She wants to talk. To you and me both."

Curious.

* * * *

Twenty-five minutes later, we walked into our office. No one was in the lobby, so we made our way toward the back, where we heard laughter coming from the office of Kenny Hale—our technology guru. I followed Toni into Kenny's office. He was at his desk with Kelli sitting across from him.

"Hey, guys," Kenny said when we entered.

"'Sup?" I said, looking from Kenny to Kelli. "Hey, Kelli."

Kelli and Toni look the same but different. Bear with me—I haven't lost my mind here. Toni's tall—a solid five foot eight. Kelli's a touch shorter—maybe five seven or so. Both girls have striking figures—something they inherited from their mom, I suppose (although I'm not sure I'm supposed to have noticed that). Both have thick, dark hair, although Kelli's is long with no bangs and more of a brunette color, while Toni's is more mid-length with long bangs and almost black. The biggest, most noticeable difference, though, is not their height or their hair, but their eyes. Toni's eyes are a brilliant blue—the color of the Hope Diamond. Kelli's are a deep emerald green. Both are beautiful. So, like I said—the girls look the same but definitely different.

"Hi, Danny," she said. She turned to Toni. "Hey, sis."

Toni walked over to Kelli. "Hi, sweetie," she said, leaning forward and hugging her sister. She straightened up and eyed Kenny warily. "I see you've met Kenny." Kelli probably missed the look. I didn't.

"Yeah," she said. "We've just been talking."

Kenny's a young guy—he just turned twenty-six a couple of months ago. He's maybe five eight and a buck fifty soaking wet. He's got an unruly mop of dark hair that he pushes over to one side. In fact, he looks just like what he is—the quintessential computer geek. When it comes to anything to do with computers, Kenny's the real deal. He's got aptitude and native talent that's off the charts. He grew up with computers in ground zero of the computer world: Redmond, Washington. I'm not certain, but I'd be willing to bet his first toy was a laptop. Knowing Kenny, he probably took it apart, tricked it out some way, and then put it back together. He's got to be one of the most brilliant PC dudes in the Pacific Northwest. His consulting services are in high demand—I'm sure he makes at least as much moonlighting for the big tech companies around here as he does from his Logan PI paycheck. Still, lucky for us, he likes the excitement of detective work. I say "lucky for us" because computer skills are a near prerequisite for PI firms these days.

Despite the fact that he's no physical specimen, Kenny is surprisingly successful with the ladies. I have a theory about this. I think that like a lot of nerdy guys, he was probably teased in high school by the jocks and shunned by their pretty cheerleader girlfriends. Back then, geeks were people to be, if not outright, scorned, at least avoided. Now, seven or eight years down the road, presto-chango! Role reversal! Now the smart-guy propeller-heads like Kenny have all the money and run around in their Porsche Cayenne Turbos. Now it's their turn to date the pretty girls while the majority of high school jocks (meaning all those who didn't get Division I scholarships) work low-paying, manual labor jobs (if they can still find them). Kenny was simply playing his new role for all he was worth. It's just a theory. Anyway, I like him. He's a good guy with a good heart.

Toni feels the same way, but to her, Kenny's a target she can't resist for some good-natured teasing. She teases him about his hair, his height, his weight, even his girlfriends. And he gives as good as he gets. He teases her about her hair, her height, her tattoos, and—until recently—her lack of boyfriends. Normally, there's a good-natured banter between the two of them. Today, though, Toni's little sister was here to talk about something, and no doubt, Toni wondered if Kenny had tried to put some kind of move on Kelli while they'd been waiting for us. I doubted this—Kenny goes out with younger women to be sure, but even Kenny has a lower age limit, which seems to be twenty-one or so. But what the hell. Toni's the big sister, and it's her job to be protective—thus, the stink eye. It continued, even as I led Kelli out of Kenny's office to our conference room.

Kenny noticed. "What?" he mouthed silently, holding up his hands.

Toni glared at him for a second, then she turned and followed us. Message sent.

* * * *

"So," I said, when we entered the conference room. "Long time no see, Kelli. I haven't seen you since your birthday."

"I know," she said. She looked at Toni then back at me. "You guys had just started going out. I'm so happy for both of you."

Toni smiled. "Thanks, sis. We're happy, too."

"And now it's time for graduation," I said. "You all ready to go?"

"Sure am," she said.

"You feel happy or sad?" I asked.

"Happy. Definitely happy."

I smiled. "That's good. What're you going to do?"

"I'm going to U-Dub," she said. "I start in the fall. I've already been admitted."

"Cool!" I said. "Outstanding! Do you know what you want to study yet?"

"Yep. I'm thinking LSJ—same as you guys." The University of Washington offers a four-year bachelor's degree in something they call Law, Societies, and Justice. Basically, it's a fancy name for a criminal justice degree. Toni and I met in early 2007 when we were seniors in the LSJ program. I was still in the army, finishing my last year as a CID special agent. It's a good education if you want to make law enforcement your career.

"LSJ—that's cool," I said. "Are you thinking about police work?"

"Pre-law," Kelli said. "I want to be a DA."

I smiled. "Excellent. Somebody to put the bad guys away. You'll make a great DA. Runs in your family, I think."

Toni smiled.

"Yeah, I think so, too," Kelli said.

"Well, that's good," I said. I leaned back in my chair. "So what brings you here today?"

Her mood sobered quickly. Where she'd been happy and smiling a moment before, she suddenly turned somber.

"I have a friend," she said. "I think she's in trouble."

Toni eyed her suspiciously, not certain if Kelli was referring to herself when she said "a friend" and, if she was, trying to determine what she meant by "in trouble." Pregnant maybe? Big sister switching back into protective mode, I suppose.

"What kind of trouble," Toni said.

"I think my friend Isabel's been kidnapped," Kelli said.

Whoa! That came out of left field! Toni and I both looked at Kelli as we scrambled to catch up mentally. "What do you mean, you think she's been kidnapped?" Toni said.

"Hold up for a second," I said, raising my hand. "Don't answer that just yet." Both girls looked at me. "Since the conversation's headed this direction, let me grab a couple of notepads, so we can take notes and do this the right way."

Toni looked at me for a second, and then she said, "Good idea."

I took a couple of steno pads from the credenza behind the conference room table. While I was up, I grabbed three bottles of water.

"Kelli, why don't you start from the very beginning," I said as I sat back down. "Go slow. Give us plenty of details. Everything you can remember."

"Okay," she said.

"Start by giving us Isabel's personal data. What's her full name?" I asked.

"Isabel Delgado."

"Do you know if she has a middle name?"

"I don't know."

"Address?"

"She lives at 4268 192nd Street in Lynnwood."

"Just around the corner from us?" Toni asked. Toni grew up in a home on 189th Street in Lynnwood—the same home where Kelli still lived with their mother.

"Yeah," Kelli said. "Isabel is in chorus with me. I got to know her last year. She's just a sophomore now, but I used to drive her to school since we live so close to each other."

"How old is she?" I asked.

"She just turned sixteen last month," Kelli said. "On May seventh."

"Physical description?"

"She's Hispanic. A little shorter than me, with long, straight, dark hair," Kelli said.

"Her eyes?"

"I think they're black."

"What's her build? Is she heavy or thin?"

"She's medium—maybe a little bit thin," Kelli said. "But she has a really good figure."

I wrote the information down.

"So what's happened?" I asked, looking up. "Why do you say you think she's been kidnapped?"

Kelli looked down at the table and gathered her thoughts. Then she looked up at me. She pushed her long hair back away from her face.

"Isabel's had it hard," she started. Toni and I both looked at her. I suppose the questions must have been obvious in our faces.

"At home, I mean." That made it a little clearer.

"She's had it hard?" I asked. "Is she being abused?" I didn't want to come off as insensitive, but I usually find it helpful to move right to the heart of the issue—eliminate ambiguities.

Kelli nodded. "She was," she said softly.

"Sexually?"

Kelli nodded. "Yeah."

"You said 'she was,'" Toni said. "And now?"

"She ran away on her sixteenth birthday," Kelli said. "She called me once and texted me a few times, but now I haven't heard from her in more than a week. I think something's happened."

I looked at her, then said, "Isabel ran away to escape abuse at home; while she was gone, she contacted you, and now she's gone silent?"

"Yeah. Nothing since her last text."

I wrote a couple of notes on my pad and then looked back up at her. "Let's break this into stages, okay? First, let's talk about Isabel's home life. Let me ask you a few questions to help fill us in."

"Alright," she said.

"Let's start by getting right to the point. Do you know who abused her?"

"Yeah. She said it was her stepfather," Kelli said.

"Do you know his name?"

"Mm-hm. It's Tracey."

"Last name?"

She shook her head. "I don't know. I know Isabel kept her father's name. Her stepfather's is different."

"That's alright," Toni said. "We can look it up. Did you ever meet this guy?"

Kelli nodded. "Yeah, a few times."

"Tell us about him," Toni said.

"I'd say he's older—probably in his forties," Kelli said. "He's a mechanic, I think. He mostly wears a uniform. He's always dirty and grungy."

"Where have you seen him?" Toni asked.

"At Isabel's house. Sometimes, I'd drop Isabel off from school late— say four o'clock or so. Izzy's mom goes to work in the afternoons and sometimes her stepfather would already be home."

"He works days then?" I asked. "And her mom works nights?"

"Yeah. I think her stepfather must get off in the late afternoon."

"What's he like?" I asked.

"He creeped me out," Kelli said. She shuddered as she said it.

"How so?"

"The way he used to look at me," she said. "He basically drooled." She shuddered again. "Just the thought of him gives me the creeps."

"Did he ever say anything? Ever try anything?" Toni asked.

"He never tried anything with me," Kelli said. "But he used to say I was pretty. Once he even said I had a pretty figure."

"Really? He said that?" I turned to Toni. "That's a pretty inappropriate thing to say to a minor."

Toni was not happy. "Yeah, you think?"

Kelli continued. "I know. I got to the point where I would just drop Izzy off at the curb. I couldn't stand going in." She stared at the wall for a second, then tears welled up in her eyes. "Izzy didn't have a choice, though. Maybe if I'd have done something, she wouldn't have had it so bad."

I looked at her and shook my head. "Done what? What could you have done? Don't second-guess yourself like that. Hell, if I did that, I'd be a wreck. You didn't do anything wrong. You didn't even know anything was happening. And if what Isabel said is true, the only one who did anything wrong was her stepfather. Don't forget that, alright?"

"Besides," Toni said. "Look at it. Now that you've discovered a problem, what are you doing? You're trying to get help—just like you should. Danny's right. You didn't do anything wrong."

Kelli sniffed. "I guess," she said.

Toni handed her a tissue from the box on the credenza.

"You ready to keep going?" Toni asked

"Yeah," Kelli said.

"You said you've known her since last year?" Toni asked.

"Yes," Kelli said. "When she was a freshman."

"Did you ever see anything with her—any sort of sign that she might have been in some sort of trouble?"

She shook her head. "Other than her creep-job stepfather, no."

"No bruises—no cuts—nothing like that?"

She shook her head again. "No, nothing. Not that I ever saw, anyway."

We paused, and then I said, "Did you guys hang out other than at school?"

"Yeah, sometimes. We'd go to the mall sometimes."

"Alderwood Mall?"

"Yeah. It's right by our house."

"Anything else?"

"We went to the movies a few times, too."

"When did she tell you about what happened at her house? About her stepfather?"

Kelli sniffled. "Not until after she left."

Toni and I both scribbled on our notepads. After a few seconds, Toni said, "Tell us about Isabel leaving home."

"Okay. I called her on her birthday, but she didn't answer, so I sent her a text. She called me back later the same day. She was like 'Kelli—I ran away.'"

"And then she told you what happened?"

Kelli nodded. She started to cry again. "She said it was because her stepfather raped her," she said.

"She said that?" I asked. "In those words?"

Kelli's face was red with anguish. "Yes," she said. Toni got up and put her arm around her sister as Kelli sobbed quietly into her tissue.

A couple of minute later, she composed herself and continued. "She said she wasn't going to put up with him anymore, so she ran away. I offered to come and pick her up, but she wouldn't tell me where she was—at least not then. I think she was afraid that if I knew, I might rat her out accidentally. I told her she could come stay with us, but she said that she didn't want us to get in trouble. She thought that her mom or her stepfather would come over looking for her. She made me promise not to say anything to anybody."

"Did they?" I asked. "Did her parents come looking for her?"

She shook her head. "No."

"So she's been gone a month, and they haven't even come looking? Do you think that her mom or her stepfather would have come to ask you if you knew anything?" Toni asked.

"Sure," Kelli said. "They know about me. They know Izzy and I are good friends."

"What happened next?" I asked.

Kelli opened her purse and pulled out her phone. She opened the text message window.

"A couple of days after she called, she sends me a text." She handed me the phone. Toni leaned over, and we both read it.

Isabel Delgado   5/9/12   7:32 PM
Met a cool girl named Crystal at the mall. Staying with her and her boyfriend Donnie for now. IOK. :^) LYLAS

"I don't know much about texting. IOK stands for 'I'm okay'?" I asked.

"Yes," Toni said.

"How about LYLAS?"

That one stumped Toni. Kelli said, "It means 'Love you like a sister.'" She sniffed and wiped her nose. "Now scroll down," she said. I did. The next message was one day later.

Isabel Delgado   5/10/12   4:56 PM
Went shopping for clothes—Crystal loaned me $$. Looking good! :^) LYLAS

"Again," she said. "A week later."
I scrolled down again.

Isabel Delgado   5/18/12   11:24 PM
Kicking it with Donnie's friend Mikey. He's the bomb, and we're into each other. :^) LYLAS

"And then the last one," she said. "A week ago."
I scrolled down again.

Isabel Delgado   5/28/12   5:17 PM
Kelli—2G2BT. :^(LYLAS

"What does this mean?" I asked.
"2G2BT? It means 'too good to be true.'"
"Too good to be true and a little frowny-face thing," I said. "I wonder what she meant by that?"
"Something must have happened," Toni said. "Something she didn't like, by the sound of it."
"Seems that way," I said. I thought for a second. "It's amazing how four little text messages can tell a story like that." I punched the intercom button and called Kenny into the conference room. When he arrived, I asked Kelli, "Do you mind if I get Kenny to pull copies of your text messages off your phone?"
"No," she said. "That'd be okay."
"And can you give us Isabel's cell phone number?"
"Yeah," she said. She read the number off, and all three of us wrote

it down.

Kenny left with the phone. I turned to Toni. "What do you think?"

She thought for a second and then said, "Sounds like we need to find Isabel."

I nodded. "I agree," I said. "The sooner, the better."

Kelli smiled, tears flowing again. "Thanks, you guys. Thank you so much."

I smiled at her. "We'll find her." I thought for a second. "But if we do," I said, "where will we take her? We can't very well take her back to her home."

"First things first," Toni said. "Let's focus on finding her for now. Then we'll worry about where to take her."

I nodded. "Good plan. Let's do it."

So we started hunting for Isabel.

Chapter 2

"JEEZ—THIRTY-FIVE yards? I can barely see that far," Detective Goscislaw "Gus" Szymanski said as I recounted the story. Gus and his boss, Lieutenant Dwayne Brown, were treating Toni and me to an early birthday lunch. I was a week away from turning the big three-oh.

"That's right," Dwayne agreed. "Thirty-five yards—that's why God invented sniper rifles with big scopes."

"How long did you have?" Gus asked.

"Two seconds," Toni said.

"Holy crap," Gus said. "Takes me longer than that to move my coat back just to reach my gun."

"We didn't have to draw," Toni said. "We got to start from low ready."

"Still," Dwayne said, shaking his head. "That's crazy fast for that distance."

Dwayne heads up the SPD's Special Investigations Unit, and Gus is his partner and assistant. They work a variety of cases—mostly those that SPD brass deems politically sensitive. Dwayne and Gus make an unlikely pair. Dwayne's a forty-something, good-looking black man with more than twenty years on the Seattle force. He's a sharp professional. The fact that he's naturally smooth in front of a television camera makes him a good representative for the police department in touchy situations. I've known him for six years—we used to work together from time to time when I was with the U.S. Army Sixth Military Police Group (CID) stationed at Fort Lewis in Tacoma. Dwayne was a detective at the time, and we found ourselves assigned to the same cases on four or five occasions. Although the years had caused Dwayne to become a little less lean than he used to be, he was still an impressive figure, not to mention a very slick dresser.

Gus—now Gus was a different story. Toni and I had met Gus last summer when we worked on the disappearance case of Gina Fiore. Like me, Gus served in the army as a grunt before going into law enforcement. He was with the First Infantry in Desert Storm in Kuwait and Iraq in the early '90s. Dwayne and Gus are a picture in contrasts. Dwayne is refined and classy-looking. Gus usually looks a little disheveled–he'll never be accused of being either refined or classy, no matter how hard he tries. And, more than most, he's completely smitten with Toni.

"And you went first?" Gus said to Toni.

"Yep."

"And you hit the target?"

"In the chin. Just below actually—in the neck. A seven-point shot."

Dwayne whistled. "That's damn good," he said. "Damn nice shooting with a handgun at long range. You beat the clock?"

"One point eight seven."

"Son of a bitch," he said. "That's awesome. You shoot what—a Glock, right?"

"Glock 23," she said.

"That's the .40-cal?"

"Yep."

Dwayne held up his hand, and Toni happily high-fived him. "Damn good shooting," he said again. He turned to me. "And you?"

"I went next."

"No shit. I figured that out all by myself. What happened when you went next?"

I didn't say anything. Finally, Toni stepped in. "What happened is deadeye here raised his gun and fired in almost the exact same motion. Hit the target right between the friggin' eyes. One point zero four seconds."

"From thirty five yards?" Gus said with appreciation. "Head shot—right between the eyes, no less—from thirty-five yards? In one second?"

"One point zero four from beep to boom," Toni said. She shook her head. "I knew I was screwed when I missed the center mass ten ring. I left him an opening." She glanced at me. "He doesn't need much."

"Well," I said, "I wouldn't exactly call your shot a miss. Your guy wasn't walking away."

"Yeah, but I liked the way you rubbed it in. You could have played it safe and shot center mass for a relatively easy ten. But noooo. Instead, you pop the target right between the eyes. Show-off."

"Damn," Gus said.

"Well," Dwayne said, setting his Coke down, "I don't know about you, Gus, but I feel much safer knowing that these two sharpshooters are around. Bad guy'd be a fool to take us on now."

"Let's hope it never comes to that," I said. "I sure don't want to have to shoot anyone." I meant it. I had enough of that in Afghanistan and Iraq to last a lifetime.

"True," Gus said. "Still—better to be able to shoot and not have to than to have to shoot and not be able to. Here's to sharpshooters!"

None of us were drinking alcohol, but we still touched glasses.

"And you want to know the really amazing thing?" Gus said.

"What's that?" Dwayne answered.

"This hot-shit shooting is coming from a guy who's nearly thirty years old!"

Dwayne and Toni laughed. "That's right!" Dwayne said. "Next thing you know, you'll be needing glasses—bifocals even. Happy birthday next week."

"Hear, hear!" Gus added.

We clinked glasses again.

"Thank you, guys," I said. "I feel older already."

"Yeah," Dwayne said. "'Bout time you settled down."

I smiled.

"Damn straight," Gus said. "Clock's tickin'." He looked at Toni, then back at me. "Speakin' of which, now that the two of you are together . . ."

"Something that makes me very happy, I might add," Dwayne said.

"Me, too," Gus added. "Although you know my door's always open, darlin'," he said to Toni, "'case this guy here does you wrong."

"Good," Toni said. She looked at me and smiled. "I may have to hold you to that."

"Right," Gus said. "Anyway, now that the two of you are together, what's next? Any plans?"

I shrugged. "I'm happy," I said. I turned to Toni. "Real happy. You happy?"

"Not counting you outshooting me? Again?" she said. "Other than that, yeah, I'm happy." She leaned over and kissed me. I get a little light-headed whenever she does this. People always look at Toni—men and women. But when she kisses me, or even holds my hand, then they look at me, too. And then they must say, "I don't get it." I admit, it's a pretty heady experience. I kissed her back, and then I turned to Gus.

"There," I said. "See? We're both happy."

"I can see that," he said.

"Plans will take care of themselves," Toni said. She smiled at Gus. "But I appreciate the offer of a safety net."

Gus beamed.

"Guess we're all happy, then," Dwayne said.

I thought about it and realized I'd never been happier—not even close. Toni and I had "crossed over" from friends to something much more than friends the previous Saint Patrick's Day when I was laid up in the hospital with a concussion. Up until that point, we'd been classmates, and then friends, and then working associates. And the four years up to that point had definitely been hands-off between us, out of respect for the doctrine of separation of work and romance. That's the way I was taught in the army.

Of course, all that changed on Saint Paddy's Day. Something about lying in a hospital bed—coming to grips with your own mortality—makes you understand what's important and what's not in your life. Lying there, hooked up to all those machines, a light had suddenly gone on, and I had realized then that Toni was the most important thing in my life. Being mortal, I didn't necessarily have unlimited time to get my ass in gear and let her know. I realized then that my own "no fraternizing" rule was bullshit, and it was going to cost me the best thing I'd ever known. Thank God I came to my senses and broke free. Life is short, and it's best not to waste time.

So Toni and I may have been hands-off before then, but we've damn sure been hands-on ever since. I glanced at her. She looked back and smiled—a real heart-melting, reserved-only-for-me smile that made my heart flutter. Yeah, I was happy. I was damn happy.

But the question of plans was an interesting one. What *was* supposed to happen next? No doubt, things were good between us. Yes, I'd taken what for me was a pretty big step by initiating our relationship a few months ago after literally years of status quo—a "one giant leap" kind of thing. And yes, we were both happy. Cool. But did that mean I was supposed to keep the relationship moving forward? Or were we now entering the next round of status quo? And if so, how long should I expect it to last? Years again? Or was I already supposed to be taking another step?

The problem surfaced—if only in my mind—every time she came over. We were "together," but we didn't live together, nothing like that. She had her place; I had mine. She stayed over from time to time—that was nice (damn nice, actually), but eventually, she always ended up going home—to her home, that is.

All these questions—questions I never even dreamed I'd be considering until a short while ago—were starting to weigh heavily. Then again, I *was* approaching thirty. Clearly, I was in uncharted territory.

* * * *

After lunch, Toni and I went back to the office where I spent the next half hour answering e-mails and returning phone calls. I entered a few invoices into our accounting system—as a business owner, I wear many hats. As I looked over the check register and checked my bank balance, it became pretty clear that Logan PI was going to be needing some work pretty soon—the kind of work that paid. I've long since come to understand that the business's cash position doesn't grow in a nice steady line. Far from it, actually. It bounces up and down in a wild sawtooth kind of way. Fortunately, most times, it trends up. When we get ahead of the curve, I draw funds out and stash them into my savings reserve. That's the good news. The bad news is that with four employees on the books plus the office rent, the overhead is relentless—the meter never stops ticking. We need to keep this machine busy, that's for sure. Looking at the computer screen, I could see that if we didn't start pulling in some paying jobs pretty soon, I'd have to tap the reserves. I thought back to the couple of times in the past four years that I'd had to do that. Going backward leaves a bad taste. I hate it.

My phone rang, startling me back to the here and now.

"You ready?" Toni asked over the intercom.

"Yeah, I'll be right out."

Speaking of non-paying jobs, we'd decided to make a quick run up to Isabel's house in Lynnwood. Her mom worked swing shift at a nearby hospital, and we hoped to catch her before she left for work. If we could spend a few minutes with her before her husband got home, we hoped she might answer some questions for us. I grabbed my keys and a notebook, and we hit the road. We slogged our way through Lake Union traffic and twenty minutes later, we were on I-5 headed north.

"What do you think we'll find?" Toni asked as we crossed Portage Bay on Lake Union.

I thought for a second. "From what Kelli told us, my guess is we'll find a pretty dysfunctional family."

Toni nodded. "Safe guess. Do you think the woman will talk to us?"

"Hard to say," I said. "Remember, we've only heard one side of the story—and that second hand to boot. What Isabel said to Kelli is a serious charge, to be sure. But just to be safe, I don't think we should be jumping to any conclusions as to whether or not it's true—at least not until we talk to some of the other people involved. We don't have enough information yet."

Toni nodded again. We drove north for ten minutes or so without talking, listening to more of the new Brandi Carlile album.

We had just passed the Edmonds ferry off-ramp at Highway 104 when Toni turned to me.

"Thank you," she said.

I glanced at her. "For what?"

"Thanks for taking the time to look into this."

I smiled. "For you? Anything."

"That's nice, but this job doesn't pay, and I know we need some paying jobs." I hadn't gone over our financial picture with Toni, but it didn't come as any great surprise that she'd been able to figure it out. She's quick, and she doesn't miss much.

I shrugged. "We'll be fine," I said. "We have some things coming up."

She was quiet for a few seconds, and then she said, "Well, thanks, in any case. You don't have to do this."

I smiled. "I want to. It's important to you. And if it's important to you, it's important to me. Besides, I'd probably be all over this anyway— runaway abused teenager and all. That's not really something you can say no to. Let's just do a little checking around and see if there's anything there."

* * * *

We got off the freeway at the Alderwood Mall Parkway exit in Lynnwood. I hung a quick left on 196th and three minutes later, we pulled up in front of Isabel's house on 192nd Street. The neighborhood was a subdivision of single-family homes that looked to have the inexpensive, low-detail style that was prevalent in the early '70s. Still, the landscape was mature and, for the most part, the homes were well kept. Isabel's home at 4268 was one of a handful of exceptions—it was definitely in need of repair.

The brown paint on the two-story home was faded to a grayish tan. The white trim was peeling. The door, also white, was worn and scuffed. The front lawn had more holes and weeds than lawn.

A light blue, ten-year-old Nissan sat next to an old pickup truck in the driveway. The primer-covered truck clearly hadn't moved in quite some time—if the dirt and cracked windshield weren't enough of a giveaway, the fact that both tires on the right side were flat was. The truck had a definite list and appeared to be banking like a motorcycle into a gentle right sweeper.

"Home, sweet home," Toni said.

"It's a shithole," I agreed. "But I've seen worse."

Toni nodded. "I believe it."

We got out of the Jeep and walked to the front door. I rang the bell.

A few seconds later, an attractive woman opened the door. She was a couple of inches shorter than Toni, and she had dark, wavy hair. She was dressed in business clothes—royal blue blazer, a green skirt with a white top. She looked to be perhaps forty years old

"Good afternoon, ma'am," I said. "Are you Marisol Webber?" Kenny had looked up the property owner records before we left so that we had full names.

As soon as I spoke, the woman's eyebrows arched, and she sucked in her breath.

She nodded. "Are you police?" she asked. "Are you here about Isabel? Did something happen to her?"

"No, ma'am," I said, shaking my head. "We're not the police." I handed her my business card, and Toni did the same. "We're private investigators," I said. "But you're right—we are here about Isabel. We wondered if we might be able to ask you a few questions about your daughter."

"You're not police?" she asked again. She studied our cards carefully. I shook my head. "No, ma'am."

"We're here because a friend of Isabel's contacted us," Toni said. "She said Isabel is missing, and she's concerned about her. We were asked to look into things."

"Who?" Marisol asked. "Who hired you?"

We didn't want to reveal Kelli's name to Isabel's mother, and especially not to her stepfather. "I'm afraid we're not able to say," I said. "Our client asked to remain anonymous. At least for the time being. They want to protect their privacy, but they are very concerned about Isabel. I'm sure you understand."

She looked at me, confused.

"Would you mind if we came in and asked you a few questions?" Toni said.

Marisol hesitated. She glanced up and down the street quickly. "Okay," she said. "But just for a few minutes. I have to go to work."

"Thank you," Toni said.

Marisol led us inside to the living room. The home was clean and neat. Toni and I sat on an overstuffed, floral-print sofa. Marisol sat in a chair across from us.

"Marisol—," I started to say.

"Please, call me Mary," she said. "I'm not used to Marisol anymore."

I smiled. "Okay, sorry, Mary." I opened my notebook. "Can you start by confirming for us that Isabel is missing?"

She stared at me for a moment. "She's not home, if that's what you mean."

I cocked my head. Word games? C'mon. "Alright. Let me ask it another way," I said. "Do you know where Isabel is?"

She looked out the living room window for a second and gathered her thoughts before turning back to me. "She left," she said. "Isabel ran away from home—maybe a month ago now."

I nodded. "Thank you. That's our understanding as well, but I needed to confirm it with you."

"During that time, have you heard from her?" Toni asked.

"She called once and left a message on my voicemail," Mary said. "She said she was okay and that she'd call back later."

"When was that?" I asked.

"A couple of weeks ago."

"And has she called back since then?"

Mary shook her head. "No. Not yet."

"Does she have a cell phone?" I asked. I knew she did, but I wanted to hear what her mother had to say.

"Yes."

"Have you tried calling her?"

"Yes, of course. It just goes to voicemail. Isabel doesn't call me back."

"Have you filed a missing person report with the police?" Toni asked.

Mary stared at her for a moment. "No," she said.

"Why not?" Toni asked.

"I can't control her," Mary said. "She's sixteen. She's making her own decisions now."

I arched an eyebrow and then shook my head. "I'm not sure the law's going to look at it the same way you do," I said. "Matter of fact, I'm pretty sure that the law would say you're supposed to file a missing person report if your minor child disappears."

She said nothing, and the quiet began to grow in intensity.

This interview was off to a bad start. Toni sensed this as well, so she stepped in.

"Mary," she said, "we're not here to cause you any trouble, believe me. All we want to do is to help Isabel. Let me ask you this. Why would Isabel leave? Did something happen?"

"Yeah," Mary said. "I guess she just grew up. She decided she doesn't want to be here anymore. So she left."

"Nothing happened around here to make her want to leave?" Toni asked.

Before Mary could answer, Toni continued. "Usually, kids don't just up and leave for no reason. Usually, something happens that makes them feel like they need to leave. It doesn't always make sense to us as adults, but it does to them. Did something happen that made Isabel feel like she needed to leave?"

Mary looked at Toni. "What do you mean? Something like what?"

"Anything," Toni said. "Anything at all that might have caused Isabel to feel like she needed to leave home."

Mary hesitated and then shook her head. She didn't say anything.

"Did the two of you get along?"

Mary closed her eyes tightly. Was she trying to hide something? She nodded. "Yeah, we got along fine. We've been through a lot together."

"So you'd say the relationship between the two of you was good?" She nodded. "Yes."

"Did the two of you talk about things?" Toni asked. "I mean, if Isabel had a problem, would she come to you with it?"

Mary thought about this for a moment. "Well, first off—I work swing shift. I'm only home for two nights a week, so we never had the chance to talk too much. But other than that, yeah—I think we were okay."

"So you don't think she had any problems with you, right?"

Mary looked away for a moment, and then she shook her head and said, "I don't think so. She had no reason to have any problems with me."

"How about your husband? Did Isabel get along well with him?"

Mary didn't answer, but I could see tears start to form in her eyes. Toni noticed, too, so she slowed down and changed directions.

"How long have you been married?" Toni asked.

"Almost five years," Mary said.

"And during this time, have you always worked late?"

"Yeah, at Lynnwood Memorial in the admitting office."

"Okay," she said. "And your husband—does he work swing shift also?"

Mary shook her head. "No, he works days. He goes in at seven and gets off at four. He's a mechanic at Auto Express."

"So basically, he's alone with Isabel almost every night," Toni said.

Mary realized what Toni was getting at. She slowly started to nod her head.

"Did Isabel ever talk to you about any problems she might have had with your husband?" Toni said.

Mary shook her head. "No. She never said anything."

Toni stared hard at her. "Would she have? Would she have said something?"

Mary thought for a few moments and then shrugged. "I don't know. I hope so."

"Well, let me ask a different question. What do you think? I mean, do you think it's possible that something happened between Isabel and your husband? And if it did, could that something have caused Isabel to run away?"

Mary's eyes filled with tears again, and she clenched her hands together tightly. She turned to look at me and then turned back to Toni. "I don't think so," she said.

"If you don't think so," Toni said, "why are you getting so emotional?"

"I don't like what you're implying."

It was quiet for a few seconds. "It's ugly," I said. "And we're sorry."

"Look," Toni said. "Mary—I don't know what kind of relationship you have with your husband. But I'm asking you, for just a moment, to put it aside. Think only about Isabel for just a moment. She's out there somewhere. She's alone, and she needs your help like never before. She's your daughter. Speaking completely honestly, do you think it's possible that something happened between Isabel and your husband? Something that caused Isabel to leave?"

Mary looked up at the ceiling and thought for a second. "It's possible, I suppose. Maybe."

Toni nodded. "Okay, Mary. This won't be easy for you to hear, but you're Isabel's mother, so you have the right to hear it. I want you to know that our client told us that Isabel specifically said that your husband raped her the night before her sixteenth birthday."

* * * *

Mary bit her lower lip and continued to look up at the ceiling. The tears now flowed down her face.

Toni continued. "We were told that Isabel said he raped her, and that

that's why she ran away."

Mary dropped her head and stared at the floor. She shook her head silently.

"In your opinion," Toni said, "could that have happened?"

Mary hesitated, then, after a few seconds, she slowly nodded her head. "I didn't know," she said quietly.

"You didn't know, but did you suspect something like this was happening?"

She shook her head. "I didn't even suspect," she said. "I wasn't suspicious. I never put things together. . . . But it fits." She paused to take a deep, hitching breath. "She changed," she continued. "Izzy changed."

"How so?"

"She was more withdrawn—more inside herself. When she was a little girl, she was always happy and outgoing. She had lots of friends. She loves to sing—she used to sing all the time. The past few years, she's more quiet. She stays up in her room. I thought it was because she was getting older—growing up."

"And now?"

"Now I don't know," she said quietly. "It's happening too fast. I don't know what to think."

It was quiet for a few seconds, and then Toni said, "Mary, if this happened—and it sounds like it might have—or at least it could have. Anyway, if it happened, this is a very serious crime."

"I didn't know," Mary said again.

"I understand," Toni said. "And like we said earlier, we're not here to see you get in trouble."

"That's right," I said. "If Isabel didn't confide in you, and if you didn't have clear evidence as to what happened, I don't think you have any legal worries. But that's not really the issue with us anyway. The police and the district attorney worry about that kind of stuff. We've been asked to look into Isabel's disappearance. I'm sure our client is more interested in finding Isabel than in the legal aspects of this case."

Mary nodded.

I continued. "But that said, there's a few things that need to happen now—a few things you should do to protect yourself."

She looked at me.

"First off, you need to file a missing person report right away. Do you understand?"

"Okay."

"You'll do that with the Lynnwood Police Department," Toni said.

Mary nodded.

"Even if your husband doesn't want to. Do it on your own. Do you understand?"

"Yes."

"It's important, because we'll be talking to the police tomorrow or the next day as part of our investigation. You don't want them to hear from us that Isabel is missing. They should hear this from you. Today. Got it?"

"Yes."

Let me ask you something," I said. "Is your husband—Tracey's his name, right?"

She nodded.

"Is he physically abusive towards you? Has he ever hit you?"

Mary's face contorted and she started crying again. She nodded.

I took a deep breath and let it out slowly. "I understand," I said. "Then we'll need to be very careful. Will he become violent if he knows you talked to us?"

She shook her head. "Probably not just for talking," she said. "He doesn't do it very often." She paused and then added, "I sure can't tell him what we talked about, though."

"No, you don't want to do that. If he or anyone else asks, you tell 'em we stopped by to ask some questions about Isabel, but you didn't tell us anything other than she's gone and you don't know anything else. Okay?"

She nodded. It was silent for a moment, and then she said, "He's not a bad person, you know."

I looked at her, shocked at what I'd heard. "Who's that?" I asked.

"You mean the guy that beats you up and raped your fifteen-year-old daughter? That guy? Come on, Mary. You're going to sit here and say he's not a bad person?"

Toni put her hand on my arm to get me to back off a little.

Mary looked at me.

I made sure I was well under control before I continued. "Don't kid yourself," I said. "Bad people don't come with a sign stapled to their chest. You admit the guy's violent around you. That's bad enough. But if he molested or raped your own daughter? If he did that—and she says he did—then Mary, I think he's a monster." I paused and then said, "Think about it. I look in your eyes, and I can see that you're scared of the guy. Terrified, really. Am I right?"

She looked at me without speaking. Her eyes said I was right.

"Well, scared as you are—remember—you're an adult. You're a grown woman. Imagine how it must feel to a little girl—a fifteen-year-old girl—knowing she has nowhere to go, no one to turn to."

Mary stared at me. Her face was red and puffy from crying.

"I'm willing to apply the innocent-until-proven-guilty rule to the guy. I don't know him. And I don't know Isabel well enough to know if she's telling the truth or not. But you do, don't you? You know."

She continued to look at me.

"You do for sure," I continued. "And I can see in your eyes that you believe her. You believe your daughter."

It was quiet for a few seconds, and then she asked, "If he did something—something to Isabel—what will happen to him?"

"Listen," I said. "If it can be proven that your husband raped your fifteen year old daughter—that's called second-degree rape in Washington state. It's a class A felony. He could go to prison for ten years or more, and he'll have to register as a sex offender for the rest of his life." I paused and then added, "And if you ask me, that's damn lenient. There's nothing he can do to pay back what he took from your daughter."

She sniffed and thought about this for a second. Then she said, "What if it can't be proven?"

I thought about this for a second. "Then I guess life goes on," I said. "Even if it can't be proven, you'll still know the truth. You'll have to decide what you want to do—whether or not you want to live with the guy. But it will be your choice."

She nodded. I felt sorry for her. She went to work every day. She was doing her best to provide for her family. Unwittingly, she'd allowed a monster into her home. She'd have to come to grips with that and, I hoped, do the right thing. But it would be hard to come to grips with and even harder to confront.

"Would you mind showing us Isabel's room?" Toni asked.

Mary nodded. "Okay." She gestured toward the stairs. "It's upstairs."

We followed her upstairs and down the hall. Isabel's room was on the front side of the house.

"She kept it a little cluttered," Mary said as she led us through the doorway. We looked around and surveyed the room.

"Oh, I don't know," Toni said. "It looks just like a teenage girl's bedroom's supposed to look."

A large Justin Bieber poster was on one wall; a Selena Gomez poster on another. Isabel's dresser held several bottles of inexpensive perfume. A bulletin board was mounted on the wall next to the dresser mirror.

Toni and I noticed a strip of four pictures on the bulletin board—the kind of photos you get from a booth at a mall. Kelli Blair and another dark-haired girl were posing in them—clowning around. Other than the posters, these were the only photos in the room.

"Is this Isabel?" I asked, pointing to the pictures.

Mary nodded. "Yes. Isabel's the one on the left. That was earlier this year I think."

Isabel was a pretty girl. In the photo, she and Kelli were cracking up—looked like they'd been having a great time.

"Who's this other girl?" I asked. Seemed like a natural question, and I wanted to keep Kelli's relationship with us hidden.

"That's Isabel's friend Kelli," Mary said. "She lives nearby."

"Do you know her last name?" I asked.

She thought for a second and then said, "Sorry. I don't"

"Well, maybe we can get it at school. Would you mind if we borrowed this picture and made some copies?"

"No, I don't mind."

I unpinned the photo strip and stuck it in my notebook. The pictures served two purposes. First, we needed a good picture of Isabel to show around if we were going to be looking for her. Second, I'd just as soon leave no reminders of Kelli in Isabel's room—reminders for her stepfather to glom onto.

We had what we needed, so we headed back downstairs.

At that moment, a shiny white Ford F150 pulled up in front of the house.

"Company," Toni said.

"Oh my God," Mary said. "It's Tracey. He's home from work."

"It's okay," I said. "It's not a problem. Somebody was bound to come looking for Isabel, right? That's us. We'll stand here like we were just getting ready to leave. You've got our cards. Stash them in your purse there, and call us anytime you want. After today, we won't be back in contact with you unless we absolutely have to. If we do need to get ahold of you, we'll call you while you're at work. If you can't talk, we'll leave a number and you can call us on a break or something."

She nodded. "Find her," she said. "Please."

I nodded. "We will."

I watched through the living room window as Isabel's stepfather got out of his truck and started walking toward the house.

* * * *

Tracey Webber was tall—maybe a couple of inches taller than me, and I'm six one. He was a big guy, and he had a bit of a belly—but there was a lot of muscle there, too. My guess is he weighed two-thirty or so. He wore black work boots, dark blue mechanics pants and a matching shirt with his name stitched on the left breast in silver cursive. The shirt was untucked, and both shirt and pants had grease stains—some looked recent; some looked like they'd been there awhile. He was dirty and sweaty and he looked like he'd had a long day. He stopped as he came through the door and checked us out. He had the confident big-guy swagger of a man who'd been through many scraps and knew he could take care of himself. He also had a mean face.

"Hi, honey," Mary said as she walked over to greet him. She stopped short of hugging him when she saw up close how grimy he was.

Webber said nothing and looked past Mary toward us. "Honey, these people are private investigators," Mary said, anticipating his questions before he had a chance to voice them. "They've stopped by to ask some questions about Isabel."

He seemed to consider this for a second, before he said, "Why?"

The fact that his sixteen-year-old stepdaughter had been missing a month wasn't a big deal for him, I guess. Either that, or he already knew why and was just playing dumb.

"Mr. Webber," I said, "I'm Danny Logan. This is my associate Toni Blair." He looked us over. I should say, he glanced at me briefly but took his time checking Toni out. This was something I'd gotten used to, but I didn't like the look in his eyes. Still, I'm a professional—I bottled it up. "We've been retained to look into Isabel's disappearance," I said. True—not counting the retainer part.

When I mentioned Isabel's name, he turned back and looked at me, a little more carefully now. His cold, penetrating blue eyes sized me up. So far, my thirty-second snap judgment was that Tracey Webber was a purely physical guy—someone not too burdened by cerebral concerns. I'm usually pretty accurate with these assessments.

"What's to look into?" he said, breaking eye contact with me and moving to the bar that separated the kitchen from the living room. "She ran away. Been gone a month now, and it don't look like she's coming back." He set his keys on the counter and looked back at us. "Want a beer?"

"No, thanks," I said. He walked around the bar into the kitchen, where he got a bottle of Rainier Beer from the refrigerator. He twisted the top off and left it on the counter. He took a long pull from the bottle before turning around.

"Who'd you say you're working for?" he asked, as he walked back into the living room.

"We didn't say," I said. "Our client wishes to remain confidential."

"Hmm," he snorted. "That's pretty chickenshit. What're they hiding from?"

I smiled. "A pretty fair number of our clients wish to keep their identities hidden. You shouldn't read anything into that," I said. I wanted to try to take control of the conversation. "We were just about to leave, but since you're home, would you mind if we ask you a few questions? We talked to your wife for a few minutes, but she wasn't able to shed much light on the situation, since evidently she works swing shift and isn't home much."

He looked at Mary, then back at me. "Let's do it," he said, confidently. He took a long drink from his beer—probably draining half the bottle. "Think I'll have a seat. Been standin' all day long."

"By all means," I said. He plopped himself onto a bar stool and took another shot from his beer bottle, draining it all the way. Then he smacked it down on the bar. He wiped his mouth with the back of his hand and looked up at me. I halfway expected him to belch, but he didn't.

"Fire away, Chief," he said.

"Okay. As I said, we're trying to figure out where Isabel went. If we can find her, we're hoping we can talk her into coming back home."

"Hmmm," he snorted. "Good luck with that."

"Why do you say that?"

"Seems to me she's been acting like she couldn't wait to get away from here for the past two years or so."

"What makes you think that? Has she run away before?"

He shook his head. "Nah. She never ran before. She just comes home from school and then scoots on up to her room and closes the door. She acts like she don't want nothing to do with this family."

Can't imagine why not. "Understood," I said. "Teenagers can be a handful."

"Damn straight," he agreed.

"Tell me," I said in as non-threatening a tone as I could muster. "What was your relationship like with Isabel?"

"What do you mean?"

"Well, you and Mary have been married what—five years now? Almost five years? That means you've been around Isabel for almost a third of her young life. You've gotten to know her. You've had the chance to interact with her. Did the two of you get along?"

He seemed confused at first, but then he shrugged his shoulders and said, "Yeah. We got along fine. I'd get home—she was already home or sometimes she'd get home later. Like I said, she'd walk right straight through and march on up to her room. She didn't have much to do with me."

"Did she have any disciplinary problems?" I asked. "Did she ever get in trouble? Did you ever have to punish her?"

He shook his head. "Nah, she was a pretty good kid when it came to stayin' out of trouble. She didn't cause no problems—she was just real quiet and kept to herself. Spent all her time up in her bedroom."

"Okay," I said. "Let me ask you—it's a little after four now, and you just got home a little while ago. Is this about the same time you get home every day?"

"Yeah. More or less."

"So seeing as how Mary works swing shift, that makes you the parent who probably spent the most time with Isabel. Did she ever confide in you? Tell you about any problems she might have been having in school? Something that might have made her want to run away?"

He pretended to think about this for a few seconds. I say "pretended" because he made a good show of staring off into space for about ten seconds, seemingly lost in thought. I figured this was a good eight seconds past his maximum attention span. Finally, he shook his head and said, "Nah—she never said anything. Like I said, she kept to herself."

"I understand. Do you know if she had any friends? If she did, maybe we can talk to them and help look for her that way?"

He shrugged. "I don't know any of her friends," he said. "She got rides to school and back from a girl who lives somewhere around here, but that's about it—leastwise, as far as I know."

"That's fine," I said. "We'll check at her school. They might be able to help us locate some of Isabel's friends."

I looked down at my notes, then back up at him. "That's pretty much it for me—I don't really have anything else—we're actually just getting started on our investigation. Is there anything else you can think of?" I asked. "Something else you might be able to add?" My point in talking to him hadn't been so much to get any information out of him—I didn't expect that would happen. Mostly, I just wanted to deflect his attention from Mary.

He looked at me and then shrugged. "Sorry, Chief," he said.

I looked at Toni. "Anything else you can think of?" I said.

She shook her head no.

"Well, okay then," I said, smiling. "I guess that'll do it for now. Thanks for helping us out. We won't keep the two of you any longer." I took a step for the door.

Mary opened it for us. "Sorry I couldn't be more helpful," she said.

"No problem," I said. "You can't be two places at the same time. Gotta work. I know what that's like. I turned to Tracey. "Mr. Webber, thanks again for your help. If we find anything, we'll keep you posted."

Webber didn't respond. Apparently, he hadn't fully appreciated the way Toni fills out a T-shirt when he came inside and checked her out. Now that he'd had a chance to take a second look, he was definitely noticing. In fact, he couldn't take his eyes off her chest. I stared at him for a second, amused by his complete lack of tact. A few seconds later though, I'd had enough. I felt myself entering familiar territory—what I've come to call "the windup." I snapped my fingers together twice, loudly.

The sound apparently penetrated his feeble brain, and he looked up. I pointed to my eyes with two fingers. "Eyes front and center, big guy," I said. "Don't be crude." He looked at me for a second or two with a look that was half stupid/half predatory until what I said registered. Then the look was replaced by a mean, ugly sneer.

Before anything further could happen, Toni grabbed my arm. "You folks have a nice day, now," she said, and she fairly shoved me out the door.

* * * *

"I think my skin is going to crawl right off my body," Toni said. We were driving south on I-5 on our way back to the office.

"He's an ass-bag," I said.

"True. I've only just met the guy, and already I think he's guilty."

I signaled and changed into the fast lane. "Me, too. We're not without reasons, though. You've got Isabel speaking directly to Kelli, saying the guy raped her. And you've got Isabel's mom—the guy's own wife—saying she can believe it."

"And oh, by the way, he's also beat on *her* in the past, too," Toni added. "What an animal. And I must say, that's an insult to animals everywhere."

"Agreed," I said. "An all-around upstanding kind of guy. And then, the smug prick thinks he's going to match wits with us while the entire time he mostly just wants to stare at your boobs." I thought for a second and then added, "Thanks again for pushing me out of there. You were just in time. You saved him."

"No problem. I meant to tell you—you should be more careful."

"I should be more careful? What do you mean?"

"Yeah—the little finger-snapping thing? Did you forget you've got a gun on your belt? That makes it your job to stay out of fights—not start them."

I thought about this. "You're right, except I wasn't trying to start a fight."

"*You* may not have seen it that way, but that pea-brain Neanderthal back there might have. You definitely don't want to get into a fight with a big guy like him when you're carrying a gun, just because your macho pride gets tweaked or because you think you're defending my honor. Believe me, I handle lots worse than him nearly every day."

I thought about this. She was right. Ironically, when you strap on a sidearm, you take on the responsibility of having to work even harder to stay out of confrontations than would be the case if you were unarmed. When you carry a weapon, too many things can go wrong when the situation gets unstable—such as in fight. I knew better. "You're right. I'll try hard to dial it back."

"Besides," Toni said. "You'd undoubtedly kick his ass. Then you'd probably get arrested for assault. That would suck—getting busted because of a douche bag like Tracey Webber." Toni and I both practice the Israeli martial art known as Krav Maga. I learned it in Afghanistan. When I got back, I was surprised to find a studio in Bellevue where I could continue my training. I had introduced Toni, and now she's nearly my equal. In the last four years, neither of us has ever had cause to pull our firearms in the heat of battle. On the other hand, we've both used our Krav Maga training numerous times. It works.

"Agreed."

"Better we get the cops to arrest him for rape."

"Agreed again."

We drove in silence for ten minutes, which gave me time to think about this case. The more I thought about it, the more upset I became.

I'm only twenty-nine—at least I'm still twenty-nine for another week. Still, despite my tender years, I've faced down some really bad guys in my time. I spent three years in the U.S. Army as an infantryman—a grunt. I loved it. Of course, I hadn't bargained on the U.S. going to war after I joined, and I sure as hell hadn't bargained on me going into combat in Afghanistan in 2002 and then again in Iraq in 2003. But what the hell—I went where they sent me, I did my job, and I made the best of it. While I was deployed, I ran into some truly memorable, badass people. Local guys with no technical sophistication at all, but who made up for it with a pure, white-hot hatred of me and my guys and everything we stood for. They'd do anything—and I mean anything—to kill us. They almost got me twice—resulting in me getting two Purple Hearts inside of four months in Iraq. And even though I believed in our cause, and I sure as hell didn't agree with the religious and political nut-jobs who tried so hard to kill me for three years, at least I came to understand said nut-jobs.

Then, after my unit returned stateside at the start of 2004, I switched careers and went into the U.S. Army Criminal Investigation Division. I was introduced to a whole different type of badass. I spent the next four years chasing down and convicting U.S. Army personnel accused of all manner of felony charges—a real microcosm of life on the "outside." Mostly, these people were either hooked on drugs or they were looking for an easy way to get rich—sometimes both. With only a few exceptions, most of these people weren't out to hurt anyone, but they were damn sure dangerous when you tried to put them in jail.

But with all these bad guys to choose from—overseas and domestic—the ones I grew to hate most were the soulless pricks who seemed to get off by preying on people less powerful than they were—what I call the law of the jungle predators. These guys have no grand political or religious objective. This makes them worse than terrorists in my book. Most of them don't care about money. This makes them worse than your typical criminal. Here's an interesting example that'll make my point. Pretend, for a moment, that Ted Bundy isn't being slowly roasted in the pits of hell. Pretend, God forbid, that he's still here with us and that he's at a game show. Ted gets to choose between two doors. And he gets to know what's behind each before he does. Behind door number one is a big bag of money. Behind door number two, a helpless twenty-two-year-old co-ed. Which door do you think Ted chooses? I rest my case. These sick bastards have an insatiable need to satisfy their own lusts. Nothing else matters. They don't care about their victims—don't even think about them, actually. The fact that the victims are people with hopes, dreams, and aspirations doesn't even enter their sick, twisted little minds.

Another thing I've found is that there are different degrees of predator depravity out there. Some like to torture and kill their victims—

the Bundys, the Ridgeways, the Ramirezes, and the like. Some don't kill—
they just rape their victims and throw them away, leaving them for dead.
Another variation is the guys who beat their wives or girlfriends—just
because they can. Others get off on stealing the pure innocence of a
defenseless child. All of these so-called people are really not people at all
in my book. They're monsters, and they're a despicable waste of air and
space. I hate 'em all.

And this guy Tracey Webber appeared to fit into at least two of these
categories at the same time.

* * * *

The closer we got to downtown Seattle, the tougher the traffic became.
Finally, we slowed to stop-and-go. At five thirty, we exited I-5 at Mercer
Street. "If you don't have to go to the office," Toni said, "Let's just go to
your place. I'll cook."

My place. There it was again. The idea of Toni fixing dinner didn't
sound bad at all. Dinner would be nice. After dinner would probably be
nicer—maybe much nicer. And then, she'd pack up and go home. To her
place. And that would be painful. But still, what can I say? When it comes
to Toni, I'm a junkie—I can't get enough. Even if it might be bad for me
later.

"I already talked to the guys in the office," I said. "Doc said they'd
lock up, so we're good to go. Do we have everything you need?" Doc
Kiahtel is an associate of ours.

"We're good," she said. "I went shopping yesterday."

"Excellent." I studied the traffic. "Looks like we're going to be a
while. What do you say we give Dwayne a call and ask him for some
advice? Maybe he can turn us on to the person we need to be talking to."

"Good idea," she said.

I had Dwayne on speed dial. I punched in the number and a second
later, he answered.

"Special Investigations, Lieutenant Brown."

"Dwayne—it's Danny and Toni."

"Hey, guys!" he said. "What's up? Sounds like you're in the car."

"We are. We're three-quarters of a mile from home. Shouldn't take more than another half hour or so."

Dwayne laughed. "You should just pull over and walk."

"Exactly," I said. "Hey, thanks again for lunch today. That was nice."

"It was our pleasure. Besides—it's your birthday. Or it will be soon. And besides that—we owe you. We keep making you buy lunch at the sushi joint, and you just keep doing it. We were starting to feel a little guilty."

"What? You've just been using me as a meal ticket?"

"Hell yeah," he laughed. "We're cops. We'll take all the free lunches we can get."

"Well, it's nice to know that at some point your conscience kicked in."

Dwayne laughed again. "At some point. But then again, maybe it's just because it was your birthday—who knows?"

We both laughed.

"That why you called?" he asked.

"Nah," I said. "We need your advice."

"Shoot."

"After we left lunch today, we met with Toni's little sister, Kelli."

"I didn't even know you had a little sister, Toni."

"I do. She's eighteen—graduates high school next week."

I said, "Anyway, we met with her this afternoon. She told us that a friend of hers called her and said she'd run away from home because her stepfather had raped her. We went and talked to the mom and the stepfather this afternoon. We got the mom before the stepdad came home. She admits that it's possible, and she also said that stepdad has beaten her—the mom—in the past. We're wondering who we should be talking to at SPD."

"Simple," Dwayne said. "If you're talking about the missing child, you need to talk to Nancy Stewart. Nancy's the lieutenant in charge of our

Vice and High Risk Victims Unit. She may want to bring in someone else, depending on the exact nature of the case, but I'd start with her. She's an expert at that sort of thing. And she's a real nice lady, too. Need me to set something up for you guys?"

"Yeah, we'd really appreciate it."

"Let me call you right back."

Ten minutes and two hundred yards later, he called back.

"You're set," he said. "She has a meeting first thing in the morning, but she can see you at eleven. That work?"

"That's perfect. Thanks, Dwayne." It was really nice to have friends in high places.

Chapter 3

I'M A PRETTY serious distance runner—have been ever since high school. My specialty now is half marathons. Seems that whatever your sport—baseball, football, running, you name it—at a certain level of performance, your body composition becomes a serious limiting factor. One of the keys to performing well is making sure your sport matches your body type. For me, it seems like the 13.1-mile half-marathon distance is ideal—it fits the best. It wasn't always this way. In high school, I ran shorter, speedier distances, like the mile. Now, twelve years later, I like the longer races. They're long enough that I can eventually run away from the pure speed guys (the 10k guys). And they're short enough that I can still out-muscle the pure distance guys (like the marathoners). It's the perfect distance for me. I like to compete in one race a month or thereabouts.

My personal best time of 1:12 means I'm usually fast enough to be near the front of the pack—top ten or so—but usually not fast enough to win. It's right there—but it's just out of reach. Sometimes—generally right after I finish just out of the top five—my friends will be impressed on the one hand and offer advice on the other—advice like maybe if I'd trained just a little longer (like those other guys), I could have made the podium. I don't think so. If I actually believed that more training would enable me to finish higher, I might try to carve out some more time. The reality is, at some point, it's back to those natural, God-given physical limits. When that happens, all the extra training in the world won't let you run like Usain Bolt or swim like Michael Phelps. You either got it, or you don't. I'm okay with this. I accept it. Fact is, most people never explore the edge of their own limitations. Even though I don't win very often (three times in the last five years), I run because I like to find that edge. I keep at it.

Which is a long-winded way of explaining why I train year-round. The training keeps me in great shape all the time. Of course, the training also has the side benefit of allowing me to eat pretty much whatever I want without having to worry about it, and this is pretty cool, too. Maybe someday that will change—but for now, it's working.

My training schedule is carefully structured to have me reach my athletic peak at various times in the year that coincide with the biggest races. It varies by time of year and by day of the week, but the pattern is similar year-round—I run shorter and harder on Tuesdays and Thursdays, longer and slower on Wednesdays. Fridays and Sundays are easy days. Saturdays are a bear—long and hard both. And Mondays— blessed Mondays—are a day of rest with no running at all. Today being Wednesday, the workout was a longish run at a moderate pace. For me— at this time in the season—this meant about ten miles in about an hour and fifteen minutes or so. I finished by 7:20, showered, and hit the office at eight o'clock on the dot. I walked straight into the conference room for our morning staff meeting.

After everyone was seated, I looked around the table. Kenny was there. I nodded to him. Then I turned to the tall, dark-haired man with shoulder-length black hair seated next to him. "How's it goin', Doc?" I asked.

He looked at me, smiled and then gave me a single nod—a fine answer for Doc—no words required.

Joaquin "Doc" Kiahtel is a Chiricahua Apache—claims to be a direct descendant of Cochise. I met Doc while we were both stationed at Fort Lewis just outside Tacoma when I worked to clear him from a little misunderstanding with some patrons of a local drinking establishment.

We proved that Doc was acting purely in self-defense—even if all four of the guys who attacked him ended up in the hospital. Knowing what I know now about Doc's background in the Army Rangers, I understand Doc actually exercised considerable restraint in the altercation: he didn't kill a single one of 'em. Later, I got to really know him, and we became friends. Doc's Special Forces background led me to offer him a position as director of security at our firm after he was discharged. I'm lucky that he accepted.

For the longest time, Doc was a solitary guy. It literally took him years to recover from the loss of his girlfriend who was killed by a hit-and-run driver in Fort Lewis in 2006. We got used to seeing Doc by himself. Then, two months ago, Toni and I met him at one of our favorite camping spots on the Olympic Peninsula and to our complete surprise, we found that he was accompanied by a woman! And a beautiful one at that! Toni and I were both struck nearly speechless when Doc introduced us to his "girlfriend," Doctor Prita Dekhlikiseh—he just called her "Pri." Unlike Doc—I mean Joaquin—Pri's a *real* doc—a USC medical school grad and emergency doctor at Harborview Medical Center. Doc met her when the paramedics delivered me there after I was hit in the head with my own baseball bat. He never said a word about Pri until that camping trip.

If I hadn't been unconscious at the time, I'd have noticed Pri myself—she's hard to miss at six feet tall. Like Doc, she's also a Chiricahua Apache, although she's from Oklahoma, and Doc is from New Mexico. Because of her, the last couple of months may have been the happiest I've ever seen Doc. When it comes to Pri, I'm a fan. I'd like her anyway, but I especially like her for what she means to Doc.

Also seated at the table was Richard Taylor. Richard's a tall, lanky man in his early seventies. He's a former Seattle Police Department detective who, twenty-four years ago, retired and opened a private investigation agency called Taylor Private Investigations. Toni and I met him when he was a guest lecturer at a police procedural course in our last year at U-Dub. When Richard told us he wanted to retire at the end of 2007, my wheels had started to turn. I made him an offer to buy him out when we graduated in December 2007. Three months later, Taylor Private Investigations became Logan Private Investigations.

With twenty-eight years at the Seattle PD, and with another twenty-four years in private practice (the last four with us), Richard is a walking Seattle criminal justice encyclopedia. I mean, the man knows everybody. He knows the history and background of every bar and nightclub in the area. He knows secrets: who owes what to whom, who slept with whom, where skeletons are buried—you name it. As an accurate information source, he's completely irreplaceable.

And the really cool thing? Even though he's officially retired and thus, done with the pressures of owning a business, he still likes to sit in on our cases and give us the benefit of his experience—for free! He says it keeps his mind active. I say, great. All I have to do is give him an office, a desk, and a phone. We're a whole lot stronger with Richard on our side. Not to mention the fact that he's also become a great friend.

"How'd the qualifying go?" he asked.

"It went great," I said. "Matter of fact, we both shot perfect scores."

"Then he beat me in the tiebreaker," Toni said. "Again."

I smiled at her. She stuck her tongue out at me.

"Does Gunny Owens still run the qualifying?" Richard asked.

"Sure does," I said. "Speaking of which, you ought to be due pretty soon, aren't you?"

"July. I've got to go down there in July."

"Piece of cake, right?"

He smiled, his blue eyes sparkling. "Is there any doubt in your mind?"

I shook my head. "Nope. None at all." I turned to the group. "Everybody's here. We'll just get right into it," I said. "Let me start by saying that I was going through the books yesterday and, as you may know, the coffers are getting a little thin around here. We haven't had a good-sized job in a while. That's the bad news. The good news is that I don't think I'm going to have to dip into reserves because I think there are two nice jobs coming right up. I've got an appointment next Wednesday with Ferguson and Sons."

"With whom?" Kenny asked.

"Ferguson and Sons is the largest restaurant-supply distributor in the Puget Sound," Richard said. "They've been around for about a hundred years. The name should probably be Ferguson and Sons and Grandsons and Nephews and Nieces and whatnot." He turned to me. "What's their problem?"

Suddenly, Toni gave a little scream. She shoved herself back from the table.

"Oh, shit," she said. "A spider just dropped down and landed on my damn notebook."

Everyone looked. A small spider—less than half an inch across—sat on her notebook, unsure of what to do next.

Kenny leaned over to look. He started laughing. "That?" he said. "You're afraid of that?"

She turned and fixed him with an evil glaze. "I. Don't. Like. Spiders." Each word was carefully enunciated.

Kenny laughed again.

Doc was sitting closest to the balcony door. "Doc," I said. "Put that little dude outside, will ya?"

He got up and scooped up the notebook, spider and all.

"Don't kill it," Toni said, suddenly concerned.

Doc glanced at her. "I don't kill spiders."

"No," Toni said. "No, you don't. Sorry."

Doc walked outside onto the balcony where he tipped the notebook up onto the balcony rail. The spider, now clear as to which way it should go, calmly walked off the notebook onto the rail. As if satisfied of its surroundings, it walked slowly over the edge of the rail, down the side and then, upside down, along the bottom, where it stopped—most likely surveying the site for a new web.

"There. Everyone satisfied?" I asked.

Toni nodded.

"Good," I said. "Let's continue. Where were we?"

"I was asking about what kind of problems Ferguson and Sons were having," Richard said.

"That's right," I said. "It's the usual stuff. Apparently, they have inventory walking out of their warehouse. They want us to set up hidden cameras and monitor their warehouse staff. We'll go in late at night when they're closed and wire the place up. We might even need to order new vinyl panels for one of the vans so we can do a little undercover work."

"Pretend we're some kind of restaurant-supply outfit?" Kenny said.

"Exactly."

"Sounds like it could be a nice job," Richard said.

"Very nice," I agreed. "Pretty good-sized project."

"You mentioned two cases?" Richard said.

"Right. The other item is my dad said he has a case he's working on, and he's going to need us to look into some stuff—but he was his usual vague self and wouldn't be more specific than that."

"It's probably a high-profile case, and he just doesn't want to get ahead of himself disclosure-wise," Richard said.

"Could be," I said. "You know my dad—strictly by the book."

"This is true," Richard said.

I continued. "Meanwhile, we've had something else pop up that might keep us busy for a week or so while we wait for the Ferguson job to get started."

This got everyone's attention. We typically go over all new cases as a group. These are all smart people, and I value their opinions. I wouldn't quite go so far as to say we're a democracy around here—final decisions are my domain—but I definitely take group input, and I listen to what these guys say.

"You all know Kelli Blair? Toni's little sister?" Everyone nodded. "Yesterday after we finished qualifying, she asked if we'd meet her here at the office. She told us a friend of hers—Isabel Delgado—had run away from home." I recounted Kelli's story to the group, leaving nothing out, including the claim that Isabel's stepfather had raped her.

"*Pinche cabrón,*" Doc said.

"Agreed," I said. "So based on what Kelli said that Isabel said, Toni and I drove up to Lynnwood late yesterday afternoon. We talked to Isabel's mom and then, later, her stepfather showed up as well."

"Really? How'd that go?" Doc said.

"The mom's okay," I said. "She seems pretty much a classic case of 'Battered Person Syndrome.' You all familiar with that?"

"No," Kenny said.

"Basically, BPS is when a person who should otherwise know better and be able to defend themselves doesn't, basically because they're afraid of or intimidated by the person doing the abusing. In this case, Marisol Webber is afraid of her husband, Tracey Webber. He's beat her in the past, but she hasn't done anything. Why? She's afraid, and she's intimidated. Battered Person Syndrome."

"What about now that he's raped her daughter?" Doc asked.

"She says she didn't know about that, but it also didn't seem to surprise her much," Toni answered.

"Right," I said. "But even not counting that—just focusing on the fact that her husband beats on her—still, she does nothing. She can probably be helped with intervention and with counseling and guidance. But short of that, she's stuck—at least for the moment."

"By the way, the stepfather is a complete douche," Toni said. "I felt like I needed a shower after he got there."

"He ogled Toni pretty good until I snapped him out of it," I said.

"You hit him?" Doc asked, hopefully.

"No. I snapped him out of it." I recounted the "snapping the fingers" episode. Toni jumped in and took credit for saving the day.

"Yeah," Toni said, "I didn't want to have to bail him out of the Lynnwood jail. But let's get back to Isabel. Apparently, she doesn't suffer from the same problem as her mom. She's obviously not paralyzed into inaction. Looks like she said, 'screw that, I'm out of here' after Webber raped her. She ran."

"I think it would be interesting to hear from Isabel," Richard said. "In my experience, when a child is abused—raped in this case—there's often been a long history of abuse at play. It's hardly ever an isolated case."

I hadn't paused to consider the notion that Isabel's rape might have been more than just a one-time event. "The idea that that little girl had to live in the same hell-house as that monster, with her mom at work and unable to protect her, is fucking staggering," I said.

Toni nodded.

"How long have her parents been married?" Richard asked.

"Five years, give or take," I said.

"And she just turned sixteen?"

I nodded.

"What do you want to bet that poor little girl was abused the whole time?"

It was silent for a few moments as we all considered this.

I shook my head. "That almost makes me ill. I'd like nothing more than to see this guy rot in prison for rape, child abuse, domestic violence—anything else they can pin on him."

Everyone nodded. "But in order to get him there," Richard said, "we have to find Isabel and convince her to testify. And frankly, even then it could be sketchy. It could end up being his word against hers. When they understand the courtroom ordeal that they're about to subject themselves to, a lot of victims decide they don't want to put themselves through it. They refuse to testify."

I nodded. "I know. But before we get too concerned about that, I think we should focus on the most important thing, which is finding Isabel and seeing that she's well taken care of. Getting her stepfather busted would also be nice, but I'm afraid that will have to be the icing on the cake."

"Agreed," Toni said.

I said, "And our more immediate problem is that it seems like when Isabel left, she may have jumped out of the frying pan and into the fire."

"I don't think that old cliché fits," Toni said. "But I'll borrow from it and say that Isabel jumped out of one fire and maybe landed in another."

I nodded. "Fair enough. Based on her text messages to Kelli, it seems as though after Isabel ran, she got hooked up with someone she thought was pretty cool, and then for some reason, she indicated that she was wrong."

"Without even knowing all the details, I have a theory where my money lands," Richard said. We all looked at him.

"Two-thirds of all young girls who run away from home end up involved in prostitution, and the risk is especially high for kids who have been abused. Sadly, this case has all the markings. I'd say there's a very strong probability that Isabel's gotten herself scooped up by one of the gangs that control prostitution here in Seattle."

"Two-thirds?" Toni asked. "I think Danny and I both suspected this might be a possibility, but I'm surprised at how common it is."

"It's a tragedy of epidemic proportions," Richard said.

No one spoke for several seconds. Finally, I said, "Well, all the more reason I'd like to find her. I can't imagine the outcome for most of those girls, but it can't be good. We need to find Isabel before she's consumed."

"Do we have the resources?" Richard said.

I shrugged. "We have the resources," I said, "but the problem is the job doesn't pay. This would be a charity case."

"Her parents sure as hell aren't going to pay," Doc said.

"Agreed," I said.

"Well, the good news is that we've got a free week anyway, right?" Kenny said. "Ferguson's not until next week. We have a gap."

"Exactly," Toni agreed. "I say we go get her."

"I agree," Doc added. "Besides, if we find Isabel, maybe she'll testify against her prick stepfather so he ends up in prison."

I nodded. "That'd work. Like I said, though, finding Isabel is job one. Getting her stepfather sent up is icing on the cake."

"Icing is good," Doc said. "Sometimes, it's the best part."

Chapter 4

OUR STAFF MEETING finished up fifteen minutes later. I spent the next hour in my office, paying bills and catching up on e mails and paperwork. I finished up by quarter after ten, and Toni and I hit the road. We were on our way to meet Nancy Stewart at the Seattle Police Department headquarters on Fifth Avenue in downtown Seattle. The plan was to meet Dwayne and Gus in their office by 10:45 and then have them take us up to meet Nancy.

Toni and I take turns, by date, picking music. Today was an even-numbered date—June 6—so that meant it was Toni's day to choose. I get the odds. Toni says that makes more sense. Go figure.

Although the "picker" gets to choose anything he or she wants, we try to pick something that the other one doesn't hate. Today, Toni chose The Black Eyed Peas' *The Beginning* CD—one we both like. She fast-forwarded to "Just Can't Get Enough" and hit the play button just as I pulled onto Highway 99 southbound.

I'm not what you'd call an old hand at relationships, but I can say that when you get together with someone you've been good friends with for many years—like Toni and me—there are many benefits. One of these is that you already know what the other likes and doesn't like. You already know where you fit and where you need to be careful. For us, we're already comfortable with not filling every moment with conversation.

The absence of conversation is not always a bad thing. We both like to just sit back and listen and think—not having to invent small talk to fill all the blank spaces. Which is why I was able to just drive and listen to the music as we cut through the heart of downtown before dipping into the tunnel that ran beneath Denny Way.

I thought about Isabel as the traffic noise bounced off the tunnel walls and drowned out the music. I was blown away by the figures Richard had quoted in our meeting earlier, and I was having a hard time getting my mind around the full magnitude of the problem. In and of themselves, the statistics are bad enough—horrifying actually. But it's worse—much worse—when you look deeper. Each number on the statistics page is its own tragedy; each number represents a separate life with its own potential. Each young person represented by a number has her own hopes and dreams. Yesterday, I'd stood in Isabel's room. I'd seen the little-girl stuffed animals, the young-teenage posters on the wall, the young-woman perfume on the dresser. For me, even though I'd never met her, Isabel wasn't just a number. She was real. I was damn grateful that my team was as enthusiastic about going after her as I was.

* * * *

We'd just pinned our visitor badges on in the sixth floor lobby at the Seattle Police Department when Dwayne walked through a restricted-access door and greeted us.

"Morning, guys," he said, smiling. He was dressed sharply in a navy suit with very faint pinstripes. He wore his gold badge pinned to his lapel pocket.

"Long time no see, boss," I said. "We don't see you in three months, and now it's twice in two days."

"I know, I know," he said. "You're fixin' to wear out your welcome." He laughed when he said it, but I hoped he didn't mean that the introductions and favors he provided for us were getting a little annoying.

"Hope not," I said.

"Nah," he said, chuckling. "You're good." He must have sensed my concern. "We're happy to help. Besides, as I said, we appreciate the free lunches you give us for payback."

"Especially happy to help your partner," Gus said as he entered the lobby. "My dear," he added, "you look beautiful, as always."

"Thank you, Gus," Toni said. She did look especially nice today. She wore black jeans; above, she wore a lavender-colored top layered over a white T-shirt. She was beautiful. Then again, I'm probably not the one to ask. I think she looks beautiful every day.

"I'm afraid we have to be pretty quick this morning," Dwayne said. "We've got a case we're working on."

"Let's go, then," Toni said. "We appreciate you guys making the introductions for us."

"You kidding?" Gus said, holding out his arm for Toni. "I don't care what the boss says. I'd rather escort you around than do police work any day."

Toni smiled and took his arm. "Lead on, kind sir," she said. Gus beamed and headed for the elevators.

Dwayne and I followed. Dwayne shook his head and laughed softly. "That guy brightens up whenever she's around like nothing I've ever seen. Just like a daylily that opens up in the morning when the sun hits it."

"She has that effect," I said.

* * * *

The Vice and High Risk Victims Unit is located on the tenth floor of the SPD building. Dwayne announced us to the receptionist, who made a phone call. A couple of minutes later, a short, middle-aged woman with shoulder-length blond hair came out to greet us. The woman wore a beige tweed dress suit over a black blouse. Her police badge was clipped to the pocket of her jacket.

"Hi, Nancy," Dwayne said, smiling broadly. He stepped toward the woman and gave her a warm hug.

"Hello, Dwayne," she said, also smiling. "It's so good to see you. I have to say, I was pleasantly surprised to hear from you yesterday."

"It's been a while," he said. "Here we are, just four floors apart, and it's like we're in two different cities."

"So true," she said.

"You know Gus, right?" Dwayne said.

"I do," she said. "Gus—good to see you." She smiled and shook his hand.

Dwayne turned to us.

"Lieutenant Nancy Stewart, I'd like you to meet Danny Logan and Toni Blair. They're with Logan Private Investigations."

"Danny Logan," Nancy said, stepping toward me and offering her hand. "I've heard of your company. I know you by reputation."

"Uh-oh," I said, shaking her hand.

She laughed. "All good," she said. "Nothing bad. You guys are held in high esteem in this building. All the old guys around here know Richard Taylor, of course. And now, you guys are making quite your own name for yourselves. You seem to be very professional—very effective."

"Thanks," I said. "We work hard at it."

She turned to Toni. "Hello, Toni," Nancy said. "It's very nice to meet you."

"Nancy and I used to work in the same unit," Dwayne said. "That would have been in . . ." he looked at the ceiling, thinking.

"That was some time ago," Nancy said, interrupting him. "Let's just leave it at that, okay, Dwayne? No sense dating ourselves."

Dwayne laughed. "Okay," he said, holding up his hands in surrender. "That works for me."

"Are you guys going to be joining us this morning?" Nancy asked Dwayne.

Dwayne shook his head. "No, I wish we could, but we can't," he said. "We've got a meeting with the DA at eleven."

"Good luck," Nancy said.

"Thanks," he said. "But I do want to get together and do lunch. We can talk about the good old days. I'll bet we've got a lot of catching up to do—a lot of secrets to share."

"Shhh!" Nancy said, smiling. "It's a date."

Dwayne and Gus left, and Nancy escorted us back to her office.

"That Dwayne is a fine man," she said, as she took a seat at a small table in her office.

"He's great," I agreed. "He and Gus both."

"Dwayne saved my life once," Nancy said. "Knowing Dwayne, I'll bet he didn't tell you."

I shook my head.

She thought for a couple of seconds. "Bad situation. Very bad— April 7, 1997. I'll never forget." She looked at us. "You should get him to tell you about it one day."

"Dwayne's a pretty modest guy," I said. "He doesn't blow his own horn much."

"Well one day, you ask him about Raymond Allan Johnson. Mr. Johnson—may he rot in hell—nearly had my number. Dwayne fixed it for me. I'll owe him forever." She thought for a few more seconds, and then she focused on us and smiled. "But you're not here to hear about my old war stories. Dwayne tells me you guys have a problem that falls into our purview."

I nodded. "I'm afraid we do."

I was just about to launch into the story when a handsome black man in his mid-thirties entered the office. He wore a badge clipped to his belt, alongside a holstered Glock. "Sorry," he said. "I couldn't get off the phone."

"Danny and Toni, this good-looking young guy is my assistant, Detective Tyrone Allison." We shook hands and Tyrone pulled a chair up to the table.

"Ty, your timing's good. Danny was just about to start explaining what's happened." She turned to me. "You ready?"

"Yeah," I said. "Thanks. Yesterday, Toni's little sister, Kelli Blair, approached Toni and me. Kelli said she was worried about her friend,

Isabel Delgado." I went on to explain Isabel's story to Nancy and Tyrone, all the way up through the details of our visit to Isabel's house. When I was done, I showed them copies of Isabel's text messages to Kelli. After they'd read the messages, they looked at each other for a second, and then Nancy looked at me.

"What's your initial impression?" Nancy asked. "What do you think happened?" If I was reading her correctly, she was probing, trying to figure out how to deliver bad news, wondering how to break it to us.

I nodded. "Let me start by saying you should know you can speak plainly to us—you don't have to worry about saying anything that will shock or offend us."

She nodded, and I continued. "That said, we're starting to think that it's possible—maybe even probable—that Isabel's gotten herself caught up in some sort of underage prostitution racket, perhaps with a gang." I looked at her. "We believe that Isabel probably felt like she needed to run away to escape her stepfather. She hooked up with some people and at first, her text messages seem to indicate that she was happy. Then, at some point, Isabel apparently came to some sort of realization that things weren't as rosy as she'd been led to believe. No word since then."

Nancy seemed to relax, knowing that she wasn't going to have to deliver unexpected news. "I'd say there's almost no doubt that that's exactly what's happened," she said. "As a matter of fact, this seems like a classic case of a runaway being scooped up. Let's start at the beginning. We usually figure that a runaway girl has less than forty-eight hours before a pimp approaches her. Of course, the pimp won't actually say he's a pimp—he'll just offer shelter, clothes, food—stuff like that. A huge number of these girls don't have any alternatives. The pimp's initial offer is like a life ring to a drowning person. The next thing she knows, the girl's completely caught up in the life."

I leaned back in my chair. "Until yesterday," I said. "I hardly knew anything at all about this. I had no idea the problem was so big."

She nodded. "It's very sad. We probably have somewhere around one thousand minor-aged girls actively being prostituted in Seattle right now.

Basically, they're sex slaves. And it's growing faster than we can stop it."

I shook my head. "It makes me wish there were more we could do. But at least with regards to Isabel Delgado, maybe we can help out."

"We'll take one-at-a-time victories," Nancy said. "Sometimes, we'll arrange stings where we can get five—maybe ten girls even. But one-at-a-time works well, too. Everyone we can pull out is one young life potentially saved."

"Speaking of that," Toni said, "what happens to these kids after you arrest them? We were wondering what would happen to Isabel when we find her."

"We don't actually arrest all that many kids anymore," Nancy said. "Not unless it's the only way to help them. A few years ago, the law enforcement community finally came to the realization that thirteen- or fourteen-year-old girls being coerced and manipulated by an older man into prostitution aren't really the criminals in the equation. They're actually the biggest victims of all—even if they are doing something illegal. That's when we changed the name of our unit from just plain 'Vice Squad' to 'Vice and High Risk Victims Unit.' It turns out that the *kids* are the high-risk victims—have been all along. They're subjected to physical violence from either the johns or their own pimps. They're exposed to deadly diseases. If they live through it, they almost always have emotional scars that last the rest of their lives. It's enough to make you cry. You wouldn't have thought that it would have taken law enforcement so long to figure that out, but bureaucratic inertia sometimes takes a while to overcome."

I nodded. "I was in the army," I said. "I understand how large organizations work. Let me ask, then, where do the kids go now if they don't go to juvenile hall? Some sort of shelter?"

"A shelter or back to their home if it's possible, although a lot of the kids can't go home. Like with Isabel, a lot of kids had their problems start at home in the first place."

I pictured Tracey Webber. "I agree 100 percent with that," I said. "There's no way Isabel can go back home with her stepfather still in the picture."

"Agreed," Nancy said.

"Any hints on the best way to tackle finding Isabel?" Toni asked. "I think we're basically planning to treat it like a missing person case."

"We don't spend much time hunting down specific individuals," Nancy said. "But I think you're probably on the right track. You said the mother was going to file a missing person report? When she does, that will get the case entered into the NCIC and WACIC databases. After that, like you say, it's pretty basic stuff—a lot of interviewing and legwork."

"But it's made all the more difficult because your subject is a minor," Tyrone added. "She's not going to be leaving any electronic traces—no credit cards, no bank withdrawals, nothing like that."

Nancy thought about this for a second. "On the other hand, there are a few things that might help you out. First, if there's a gang involved—and odds are that there is—then you might be able to work another angle and get some help from our Gang Unit. They might have some information on the gang itself. Can I see those text messages again? What were the names of the people Isabel ran into?" She looked over the transcripts.

"Crystal, Donnie, and Mikey." She turned to Tyrone. "Any of these sound familiar to you?"

He thought about it and then shook his head. "No." He looked at me. "But don't read anything into that. Unless we're dialed in on someone as a subject of one of our investigations, we probably wouldn't bump into them during our normal course of business, and we'd have no reason to know their names. The Gang Unit might, though. They bounce around in those circles all the time. I'll hook you up with those guys before you leave."

"Thanks," I said.

Nancy continued. "The second thing is that, as I was saying, whoever Isabel's gotten herself involved with is going to try and prostitute her— most likely on the Internet. That may be what led to this last message— the one that reads 'too good to be true.' She may have finally been exposed to the big picture—the timing seems about right. She might have even tried to resist. As distasteful as it is, I'd start monitoring the Backpage.

com website. Leave us a picture, and we'll keep an eye out, too. That's something we can do—we monitor Backpage all the time anyway. That's where most of the pimps run their ads. There's a reasonable chance that you'll see a picture of Isabel in some provocative pose posted there. Brace yourself."

The thought disgusted me, but the tactic made sense.

"Another lead we can give would be to talk to Annie Hooper at Angel House. Angel House is actually a series of houses that the city has recently purchased and fitted out as safe long-term places where these girls can live while they're trying to break free from their pimps. They keep the locations pretty secret, and they're heavily securitized, although from the outside, they look just like a regular house. Each house takes six or eight girls. They're able to stay in a safe, structured place without having to worry about their pimps coming after them. If you'd like, I can call Annie and see if she'd agree to a meeting."

"That would be great," Toni said.

"Annie likes to encourage her girls to speak out. She feels that it can be therapeutic for them if she can get a girl to the point where she's actively trying to help other girls break free. It's possible one of her girls might recognize these names. If it's okay with you, I'll pass on that information as well and get back to you with meeting arrangements."

"Fantastic," I said. "That'd be a big help."

"I wish we could do more," she said, "but we're not set up to hunt down individuals. It sounds like what you were planning is the right approach—you need to do some missing-person-type work to try and find Isabel."

"Agreed," I said. "We specialize in missing persons. I'm betting that we'll find her."

"Good. When you do, I'd like you to call us before you try any sort of intervention. It could be that us going after her pimp might be the safest way to rescue Isabel. Besides, if Isabel's pimp is a gang member—highly likely—then that makes it quite probable that he's armed and dangerous. We can certainly match our resources to the specific problem. We should definitely work together."

"Agreed," I said again. "We'll gladly take whatever help you're willing to provide."

Chapter 5

NANCY CALLED ANNIE Hooper before we left and put in a good word for us. It must have worked because Annie agreed to meet us for lunch at noon at a popular Caribbean-style restaurant in Fremont called Paseo. "Do you know where it's at?" Toni asked as we headed north. I was trying to get on Highway 99, but it was closed throughout a good part of the city for construction work.

"Yeah," I said. "It's on Fremont Avenue just north of Forty-Second Street. Just off 99."

"You ever been there?"

"No. But they have one in Ballard—I've been to that one. It's spicy stuff. You'll like it."

"Good," she said. We fell back into silence for a few minutes.

"Did you ever do it with a prostitute?" she asked.

I suppose I should have seen this coming.

"Why do you ask?"

"I'm just curious."

"Would it make a difference to you if I had?"

She thought about this. "Maybe," she said. "Depends on the circumstances." She turned to me. "Why? Did you?"

I stared straight ahead and didn't answer for a minute. She continued to look at me.

"I came close once," I said. "Long time ago." I paused for a few moments.

"What do you mean—'close'?"

I turned onto Aurora at Denny. I finally had a clear ramp to get on 99 northbound. "It was at Fort Benning in Georgia. We'd just graduated from Advance Infantry Training like two days before New Year's. I was all of eighteen years old. We'd all just received our new assignments and were set to ship out the next week. Three of my buddies and I had passes for New Year's Eve, so we were out to do some celebrating. Naturally, we got completely shit-faced at one of the local redneck bars down there and—well—there was this place you could go—this house. One of the guys heard about it, so we got a cab to take us there. Turned out to be a full-on whorehouse—set way back up off a country road. Had a red light out front and everything. The place was full of soldiers—soldiers everywhere. We actually had to wait our turn. But they had beer and loud music, and everyone was hootin' and hollerin' and having a good time, so we didn't care. I was young and stupid."

"What happened?"

"We finally got our turn and went inside," I said. "They had this lineup of girls—women really—they were older than I'd expected. They all looked like they were in their thirties—maybe forties even." Despite being halfway drunk at the time, I remembered the lineup. I guess something like that is one of those things that gets permanently burned into your mind's memory chips.

"Were any of them cute?"

I shrugged. "A little, I suppose. They weren't ugly. Remember, I was a little shit-faced by then. Anyway, I was last in our group to pick. When it got to be my turn, I looked at the four women who were standing there." I shrugged, seeing the women in my mind. "They were okay-looking, I suppose. They were all wearing this slinky lingerie, supposed to make 'em look sexy. And as I looked at them, that's when it hit me." I shook my head. "They didn't look sexy. Far from it, really. They actually looked kind of sad. I looked in their eyes and *bam!*—the switch got thrown, and

I was instantly turned off." I paused for a moment, remembering. "They all had sad eyes. It changed things for me—kind of woke me up, I guess." I paused for a moment, remembering. "So then I just turned and walked back outside. I had another couple of beers and waited for my friends."

Toni thought about this for a few moments, then she said, "Do you imagine under different circumstances—?"

I shrugged. "What is this? A test? Who knows. I do know that that's the closest I've ever been to being with a prostitute. And there've been plenty of opportunities since then."

"Like you got close to the fire once, and you don't want to go back."

"Got that right—I definitely don't want to go back. It was twelve years ago and today—just thinking about it—mostly all I see are those sad eyes."

* * * *

"We're buried." Annie Hooper was sitting across from us at an outside table at Paseo, explaining the shortcomings of Angel House. We'd just finished lunch. Annie was a cute, vivacious woman, I'd say in her early forties. She had wavy red hair that fell to her shoulders. Her bright, infectious smile was made all the more endearing by the band of freckles on her face. She wore a black dress with a black necklace. "We're up to six houses now—that means beds for thirty-six girls—a couple more in a pinch. And that means that at any one time, I probably have four more girls on a waiting list—girls I don't have room for."

"There's that many girls trying to get straight?" Toni said.

"That's right. The girls are all minors—by our charter with the city, we can only accept minors. Nearly all of them have been working for pimps. We give them a safe, secure home. We try to keep the locations secret to keep the pimps from coming by. They tend to find out anyway, but we have cameras, alarms, and heavy locks—and nearly instant response from the police. If a pimp shows up, he gets hit with a restraining order and a pretty firm warning. After that, most of them figure it's not worth the trouble, and they don't show up again. Most of them seem to get the message. At least so far. We're diligent." She smiled. "And maybe, just a little lucky."

She paused and then continued. "Anyway, we work with the girls. We have classes and counseling for them. We encourage them to get their GEDs. The houses have normal house-type rules and structures, but we don't have real heavy-handed enforcement. And it's all voluntary—it's not jail. The girls are all there because they want to be. If they want to leave, they can. But if they want to stay, they have to follow the rules."

"How successful are you?"

"Let's have Carla answer that," Annie said. She turned to the dark-haired girl sitting to her left. When we'd arrived, Annie had introduced herself and Carla Nguyen. Carla was a pretty Asian girl, probably about eighteen years old. She lived at one of the homes in the Angel House network.

"It works pretty good," Carla said. "The girls are uncertain when they first get there, but they're surrounded by other girls who've already been through it. After a while, most of the girls take it pretty seriously."

"You went through all of this?" Toni asked. "Out on the streets?"

Carla nodded. "Yeah. I worked. I had a pimp."

"How long, if you don't mind me asking," Toni said.

"I don't mind," Carla answered. "Four years. I started when I was twelve. I got arrested for the fourth—no, the fifth time when I was sixteen. That time they told me I could come to Angel House. The first house was just opened then. I got to meet Annie." She turned and smiled at Annie, the love and respect easy to see. "I've been there almost two years. My time's about up now."

"You're happy?" I asked.

She smiled. "Yes. Happier than I've ever been in my whole life. For the first time, I feel like I'm in control of my own destiny. I got my GED. I'm already enrolled in U-Dub for the fall semester."

"That's great," Toni said. "Danny and I went to U-Dub, and my little sister's going this fall, too. What are you going to study?"

"Psychology, I think," Carla said. "I want to be a therapist. I want to be a counselor for girls in the same position I've been in."

"See?" Annie said, fairly beaming. "What a success story. And Carla's not the only one. All of these girls are special—every one of them. They all have something to offer this world. They just need a little love and encouragement—sometimes the first they've received in their young lives. And protection. They need to be protected. They need people to stop taking advantage of them. We give them that at Angel House."

"Sounds awesome," I said. "A very noble cause."

"Thanks," Annie said. "It's hard work, but I go home proud."

"And thank you for agreeing to meet with us on such short notice," I said. "I think Nancy told you about our particular problem."

"She did. Carla and I talked about it on the way over."

Carla nodded. "Since I got to Angel House, I've talked to a lot of girls who got picked up at the Mall and the Alderwood Mall," Carla said. "I'm pretty sure that there's a gang working up there—they call themselves the North Side Street Boyz. That's Boyz with a 'z.'"

"Do you know anything about this gang?" I asked.

She shook her head. "No—only that they hang out at the north-side malls a lot."

"And you think they're basically recruiting these girls and pimping them out?" Toni said.

She nodded. "Yeah."

"How's it work?" I asked. "After they get recruited, do the girls live with the pimps?"

"Some work it that way," she said. "Sometimes, if it's a gang of guys, they live somewhere else, and there's like a house boss who lives with the girls. I think that's the way it is with NSSB."

"Would they at least live close together in that case?"

Carla thought about this. "I don't know," she said. "It makes sense, I guess."

I nodded. "In our case, the only names we have to go by are a woman named Crystal, and two guys—one named Donnie and one named Mikey.

Have you ever heard of these people?"

"I haven't. But I'll ask around when I get back home. Probably one of the other girls has."

"I'm going to give you another name, too," Annie said as she wrote something down on the back of her business card. "Reverend Arthur Jenkins. Reverend Art lives in the area where a lot of the gang members are from. He's pretty close to a lot of the current gang members."

"Where would we find him?" I asked.

"He's the pastor at the Twenty-Third Street Baptist Church on Capitol Hill. If you'd like, I'd be happy to give him a call for you and introduce you."

"Fantastic," I said. "We could use all the help we can get."

"Reverend Art might know these guys," Annie said. "And he's a wonderful, caring man. I think the guys in the gang respect him, but still he won't protect one of them if they're involved in running prostitutes."

"That'd be great," I said. "Meanwhile, let me ask another question. Apparently, Isabel's been gone about a month—that is, she was recruited about a month ago. Carla, can you describe the process of what happens after someone gets recruited? Maybe the first month?"

"I'll try," she said. "First, they'll try to make her comfortable—safe and secure. They'll treat her nice and buy her things. She'll start to feel special. Then, the pimp will probably have sex with her. Even if she's scared, she'll go along because he's been so good to her. She won't want to disappoint him. He'll keep treating her nice, and then she'll start to think she's in love with him. He'll even tell her he loves her."

"And all this happens when?" Toni asked.

"I'd say the first couple of weeks," Carla said.

"Wow, they move fast."

She nodded. "Yeah. Then, not very long after, he'll tell her he needs her to have sex with a friend of his. As a favor to him. She'll do it because she wants to make him happy. Then it'll be another. Next thing you know, she'll have her picture taken, and he'll tell her she has to start going out on dates. He'll give her a quota. He'll tell her that she can't come home until she brings in her quota. And she'll want to come home, believe me. When she does, he'll make her turn over all the money. She can't keep anything."

"So she'll be totally dependent on the pimp?" I asked.

She nodded. "She'll love him, and she'll think he loves her. She'll do anything for him."

"And what happens if she doesn't?" Toni asked.

"Then he'll get mean," Carla said. "I've been punched. I've been burned with a cigarette. One time he made me stand naked in front of other girls while he beat me with a belt. Another time, when I complained, he called some of his friends over and they gang-raped me. He even threatened to sell me to another pimp in California."

"Did you ever get to the point where you wanted to just leave?"

"Not really," she said. "At least, not until I was a lot older. Once you're in it, it's kind of all you know. Besides—through it all, I felt like he cared about me. He was like, 'you know I love you baby, but I need you to do this for us.' I know now that he was lying—he didn't love me. Well, maybe he did. I don't know, even now. It's weird, you know? But I know now that whatever he thought of me, he cared a lot more about himself. And he cared a lot more about using me to make himself money."

"But still," Toni said, "while you're there, you do what he says."

She nodded. "Yeah. You don't feel like you have much of a choice. You don't want to make him upset partly because you love him—or think you do. And partly because you're afraid of him."

"How many guys would you have to see?" Toni asked.

"Until I made my quota, which was usually $500," Carla said. "If it was a good night, I could make that with two or three guys. If it was a bad night, it might take ten."

"Did you have to walk the streets?"

"Sometimes. Not too often. Mostly we had dates with guys who called in from the Internet ads. We'd get our pictures taken in a sexy pose, and he'd put it up on Backpage. We'd get tons of calls. If we had a gap and weren't close to making quota, then they'd drive us over, and we'd hit the streets."

"Where?"

"Mostly a place we called the Track. It's between Lake Union and downtown. Kind of by the Space Needle."

"And you did this every night?"

"Pretty much. I figure in four years I was with four thousand guys."

"What?" Toni asked, incredulously. "Did you say four thousand guys?"

"Yeah. Figure three to five guys a night—six days a week. Sometimes more."

"Pretty mind-blowing, isn't it?" Annie asked.

I shook my head. "It leaves you speechless."

"We figured it out—we think I made my pimp probably a half million dollars," Carla said.

"Half a million!" I said.

"That's right. And I wasn't his only girl."

"How many girls did he have?" I asked.

"Most of the time, three or four," she said.

"And they all worked the same way?"

She nodded. "Pretty much."

"So that works out to what—" I calculated in my head, "—$1.5 million in four years—that's almost $400,000 per year for the pimp! Wow. I guess that explains why they're drawn to it."

Annie nodded. "They make a lot of money off these girls."

"And you didn't get to keep any of the money?" I asked.

She shook her head. "We got an allowance—twenty-five dollars per week. If we did something really good—like bring in a really big night—we might get a bonus: fifty dollars or something. But mostly, we didn't get anything." She paused. "I mean, he bought food and clothes, but we didn't get any money."

"Carla," Toni said, "let me get your opinion. In her last text message, Isabel says that it was 'too good to be true.' What do you think was happening?"

"This was like three weeks after she was recruited?" Carla said.

"Yeah. It was on May 28, and she was picked up sometime around May 7."

"It sounds like they were telling her she was going to have to go to work, and she didn't want to go."

"Did you ever see that before?"

"Yeah, a few times. It happened to me. I was twelve. I didn't want to have to start meeting other men."

"What happened?"

"I got beat up. Usually, that's what happens."

"And you had to give in?"

She nodded. "Yeah. He beat me—said he'd kill me. He said he'd kill my family if I ran. So I did what he said. It's not like I had much of a choice. This always happened when I pushed back. Later, he'd come and make up, and then things would be good for a while. As long as I did what I was supposed to."

"And what about the men you were forced to see?" Toni asked.

"They were the worst," Carla said with disdain. "I've been beaten by johns. I've been stabbed twice. I've been choked. I've been raped three times. I even got thrown out of a moving car once. We were just like garbage to them. Basically, they suck."

"I'm so sorry someone put you through all that," Toni said. "Thank God you made it through in one piece."

Carla smiled. "I did," she said. "I made it." She reached her hand across the table. Annie took it and gave it a squeeze.

I watched them. Carla's nightmare was over—at least the physical part. I suspected that the mental part might take longer to deal with. A young girl can't be forced into sex with four thousand men in a four-year period and come out without serious emotional scars. These were going to take a while—maybe a whole lifetime—to overcome. Thank goodness for caring people like Annie Hooper—people who gave a damn and weren't content to turn away and pretend the problem didn't exist.

But Carla was safe now. For Isabel, though, it was different picture. Unless we could find her and pull her out—and do it fast—Isabel's long nightmare was just about to begin.

Chapter 6

WE WERE ON a roll. When Annie called Reverend Jenkins to see if he'd be willing to talk to us, his administrative secretary said that the Reverend would be in a bible study meeting until two thirty, but that he'd be free to see us afterward for a few minutes. The Twenty-Third Street Baptist Church is located right on Twenty-Third just a little south of Madison. We had just enough time to return to our office and make a few phone calls before we hit the road again, this time headed south. We arrived five minutes early and found a parking space down Twenty-Third and across the street on Howell. By the time we walked back across the street, the study meeting had apparently just adjourned because a small crowd was gathered on the steps in the small courtyard outside the church's office. Reverend Arthur Jenkins was immediately recognizable. He was a tall, thin, very nice-looking black man in his fifties. His dark hair was short and touched with a brushing of silver. He was clean-shaven. He wore a white short-sleeved shirt with black slacks and a black tie. The Reverend was surrounded by a small throng of five or six mostly gray-haired ladies. Even as we approached, his ready smile and warm laugh made it easy to see why he appeared so well loved by the women.

"And you'd do well to remember that, sister Evelyn!" we overhead him say to one of the ladies as we approached. He had a deep, soothing voice. Evelyn and all the other women laughed like schoolgirls on a playground, clearly enjoying their time with this charismatic man. We watched them chat for a few minutes as the group dispersed.

Reverend Jenkins ignored us until the last woman turned to leave, preferring to give her his undivided attention. Only when they said good-bye did he seem to notice us—although he'd surely seen us standing to the side, waiting.

"Reverend Jenkins," I said, as I approached. "My name is Danny Logan." I nodded to Toni. "This is my partner, Toni Blair. We were hoping to speak to you for a couple of minutes."

He nodded. "Luella slipped me a note saying you'd be coming by," he said, as he stepped forward and shook our hands. "What can I do for you two?"

"Sir," I began, "we're private investigators. Toni's sister came to us with the story of a classmate of hers who ran away from home last month on her sixteenth birthday, apparently because she was having problems with her stepfather. We were touched by—well, frankly, by the tragedy of the story, so we agreed to look into it. We've since come to believe that as bad as her home life was, she may have now gotten herself into even worse trouble. We think she's been recruited into what appears to be a gang involved with the prostitution of under-aged girls. We're hoping to find her and get her out of there before it's too late."

He studied me intently for a moment. Then he said, "That's a worthwhile endeavor, isn't it. And you're hoping I might be able to shed some light on the gang members for you?"

I nodded. "Yes, sir. That's it exactly."

"What do you hope to do if you find them?" he asked.

"Well, naturally, we want to rescue the young woman."

He studied us for a moment, and then he nodded. "Good. I'll be happy to do what I can," he said.

"Thank you very much," I said. "We appreciate it."

"I'm not sure how much help I can be," he said, "but I'll do what I can. Let's go inside, shall we?"

We followed him inside the office and classroom area of the church.

He led us down a hall that was nearly completely covered with photos.

"The church has been here a long time, hasn't it?" I asked, as I noticed a picture of Reverend Martin Luther King Jr. on the wall.

"It certainly has," he said, pausing while I studied the photo. "The church is eighty years old next year. Of course, this isn't the original building. The first building actually burned down in 1934. Then, we outgrew the next one in the seventies. We built this one in 1975."

"Very impressive," I said, turning to him. "How long have you been here?"

"Fifteen years this past April," he said.

I smiled. "Well, judging by the mood of the prayer group that we saw, you appear to be doing a good job."

He laughed. "Thank you. We have ourselves a good old time. I'll let you in on a little secret: when you say 'bible study' to most people, they almost immediately form an image in their minds of a quiet, somber, studious-type group, all huddled up over their well-worn King James. Except for maybe a Benedictine monk, who'd want to act like that? So around here, we spice it up. We make it a little more human. Think about it. Who gave us our sense of humor?" Before we could answer, he continued. "It was the good Lord, of course. He made it so that we can laugh and have a good time. And we figure that since the Lord saw fit to give us a sense of humor—the ability to laugh and to be happy—why, then he must have wanted us to use it. So we decided to have some fun with our bible study group—lighten things up a bit."

"Looks like it's working," I said. "Everyone seemed pretty happy outside there. Who knows—might even make me want to come to a meeting and check things out."

"You're welcome anytime!" he beamed. He opened his arms up wide. "Come on down, brother Daniel!" He smiled for a second, then he said, "You know that Daniel is a historic biblical name, don't you?"

"Of course," I said, smiling. "I've got my own book in the Old Testament."

He laughed. "Indeed you do, young man. Indeed you do."

Toni looked at me. I could tell she was much impressed with my biblical acumen. I'm full of surprises.

We followed Reverend Jenkins through an office area where two women were seated.

"Luella," he said, "I'm going to be with these folks here for about thirty minutes or so. How's that fit in?"

"You're good," Luella said. "Your next meetin's not till three thirty."

"Thank you."

He held the door for Toni and me, and then closed it behind us.

* * * *

"Have a seat here," he said, pointing to a couple of chairs across from his desk. The surface of his desk was neat and organized—a man after my own heart. The walls, like the hallways, were covered with photos. What impressed me was the fact that there weren't any pictures of politicians, no celebrities, no famous people at all. Instead, except for a PhD in Theology diploma from Liberty University, the common theme of the photos was Reverend Jenkins and children. Either in a classroom, or on a playground, or at a hospital, I didn't notice a single photo without a child.

When we were all seated, I said, "Thanks again, Reverend Jenkins." I nodded to the diploma. "Or should I say 'Doctor Jenkins'?"

He smiled. "Don't do either one of those," he said. "I always thought that 'Doctor' sounded a little pretentious—particularly around here. We're a long way away from any ivory towers. Just call me Reverend Art. That's what everyone calls me around here."

"Okay," I said. I nodded in the direction of the wall. "Looks like you have a soft spot for kids."

He smiled again. "I do," he said. "I do indeed."

"Any children of your own?" Toni asked.

"Six," he said. "Six children—all under the age of seven."

"Wow," Toni said. "How—?"

Before she could finish, Reverend Art said, "Before you accuse me of either spousal abuse or polygamy, they're all adopted. We have our own little Rainbow Coalition going in the Jenkins household. We've got three sets of siblings—two from Vietnam, two kids from right here in the neighborhood from a member of our congregation who ran into some legal problems a while back, and the twins—two little ones we just adopted from Romania."

"Your wife must be really busy," Toni said.

"She is, she is," he said, laughing. "Maybe it is spousal abuse after all?" He laughed again, a twinkle in his eye. "Nah, she loves it. She considers it God's work. And, of course, she's right. We are truly blessed. People are always saying what a wonderful thing we've done for these children, but I'll let you in on a little secret. No one seems to recognize that we're getting back twice as much as we're giving out with these little ones."

"Even so," I said, "you and your wife are to be commended. It really is a wonderful thing you're doing for these children."

"Well," he said, "just as you're trying to do the right thing for this missing girl." He smoothly segued into the purpose of our meeting. "Tell me about her and what's happened."

We spent the next fifteen minutes filling Reverend Art in on Isabel— her attempt to flee the horror of her home life, the text messages that told their own ominous story, and our meetings with both Nancy Stewart and Annie Hooper.

"Isn't that Carla Nguyen an impressive young lady?" Reverend Art said. "She's a poster child for what motivates a lot of good people to step up and get involved."

"She's been through a lot," I agreed.

"She's been through a living hell," he said. "And she's making her way back. Step by step, she's turning back into a sweet, caring girl. Young lady, really." He thought about it for a minute. "She'll never be able to forget what she went through—what was done to her—but she's learning how to deal with it."

"It seems like she's not going to let it define her," Toni said.

Reverend Art looked at her. "Exactly. It's not who she is. It's what was done to her, but it's not who she is." He turned to me. "So now, we've got to yank Isabel out of this situation before she falls into the same trap."

I nodded.

"And Carla said something about the North Side Street Boyz? And you said Isabel's text message says the names were Crystal, Donnie, and Mikey?"

"Yes. Does any of that ring a bell with you?"

He leaned back and nodded. "I'm afraid it does," he said. "Part of it, anyway. I don't know anyone named Crystal. But the North Side Street Boyz is a gang that split off from a Central District gang that called themselves the Madison GDs."

"GDs?" I asked.

"Gangster Disciples," he said. "They're like the Bloods and the Crips. They started in Chicago, and they're pretty much nationwide now. Anyway, there's a young man named Donnie Martin, used to live around here. Based on what you're saying, I imagine he's the 'Donnie' referred to in Isabel's text message. He was a member of the Madison GDs. Some time ago, he splintered off and formed his own gang in the area north of the U-District. Down here, the GDs focus mostly on drug dealing. I understand Donnie's taken the NSSBs in a whole new direction—they're totally focused on prostitution. Basically, they're organized pimps."

"Any idea how big they are?" I asked.

He thought for a moment, and then he shook his head. "I don't know for sure. Probably not very big, be my guess. Donnie never impressed me as the organizational type. I don't think he was overly worried about growing anything. Except his own wallet, maybe."

"So you know this Donnie Martin personally?" Toni asked.

"Oh, yeah, indeed I do. In fact, as a youngster, around about ten years ago, he used to come to Sunday school here off and on. His aunt was a member of our congregation, and he mostly stayed with her back then. Sadly, she passed away earlier this year—I think it was February. Of course, Donnie hadn't been to services in years, but he came to her funeral. He was driving a white BMW with tinted windows. He was dressed really sharp. I asked him what he was up to, and all he'd say was that he'd moved up north. So later, I started asking around—kind of subtle-like."

"People talk to you?" I asked.

He smiled. "I'm the pastor, aren't I?" he said. "I'm not ashamed to say that I have no problem snooping information from the members of the church in order to protect them from some of the bad apples around here. And, of course, they talk. Most of them, anyway. Sometimes, the gang members come back and spread some of their money around. That tends to quiet folks down a little. But not everyone, and not forever. So I talk. And I listen. A little hint here, a little hint there, eventually the whole picture starts to emerge."

"Do the guys themselves ever talk to you—other than Donnie at his aunt's funeral?" I asked.

He smiled. "When they were children, they did. When they grow up—well now, that's different. They don't have so much to say now. Every now and again, one of these guys will step back in for a talk. And if they're trying to do something positive with their lives—why then I'll help 'em, of course. But if it's just business as usual for them, then they know about me and who I am. They know better than to tell me anything if they're involved in something illegal. I'll turn from their best friend into their worst enemy in a quick minute."

"What do you mean—they know about you and who you are? You mean in your role as a minister?"

He looked at me. "Annie didn't tell you?"

I was puzzled. "No. Tell us what?"

He smiled. "I was one of 'em," he said. "I was one of these guys. Before I was ordained, I spent seven years in Folsom State Prison in California for drug trafficking. I spent seven years of my life in prison because I was moving drugs for the Stone Canyon Bloods in east LA. I did that every day for years, and I finally got nailed. Praise God I didn't get killed. I was in the gang for almost twelve years before prison, and for another couple in prison before I woke up. These guys up here?" He stopped and smiled. "They got nothin' on me."

* * * *

"For some reason that I don't understand and cannot explain, the Lord Jesus Christ has seen fit to give me not one life but two—the first life before I accepted Him as my savior, in which I didn't do a single thing I am proud of—at least, nothing that comes readily to mind, and the second life after I accepted Him—in which I've made it my life's work to make up for the first one. Maybe God wants this humble servant to be His instrument in my small part of the world—I don't know. But I know one day, sitting in my cell by myself, that a light went on—figuratively speaking. You may think I'm crazy, but I actually heard a voice—all but commanded me to change my ways. There was a faith-based group within the prison, and I joined. Not long after, I left the gang for good. I took my newfound faith in the Lord, I got my GED, and then I actually used the rest of my time to get a bachelor's degree in divinity from Lincoln College. When I got out, I became an ordained minister."

"That's a pretty incredible success story," I said.

"I'll say," Toni added. "A remarkable turnaround."

"Could've turned out a lot different," Reverend Art said. "I owe it all to a power bigger than little old Arthur Jenkins. I owe it to the Lord." He paused, lost in thought. His eyes were closed—perhaps he was praying. I couldn't tell. Then, he opened his eyes suddenly. "And to some good people who saw something worth salvaging in me. But one thing's for certain," he added. "I am left with a pretty thorough knowledge of what makes these young people around here think the way they think and live the way they live. I've been there. And I can tell you—it's real simple. In fact it comes down to two things: money—," he held up one finger, "—and respect." He held up another. "These guys think if they get one, the other's gonna follow."

"And being a pimp gets them plenty of money."

"Oh, it sure does. A lot of money. From their perspective, it's like selling drugs, only better. After you sell the drugs, they're gone. These guys sell these girls over and over again. Carla tell you how many times she got sold?"

We nodded.

"That's tragic," he said. "Another thing. With drugs, you actually have to get your hands a little dirty. You got to make pickups and deliveries. There's guys with guns all over the place. With pimping, the girls do all the dirty work. The guys stay home and get stoned. All they have to do is keep the girls in line. It's a perfect gig. That is, long as you don't care that you're stealing somebody's soul."

"And you think this sounds like it could be Donnie Martin in this case?"

He looked at me and nodded. "Yep," he said with resolution. "If it's the North Side Street Boyz who are involved, I'd say it's almost certain. This is right up Donnie's alley."

Great, I thought. *Now it's confirmed.* "What can you tell us about this guy?" I asked.

"He's probably twenty-one now, maybe twenty-two. Tall guy. Good-looking. Turned into a sharp dresser. Spent some time in juvenile detention—a couple of years. I wish I had an exact address for him now, but I don't—best I can give you is a general area."

He paused and thought for a second before he continued. "Like I said, I talked to him at the funeral. I can say that he may be a disturbed young man, but he's smart. Course, he won't tell me too much, but I remember he did say that he's living north of the university. Says he's working in 'entertainment.' Yeah, right. So later, I start talking to people, piecing things together, you know what I'm saying?"

We nodded as we both wrote down the information in our notebooks.

"Here's what I find. You know you got your typical gangbangers all over the south side of Seattle getting into prostitution right and left. But Donnie? No. I find out that Donnie's gone north, just like he said. Everybody else working south; Donnie's working north. Smaller market but almost no organized competition. He's probably got everything north of Lake Union marked as his territory. Apparently, he and some other guys run a string of prostitutes up there."

"Would one of those other guys be this Mikey character?" Toni said.

"Mikey," Reverend Art said, slowly. "Yeah. I think that'd most likely be DeMichael Hollins. He's Donnie's usual sidekick. He grew up here in the neighborhood, too."

We wrote this down.

"What're these guys' natures?" I asked. "What are they like? Are they dangerous? Psychos? The kind of guys that hurt people for fun?"

He leaned back in his chair. "Wow," he said. "Let me think about that. I've got to try and recall my college psychology classes here." He pondered the question for a few moments, and then he leaned forward and said, "I wouldn't say these boys are crazy—not in the clinical sense, anyway. I don't believe they were born with some sort of physiological deficiency that made them into the guys they are now. That's the good news. The bad news is, it doesn't matter. They still show many of the same symptoms. Mostly, I think they're just fools who grew up without the proper guidance and developed the wrong moral compass. It happens all the time around here. They didn't start out bad—they just grew into it."

"You're right," I said. "In the end, what's the difference?"

He smiled. "Maybe something in the nature of reformability, I suppose. Can't really cure a guy with a loose screw in his brain. But you might be able to reshape someone who grew up bad. Look at me. I was a pretty bad dude, myself. Not like Donnie, but I was no saint. I wasn't mentally ill, though. So when the calling came, I was able to answer, praise the Lord." He paused for a moment, and then he said, "But as to your real point—what's the difference? Ain't no difference at all if either of 'em's got the drop on you. Don't matter if the guy holding the gun is a natural-born psycho or if it's someone who just grew up mean and stupid. Either way, they don't care about you, and you're going to be dead right quick."

He paused again.

"Just so you understand clearly," he spoke slowly, "I can flat out guarantee you that Donnie for certain—and that probably means the other guys, too—they're all armed to the teeth. I know Donnie well enough to say that he's not afraid to pull out his gun and start shooting if he feels threatened." Reverend Art leaned forward. "And the thing of it is, he's likely to feel threatened over almost anything—you can't tell. He's like one of them rattlesnakes some of those crazy preachers in the South hold. They pick it up and stroke it twenty-five times. Snake's cool with it. Flicks his little tongue out at 'em, but he don't do anything else. Then they pick it up the twenty-sixth time—wham! Snake bites 'em right in the neck for no reason anyone can see. Snake knows—but no one else can tell." He leaned back and looked at us—first one and then the other. "Case you're not getting me, don't take this kid too lightly just because he's young. Word on the street is that he's vowed to never go back to jail. He says he'd rather die shooting. He's a dangerous young man. I agree 100 percent that you need to get in there and rescue Isabel, or else Donnie's going to consume her like Satan himself. But when you do, understand that Donnie's not just going to sit back and watch you. He's going to put up a fight."

I nodded. "Thanks, Reverend Art. We'll watch out."

Chapter 7

I WAS HOME by myself later that night. I'd just popped in *Songbird* by Eva Cassidy. As is my usual custom, I automatically skipped over track one—"Fields of Gold." Don't get me wrong, I like the song. I'm not what you'd call a "weeper" (okay, just a little) but to this day, I can't listen to Eva Cassidy sing "Fields of Gold" without breaking down and becoming a useless, blubbering fool. Doesn't matter where I'm at or who I'm with— if that song comes on, I have to get out before I lose it. Even if they played it at a friggin' Seahawks game, I'd still have to bolt for the tunnels (me and probably forty thousand other people). I love all her music, but with that particular song, she reaches into me and touches something, and I'm a goner. I think it probably starts with Eva's incredible voice. Then I think of her sad story, and then I move to thinking about all the friends I lost in combat, and then I think of lost relatives, and then it just spirals completely out of control altogether. Happens fast, too. It leaves me a wreck. So I generally do the safe thing and skip it.

Especially tonight. Toni was having dinner with her mom and sister. Cool. I mean, I need my space, right? Give me time to get some stuff done around my place. Guy stuff. So I picked up my guitar and twanged through a couple of songs I'd been working on. I'm a decent guitar player, but it wasn't happening tonight, so I put it away. I picked up an epic James Jones novel I was halfway through, read about half a page, and then I stalled out, so I set it down. I sat there on the sofa and looked around for a minute. I got up and turned the stereo off and the television on. Five minutes later, bored, I got back up and turned the TV off and the stereo back on. I went down and sat at the table with my laptop.

Eva sang "Wade in the Water" while I stared a hole right through the computer screen, lost in thought. Damn! What was the matter with me? What the hell was going on around here?

I shook my head and refocused on the computer. Maybe I could do some work. I'd already mapped out the NSSB area north of the U-District where Reverend Art had said Donnie was living. Tomorrow, Toni and Doc and I were going to split up and start canvasing all the businesses. Our idea was to start showing pictures of Isabel around to the shop owners in hopes someone might recognize her and help us zero in on her. A bit of a long shot, to be sure. But at least we'd be doing something.

Now, I found myself staring at a map of what the Seattle Police Department calls the Track—a high-activity prostitution area just south of my apartment. The area—bounded on the north by Mercer, Westlake on the east, Fifth Avenue on the west, and Lenore on the south—is primarily a business district loaded with business-type hotels, meaning Holiday Inn, Travelodge, Comfort Suites—that sort of establishment. At the same time, it's such a high-profile area for prostitutes that the city has actually designated it as what they call a SOAP zone—"Stay Out of Area of Prostitution." Penalties for prostitutes with arrest records who are arrested again in a SOAP zone are high.

I never knew it before, but this area almost reaches my front door. When I saw this, I was suddenly struck with an idea. I'd never noticed any prostitution-type activity around my place before, but I suppose it could happen. But if it was happening, how did it take place? What did it look like? I decided to hop in the Jeep and take a cruise around the Track for an hour or so, just to see what I could see. I was under no illusions that I would find Isabel out there, at least not tonight. Hell, for that matter, I'd only seen one little picture of Isabel before, and I wasn't sure I'd be able to recognize her on sight anyway. But maybe I would see some activity.

I was thinking that perhaps I might be able to get a sense as to what the girls went through on the streets. I didn't plan on talking to anybody or even stopping. Just observe, maybe get a feel for the area.

Of course, getting out and doing a little recon could have another benefit. It might help me to get my mind off Toni—at least for a while.

I shut off the computer and the stereo, strapped on my sidearm, turned out the lights, and shut the door behind me. I had no idea what to expect.

* * * *

Maybe I'd formed pictures in my mind of the stereotypical scenes of streetwalkers standing in dark doorways, approaching cars as they slowed down for stop signs. Nope—I didn't see anything like this. Maybe the fact that it had rained earlier had something to do with it, I don't know. Fortunately, the rain had stopped, but the streets and the sidewalks were still wet. I drove around for maybe half an hour, and I think I saw three or four girls who looked more like secretaries than prostitutes. I saw no prostitutes or, I should say, no one who I thought looked like a prostitute. I suppose I should mention that I have very little experience identifying prostitutes, so it's possible that I wouldn't recognize one even if I saw one.

After about a half hour of burning gas with this fruitless exercise, I had a sudden, enlightening thought. I am a detective, after all. Eventually, I figure shit out. Here was my thought. If the Track fell within an official SOAP area, the girls probably knew this. If they were going to get busted, they didn't want it to be here. So they probably didn't make a habit of streetwalking in areas that were heavily patrolled by the police, as this area appeared to be. I'd have to get a little smarter if I wanted to discover any activity. See how this detective stuff works?

So I drove into the parking lot of a hotel called the Snuggle Inn, right off Aurora, right in the heart of the Track. The place looked like a typical suites-type business hotel—one of those where all the rooms have Wi-Fi and little mini-fridges tucked beneath a counter that holds a mini-coffee pot and a small basket of coffee packets with brand names no one's ever heard of. The hotel was only a few years old, still neat and clean. It consisted of four buildings surrounding a central courtyard with a swimming pool.

I drove around to the back and found a space near the stairway. Then I switched off the lights and waited.

Ten minutes later, a girl walked past. Was she a prostitute? I couldn't tell. I didn't get a chance to see her face as she passed in front of the Jeep, but I watched her walk up the stairs and saw her knock on one of the doors and be let inside. Then, thirty minutes later, the door opened, and she walked out.

As she walked down the stairs, she was facing me, and I could see that she was a cute blond girl. She wore a bulky coat over loose, billowy pants that appeared to be gathered at the ankle. As she passed beneath the outside lights, I could see that she was heavily made up—it was impossible for me to tell her age–she could have been sixteen or she could have been twenty six. She turned and walked back to the front entrance, a path that would take her right past the front of the Jeep.

When she reached the edge of the Jeep, she noticed me. She slowed down and looked at me. Our eyes locked, and I knew. She paused for a moment, but I didn't move, so she picked up her pace and hurried past the Jeep. I probably scared her—she must have thought I was at least a little strange, sitting in the dark parking lot. She turned the corner and walked quickly away, silhouetted in the gap between the buildings by the overhead lights.

* * * *

I'd been home maybe fifteen minutes when the phone rang. Caller ID: Toni.

"I'm home," she said. "Safe and sound." I'd asked her to call when she got home. Don't ask me to explain this sudden propensity to worry about her just because I'm not there. Truth be told, she's more than capable of taking care of herself. Still . . .

"Good," I answered. "I'm glad."

"You miss me?"

"A little."

"Just a little?"

"Well, I had a good book."

"Bastard."

I laughed. "Just kidding. I missed you. A lot. How was your dinner?"

"It was nice. Mom's good. Kell's all antsy about us finding Isabel."

"It's only been two days," I said. "Tell her I'm supposed to get my magic wand out of the shop tomorrow. Then, I'll just go ahead and give it a wave, and Isabel will appear."

"Very funny."

"It's not like we're sitting on our hands. It won't happen overnight."

"I know. But she doesn't. And besides, patience isn't her strong suit."

"Did you explain things to her?"

"Yeah, she's cool. She'll be okay. For a while."

It was silent for a few seconds.

"What'd you really do tonight?" she asked.

I chuckled. "Really? I played the guitar. I read. I watched TV. Then I did some work."

"You *were* busy," she said. "What kind of work did you do?"

"I did a little prep work for our canvas tomorrow. Looked at maps. Looked at aerials, that kind of stuff. Then, I got a crazy idea and decided I'd go for a recon drive through the Track. You know where that is?"

"Yeah. You see anything useful?"

"It was weird. There were actually more SPD squad cars than there were people. The area seems to be really heavily patrolled. I didn't see any prostitutes."

"Uh, gee whiz. Maybe that's because it's so heavily patrolled," she said.

"Duh."

"Besides, most of the girls probably work through the Internet now, anyway."

"I figured all that shit out all by myself about half an hour after I started driving around. That, plus the fact that the entire area called the Track falls into a special anti-prostitution zone."

"A SOAP zone?" she asked.

"You know about SOAP zones?"

"Duh." Again with the "duh."

"Touché. I should have known. Anyway, after that, I went and parked at a little hotel, just to see if I could see anything there."

"Did you? See anything?"

"Sure enough. A few minutes after I park, a girl walks past me, walks up the stairs, and knocks on a door. Door opens—she heads on in. Half hour later, out she comes."

"Could you see her?" she asked.

"On the way out? Yeah, I could see her."

What'd she look like?"

"I think she looked like a prostitute," I said.

"Really? How could you tell?" she asked. "What does a prostitute look like? Dress? Makeup?" She asked.

"Makeup, for sure. She was dressed pretty plainly, but she was heavily made up. But that wasn't it. You want to know what the big tip-off was for me?"

"What?"

"When she was walking past, she walked right in front of the Jeep. When she got there, she slowed down—almost stopped. Then, just for a second, she looked right at me, and our eyes locked. The thing that got me—it was her eyes. She had the same eyes as I remember from Fort Benning. The same sad eyes."

Chapter 8

THE NEXT MORNING, Thursday, June 7, I called Nancy and passed on the information Reverend Art had provided, particularly the names Donnie Martin and DeMichael Hollins, along with details about the North Side Street Boyz. She said she'd spoken to the gang-unit commander and that he was in the process of talking to the two detectives in charge of the north area. She agreed to have them call me directly.

After the call, the Logan PI team held a short meeting in the office before breaking up for the day. Reverend Art had said that NSSB was active in the area north of the U-District. Our plan was for Doc and Toni and me to leave the office at nine thirty or so and drive over to the Ravenna area, which abutted the U-District on the north. Kenny'd done a little research, and in addition to the 8 x 10 photos of Isabel he'd printed for us from the mall photo-strip photos, he gave each of us a list of half a dozen shopping centers to canvas. We decided to pay particular attention to drugstores, coffee shops, beauty supply stores, hair salons, and clothing boutiques—the kinds of places we figured Isabel, Crystal, and the other girls would visit and be remembered.

Walking the street, talking to shopkeepers, showing pictures around—this is about as low-tech old school as it gets for detective work. It's pretty much the way it's been done for a hundred years or so. Granted, it's a little crude, and it's not terribly efficient. But when you're looking for a low-profile missing person who either by choice or by coercion is off the grid, it's still the best way to develop leads and get the ball rolling.

Ironically, even though she was just sixteen, Isabel wasn't completely off the grid. For starters, she'd left home with a cell phone. Kenny'd had some luck in the past using a cell phone to locate a missing person. The easy way to do this requires the missing cell phone to be equipped with GPS (most new phones are) and its owner to either have installed an appropriate app or subscribed to an appropriate service. If one of these things has happened—and if the owner of the phone gives his consent—then the cell phone can be remotely commanded to "ping" its exact GPS coordinates. This can be very useful in many situations—parents keeping track of their kids, for example. The drawback—at least from our perspective—is that absent the owner's advance consent—something that's basically impossible to obtain if someone's gone missing—the phone won't respond to a ping request.

Of course, law enforcement agencies have the ability to get around the consent requirement. And, thanks to Kenny Hale, so do we. Not legally, but from time to time I'll make the judgment call that the ends justify the means. I won't use it to track down someone running from a creditor. And I won't use it to track down someone I think is just trying to get away from someone else—most often a wife trying to ditch a husband. But in the case of a sixteen-year-old girl who's potentially being brutalized by gangbanger pimps, then the decision's a no-brainer. I'm all over it.

I walked into Kenny's office. "I've got some things I need you to check out while we're out walking," I said.

Doc was there, too. "No walking for him?" he said.

I shook my head. "He gets out of it."

Kenny smiled. "Oh, darn," he said. He turned to Doc. "You should have paid more attention in math class, dude."

Doc gave him a little stink eye, and then he got up and left.

"Here's the deal," I said. I gave Kenny Isabel's cell phone information and told him to pull the billing records and start working on trying to ping the phone while we were gone. Hopefully, she still had her phone, and it was turned on.

"Next thing, the police said another way Isabel might pop up on the grid was when her pimps decided it was time to try to put her to work. They would need to advertise, and now that Craigslist has stopped accepting these kinds of ads, there's pretty much one game in town—"

"Backpage.com," he said.

I looked at him. "You're familiar with it." It was more of a statement than a question.

He shrugged. "Isn't everybody?" he asked. He noticed the look I was giving him. "I don't look at the personal ads," he protested. He paused, then he added, "Well, okay, maybe I look, but I never call them." This I could believe.

"Just shut up while you're still ahead," I said. "Listen. If Isabel said things were too good to be true because the pimps had suddenly tried to put her to work, then it's very possible that the pimps had already started to run ads. So, while we're gone, I want you to start combing through all the ads. Take a look at the photos, and see if you can find one that matches the picture we have of Isabel. Look all the way back through mid-May if you can."

"Got it," he said.

"And while you're at it, take a look at the DMV records to see if Donnie Martin or DeMichael Hollins pops up."

He nodded.

With all the instructions given and everyone prepared, we hit the road at exactly nine thirty.

* * * *

If you divide Seattle up into quadrants using I-5 as the east-west divider and the Lake Union/ship canal waterway as the north-south divider, then you'd find the University of Washington nestled toward the center of the city in the upper-right, northeast quadrant, right along the waterway. The entire area surrounding the university—from Lake Union on the south to Ravenna Boulevard on the north and from I-5 on the west all the way to Lake Washington on the east is called the U-District. The area immediately north of the university is dominated by dense student housing and commercial shops, most of which exist to support the students or the thousands of workers who are employed in and around the university.

As I drove through the tight, crowded streets on my way up to my first shopping center on Ravenna Boulevard, I immediately saw what a smart idea it had been for Donnie Martin to base his operations around here. What better place to hide a group of teenaged girls but right smack-dab in the middle of thousands of other young people. The University District is a teeming cauldron containing an eclectic, funky mix of people. Eccentric dress, eccentric behavior, eccentric hours—hell, eccentricities are the norm for people around here. In fact, around here, it's the normal people that stand out. Donnie's girls could basically come and go as they pleased, with no one even noticing them. For that matter, the gang members themselves would also become effectively invisible in this area. In some areas of the Puget Sound, three or four young black men living in a house frequented by young pretty white girls would definitely *not* go unnoticed. But here—here in an area surrounded by an eclectic mix of young people, they would blend in.

I parked at my first designated shopping center and started talking to people and showing them Isabel's photo. For the next two hours, I went door-to-door, showing the picture and asking if anybody recognized her. I visited four shopping centers. I got the same answer over and over. People were polite—some even seemed concerned. But no one could remember ever seeing Isabel. Doc and Toni had the same experience.

"It's not surprising," I said, as we gathered over lunch. We'd selected a Mexican restaurant on Ravenna Boulevard just after noon. "Did you notice how many shopping centers there are around here?"

Toni nodded. "A lot. There's a lot that can go wrong—get in the way of us finding Isabel," she said. "We could be hitting the wrong stores, for starters. Or Donnie Martin might not be letting Isabel out."

"Or the store people might not be telling us the truth," Doc said.

I nodded. "Most of the people I talked to sounded pretty sympathetic," I said. "After I told them that Isabel was just sixteen."

"I got the same thing," Toni said. "Still, we're only just a little better off than if we were looking for a needle in a haystack."

"You're a city girl," I said. "You've never even seen a haystack."

"I most certainly—," She was interrupted by my cell phone. Caller ID: Kenny.

"Hold that thought," I said to her. I tapped the talk button on the phone. "What's up?" I said.

"Hey boss," he said. "I got nowhere on the cell phone so far, but right away I think I've got a match on the personal ads."

"No shit?"

"Yeah. I mean, I can't be certain, but I've found an ad on Backpage, and the girl on the ad sure looks like the picture of Isabel we have. Looks older—sexier to be sure. But it still looks to me like it could be her."

"Excellent. Good work, dude."

"Thanks. You guys get any hits?"

"Not a one. Hold on for a second." I turned to Toni. "Kenny thinks he has a match."

"Cell phone or Backpage ad?" Toni said.

I nodded. "Backpage. He says the girl in the ad looks older and sexier than the picture we have of Isabel, but he thinks it's her."

"I'll call Kelli and have her come in," Toni said. "She's the one who really knows what Isabel looks like."

"She can come in now? No school?"

"I think she's done," Toni said. "But even if she's not, she had a short schedule this last semester. Mornings only."

"Good. Go ahead and do it," I said. I brought the phone back up. "Kenny? You still there?"

"Yeah."

"We're going to finish up with lunch, then we'll be back in the office. Probably just a little after one or so. Toni's calling Kelli so she can come in and confirm the ID."

"Cool. I'll be ready."

"Well done, dude," I said, before hanging up.

Toni made her call and said that Kelli was "very anxious" to come in.

* * * *

We all walked into Logan PI together at 1:15 p.m. Kelli was already there, talking with Kenny in the lobby. We said hello to Kelli, and then I turned to Kenny. "You ready?"

"Yeah. I'm all set up on the big screen in the conference room."

I nodded. "Good." I led everyone back. It was nice outside, so while the others took their seats, I closed all the blinds to darken the room, but I propped the outside door open a little to let in some fresh air.

I sat down and said, "Okay, Kenny. It's all yours. Show us what you found."

"First," he said, as a picture flashed on the screen, "here's the picture of Isabel that her mom provided for us." The blowup was from the picture strip, and it showed Kelli and Isabel together. "I scanned it and then used Photoshop to clean it up a little. Lightened this area, darkened that one. Basically sharpened up the focus and enhanced the contrast. It's how I normally treat ID photos."

The image changed. "Next, I cropped this enhanced image into a headshot of Isabel. This is the picture you guys have been carrying around all morning." The picture was hardly recognizable as being from the snapshot. Kelli was gone, cropped away. Isabel's image was much clearer and had much better contrast. Kenny continued. "When I crop it and then enlarge it like this, the resolution starts to work against us, and you see the start of a little pixilation, but I smoothed it up a little, so it's still pretty decent. Better than a newspaper, for example. So hold that image. Now, let me switch and go to the Internet." He closed the photo and opened up the Internet. "Here's Backpage.com. Backpage is a nationwide site. You tell it what metro area you're in, and it feeds you ads just for your area. You can see here that I've picked Seattle." He waited for the site to catch up. When it did, he said, "Now you see these categories? Most of their categories are legit, but you see way over here on the right is a section called 'Adult.' We'll pick the Escorts category from the Adult section."

A screen titled "Disclaimer" popped up. Kenny continued, "Now you get this hokey little disclaimer page where you have to swear you're at least eighteen. Like this is going to slow someone down, right? Just for shits and giggles, we'll say we agree," he clicked the appropriate button, and the screen changed. "And we're in. That right there appears to be the extent of their age screening."

"Now over here on the left, you can see that there's a long list of advertisements. And these ads are all real-time. Someone posts an ad, and it pops right up. You can see that they're separated by the days the ads were posted. I counted up today's ads a little while ago. As of eleven o'clock this morning, there'd already been sixty-something posted for so-called escort services. And that's just for Seattle, remember."

"Now let me show you some of the ads." He clicked on the top headline. Immediately, the screen was filled with very provocative photos of a barely dressed woman on the right and a bunch of text on the left that left little doubt as to what the woman was willing to do—which seemed to be pretty much anything somebody'd be willing to pay for.

Kenny closed the page and clicked on several more. The faces changed, but the message remained consistent.

"Sometimes the photos hide the faces, sometimes they don't," I said.

"Yeah," he said. "It's about one-third hidden, two-thirds not hidden."

Toni said, "When it says '200 roses H—120 roses HH' does that mean—"

"It's a simple little code. I'm pretty sure it means $200 for an hour—$120 for a half hour," Kenny said.

"Holy crap," she said. "That's what I thought it meant. They're just out and out advertising sex for sale. It's like a catalog for prostitutes."

I nodded. "That's exactly what it is," I said.

Kenny closed the ad. "I showed you all these because I wanted you to be a little prepared for this next one." He scrolled down and clicked on an ad. It opened up and immediately, Kelli gasped.

"It's her," she said, her eyes fixed on the screen. "It's Izzy."

The ad showed Isabel in several provocative poses wearing a string bikini bottom and a very skimpy string top. She was smiling seductively into the camera. The ad wording looked similar to the other ads.

"Let me do this," Kenny said. "I captured the face from the Backpage photo. Then, I enlarged it, enhanced it, and cropped it." He split the screen in half. On the left half, he brought up the ID photo of Isabel we'd been using. Then, on the right, he showed the image he'd captured off the Backpage ad.

"They look almost identical," I said.

"It's her," Kelli said again, her voice steely.

"Are you certain?" I asked.

She nodded but didn't speak.

I looked at her. "Are you okay?" I asked.

She nodded again, face resolute. "I'm okay. But I want to kill the guys who're making her do this."

"Don't do that," I said, trying to joke with her to lighten the mood. "We'll get 'em. We have to take it one step at a time, but we'll get them."

"When do you suppose this picture was taken?" Doc asked.

We thought about this for a moment, and then Toni said, "I'd bet this was taken somewhere between ten days and two weeks ago. Think about it. It had to be long enough after these guys picked her up for her to feel comfortable enough wearing clothes like that to pose for someone taking pictures. She doesn't look like she's under any duress here."

"Although that might be hard to tell," I said.

"True. But for the moment, all we have to go on is what we see."

I nodded.

"So the picture would have been taken—what—a couple of weeks after she got picked up? When was the text saying that she liked Mikey?"

"May 17," Kenny said.

"May 17. And what—ten days later she's writing to say that it was too good to be true?"

"May 28."

"So my guess is that sometime in that window—starting around May 17 and definitely ending by May 28—that's when this picture was taken."

"But I don't understand," Doc said. "That last text message said it was 'too good to be true.' If that was how she felt, I would have thought that she'd somehow try to leave or at least not go along with these guys. But that doesn't make sense when you see they're still running the ad."

"I guess she just ended up doing what they told her to do," Toni said. "Carla said the pimps have ways of dealing with girls who resist."

The room grew silent as we stared at the ad and considered its implications. "Any thoughts? Any ideas? Any directions?" I had a pretty good idea, but I wanted to see if someone else would come up with it.

"It's time for a little sting," Toni said. I should have known Toni would reach the same conclusion. We tend to think a lot alike.

"Exactly," I agreed. "We need to run it through Nancy, but I think we just call the ad and pretend like we're a tourist in from Podunk and we're looking for a little companionship while we're here. We make a date. When Isabel shows up—we do a little intervention. Nancy grabs her—problem solved."

"Well," Toni said, "first step, anyway. There are still the long-term problems that need to be resolved."

I looked up at the ad photo—at Isabel looking off into the distance over my head, smiling suggestively, trying hard to look like her idea of a sex symbol.

I turned to Toni. "One step at a time, right?"

She nodded.

* * * *

After the meeting, I went to my office and put a phone call in to Nancy Stewart. They patched me through to her cell phone—she and Tyrone were away from her office. I explained to her what we'd found and that we had a plan we wanted to run by her. To my surprise, she offered to stop by our office. She and Tyrone were on their way to a meeting in Ballard at the moment, but Nancy thought that they'd be done by three o'clock and could probably make it to our office by 3:15 or 3:30 p.m. I was pleasantly surprised. The police coming to our office instead of the other way around is like the mountain jumping up and coming to Mohammed—it's happened maybe three times in the past four years.

And they were right on time—they walked into the office at 3:15 sharp. Toni and I greeted them and walked them back to the conference room.

"You have a beautiful view from here," Nancy said, looking out the window to the southeast. Our office is on the south end of the second floor of an old building, situated right on Lake Union. In fact, the building is built on pilings, and it actually sticks out over the water. A large balcony wraps around the southeast corner of the building. The conference room faces south; my office is on the end facing east. The balcony services both spaces. Today, as most days, a number of small boats moved quietly across the water. Some of the boats were sailboats, some were powerboats, some were even rowboats.

"Thanks," I said, stepping out with her onto the balcony. "We leased the space four years ago. First thing we did was basically gut it and redo it. But the view was already here, of course. In fact, that's why we picked this place."

A Kenmore Air seaplane taxied away from the dock just a hundred yards or so south of our office. The little plane maneuvered into the middle of the channel, where the pilot pointed the plane into the wind and gunned it. The engine roared, drowning out any thoughts of further conversation for a few seconds.

After it had taken off, Nancy said, "Boy, I tell you, I'd be out here every chance I could get."

"Are you a boater?" I asked.

"My husband and I live for it," she said.

"I think I could be a boater," I said, "It looks really peaceful. But it's not something I have much experience with. I do like watching, though. Matter of fact, in the summer—probably starting next month—I like to bring my laptop outside my office right around the corner there." I pointed to where the balcony wrapped around the side of the building. "Then I just do my work from outside."

She shook her head. "You're lucky."

Kenny poked his head outside and waved.

"No doubt," I agreed. "It looks like we're set up for you now. If I can tear you away from the view, let's head on inside."

"Back to the salt mines, right?" she said, laughing.

"You got it. This shouldn't take too long."

Inside, everyone took a seat. I made the introductions, and then I got started.

"We had a busy day yesterday," I said. "After meeting with you guys in the morning and then with Annie Hooper, and then with Reverend Jenkins in the afternoon, we decided it'd be best to split our efforts this morning. So Toni, Doc, and I took the reference picture we have of Isabel, and we hit the streets. Or, more accurately, we hit the shopping centers up in the north part of the U-District. We were looking for anyone who might have recognized Isabel. Unfortunately, we struck out in spectacular fashion. Between the three of us, we talked to seventy-five stores and none—not a single one—had seen Isabel. It was a complete bust. The good news is that while we were out getting our exercise, Kenny here was actually hitting pay dirt. Kenny—why don't you take Nancy and Tyrone through the same presentation you gave to us earlier this afternoon."

"Okay," he said. He turned to Nancy. "Like Danny said, before he left this morning, he gave me some direction about how he wanted me to start searching the online advertising spots so that I could compare the pictures in the ads with the reference picture we have of Isabel."

Kenny walked Nancy and Tyrone through the entire process—how we obtained the original and all subsequent photos, how he'd gone through Backpage.com, and how he'd discovered the ad with Isabel's photo.

"We actually brought Toni's sister Kelli in to confirm the ID," I said. "We didn't want there to be any confusion as to the identity. We're now certain the girl in the picture is Isabel Delgado."

Nancy nodded slowly. "Well, the pattern certainly fits."

"It would seem to," I said.

"But wait a second," Tyrone said. "Don't I remember you saying there was an e-mail indicating that she wasn't very happy?"

I nodded. "Good memory. Yes—there was a text message. It was dated May 28." I went on to explain to them when we thought the ad photos were taken and what we saw were the possible scenarios now.

Nancy nodded. "That makes sense," she said. "Most likely, they 'convinced' her. That means they coerced her, maybe even beat her up until she agreed. These guys are real good at that." She paused for a moment as she looked at the ad.

"May I?" she said to Kenny, as she reached for the mouse.

"Sure."

Nancy opened up several pages, then returned to Isabel's ad. "You know," she said, "the website's sole effort at self-policing is to have the person who places an ad check a box saying that they and the person in the ad are both eighteen or over. That girl—" she pointed to the screen, "—that little girl is clearly not eighteen. This so-called system is failing our young people. It's turned into the single, primary vehicle that allows them to be exploited by these predators." She was visibly angry. "But at least Backpage.com and its owners are making a nice, fat profit. Whenever the legislators in Olympia or at other statehouses across the country try to enact laws to hold them responsible for what they print, they immediately scream bloody murder and start invoking the First Amendment."

"Somehow, I don't think this is what Jefferson had in mind," I said.

"I don't either," she said with disgust. A second later, she regained her composure. She turned to me. "So you said you had a plan. Let's hear it."

Chapter 9

"WE WERE THINKING we should just call the ad and set up a date with her," I said.

Nancy nodded. "A sting. That's usually the way we do it. We run through the ads all the time. We make dates just like this." She stopped and studied me for a second. "Just to be clear, though, when you say 'we' should just call the ad, I assume you're meaning SPD, right? We'll need to run the show."

I nodded. "Understood. That's the way we'd prefer it."

"Good," she said, apparently relieved to find that Logan PI wasn't in the process of planning any sort of independent action. "The way it usually works is that we'll pick a business hotel inside the Track. Are you familiar with the Track?"

I nodded. "I scouted out the area last night."

"Good. We like to pick a hotel that has adjoining rooms so that we can stage from right next door until the signal. We'll hide a couple of cameras in the target room beforehand. We'll have four officers on-site. One will pose as the john, the other three will be waiting for his signal in the adjoining room. You two," she looked at Toni and me, "can hang out with us there. We'll position four or five plainclothes officers outside to control the parking lot."

"I saw a place last night called the Snuggle Inn," I said. I described what I'd seen with the girl knocking on the door and then exiting thirty minutes later.

"That's the way it happens," Nancy said.

"So we make a date and once she comes inside, do you have to wait for her to solicit?" I asked.

"Depends," Nancy said. "If we think the girl is a minor, then the officer who's playing the john will give us a signal, and we can go ahead and take the child into custody immediately—as soon as the door shuts. If there's a missing person report on a minor—which, by the way, there is now in Isabel's case—then it's not a prostitution bust—it's a runaway case. On the other hand, if we think that we're dealing with an adult and not a minor, then we wait for the pitch."

"May as well get a bust out of it for all your hard work," I said.

"Exactly. But if she's a minor, by us not arresting her for prostitution, eventually the child's a little more willing to work with us—provide information, participate in counseling—that sort of thing," Tyrone said. "Once they understand they're not being busted."

"That said," Nancy added, "the operative word is 'eventually.' Please understand that at first, Isabel might not be very happy to see us."

"Isabel actually might not be so bad because she's new," Tyrone said. "But Nancy's right—if a girl's been working for any length of time—say at least a year—then most of the time they're going to be pretty belligerent at first. They are so totally brainwashed by their pimps, that even while they're basically being held as sex slaves, they don't look at themselves that way. Until they get a little older, anyway, they see themselves as survivors. They think that what they're doing is working for them, and they don't want to rock their own boat. It usually takes them a while before they loosen up."

"When could we do this?" Toni asked Tyrone. "Tonight?"

He nodded. "Why not. None of us have anything better to do on a Friday night, right?"

"Works for me," Nancy said. She turned back to Toni and me. "Most of the time, these 'dates' are pretty spur-of-the-moment kind of things—

not a lot of advance planning by the johns. They come into town and make the call in the afternoon when they get here—usually want someone either right away or maybe later the same night."

"So you're saying the best time for the date is—?" I said, letting it trail off into a question.

Tyrone shrugged. "We usually shoot for something between seven and ten."

"Where do we make the call from?"

"You'll notice that most of the ads say something about 'No Blocked Lines,'" Tyrone said.

I nodded. I'd seen that.

"The pimps won't answer calls from lines with blocked caller IDs," he continued. "So we just have a bunch of bogus IDs on secure lines set up with the phone company that we use for this sort of thing."

I nodded. "Who makes the call?" I asked.

"We have four or five guys on our staff we use, including yours truly," Tyrone said. "We rotate—depends on whose turn it is to be the john."

"The best thing would be if you guys just followed us down to our office now," Nancy said. "Assuming you want to be in on the call in the first place."

I thought for a second. "I'd like to," I said, "but I don't think our listening in on you guys while you set up the date is going to add much. I mean, neither of us has ever even heard Isabel speak. It's not as if we'd recognize her voice or anything like that."

Nancy nodded. "Understood."

"Besides," Toni said. "I think Danny and I need to call Isabel's mother and let her know what's happening—that we have a lead. She's basically a good woman, but she needs help in her own way. She's going to have to figure out how to stand up to her husband. It's possible that knowing we're getting close to pulling Isabel out of trouble will help strengthen her resolve."

"Well, you should go ahead and talk to her, then," Nancy said. "I'd be a little vague on the details. But, after all, she *is* Isabel's mom. She has a right to know, and we'll certainly have to involve her once we've pulled Isabel out of there."

Toni nodded.

"Next question. How will we make a positive ID?" I asked. I was a little concerned that Toni and I might have trouble recognizing Isabel. All we'd ever seen was the picture strip with Kelli and the Backpage ad.

"You said your sister knows her?" Nancy said to Toni.

Toni nodded. "Yes," she said. "Kelli's good friends with Isabel. She'd know her for sure."

"How old is your sister?" Nancy asked.

"Eighteen."

"Good. Would she be willing to come along?"

"Oh, yeah. She'd do anything to help Isabel."

"Okay, that's settled then."

I nodded. "This sounds great. Give us a call when you've set up the date."

"Will do," Nancy said. "We'll let you know when and where. We'll want to be in place at least sixty minutes before the time of the date."

"What will happen to Isabel?" I asked. "After you have her, where will she go?"

"We'll take her to the King County Juvenile Detention Center first," Nancy said. "She'll have to spend the night there—I'm not sure I can get longer-term arrangements made this late. I'll put a quick call in to Annie Hooper now, but it's probably too late for today. Tomorrow, though, we'll talk to her."

"There's no way she can be allowed to be sent back home," Toni said.

"I know," Nancy said. "Annie will have some ideas."

"She told us she's got a long waiting list," I said.

"Yeah, she does," Nancy said. "But she knows about the other facilities, too. All the facility directors talk to each other. It would be nice to see her in a place where she can get her life back together."

"Sure would," I said.

* * * *

At a few minutes before five, Tyrone called. "We're set," he said.

"No problems?" I asked.

"None. She answered—said she was available tonight at eight thirty."

"Perfect. Where we doing this?"

"We got adjoining rooms at the Snuggle Inn," he said. "The same place you told us about. The target room is 301. Our staging room is next door at 303. When you get there, just park somewhere in the lot on the north side and then come on up to room 303. You want to be there no later than seven thirty. After that, we won't want any comings and goings."

"We'll be there," I said.

"Good. Cross your fingers."

* * * *

"Let's call Kelli," I said, as I walked into Toni's office. "We're on for eight thirty, but we need to be there no later than seven thirty."

"So she needs to be here by seven," Toni said.

I nodded. "That'll work."

Toni put her phone on speaker and made the call.

When Kelli answered, Toni explained what was going on and then asked her, "You want to come with us and help ID Isabel?"

Kelli agreed immediately. Five minutes and twenty questions later, she had all the information she needed.

"Now, let's give Marisol a call," I said.

"I wish we could talk to her face-to-face."

"Me, too. But it's too late. There's no way we could make it to Lynnwood and back in two hours—not in rush hour. Have you got her number?"

"Yeah, I wrote it down on my pad." She opened a file on her computer. Our general policy is to scan our notes onto our server as soon as we're able. It gives us a good backup, and it also makes it easier to find and share information. She quickly located the number and dialed Marisol's cell phone.

Marisol answered and told us she'd call back in five minutes. Right on time, our phone rang. "I took a break," Marisol said. "I wanted to get to a quiet place where I can talk."

"You're good now?" I asked.

"Yeah. Did you find Isabel?"

"We think so," I said. "If everything works out right, we're going to see her a little later this evening."

"Will I be able to see her, too?"

"Probably tomorrow," Toni said. "We're working with the Seattle Police Department on this."

"Is she okay?"

"We don't have any information one way or another," I said. "We haven't personally spoken with Isabel. The police did."

"I don't understand," she said. "If you didn't talk to her, how is it that you're meeting her tonight?"

"All I can say is that we're working with the police on this."

"Did she do something wrong? Is Isabel in trouble?"

"No, Mary. At least, no one's saying anything like that," I said. I looked at Toni and shrugged before I continued. "There's a concern that Isabel may have fallen into some bad company. We're working with the police to pull her out of that before anything bad happens."

"Oh my God," Marisol said. I was a little suspicious of Mary's sudden concern about Isabel. After all, she'd allowed thirty days to elapse before she told anyone anything at all about Isabel running away—and then perhaps only because we confronted her. But I wasn't going to sit there and pass judgment. Like I said, I didn't know how or why Marisol felt the way she did. Maybe she'd had an epiphany. I suppose it was enough that she was concerned now.

"Don't worry," I said. "We're going to get her. And once we do— once she's safe and sound, then you'll be able to see her. You'll be able to start putting your lives back together—," I paused for an instant, "—both of you."

"What's going to happen to her? Where will she go?"

"You know she can't go back with you," I said. "Not with him around."

She was quiet for a second, and then she said, "I know."

"There are places that are set up to work with young girls like Isabel," Toni said. "We'll be working hard to find a spot for her in one of those places. Hopefully, we can get her into one of them tomorrow."

She was quiet for a second. "Thank you," she said. "What time is all this supposed to take place?"

"The meeting is set for eight thirty," I said. "We should be calling you by around nine with more information."

"Good," she said. "Please don't forget."

Toni smiled. "Don't worry. We won't forget."

Chapter 10

WITH MY LITTLE excursion at the Snuggle Inn the previous night still fresh in my mind, I was familiar with the property's layout. The small hotel is bordered on either side by similar business hotels—a Holiday Inn to the south and a Comfort Inn to the north. My guess is that except for the names, the hotels themselves are probably pretty much interchangeable. Toni, Kelli, and I pulled into the north-side parking lot at 7:25 p.m. It was still daylight outside—the sun doesn't set until after nine at this time of year. A light, misty breeze had rolled in, and it was cool enough for jackets—probably in the mid-fifties. We hopped out and walked up the stairs to room 303. I knocked and a couple of seconds later, Nancy opened the door. "Come on in," she said, smiling. "You can hang your jackets in the closet there. And help yourself to some pizza," she said, pointing to two large pies on the table. Kelli moved that way immediately. "There's soft drinks in the fridge," Nancy said.

"Thanks," Kelli replied.

I looked around the room. The police had removed the television from on top of the dresser and replaced it with a thirty-inch computer monitor and a laptop PC. The monitor was split into four windows, each showing a different angle of the room next door. The laptop was connected to some sort of wireless device.

"Come on next door, and I'll show you our setup," Nancy said.

Toni and I followed her through the open connecting doors. Room 301 was a mirror image of the room we'd just left, only with no surveillance equipment. A garment bag was draped over one of the two chairs, and a briefcase sat on the table.

"We try to make the room look reasonably authentic," Nancy said. "If we're taking a juvenile down, there's not much to worry about—we basically pop 'em as soon as the door closes. But we never know for sure if we're going to open the door to a minor or to an adult, in which case we would need to wait for her to make a pitch. When we first started doing this, we weren't as good as we are now. We wouldn't have any props showing. And we found out that the lack of authenticity caused our subjects to sense something was wrong. Then they would get antsy, and the pitch would never happen. They'd walk, and we would have just wasted our time. So after that, we learned. Now we set the room all up to look like the real deal, like it's being rented by a traveling businessman."

"These people must be pretty wary, just by their nature," Toni said.

"Some of them," Nancy said. "Some are surprisingly oblivious. We just plan for the worst."

"Good idea," Toni said.

I looked around the room. "Nancy, I know there are four cameras in here, and I still can't see them," I said.

She smiled. "Pretty nifty, huh?" she said. "Look here." She pointed to a vase that sat on the dresser. "See these little designs? Look closely at this one."

When I inspected the vase more carefully, I was able to see that the circle in one of the diamond-and-circle patterns was actually the lens of a tiny camera. I was impressed. "Damn. That's amazing," I said. "James Bond would be proud."

She laughed. "Wouldn't he, though? This innocent-looking vase is really an RF feed video camera. It's all solid state—completely silent. Look inside, and you still can't see the camera." I peered inside the vase— she was right.

"That's pretty impressive," I said, as I looked at the tiny camera. I handed the vase back to her, and she placed it back on the dresser.

"And it's HD, too. Also has a built-in microphone so it picks up the audio. Sends it all to the laptop next door." She aligned the camera and then called out, "How's that, guys?"

"Good," someone answered from next door.

"And there are three others?" I asked.

"Yep. In the coffee basket over there, on the desk by the phone, and in the bathroom. We cover the whole place—one person watches the monitor while the other places the cameras and checks the audio. We can be out of here in under a minute. Use to take over an hour." She turned to me. "You were CID, right? Fort Lewis?"

I nodded. "I was."

"Ever do one of these?"

"Not for prostitution," I said. "I participated in a couple of stolen property stings—one with SPD and the other in Tacoma. But we didn't have lead roles in any of them."

"Well, you might find this interesting, then," she said. She looked around. "Jimmy?" she called out. "Where's Bobby?"

"Yo," came an answer from the next room. A good-looking young man dressed in a business suit and holding a slice of pizza entered the room. "I'm here."

"This is Bobby Brannon. Bobby gets to play our john today."

"That's right," Bobby said. "Today, I'm Jimmy. Jimmy the john. You can just call me Jimmy John."

"Jimmy John, here—" Nancy nodded toward him and smiled, "—he gets more than his share of john assignments in these things because he's young and not very threatening-looking."

"And I'm the best-looking," he said, smiling.

"He looks like a kid," Tyrone said. "No one's scared of him. No one believes a twelve-year-old could be a cop."

"Which," Bobby said, "is another way of saying, the rest of these guys here are a bunch of crusty old mean-looking suckers, and they're all so scary, they can't even get anyone to come in the front door."

"Shut up," Tyrone said.

At eight o'clock, Nancy said, "Alright everyone, we're all set." She turned to Bobby. "You ready?"

"Born ready, boss," he said, still smiling.

"You remember who we're looking for?"

"Of course. Isabel Delgado. Hispanic teenager. Slim build."

"Good. Let's do this, then," she said.

Except for Bobby, we headed next door. Both connecting doors were closed, but only our side was locked.

"We've got four officers outside and, counting Jimmy, four inside," Nancy said. "We've got all sides of the building covered so, at least in theory, no one should be able to sneak up on us."

"Unit one, how's it look?" she said into her radio.

"We're ready. It's quiet."

Each of the other three officers outside reported in.

"So now——," Nancy said, leaning back in her chair in front of the monitor, "——now we just hurry up and wait."

* * * *

"Unit two to base." Nancy's radio crackled to life. I checked my watch—it was 8:40 p.m. We'd been in position, waiting for forty minutes.

"Go," Nancy said.

"I've got a Hispanic female approaching the south stairs."

"Roger that," Nancy said. "Unit three, can you shift position to pick up visual at the top of the stairway?"

"Roger," unit three said. "I'm on the move now." A minute later, he said, "Base, unit three. Subject just reached the top of the stairs, and she's headed your way. She's all alone—no company. Appears to be medium height, five five or so. Thin build. Dark hair. Wearing some kind of leggings and a white coat with fur around the collar."

"Roger," she said. "You guys outside stay in your positions now. Watch our backs."

Nancy nodded. "Bobby—you hear that she's at the top of the stairs?"

He looked into the dresser camera and gave us a thumbs-up. "Got it," he said into the radio. His voice was also picked up by the hidden microphones.

"You ready?" Nancy asked.

"Roger." Bobby wasn't joking now. His curt reply indicated he was all business. "I'm turning my radio off now," he said. We watched him click his radio off and put it into a drawer. He turned back to the camera. "Test, one-two-three," he said. The microphone in the vase with the hidden camera picked up his voice, allowing us to hear him clearly through the PC speaker.

Nancy knocked on the wall. Bobby did another thumbs-up in reply.

"I'm turning the PC speaker way down now," Nancy said, reaching for the volume control. "There's a bit of latency in the sound transmission, and I don't want our subject hearing her own voice echoing in the next-door room."

A minute later, even with the volume turned down low, we heard the knock on Bobby's door through the speakers. On our side of the door, Tyrone and the other officer stood ready to burst into the room.

We watched the monitor carefully. Bobby—now Jimmy—walked over and looked through the peephole before stepping back and opening the door.

"Hi, there," he said.

"Hi," the girl said. I strained and could barely hear the voice. The front door was visible on one of the cameras, but Bobby was blocking the view of the girl.

"Come in," Bobby said. "Come in."

We watched as she stepped into the room. Her hair was shorter than it had been in the photo of her with Kelli, and it fell across her face as she entered.

"Kelli?" I said quietly.

"Damn," she said. "I can't tell for sure." She studied the monitor intently. "It looks like her. I recognize her coat, but her hair's shorter. And it's hanging down in her face—I can't see her face."

The prearranged signal Bobby was to give if he thought the girl was a juvenile was to reach across his body with his left hand and rub his right shoulder, as if it were sore. The other officers would then enter the room immediately. On the other hand, if Bobby thought the girl was an adult, he was to wait for her to solicit money in exchange for a sex act before signaling. In this case, as soon as the girl stepped past him, Bobby closed the door, turned to face the camera, and started rubbing his shoulder as if it were dislocated.

"Go!" Nancy said forcefully.

Tyrone and the other officer flung the connecting doors open and burst into the room.

"Seattle Police," all the men yelled at the same time. "Put your hands up! Now!"

I could see that the poor girl was completely caught by surprise—she nearly stumbled backward. She turned back to face Bobby and quickly raised her hands into the air as she'd been told.

"Hello, Isabel," Bobby said, smiling.

* * * *

"Put your hands on the wall," Nancy ordered as we all filed into the room behind the officers.

"Do you have any weapons? Any needles on you?" Nancy asked.

The girl didn't answer.

Nancy did a thorough pat-down and then said, "Okay, go ahead and turn around."

Kelli gasped. I looked closely at the girl. She was young. She was Hispanic. She was pretty. And she was clearly not Isabel.

"You have the wrong person," she said. "I'm not Isabel. I'm Jasmine."

Chapter 11

THE GIRL—WHATEVER her real name was—looked stunned by the direction her routine rendezvous had taken. Her wide eyes scanned the room quickly. I couldn't tell her age, but I could see that she was young—no doubt a minor—Bobby at least got that part right. If I had to guess, I'd say she looked like she might have been sixteen.

Nancy radioed the officers that were stationed outside. "We're code four in here," she said. "One in custody. How're we looking?"

Each officer reported no activity.

"Call in a squad car," Nancy said. "Seal off the parking lot entry and check around. Let's see if we can find out how this girl got here. Then, meet us in the north parking lot in ten."

"Roger."

Nancy turned back to the girl. "Hi there," she said. "My name's Nancy Stewart. What's your name?"

The girl looked Nancy over and then said again, "Jasmine." She did a pretty fair job of mustering up enough bravado to mostly hide any fear she might have been experiencing.

"Jasmine?" Nancy said, her tone of voice making it clear she didn't believe this. "That's a pretty name. Is that your real name?"

The girl nodded.

"Jasmine what?"

The girl stared at her for a moment, and then slowly and deliberately, she said, "Jasmine Jones."

"Jasmine Jones," Nancy repeated. "Have you got any ID on you?"

The girl shook her head.

Nancy continued. "So how old are you, Jasmine Jones?"

"Eighteen," the girl answered.

"Got a knife," Tyrone said. He'd been looking into the girl's purse while Nancy talked. He reached in with gloved hands and gingerly pulled out a kitchen knife with a six-inch blade.

Nancy looked at it and then turned back to the girl. "You're eighteen? Really? So that'd make you an adult, right?" she said. "That means you can be tried and convicted as an adult. Is that what you want?"

Jasmine stared hard at Nancy, and then she shrugged. "For what? I didn't do anything," she said.

Nancy smiled, then she nodded. "That's true. You ever been arrested before, Jasmine Jones?"

Nancy got a hard stare as an answer.

"No answer? Well, that's okay. You don't have to answer. We'll probably find out soon enough. Are you familiar with your legal rights in a situation like this? Let me go ahead and read them to you." Nancy read Jasmine her Miranda rights.

"Do you understand these rights?" Nancy asked.

Jasmine nodded her head.

"Okay, Jasmine," Nancy said. "Here's the way I see things. First off, if you're eighteen, I'm 107." She looked at Jasmine for a second and then said, "Sorry, sweetie, you're not eighteen. What are you? Fifteen? Sixteen?"

Jasmine didn't answer.

"You don't have to answer, but I can't let you stay out on the street if I have reason to believe you're a minor. So that means, tonight, we're going to detain you and take you over to the Juvenile Detention Center. If you want to tell us who your parents are or who your legal guardian is, we'll call them, or we'll let you call them. We might be able to sort this out tonight. Understood?"

Again, Jasmine didn't answer.

"Does that mean there's no one you want us to call?"

Jasmine looked down and shook her head.

"I understand," Nancy said. "But if you're not going to help us out, it's too late tonight for us to start trying to track down who you are and where you're from. We'll get started on that tomorrow."

"You understand that seeing as how you're not eighteen, your parents or legal guardian are responsible for you, right? Do they know you're out here answering ads for an escort service? Do they even know where you are? Are you a runaway?" Jasmine didn't respond to any of these questions.

"Next thing—and this is important. Except for providing your name, you're not required to answer any of my questions. But if you do answer my questions, you're not allowed to lie to a police officer. And I think you've already lied to me. Twice. Once about your age. Once about your name. You can get in big trouble for lying to a police officer. Do you understand?" Again, Jasmine didn't answer.

"Here's the last thing. Despite the fact that you've lied to me—twice—and despite the fact that I think you're out here answering calls for escort services, and despite the fact that you had that knife in your purse—despite all that? We're not going to charge you with anything. Want to know why I didn't have my officers wait another thirty seconds for you to solicit them? You know what soliciting means, right?"

Jasmine looked at her.

"It's simple," Nancy continued. "We don't want to arrest you. Not for prostitution. Not for lying to me. Nothing like that. That's not why we're here. We want to help you."

Jasmine sniffed. "I don't need your help," she said, softly.

Nancy shrugged. "Maybe you do and maybe you don't. I can't make you accept it," she said. She paused and looked at the girl. "Jasmine, I don't know anything about you or your home situation. I know that if you've run away, we'll eventually find out. But I also know that sometimes there are reasons why you have to get away. I'm not blaming you."

The girl dropped her eyes.

"Listen," Nancy said. "I work with dozens of girls just like you. Exact same position, Jasmine. You can say what you want, but I *know* what you're doing, and I know how you live, believe me. I see it with girls just like you every single day. I know you have a quota. I know you have to come out most every night and have sex for money with guys you don't know. I know you have to bring that money back to your pimp. Jasmine—I know what you're going through, and I know how it's making you feel inside. And I'm here to tell you, it doesn't have to be that way. My one goal is to help you. You can have a better life. Your own life with your own dreams and goals. The only person you'd have to answer to is yourself. There'd be no one lording it over you, telling you what to do, where to go—whom to have sex with."

I couldn't tell for sure, but it looked like Jasmine's features were softening just a little bit.

Nancy continued. "We've helped hundreds of girls who've come before you. You can talk to them if you'd like. We can help you, too. Understand?"

Jasmine looked at her for a second, then she dropped her head and nodded. Maybe Nancy was starting to get through to her.

"Good," Nancy said. "Tomorrow morning, I'm going to come over and see you, and we'll try talking again. Jasmine, look at me."

Jasmine looked up again.

"You might not believe it, but one day you're going to look back at tonight and you're going to look at it as one of the best, most important days in your life. Tonight's the night that good people—people who really care about you as a person—are standing up for you and stepping in to help you. Tonight's the night you get to take back control of your own life. Understand?"

Jasmine looked at her and nodded.

"Are you okay?" Nancy asked.

"Yeah."

"Good. Are you sure you don't have someone you want us to call?"

She looked down and shook her head.

"That's okay," Nancy said. "You don't need to. You'll be okay tonight. You're going to ride with these guys now. They'll take you downtown. Like I said, I'll come by in the morning. If you want, we can talk then."

Tyrone and the Bobby led Jasmine out of the room to the waiting squad car.

* * * *

"That went pretty well," Nancy said. "At least she didn't scream at me. That happens sometimes." She looked up suddenly. "I hope you don't mind my not asking about Isabel just now."

"I understand," I said. "It's too early. This girl's still in a state of shock over everything else that's happened. Maybe she'll talk to you tomorrow."

"That's what I was thinking," Nancy said. "I'll give you guys a call in the morning and let you know how it's looking." She looked at Kelli. "What do you think about what you saw?" she asked.

Kelli shook her head. She had a tear in her eye. "It's sad," she said. "She's just a kid. All dressed up but still, just a kid."

Nancy nodded. "You're right," she said. "It's very sad. But maybe tonight, we saved a little girl. And if it has to be one at a time, then that's fine with me."

* * * *

It was quiet in the Jeep on the way back to the office. We didn't talk much about Isabel or anything else, for that matter. I guess everyone was still trying to recover from the disappointment of Isabel not being the girl who showed up, combined with the reality of seeing a girl like Jasmine up close—a girl who, except for her rather desperate circumstances, seemed like she wasn't much different than the girl next door.

"We have to call Marisol," Toni said, breaking the silence.

"Right. I'll do it as soon as I get home. I don't feel like making that call while I'm driving."

"You okay, Kell?" Toni asked, looking in the backseat where Kelli was seated.

"Yeah," she said. "It sucks that it wasn't Izzy."

I nodded. Too true. "Nancy said that when she talks to Jasmine in the morning, she's going to ask her if she'll talk to us about Isabel. Maybe we'll find out something then."

"What happens if she doesn't want to talk?" Kelli said.

"Then we'll just go back to canvasing the neighborhood," Toni said. "If we do that and if we have Kenny monitor her cell phone, eventually we'll find her."

"That's right," I said. Of course, I was thinking it could be a whole lot faster if Jasmine knew Isabel and agreed to talk to us about her. I crossed my fingers.

Chapter 12

AT 9:45 A.M. the next day, I was sitting at my desk staring at the calendar when my cell phone rang. Caller ID: Nancy Stewart.

"Good morning," I said.

"Hey. Can you and Toni shoot on down here to the Juvenile Detention Center?" Nancy skipped the small talk. "I've been talking to Paola—her name's not Jasmine Jones by the way, and she's not eighteen. She's fifteen, and her name is Paola Morales. I've been talking to her for about an hour now. She's starting to come around. Anyway, she knows Isabel, and she's willing to talk to us about her. She's not ready to give up her pimp—she won't go that far. But she is willing to help find Isabel. We're taking a break now while we wait for you."

"Fantastic," I said. "We're on the way."

Toni had overheard me talking, and she walked into my office as I was hanging up.

"She's cooperating?" Toni asked.

"A little, anyway. Nancy said that she knows Isabel, and she'll talk about her. She doesn't want to talk about her pimp, though."

"That's okay. It's better if she can give us some good information on Isabel," she said as we hustled down the hall and out the door.

"Agreed," I said. "Hopefully, she knows where we can find her."

"Maybe she could lead us right to her," Toni said.

"Wouldn't that be nice."

* * * *

The King County Juvenile Detention Center sits on Alder just east of Twelfth Avenue. The building consists of two distinctly different sections. The back section is the residential area. It looks like a typical, four-story apartment building except that the doors and the exterior stairwell are painted bright orange. Someone probably thought it looked artistic when they selected the colors. I think it looks pretty odd. The front section consists of offices and classrooms. This section is a single story and made of brick. We parked in the visitors' parking lot on the north side of the building and hopped out. Then we walked past the American flag and into the lobby of the front section.

Inside, the building was quiet and smelled of floor wax. In fact, the guy doing the waxing was still running a floor machine maybe forty feet down a long hallway. The tiles glistened. The receptionist sat behind what appeared to be a bulletproof glass partition—the kind like at movie box offices with the little chrome intercom speaker grill in the middle of the glass. I find it odd that someone would go through the trouble of installing an expensive piece of bulletproof glass for protection and then go and drill a three-inch hole in the glass for the intercom, right about at head level for the unlucky soul sitting behind the counter. I guess the intercom is supposed to be bullet-resistant, but I'm pretty sure my .45 would have no trouble shooting right through that hole—even with the intercom in place. I wouldn't want to trust my life to it. But I digress.

We gave the receptionist the information that Nancy had given me and were issued visitor passes and told to have a seat in a long row of blue-and-orange seats—the kind that are attached together like those in a train station. Five minutes later, Nancy popped out through a set of double doors marked Authorized Entrance Only.

"Come on back, you guys," she said.

"How's it going?" I asked.

"Pretty much like I said on the phone," she said. "Paola is a stubborn young lady. She's only going to come along just so fast—we can't push her. But if we can gain her trust by following through and making good on our promises, then she'll probably open up more and more. For now, though, here's where we stand. She seems to like Isabel. She actually seems like she's worried about her. She wants to help."

"Wonder why she's worried," I said. I was worried about Isabel when we started this case. Then, yesterday, I'd gotten hopeful. Then last night, worried again. Now—based on what I'd just heard—even more so.

"Don't know," Nancy said. "As soon as she agreed to talk to the two of you, I stopped our discussion and came and phoned you. We've just been waiting for you to arrive to pick up where we left off."

"Did you find her parents?" I asked.

"Paola is from Las Vegas," Nancy said. "She doesn't know her father, but apparently her mother is still there. They don't speak."

"That would explain things a little, anyway," I said.

Nancy stopped in the middle of the hallway and turned to face us. "It gets worse. This morning, Paola told me she was introduced into prostitution when she was eleven years old. She's fifteen now."

"Oh my God," Toni said quietly.

"Exactly," Nancy said. "This little girl has been living with one pimp or another, turning tricks as a way of life—a way to survive—for more than four years. Last year, apparently, she made her Las Vegas pimp mad, so he sold her to a pimp up here who she won't name."

"Donnie Martin," I said.

"Perhaps. I don't know if she has any sort of alcohol or drug dependency—that's something we'll find out in the next few days. But even if she doesn't, Paola's going to need treatment and counseling and schooling for several years in order to get her life back together."

"That poor girl," Toni said.

"This is so typical of what happens to these girls. Paola's a lucky one—last night really was her lucky night. For her, there might be a happy ending. At least, there's the possibility. We'll move to have the court appointed as her guardian. I talked to Annie Hooper—she's putting Paola on the list and thinks she might be able to squeeze her into one of the Angel Houses in the next day or so."

"That would be fantastic," I said.

"Frankly, it's her only hope," Nancy answered.

* * * *

Nancy led us into a room that served as a sort of small classroom. There was a table for the teacher at the front of the room in addition to four round tables, each with four chairs, spread through the remainder of the room. The entire front of the room was covered with a large chalkboard.

Paola sat by herself in one of the chairs, reading a pamphlet that read "Angel House" in bright, cheery letters. The difference in her appearance between now and last night was striking. Last night, she'd been heavily made up—apparently to look like someone's idea of a dream date. The makeup had been overdone to the extreme. This morning, she wore no makeup at all. Someone had given her a dark blue T-shirt and a pair of matching dark blue sweatpants. She looked freshly scrubbed. In fact, now she looked like a teenaged girl.

We walked over to her table. "Good morning," I said.

"Good morning," she answered. Her voice was soft and demure. We took the other seats at her table.

"Paola," Nancy said, "you remember Danny Logan and Toni Blair from last night, right?"

Paola nodded. "Yeah."

"Okay, good. Now, before I begin," Nancy said, "I'm going to turn the tape recorder on. Okay, Paola?"

She nodded.

Nancy said, "We're here on Friday, June 8th, 2012, at 10:25 in the morning. I'm Lieutenant Nancy Stewart. I'm the commander of the Seattle Police Department Vice and High Risk Victims Unit. I'm here today talking to Paola Morales. Paola is a fifteen-year-old girl we detained last night pending identification of her legal guardian. That work continues. To be clear, Paola is not under arrest. With us this morning are Danny Logan and Toni Blair, both licensed private investigators with the Logan Private Investigations firm."

Nancy turned to us. "May Paola call you by your first names—Danny and Toni?"

"Absolutely," I nodded. Toni indicated her agreement as well.

"Good." She turned back to Paola. "Like I said, Danny and Toni are private investigators. They're not police officers. Do you understand the difference?"

She nodded. "Yeah."

"In this case, they're working to find Isabel Delgado. You told me earlier that you know her, right?"

She nodded.

Nancy said, "Okay. Just to remind you of the ground rules, Paola— you're under no obligation to answer any questions at all. You're not under arrest here. You've got all the control. You're helping us—kind of like doing us a favor. This is not like TV where 'anything you say can and will be used against you.' In fact, it's the opposite. Nothing you say here will be used against you for any reason. Like I told you earlier—I'm not interested in seeing you go to jail. I think you and I are past that now, right?"

Paola smiled and nodded.

"As a matter of fact," Nancy continued, "I want to see you go to college and then come and work for me. Do you understand?"

Paola laughed. She had a little-girl giggle.

"And if you change your mind and don't want to talk about anything anymore, you can stop anytime you're uncomfortable, or you can simply say, 'I don't want to answer that question.' Anything like that will work, okay?"

"Okay," Paola said, nodding again. "I get it."

"Good," Nancy said. "So with that understanding, do you still want to talk to us about Isabel Delgado?"

She nodded. "Yes."

"Good. Then why don't I just let Danny and Toni ask you the questions, alright?"

She nodded.

"Thanks, Nancy," Toni said. She turned to Paola. "I'm Toni. It's good to meet you, Paola. Do you mind if we call you Paola?" she asked.

Paola shook her head.

"It's a beautiful name," Toni said. "I love it."

Paola smiled. "Thanks."

Toni looked to me. Guess it was my turn. I put on my best smile. "And I'm Danny," I said. "Thanks for agreeing to talk to us about what you know about Isabel."

She smiled again.

"Like Nancy said, we're looking for Isabel," Toni said. "My sister—she was also in the room last night—I don't know if you noticed her—anyway, she's a good friend of Isabel's. They go to school together. When Isabel went missing, my sister asked us to help find her. That's how we're involved."

Paola nodded. "And you guys thought it was Isabel who was supposed to be there last night?" she asked.

I nodded. "We did. We found an advertisement on Backpage.com with Isabel's picture in it. We answered that ad, thinking Isabel would show up. You showed up instead."

"They just told me to be at the Snuggle Inn at eight thirty," Paola said. "Nobody told me anything else."

I wanted to ask who told her this, but I figured she might not be willing to give that information just yet, and I didn't want to start off the conversation with her having to say no.

"Must have come as quite a surprise to you," Toni said.

Paola nodded. "Yeah."

"Tell me," Toni continued. "Why were you there instead of Isabel?"

"I'm not sure," Paola said. "Last week, I know they told Isabel that it was time for her to move over to the girls' house and go to work."

"Where'd she live until then?" I asked.

"She was at the big house across the street from the park, by the—," she stopped suddenly. "I don't want to say," she said.

"That's fine," Nancy said. "You don't have to."

"Sorry, Paola," Toni said. "I didn't mean to ask you a question that made you uncomfortable. Let me move past that. When you say that Isabel had to 'go to work,' you mean someone put an ad in Backpage.com and Isabel was supposed to start going out on dates?"

"Yeah. They probably took her picture that day," Paola said. "They have us dress up all sexy, and they take pictures all the time."

"But up until then, Isabel didn't have to go on dates?"

"No, she was new. She didn't live with us. The new girls aren't ready for dates at first."

"But a week ago, you're saying Isabel's time was up. They told her she had to move into the girls' house and go to work?"

Paola nodded. "Yeah."

"What happened when they told her that?" Toni said.

Paola shrugged. "They brought her over to show her around. We met her and stuff. We talked a little by ourselves. She told me she wasn't going to go out on any dates."

"What happened?" I asked.

"A couple days later, they moved her over to our house. It was the end of last week, I think."

"Were you able to talk to her again?"

"Yeah. She was there a couple days. I worked at night, but I talked to her in the daytime. I thought she was cool. She loaned me the coat I was wearing last night."

"And did she start going out on dates?" Toni asked.

"No. They had dates all set up for her, but right after she moved in, she came right out and told them she wouldn't go on any dates. She told them she was going to leave."

"What happened then?"

"They all got really mad. Isabel got punishment."

"What's that mean—punishment?"

"They beat her with the belt. Right in front of us. Then they threatened her family. They said they were going to kill her mom."

"What did Isabel do?"

"She got mad. She told them to go ahead, she didn't care. Then she told them to fuck off—those were her exact words. She said she was leaving." She looked down for a moment before continuing. "So then they took her to a party."

"A party?" I asked. "What's that mean? What's a party?"

She looked down and shifted her feet. She was clearly getting nervous.

Nancy noticed, too. "Paola, you don't have to answer if you don't like."

She looked up and then said, "It's alright." She turned back to me. "A party is when they take you over to the boys' house, and everybody gets high, and then you have to have sex with all of them at the same time."

I could feel my skin start to tingle—a clear sign that I was on my way to getting good and pissed. Whenever I think I'm past the point where I can be surprised by the pure depths of depravity some scumbags seem able to reach, something new like this comes along. The drugging and gang rape of a child by a group of men as a means of forcing the girl into prostitution—this was a new low in my experience. I shuddered. Poor Isabel ran away from home to escape an abusive prick of a stepfather—an animal who liked to rape her just for fun and where'd she end up? With a bunch of the worst kind of thugs I'd ever heard of. Wonderful. I noticed I was staring at the ceiling, holding my breath, so I slowly let it out and looked at the others. They were all looking at me.

"Sorry," I said. I shook my head slowly. "Paola, it makes me very sad to hear about the kind of life you've had to live. I'm so happy for you that Nancy found you and wants to help you. Really. No one deserves to go through this."

She looked at me for a second and then shrugged. "There's worse," she said.

How? Tough little girl.

Toni continued. "So Paola, after the beating and the party, then what happened to Isabel? Did she start going out on dates then?"

"I don't think so. They probably wouldn't send her out all beat-up. But I haven't seen Isabel for about a week—since the night they took her to the party."

"Do you know what happened to her?"

Paola stared at Toni for a moment before she answered. "No. I just know that she wasn't at our house anymore."

"Why would they take her away?" I asked.

"They said he was going to sell her."

"Sell her?" I asked. I didn't bother asking who "he" was.

She nodded. "I think they took her away so everyone else wouldn't feel bad."

"Who would they sell her to?"

She shrugged. "I don't know," she said. "Maybe his friends in Las Vegas. They have girls, too. They're always checking out each other's 'inventory.' That's what they call it."

"How often do they hook up?" I asked. I needed to find out how much time we had.

"I don't know," she said. "Whenever they need to, I guess."

She looked at me, right in the eyes. I looked back. For just a moment, I felt like I could see straight into her inner thoughts. They were a child's eyes, yet they weren't the innocent eyes of a fifteen-year-old. They were hard eyes, eyes that had seen way too much evil for one so young.

We talked for another fifteen minutes, but we didn't really get any more pertinent information. Paola did let slip the fact that she liked riding around in the "beemer"—which I took to be Donnie Martin's white BMW. I was already pretty sure that Donnie was her pimp. And now we knew that he had been trying to become Isabel's as well. Except Isabel— God bless her—was no eleven-year-old. She was fighting back.

PART 2

Chapter 13

AT LOGAN PI, we don't have a motto, but if we did, it would probably be: "When in doubt, get back to the basics." No question about it, we were in doubt now. No one knew exactly where Isabel was. Unfortunately, since she was too young for a bank account or credit cards that we could trace, our magic shortcuts list had pretty much been reduced to one item: her cell phone. And Kenny'd tried that and struck out. So we were left with no choice but to fall back on the basics—back to good old-fashioned nuts-and-bolts detective work. We needed to eliminate some of the unknowns.

Nancy had someone send us an audio file of the recording of our interview with Paola and now the whole Logan PI team was assembled in the conference room, listening to the playback from one of the PC speakers. We'd suffered two unfortunate setbacks in the last sixteen hours. First, of course, was the simple fact that the girl who'd showed up at the sting last night wasn't Isabel. We'd been excited to see the ad with Isabel's pictures, and we'd gotten our hopes up, only to see them come crashing down. Now, even after Nancy'd worked on Paola this morning and gotten her to loosen up a little, the only information she had offered didn't sound too good for Isabel. She'd been "punished," and Paola'd had no contact with her for a while. Worse, Paola wasn't certain that Isabel was even still around. For all she knew, Isabel might have been sold. Or she might even be on the run. Again. This was beginning to look like a bigger job than

I'd originally anticipated.

"There!" I said, focusing back on the recording. "Back it up and play that part again."

Kenny started the recording again. "They live across the street from the park—by the—," Paola's voice echoed on the recording.

"Stop," I said. "I *knew* she said something about a park." I was thinking that if we could figure out where the houses were located, maybe we could discover something about where Isabel was. Or where she wasn't—either way would be helpful.

"Good memory," Toni said. "I wonder which park she meant?"

"She wouldn't say, but we know—or at least we think we know—that it's in the area north of the U-District."

Doc was standing by a whiteboard mounted to the wall opposite the window. I turned to him and said, "Write it down anyway, okay?"

Up to this point, clues were pretty scarce, but we were still writing down what we had. So far, Doc had written:

CLUES
Donnie Martin—BMA—early twenties
DeMichael Hollins—BMA—early twenties (?)
Crystal—??
Auto: white BMW with tinted windows
multiple houses
—girls' house
—boys' house
—big house
north of the U-District

To this he now added :

across from a park

We stared at the board.

"Not much to go on," Toni said.

I shook my head. "Not much."

"Well," Kenny said. "We could always just jump in the car and drive by the houses around all the parks north of the U-District looking for a white beemer with two black guys in it."

I looked at him then at the board. Then I looked back at the group. "I suppose."

"Really?" Kenny said.

I shrugged. "It's a simple answer." I looked at the board again. "But sometimes the simple answer is the right answer—especially when you don't have any others."

"It's called Occam's razor, dude," Doc said to Kenny.

I looked at Doc and smiled. "Doc, you never cease to amaze me."

"Part of my job description," he said, smiling back. "So how many parks you think are up there, anyway?" Doc asked.

"We can look on a map and count 'em out," Kenny said.

"How long will it take?" I asked

"We can do it right now," he said. "While you wait." He opened up a map program and zoomed to the area north of the U-District.

I studied the map for a few seconds. "It's a pretty big area, but according to the map here, there aren't that many parks—maybe fifteen or twenty if you count school playgrounds."

We all looked at the map for several seconds. Finally, Toni said, "This is a big area, Danny. Are you seriously thinking about driving around up there looking for a white BMW?" She looked like she thought it was a bad idea. Looking at the map, I started to think that it might not be such a great idea. We've done this before, and it usually doesn't amount to much. Then again, we were short on clues. That said, I decided to give the creative process one more shot.

"As a last resort," I said, "we'll drive the area. But before we go burning gasoline, let's use our heads and think this through. Kenny," I looked at him, "I really need you to come through for us. I want you to go back to your office and close the door. Then, I need you to sit there where it's all nice and quiet, and just think. Figure out some little angle that we're missing—something you can use to help us find these guys and short-circuit this groping-around-in-the-dark search of ours. Then, maybe we can zoom right in on Isabel. You can search a lot faster on your computer than we can in our cars. Be a detective for us."

Kenny considered this for a second, then he nodded. "Okay," he said. "I'm on it."

"Good." I turned to Doc. "Doc," I want you to take the DMV records and the property records that Kenny found earlier and start assembling them into a report we can give to Nancy. If we find anything, we're going to need her to move on it, and she's going to need the backup."

Doc nodded. I turned to Toni. "You," I said, "you and I have an appointment with Ferguson and Sons. We've got to keep the money engine running."

* * * *

Two hours later, Toni and I were on the way back from the SODO district of Seattle where Ferguson's main warehouse is located. We'd presented them with a contract for review, and we'd agreed on a start date a week from next Monday. The stereo was on, and Toni had chosen "Something in the Water" by Chris Webster. Just as we exited I-5 onto Mercer, my cell phone rang. Caller ID: Kenny.

I tapped the speakerphone button. "Hey there," I said.

"Got something," he said.

"Go."

"I checked out the name 'Donnie Martin' with DMV, and there was nothing, so I checked 'Donald Martin' instead and bingo!—I got a match on a Donald Allen Martin on Twenty-First Avenue. Didn't you say Donnie Martin's aunt lived in the Central District?"

"Interesting," I said, thinking. "Hold on a second—I need to pull over." I pulled the Jeep into the parking lot at the Lake Union Park. "So you're thinking that Martin still has his driver's license address at his aunt's old address, then?"

"It gets better," he said. "I'm pretty sure of it because there's also a car registered to the same Donald Allen Martin at the same address."

"And?"

"2005 BMW 750i."

"Bingo!" I said.

"Wait, boss," he said. "There's more. We're pretty sure the guy we're looking for lives up north of the U-District, not in the CD. So I started thinking, what would the guy have to have at his new house—wherever it might be—that would most likely match up to the place where he actually lived? Now that I know his name, I had something I could work with."

"Did you hit something?"

"Yeah."

I waited for a second, but he didn't answer. He wanted me to pry it from him. "Come on, man, quit playing games," I said impatiently. "Tell me what you've got."

"Electric bill," he said. "The service address on the electric bill has to match up. I took a quiet little peek into the Seattle City Light records and voilà! Donald Allen Martin has power service at 6345 Fortieth Avenue Northeast—right up where you guys are looking. And I looked on the maps—the house is right across the street from the Bryant Neighborhood Playground."

"Dude, you're a genius!" I said.

"Yeah, I know."

"And humble, too," Toni called out.

We were excited again. We were back in business. Now that we had an address, it looked like a good old-fashioned stakeout was in order.

* * * *

We have three vehicles that we've converted especially for surveillance over the past four years. The first two are nearly identical windowless vans—a white one and a dark green one. Seeing as how we're particularly clever, we generally slap a colorful commercial sign on the sides of the vans to disguise us. The vans are tricky, but our mack daddy, crown-jewel surveillance rig is our 1982 Winnebago Brave motor home. No one ever suspects it.

With their work areas concealed by a curtain, all three vehicles look harmless from the outside. Inside, though, they're all business. They're loaded with audio, video, communication, and computer gear and with a bevy of recording devices. We can take clear photos from one hundred yards, clear video from fifty yards. With a boom mic, we can record a conversation from nearly one hundred yards away if ambient conditions are favorable.

In addition to being workhorses, the vehicles are also long on creature comforts—especially the Winnebago. All the vehicles feature a sink and a microwave, a mini-fridge under the desk, and—best of all—a small enclosed toilet. Anyone who's ever spent time on a stakeout in an automobile would look at a surveillance assignment in any of our vehicles and think they'd died and ascended to the right hand of God. With all these features, it's easy to remain on station for hours at a time. I figure that by rotating the crews, the vans are good for a full day in place without attracting too much attention, while the motor home should be good for three or four days without arousing suspicion. The Winnebago would be the perfect choice for watching the house on Fortieth for a couple of days.

The Bryant Neighborhood Playground, directly across the street from our target house, has a parking lot at the north end alongside 165th. By parking in the far western part of the lot, the target house would be only 150 feet from the motor home—perfect surveillance distance. At ten the next morning, I backed the motor home into a parking space such that our left side faced the target house across a corner of the park. The parking spot was ideal—close enough for effective surveillance, and far enough removed to be essentially inconspicuous. Even if someone did notice us, what was threatening about a small motor home in a park? Toni followed me in her car and pulled in on my east side, blocked from view of the house by the motor home. She left an empty space between us. We were to take the 1000 to 1400 shifts plus the 1800 to 2100 shifts on both Saturday and Sunday. Kenny and Doc would relieve us at two o'clock and cover the 1400 to 1800 and 2100 to 0000 shifts. It wasn't round-the-clock, but we only have four people, and it would have to do.

Once we were in position, we started watching the house. Donnie Martin's white BMW was parked in the driveway, alongside a red late-model Honda Accord. I called Kenny and read him the Honda's license plate number. Ten minutes later, he called back with the owner: Patricia Denise Wallace with a Kirkland address. Was this Crystal?

The house was a neat, little two story with well-kept landscaping. It appeared quiet. I fired up the high-powered video camera mounted to the roof of the motor home. The camera is hidden inside a smoked plastic dome on the roof that looks a little like a satellite dish. When I pointed the camera at the front door, I was able to nearly fill the screen with a pretty sharp image—good enough for our purposes.

We opened the main door on the "away" side to let some air in. I extended the awning, rolled out the carpet, and set up a couple of chairs. We wouldn't be spending any time sitting outside, but it made the cover story all the more convincing.

Being that it was June 9—an odd-numbered date, it was my day to pick the tunes. I couldn't get too wild and crazy, though. After all, we were scheduled for the next day as well. Best not to annoy Toni if she and I were going to be spending the better part of the next two days elbow to elbow.

* * * *

"Movement!" Toni whispered, excitedly. It was her turn at the console, monitoring the front door of the residence. I'd been leaning back, completely relaxed, in the motor home's lounge chair, listening to "Uncaged" by the Zac Brown Band. I snapped out of it quickly, though, and looked at the clock on the wall. It was 12:10 p.m. I looked at the console. A tall, thin, well-dressed black man and a white female with medium-length dark hair were coming out of the house.

"Tighten up," I said. Toni twisted the control, and the camera zoomed in closer on the two.

"Donnie Martin?" I asked.

"Watch," Toni said.

The two walked over to the white beemer and got in. A second later, the car fired up. A few seconds after that, it backed out of the driveway and headed south on Fortieth.

"It's him," Toni said.

"How do you know?"

"He got in the car. It's his car."

Duh. "Good point. You're probably right," I said. "You think that was Crystal?"

"Could be. The age fits. That woman didn't look like a teenager to me."

"True," I said. "But in the photos, Isabel didn't look like she was just sixteen, and Paola didn't look like she was fifteen, either. It looks like I'm no judge."

"It's hard. Especially since the young girls are trying to look older and the older girls are trying to look younger."

"Geez," I said. "No wonder I can't figure it out. Roll back, will you. Let's have another look at these two."

Toni went back to the two of them coming out of the house. "Can you capture that? Let's see if we can clean it up with Photoshop and print."

We kept an eye on the house for the next hour and a half while we worked on enhancing the photos. In the end, we were able to isolate each person, compensate for grain and shadows, and end up with a pretty decent ID shot. "That oughta work," I said.

"Cool," she agreed.

My phone rang—caller ID: Doc.

"What's up, Doc?" I said. I know. It's corny.

"We're two minutes out. Clear to relieve?" Doc was asking if there was any reason why he shouldn't pull in next to us now—like, for example, if the subjects were out in their front yard or something like that.

"Stand by," I said.

I panned the camera as far down Fortieth Avenue as I could. There were no cars visible and, more important, no potential bad guys standing around who might get suspicious of us being there.

"Come on in," I said. "You'll see Toni parked east of the rig. The spot on the east side of her is open. Go ahead and park there."

"Roger," Doc said.

A minute later, they pulled in. Kenny was driving. He shut his car off and hopped out. "Hey, this is nice," he said as he checked out the awning and the chairs. "I haven't seen it since you added the awning. All we need's a barbecue."

I laughed. "I should bring my Weber grill," I said. "That would make for a pretty sneaky surveillance setup, you think?"

"No shit," he said. "We'd be sitting right in front of them barbecuing Kobe burgers, completely invisible."

"Best way," I said.

Doc walked up. "I don't see a beemer," he said.

"Yeah, they left a half hour ago," I said. "A guy we think must be Donnie Martin and a white girl—might be Crystal."

"Nothing else?"

"Nope. Four hours. That was it."

"Show me," he said. As usual, Doc was all business.

We went inside. "Here's a couple of photos we took. We think this is Donnie Martin—at least he was driving Donnie Martin's car. And this is the girl who could be Crystal."

Doc and Kenny peered in. "She looks a little older," Kenny said.

"Exactly," Toni said. "If she's the bottom girl, that would make sense."

Doc nodded.

"That your log?"

"Yep. That's it. They left at 12:12 p.m."

Doc nodded. "Okay then," he said. "You guys are relieved. We got it."

"You boys play nice," Toni said, smiling.

Chapter 14

AT 8:15 A.M. on Monday, we were back in the conference room. We'd decided to end the surveillance of the house on Fortieth Avenue last night at midnight—the Winnebago was already back at the storage lot.

"Scroll through them, slowly," I said to Kenny. He was running through our combined logs for both days. We'd already been through them once; now we were tabulating visits.

"So it looks to me like Martin makes a total of seven trips. Four of those times, he's with Crystal. Twice, he brings back this guy here—," I pulled another photo out, "—who we think is DeMichael Hollins."

"And Crystal makes four trips by herself in the red Honda," Doc said. "Owned by Patricia Denise Wallace, aka: Crystal."

I nodded.

"No other girls," Toni said. "No Isabel."

"Nope."

"And I noticed something else," Doc said. "These guys don't seem to be too worked up about anything. If Isabel's gone, they don't seem too concerned, at least not outwardly. They seemed in a pretty good mood both times I saw them."

"I think you're right," I said.

"Where are they coming from and going to?" Toni asked. "The other houses?"

"Could be," I said. "They'd have to visit them sometime."

"So, like Paola said, the girls are at one of the other houses," Kenny said. "Maybe Isabel's with them."

"Perhaps. It would be really nice to know how they've got their operation set up—where everybody stays, what everyone does."

"I know a way we can start filling in the blanks," Doc said. "At least find out where the other houses are located."

"Vehicle surveillance," I said.

"Right. It will help us find out what they've got. We start following this guy Martin. See where he takes us."

I usually don't like to do vehicle surveillance because there are only four of us, and it's really hard to do a proper job of following someone in a vehicle with only four cars. It's too easy for a wary subject to ID the tail. Then, once you're made, you're worse off than when you started. "I normally try to avoid vehicle surveillance," I said, "for reasons known to all of you. On the other hand—though I don't want to underestimate the NSSB guys—they sure don't look like they're playing defense out there. If they are, they're really good at hiding it."

"What do you mean?" Toni asked.

"What I mean is that these guys don't seem to have a care in the world. They walk outside from the house to the car, and they don't even look around, for Christ's sake. There could be a whole SWAT battalion parked at the house next door, and I'm not sure these clowns would even notice."

"Your point?" Toni said.

"My point is it might be okay for us to follow them with just four vehicles. They probably aren't even looking for tails."

"Floating box?" Doc said.

"I don't know," I said. "Let's assume the other houses are nearby. Did you notice the streets in that area?"

"Yeah," Doc said. "They're friggin' skinny."

"That's right. A floating box might not work because you'd be stuck behind a slow-moving subject. Even a dimwit might get suspicious."

"So we use cheaters," Toni said. "Cheaters" are cars that are parked ahead of the subject's route of travel. They relieve the previous vehicle by falling in ahead of or behind the subject as it reaches their position.

"I think that's the best," I said. "Kenny—pop open a map of the area."

Kenny selected the proper file and zoomed to a map of our four-quadrant area.

"Go ahead and put a mark by the Fortieth Avenue house," I said.

After he did, I asked, "Now—when Donnie leaves his house here," I pointed to the red square Kenny had placed on the Fortieth Avenue address, "in which direction is he ultimately going to be headed?"

"West," Doc said.

"West or south," Toni said.

"I think west, too," Kenny said. "Maybe south."

"Why?"

"Because," he said, "that's what he did every single time on Saturday and Sunday. He never went north or east that we can tell. Besides, if he does go north or east, the area tends to change to bigger, more expensive houses. If he goes west or south, it gets to be more and more apartments and college-type housing. My guess is, he'd probably not have the girls— or anyone else—living in a nicer house than he does."

I smiled. "Well said. I hadn't looked at that angle. But it makes sense. And it reinforces my strategy. Since we're short on manpower, we're going to have to take a few chances and be willing to swing again if we miss. Here's the deal."

I detailed a plan that took advantage of the fact that there was about a 99 percent chance that Martin would leave the area either westbound or southbound, as seemed to be his pattern. We'd all be wearing our VHF radios with hands-free headsets. This way, as long as Donnie did more or less what we expected, we should be able to follow him without being detected—at least for a while. I figured we'd roll into position by 11:45 a.m. since on both days, Donnie and Crystal had left the house between noon and twelve thirty. Apparently, they went to lunch. If this was a habit of theirs, we'd be able to capitalize on it.

The office phone rang. Kenny was nearest, so he answered. He turned to me. "It's Lieutenant Stewart," he said.

"Good. I needed to bring her up to date. Put her on speaker, will you?"

"Good morning, Nancy," I said. "We were just about to call you and fill you in on what we found over the weekend."

"Good morning," she said. "Before you get started, you might be interested to hear that Annie Hooper was able to find a spot for Paola. They've just opened up a new house, and they were able to get her in. Annie made it a priority given the background of Paola's case."

"That's great news," I said. "That girl's been through a lot. Maybe now she can start to get her life turned around."

"We can only hope," Nancy said. "At least she seems like she's willing to take the step. I think it's possible that she will continue to open up over time—although that might not happen fast enough to be of much value to you in your case. Anyway," she added, "what's going on? How's the case progressing?"

"You remember I told you we were going to hunt for Donnie Martin's house—the one Paola mentioned was across from the park?"

"Yeah, sure."

"Well, we found it. I don't know if it was extraordinary detective skills, or complete dumb luck, but we matched up the name on a power bill to an address that matched the description that Reverend Jenkins provided. We checked it out and lo and behold, Donnie Martin's BMW was parked right out front. The house is located across the street from a park up on Fortieth Avenue North."

"Just above the U-District," she said. "Just like Paola said it was."

"Right. And just like Reverend Jenkins said. Anyway, we staked out the house over the weekend."

"And?"

"We saw Martin, or at least a guy we think was Martin—he was driving Martin's car anyway—and a girl—older girl—we presume it's his bottom girl, Crystal. By the way, we think her real name is Patricia Denise Wallace. I'll send you her info. Anyway, we saw them come and go together maybe half a dozen times. Also saw a guy we presume to be DeMichael Hollins. He drives a maroon Expedition. We were able to trace the registration back to Hollins. We'll send you that, too."

"Power bills and DMV info?" Nancy said, a touch of suspicion in her voice. "I don't even want to know how you guys are getting this stuff."

"Better that way," I said. "But my real point is, we never saw any other girls at the house. And since we were stationary, we don't know where these guys were going or where they were coming from. Based on that, we've decided to do a vehicle surveillance this afternoon. We want to tail him and see if he'll lead us to the other houses—including, we hope, the one where the girls live."

"That sounds logical," she said. " I know you guys know what you're doing, but I have to say this—be careful."

"Definitely," I said.

"Oh, by the way, I got a message from our gang unit—they've assigned us the guy they say is most plugged into the north side. They asked me to set something up with you guys. He's free to meet with you tomorrow."

"Great," I said. "We can make any time tomorrow work. Just let us know."

"I'll send you a text," she said.

"Good. Thanks for setting things up for us."

* * * *

By 11:45 a.m., all four vehicles were in position. I was parked in the Bryant Playground parking lot—the same lot where the Winnebago had been parked over the weekend. Only I wasn't driving the Winnebago. I wasn't driving my red Jeep, either—the consensus of the Logan PI staff being that it stood out too much (an opinion that was hard to dispute). I didn't set out to make the Jeep conspicuous—I just wanted it to be a pretty decent off-road vehicle, but by the time I'd lifted the body a couple of inches to accommodate the tall wheels and thirty-one-inch tires, well, I have to admit, it wasn't easy to hide anymore. So I drove the dark green van with *Lake Union Appliance Repair* vinyl stickers slapped on the side.

When properly executed, the rolling box method of vehicle surveillance doesn't give the subject an opportunity to ID a tail, because the tail is constantly changing. One of the vehicles—usually the closest, is the "prime" vehicle and has command. That vehicle directs all the others. The prime vehicle might not be behind the subject, it might actually be in front with additional vehicles staged on parallel side roads in case the subject turns off. The command changes constantly as the team members take turns rotating into the prime position, never staying long enough to arouse suspicion. Good communication between all vehicles is essential, as is proper staging and placement of vehicles around the subject.

We started by staging Toni across the street in a supermarket parking lot. If Martin turned to go south on Sixty-Fifth, I'd follow him as command vehicle, and Toni would follow me as backup. Doc was further west on Sixty-Fifth. He'd take off as I approached. When we got in range, I'd pull off and allow him to become the command vehicle while he was still in front of Martin. Toni would continue to stay well behind as backup. Meanwhile, Kenny was about a half mile south on Fortieth in case Martin decided to head off in that direction.

At 12:15 p.m., pretty much right on schedule, I saw the door to the house open, and Crystal stepped out, followed a moment later by Martin.

"Showtime, guys," I said into the headset. I watched as they got into the car and pulled north. As soon as he put his left turn blinker on, indicating he was turning west on Sixty-Fifth, I was immediately relieved—Martin was following his pattern. I said, "He's turning westbound on Sixty-Fifth. Kenny—start making your way westbound."

I followed him westbound on Sixty-Fifth for a mile, with Toni behind me by about one hundred yards. Kenny was about five blocks south of us, paralleling our direction of travel. When we approached Doc, I pulled off, and Doc became the command vehicle. Toni continued to trail.

Martin continued westbound for another mile, and then Doc said, "He's turning south. Looks like he's turning on Brooklyn. I'm already past."

I was just about to reach Brooklyn.

"Kenny," Doc called. "Are you at Brooklyn yet?"

"Negative."

"Then just pull up on Fifty-Fifth and stop short of Brooklyn," Doc said. "Don't cross. Cover us in case he keeps heading south."

"Roger," Kenny said.

"Toni, are you going to follow him down Brooklyn?"

"Yeah. It's a tight street, though—I'm going to hang back a bit."

"Okay," I said. "Toni, you've got command." I was looking at the portable Garmin GPS suction-cupped to the dash.

A few seconds later, Toni said, "He's slowing down. He's parking along the curb at a house across from the park. I'm going to slow down and then turn east here on Sixty-Second before I get there."

"Okay, they're getting out," she said a second later.

"Kenny," she called out. "Turn north on Brooklyn. Come up slow and do a drive-by and grab the address. The beemer is parked right in front of the house they went in."

"Roger," Kenny said.

"I'm making my turn onto Sixty-Second eastbound," Toni said. "Kenny, you have the command."

"Roger." Kenny loves the military lingo.

"Do it slow but not stupid," I said.

"Got it," he said. "I'm just going to call it out. One of you guys can write it down."

"Good."

A few seconds later, Kenny started counting the numbers. "6131 . . . 6135 . . . 6139 . . . 6143 . . . it's 6147! 6147 Brooklyn."

"See anyone outside?" I asked.

"Nobody," he said.

"Good. Keep driving. Toni, can you make a U-turn and sneak back up to keep an eye on the house?"

"Yeah. I'm already on it. I'll call you when I'm in position."

* * * *

Was this the boys' house or the girls'? I didn't know, but at least we now had an address. We could stake it out later and try to decide who actually lived there. Meanwhile, I redeployed all the vehicles in preparation for when Martin moved out again. Toni reported from her vantage point that four cars had arrived over the next twenty minutes. Each car was driven by a young black male. Using her binoculars, Toni was able to report that all of the drivers appeared to be in their early twenties. She took license numbers for all of them. Two of the drivers were accompanied by young white girls, neither of whom looked anything like Isabel. We waited. Forty-five minutes later, Toni said, "Here comes Martin and Crystal," followed a minute later by, "They're getting in. Doc—you ready?"

"I'm rolling," he said. Doc was going to take over as command vehicle, this time from behind. We figured that since Martin hadn't seen Doc's vehicle in a trail position, it might be our best bet. Toni was going to be backup again, and Kenny was back down on Fifty-Fifth—this time, pointed east.

"They're heading south," Toni said.

"I got 'em," Doc said. "I've got command. Just driving past the house. No other apparent activity."

Martin drove south until he reached Fifty-Fifth, where he turned eastbound. We followed him for another two miles as he worked his way south and east, deeper into the U-District.

"He's stopped on Nineteenth," Doc said. "They're getting out."

"Can you break off?" I asked.

"Yeah. I'll just keep going straight here."

"Okay," I said. "Don't go down Nineteenth. I'm fifteen seconds away," I said. "He hasn't seen me in profile yet. I'm going to make the turn on Nineteenth and check it out." We were running out of vehicles that hadn't already been in prime position.

I turned south onto Nineteenth off of Fifty-Fifth. Immediately, I could see the white BMW parked alongside the curb, four houses down from Fifty-Fifth. The car looked empty.

"He's parked at a house down the street. Looks like they've gone inside," I reported.

The street was heavily tree-lined, making it hard to see the address. I slowed down before the house—I didn't want to change speeds in front of it. As I approached, I looked for the address on the mailbox. Finally, just as I reached the house, I saw the box. The address was pasted to the side in inexpensive foil letters. "5387 Nineteenth," I said. "5-3-8-7."

"Got it," Toni said.

"Nobody visible. House looks like a frat house. Big brick sucker—big porch. I'm going on past."

I drove to the end of the block and stopped. I could see Doc parked around the corner.

"Think the other house was the boys' house and this one is the girls' house?" Doc asked over the radio.

"Maybe. Is there a place for me to pull in and park on the curb north of the house, someplace where I could still get a view?"

"I don't know," Doc said.

"Hey, guys," Kenny said. "I'm up here at the top of the street. How about if I make a U-turn and come back and just park up here. I can eyeball them when they come out before they even get in the car."

"That works. Doc—you're good where you are. I'd just as soon he didn't see this green van again. I'm going to go down a half mile or so here and park. Toni? Where are you?"

"On Twentieth between Ravenna and Fifty-Eighth."

"Perfect," I said. "Just wait."

Less than five minutes later, Kenny said. "Here they come. Just the two of them," followed shortly afterward by, "They're headed south again."

"I got 'em," Doc said a minute later. "They just passed me. They turned east on Fiftieth. They're leaving our area."

I thought about this. We were out of vehicles that hadn't already been in the prime position. We had what we needed. I didn't think we'd been spotted. A good afternoon.

"Everybody—let's call it a day," I said. "Break off, and we'll debrief back at the office."

Chapter 15

A FEW MINUTES before ten the next morning, Toni and I waited in the lobby of Nancy Stewart's office for our meeting with the SPD gang unit. I was reading a *Sports Illustrated* article about Texas Ranger left fielder Josh Hamilton. Hamilton's my kind of hero—a guy with superhuman powers yet still a man—a fallible human being. Part of the package with Josh Hamilton includes a fair share of goofs, screwups, and mistakes—just like the ones we all make every day. Yet—and this is the really inspirational part in my book—he still manages to find his way back—humble, contrite, no excuses, no attempts at blame shifting. His faith in God and the love and strong support of his family and friends serve as his bedrock, and—at least so far—it appears to be an unshakable foundation. I'm a fan.

"Morning, guys," Nancy said. She'd poked her head out the "Restricted Access" door, and I hadn't even noticed.

"Hey there," I said, standing. "You ready for us?"

"C'mon back."

She held the door for us and then led us back to a conference room. We walked into the room and noticed two men already seated. Both men were dressed casually—even more so than I was (I wore jeans and a short-sleeved Hawaiian shirt). One of the men looked up when we entered. He was Hispanic, probably late twenties. His dark hair was cut very short except for a slightly longer Mohawk strip down the middle. In a thousand years, I'd never have guessed him to be a cop—except for the badge pinned to his shirt and the Glock on his belt. The other guy was on his cell phone, his back turned to us. He had medium-length blond hair and even from the side, I could see he wore a short, scruffy beard. When we entered, he finished up his call and spun around in his chair.

Our eyes met, and we instantly recognized each other. "D-Lo!" he said, hopping out of his chair. "Son of a bitch! I had no idea you were the one we were meeting with today."

"Mickey Cole," I said as I walked around the table to greet him. Michael Cole, known far and wide as Mickey, had been a senior at Ballard High School when I was a sophomore. Normally, that two-year difference would have made us invisible to each other. In our case, though, we were both on the varsity track team—he threw the javelin, and I was a miler. We spent a lot of time together. "Long time no see."

"Damn right," he said as we shook hands warmly. "Last I heard, you'd gotten yourself shot over in Iraq."

I nodded. "Yeah, I zigged when I should have zagged."

"Jesus, dude. You're okay?"

"I'm fine. All in one piece. I was only out of action for a week or so."

"Glad to hear it," he said. He turned to Toni. "Hi," he said, smiling broadly. "I'm Mickey Cole."

Toni smiled. "Hi," she said. "Toni Blair. I work for Danny."

Mickey shook her hand. "Danny and I were on the track team together in high school. He was pretty good at it—damn good, actually. I sucked. I was just there for the letter."

"He's still pretty fast," Toni said.

"I'll bet he is," Mickey said. He turned to the other man at the table. "This skinny guy over here is my partner Javier Martinez. Javi and I head up the Gang Unit's north-side efforts. Nancy told us about your little sting operation. Sounds like it didn't turn out quite the way you'd hoped."

I shook my head. "No, it didn't," I said.

"Let's have a seat, and you can tell us about it."

We took our seats. "Have you ever heard of a group called the North Side Street Boyz—that's boyz with a 'z'?" I asked.

Mickey glanced at Javier and then turned back to me. "Oh, yeah," he said. "We've heard of them. Donnie "Young Love" Martin and his crew. What are those knuckleheads up to?"

I walked them through the events of the last week and a half, starting with the text messages Kelli'd received from Isabel, all the way through our vehicle surveillance. "So," I concluded, "our interest in this is finding and rescuing Isabel Delgado."

Mickey nodded. "Based on what you just described, this sounds like vintage shit from these punks. They recruit young runaway girls, force them into prostitution, and then they live off the earnings. We think they've been doing it for three years or so. They use the money to buy drugs and fancy cars. They're nothing but modern-day pimps."

"That's actually an insult to pimps, if you can believe that," Javier said. "At least most of the old-fashioned pimps split the money with the prostitutes in some fashion. These guys don't even do that. They keep everything. They're actually modern-day slave masters."

I opened the file I'd brought and slid out pictures of the three individuals we'd seen at the big house.

"That's Donnie Martin," Javier said. He held up the picture and turned to Nancy. "Have you pulled this guy's sheet?"

Nancy nodded. "He's been in trouble since he was ten years old."

"No doubt," Mickey said. "He's a bad dude. What's worse, he's not very bright. The combination makes him dangerous. I'd say he's on a one-way street. If he's lucky, he'll end up in prison for a long, long time."

"And if he's not," Javier said, "somebody's gonna take him out."

"You guys don't have any active investigations going on this guy then?" Nancy asked.

"Nothing formal," Mickey said. "You guys neither?"

Nancy shook her head. "We'd never even heard of them until Danny and Toni brought them to us. It's the exact kind of thing we're all over—particularly with the threat of trafficking."

"What threat is that?" Mickey asked.

Nancy recounted Paola's conversation about Isabel possibly being sold.

"That makes it federal, doesn't it?" Mickey asked.

Nancy nodded. "It does. The FBI runs a local task force dealing with sex trafficking of minors. They should be joining us any minute."

* * * *

Ten seconds later, a man in a suit and a woman in a dress suit were led into the conference room by a member of Nancy's staff.

"Here they are," Nancy said, standing. We all stood for introductions. "Special Agents Nicole Bryan and Jonathan Geist." Nancy introduced each of us.

"Thank you for inviting us to your meeting, Nancy," Agent Bryan said as they took their seats. She was a tall woman, perhaps mid-thirties. Her blond hair was pulled back tightly. She turned to us. "I don't know how familiar you are with what we do, but Agent Geist and I are attached to the national Innocence Lost Initiative. As such, we head up the King County Innocence Lost Task Force, which consists of the FBI, the King County Sheriff's Department, and most of the local police departments. We're here to try and stop domestic sex trafficking of children in the Seattle area. Nancy called us and told us that we might have a new subject."

"That's right," Nancy said. "Danny and Toni are trying to find Isabel Delgado, a sixteen-year-old girl who we believe has become connected with a local gang called the North Side Street Boyz." Nancy went on to explain the sting and how we ended up with Paola. "When Paola implicated the NSSB gang in trafficking, I had no choice but to notify the task force."

"Just to be clear," I said, "as I recall, Paola said she heard Isabel Delgado was going to be sold to another pimp—perhaps someone in Las Vegas—because she refused to begin prostituting herself for the gang."

"Understood. And there are no details other than that?" Agent Bryan asked.

"If by details you mean times and places of exchange, then no," I said, "no additional details. We do believe we have the addresses of the three houses where the gang bases its operation, the automobiles they drive, and—," I pointed to the pictures, "—pictures of the gang leaders."

Both agents examined the photos and took notes. When she was finished, Agent Bryan said, "Well, Nancy, I agree—this sounds like exactly the kind of case we're set up to investigate. As you know, we're just days away from pulling the trigger on Operation Cross Country VI. It's way too late to fold this into that. But I'd be willing to recommend that we start an investigation into this NSSB group now. That way, we could definitely include it in Cross Country VII."

"How long would that take?" I asked.

"It could take a while," she said. "We have to gather evidence, prepare a case."

"Weeks?" I asked. "Months?"

"Probably months," she said.

"Well, let me ask you this," I said. "You said you're about to pull the trigger on Cross Country VI, right?"

"Yes," she said.

"When did Cross Country V happen?"

She thought about it for a minute, and then she said, "December— no, November 2010."

"2010?" I said. "Eighteen months ago?"

She nodded. "That's about right."

"And how many kids got rescued?"

She considered this. "Around seventy," she said.

"Nationwide? Or just here in Seattle?"

"That was nationwide. I can see what you're getting at, Mr. Logan," she said, a little testily. "But you have to understand that it takes time for us to put a case together against these people."

"I do understand," I said. "And that's the point." I tilted my head a little and looked at her. "Where's that leave Isabel? Apparently, she's about to be sold like a slave and shipped out of state any time now. What about her?"

"I wish we could do more, but we can't swoop in and arrest these guys and make a case that will stick overnight," Agent Bryan said.

"Who cares about that?" I said. "We can definitely swoop in and rescue Isabel—this afternoon for that matter. To hell with making a case. All I care about is Isabel. I don't give a damn about NSSB."

She looked at me for a moment and then said, "Unfortunately, for us it doesn't work that way. We have to look at the bigger picture." She seemed to have channeled her patience and decided to explain things to me. I felt like I was back in elementary school. "Consider for a moment that these guys might be involved with dozens of girls just like Isabel. We have a duty to close the whole operation down. Jumping in and blowing our cover before we're ready probably eliminates that possibility. We have no choice but to carefully assemble a tight, solid case against the men involved so that we can arrest them, convict them, and put them away. In the process, we save all of their victims."

I stared at her for a moment. "And while you're doing that, what? You just ignore the people you see right in front of you who are being hurt by these men? People like Isabel?"

The room was tense. I could clearly hear the ticking of the clock on the wall as the seconds passed by. Finally, Nancy broke the silence. "Nobody's going to ignore anyone we see getting hurt, including Isabel," she said. "That said, the sad fact is that right now, it's a moot point anyway. We don't even know where she is."

"That's easy enough," I said. "Why don't you just go look? We already gave you the addresses."

"You mean get a warrant and search the houses?" Agent Bryan said. "Yeah."

"We can't do that," she said. "We don't have anything on them. We just heard about them two minutes ago. I don't think that hearsay from a fifteen-year-old would be sufficient probable cause. We'd never be able to get a warrant."

"You mean a warrant for trafficking?" I asked.

"Yes."

I turned to Nancy. "And you agree? I mean—the Seattle Police Department agrees?"

She looked at me. "For the moment—much as I hate to say it—we don't have a choice. Unless we get something more concrete, our hands are tied." She turned to face Agent Bryan. "But, Nicole, if we do come up with something more concrete—something that makes it so we think we know where that little girl is, then I *will* try to get a warrant. And I don't care if it's for trafficking or jaywalking or whatever. My first job is to protect. I won't stand by and watch one little girl become a sacrifice while we build a case against these guys. I'll find some reason to throw them in jail."

"But they might turn right around and walk," Agent Bryan protested.

"They might," Nancy said. "But in the meantime, I'll have Isabel. Safe and sound."

* * * *

"This is the exact problem I almost always have with those pinheads at the FBI," I said as I spooned my bowl of chowder. We were at Duke's Chowder House in Chandler's Cove by Lake Union, directly across the water from our office. I'd called a team meeting at one o'clock, and Toni and I were grabbing a quick lunch before. "Some of them—not all of them, but enough of them—they lose their common sense when they get their FBI badge and the secret decoder ring that goes with it."

Toni kept eating, content to let me rant.

"'We're here to arrest bank robbers,'" I said in my best FBI voice. "'We don't care if you're selling crack cocaine to little kids. That's someone else's department. We want to know about bank robbers.'" I shook my head. "That whole mindset pisses me off."

"The government compartmentalizes everything," Toni said. "And then, they assign duties and responsibilities based just on that narrow scope."

"And their culture rewards people who stick to the program and penalizes people who don't."

"Like the free thinkers," she said.

"Exactly."

"Good thing your girlfriend moved to Virginia," she said without looking up. She was referring to an FBI agent friend of mine—not a girlfriend—whom I'd spent some quality time with earlier in the year. My friend had coincidentally decided to transfer back east about the same time I came to my senses and figured out Toni was more than just a business partner to me. I could see Toni smiling, even as she refused to look up at me.

"Shut up," I said. "Gloating doesn't become you."

Now she looked up and smiled. "Just saying."

"Saying nothing. Besides," I said, "my girlfriend lives in Seattle."

"Oh, does she? Anyone I know?"

I shrugged. "Could be. She's pretty tall, dark hair, great eyes." I paused, as if I was thinking. Then I shrugged again. "Decent figure," I said, for which I received a quick kick in the shins under the table.

"Decent?" she said, feigning indignation.

"Okay," I admitted. "Better than decent." I stared off toward the ceiling, as if I were visualizing. Fact is, I *was* visualizing. "Damn fine, actually."

"You'd better say that," she said, smiling.

"Are you blushing?"

"No."

"Yeah, I think you are. Just a little."

"Shut up, Logan."

When we were finished, a thought occurred to me. "I have an idea," I said.

"Good."

"About the case."

"I assumed."

"Nancy said if she got something more concrete about Isabel's whereabouts, she'd move on it. Right?" I said.

"Yeah." Her voice took on a wary edge. "What'd you have in mind?"

"I think I might have a way of moving things along. No waiting for the FBI."

"You want to tell me about it?"

"Yeah. Let's get out of here."

Chapter 16

"THAT SUCKS," KENNY said. "You mean they won't do anything?" We were seated around the conference room table. It was 1:15 p.m. I'd just recounted our meeting with Nancy and the FBI.

"The FBI is made up of a bunch of weenies," I said. "Mostly, anyway. There are some good people there, but they're all covered up in mountains of political bullshit so high they can't even come up for air. They won't move on the NSSB for probably eighteen damn months while they 'assemble their case.' Good news—once they're done, it'll be ironclad. Bad guys will go to prison for a long time. Bad news—a half-dozen girls will slip through the net between now and then."

"Isabel being the first," Toni said.

"Exactly. And worse, dozens more girls will slip through because they're on either side of the FBI investigation—they don't exactly fit the type of crime the FBI's going after, so the FBI ignores them altogether. Meanwhile, the Feds would rather let Isabel get sold to a Vegas pimp so they can use that little transaction as evidence against the NSSB at some point down the road than step in and prevent the crime from happening in the first place. They'd never admit it, but Isabel's a pawn to them."

"That's pretty tunnel-visioned," Doc said.

I nodded. "Damn straight."

Richard shifted in his chair. "Does Nancy Stewart feel the same way? Is she somehow compelled to defer to the FBI because of SPD's participation in the task force?"

"I get the impression that she needs to go along with them in matters directly related to the Innocence Lost task force—in this case, trafficking."

"That was my impression, too," Toni said. "I don't think she has a choice. That's probably why she talked to them about it in the first place. But at the same time, I left the meeting thinking that she's definitely in charge when it comes to any other criminal activity—particularly something that's about to lead to the harm of a minor. She as much as said she wouldn't stand by and allow Isabel to get hurt—even if it messed up the case the FBI wanted to start on NSSB."

"Good for her," Richard said. "In my experience, when the FBI would roll into the middle of a case, they'd try to suck all the air out of the room. In fact, they'd act like they owned the place. Depending to some extent on whom you're working with, they don't like to be dealt with as equals—you have to stand up to them. But, then again, they are the eight-hundred-pound gorilla. There's only so much you can do."

"That's right," I said. "And that's why Nancy's not going to pursue an investigation centered around sex trafficking. Period. She can't. Not without the Feds."

"So we have to come at the problem from a different angle, then," Richard said.

"Exactly," I said. "Look at the title of Nancy's department. It says 'Vice and High Risk Victims unit. If Isabel isn't a potential high-risk victim, I don't know who is."

Richard nodded. "It's for people like Isabel that SPD reorganized that whole department," Richard said.

"So do you have a plan?" Doc said. Doc's a pretty direct guy. He grasps concepts very quickly and, after that, doesn't require much in the way of explanation.

I smiled. "Do I have a plan," I said. "Of course I have a plan. The way I see it, we're here to rescue Isabel. We don't care about legal cases. The issue is, rescuing Isabel can either happen the direct way—we go in and snatch her—or the indirect way: we give the police the evidence they need so that they'll go in and bust the bad guys and, in the process, rescue Isabel. And if it's going to happen the indirect way, then we *do* need to worry about legal cases because the police won't come out and play any other way. Does this make sense?"

Everyone nodded.

"Good. I think there's a reasonable chance—I don't know the exact odds—that Isabel hasn't been shipped to Las Vegas or wherever just yet. I say that because if they beat her up last week, they might want her to recover a little before they try to sell her."

"In order to get top dollar?" Kenny asked.

I nodded. "It's despicable, but it's logical. And, if that's the case, that means she's still around—very possibly at one of the three known NSSB houses. I propose we mount a tactical operation in which I go into each house on a clandestine basis." This got everyone's attention. I continued. "Best case—I find Isabel right then and there and bring her out with me. Otherwise, I look for evidence that she was there. If I can't find either of those, then I look for any other incriminating evidence I can find. I take a few pictures, and I leave."

"Obviously, evidence obtained like that is most likely of no value in court," Richard said.

"Assuming I don't find her outright, you're probably right. With luck, I will find her."

"For what we're doing," Toni said, "it doesn't matter if the evidence is legally admissible or not. We're not trying to convict anyone. And besides, even if the evidence isn't legally useful, it still gives us some good intel. And that helps us create our next step. If we have solid information as to what we're looking at, it will be that much easier to be able to develop a plan to obtain evidence that is useful in court—evidence that will motivate the police to get involved."

"Evidence aside, it might be prudent to consider the fact that breaking and entering is illegal in this state," Richard said. "Never mind the fact that the idea of breaking into a known gang house poses its own problems, right from the start. Do you think there might be an element of danger involved?" I liked Richard's sarcasm.

"Your second point addresses your first," I said.

He tilted his head. "Explain."

"I don't think it's very likely that I'd get caught. But even if I did, I don't think the gang is likely to call the cops. I think they'd be more inclined to dispense a little cowboy justice, right?"

He nodded. "That's supposed to be a comfort?" he asked. "Your first point bolsters my second. The danger is doubly high."

I smiled. "Which is exactly why I'm not asking for volunteers on this mission. I'm doing it myself."

"I volunteer," Doc said, raising his hand.

"Me, too," Kenny said.

"Me, three," Toni said.

"You guys are all cowboys. I said I'm *not* asking for volunteers. I'm going in myself—by myself. We'll set up a good, tight perimeter operation and minimize the danger. I'll get in, see if Isabel's there or if there's any trace of her, snap a couple of photos, then get out. Anything goes wrong, you guys come get me. Maybe we'll get lucky, who knows. At least we won't be sitting around twiddling our thumbs, waiting for something to happen."

* * * *

At 3:45 p.m., I decided to enter the big house. I was sitting with Kenny in the parking lot of the Bryant Neighborhood Playground—the same place we'd parked the Winnebago last Saturday. We were in our white van with *Rainier Valley Water Damage Repair* vinyl stickers slapped on the side. Kenny and I had been watching the house on Fortieth Avenue for an hour. We'd seen no signs to indicate it was occupied. The white BMW was gone, as was the red Honda. No one had entered or left the home since we'd been there. We could see no lights on inside.

"There's no cell phone signals that look to be coming from that direction—at least nothing close," Kenny said, staring closely at an instrument he used to direction-find cell phone signals. "I'd say you're good to go."

"Toni? Anything?" I spoke into my hands-free headset. Toni was parked about two blocks south on Fortieth. Her job was to look for the white BMW or the red Honda in the event that they returned home. If she saw them, she was to sing out on the radio.

"Clear," she said.

"Doc?" Doc was parked on Sixty-Fifth, where he had a clear view of cars approaching Fortieth from the west.

"Clear," he said.

"Okay, boys and girls," I said, hopping out of the van. "I'm going in." I slid the van door closed. "Kenny—you're the last line of defense. If Doc or Toni misses anybody, you're the only one left to call me up and tell me someone's coming. Don't you fall asleep or let your mind go wandering off. You got it?"

"Ready, boss," he said. The words sounded faint and quiet in my headset. I walked across the edge of the park and across Fortieth. The house looked empty.

I continued up the pathway to the front door and stepped up on the porch. I listened hard, but could hear nothing coming from inside. I stepped up and knocked on the door. If anyone answered, I'd pretend I was with Rainier Valley Water Damage Repair and was looking for a nonexistent address. I wore a uniform shirt that had *Ryan* printed on it.

I waited, but no one answered. "Nobody's home," I said. "I'm going around."

I had reached the side of the house when my radio crackled. "Danny?" Toni said.

I froze. "Yeah." The BMW was returning?

"Make sure your cell phone ringer is off."

"Jesus Christ, Toni—you scared the shit out of me," I whispered. "Sorry."

"My cell phone ringer is off. Thank you." I walked down the side of the house and reached a gate about midway. I looked over the back and checked for dogs. A yappy dog, or worse—a big mean one—would have ended this operation before it even started.

Thankfully, there were no dogs. I opened the gate and went inside. The home was well screened from its neighbor by a hedge of red-tipped Photinias that must have been fifteen feet high. There were probably whole colonies of animals that lived inside the hedge that never saw the full light of day their whole lives. It was thick enough to be completely opaque.

There were three windows on the side of the house on the other side of the gate. I checked each of them carefully as I passed. We were pretty certain the house was not alarmed. When we'd watched the house over the weekend, they certainly didn't act like it was alarmed when they left. Usually, when someone sets an alarm before they leave, they hustle on out in order to beat the arming countdown. It's a pretty distinctive set of motions. In the case of this house, Martin and the others would leave the door open, come and go, forget something and go back, all the while with the door open and no apparent concern for an alarm countdown. As we expected, there were no alarm company signs, no window foil, no magnetic contact switches, no apparent embedded magnets. No guarantee, but a good sign. All the windows were locked, though.

I reached the rear of the house and checked out the backyard—no dogs, no people. I made the turn and stepped up onto a deck. I continued checking windows. The home looked secure until I reached a window that definitely was not original. Instead of the casement-type windows I'd seen on the other openings—the kind where you spin a little crank to open and close it—this window was a cheap aluminum-framed slider. Once locked, casements are almost impossible to jimmy open without breaking the glass. Aluminum sliders are usually a piece of cake, though. I simply pushed hard on the window frame, causing it to bow until the locking lever cleared the frame. Then, I slid the window open, just like that. Fortunately, it slid quietly.

I pushed the curtain aside and leaned inside. The window opened into a utility room with a washer and dryer. Another door on the opposite side of the room led into the house. I checked my landing area, then I sat on the window ledge and simply spun on inside.

I walked across the room and listened for a second before opening the door into the house. I stepped inside and found myself in the kitchen. I didn't move—just listened for a full minute. Satisfied for the moment, I stepped forward and scanned the area. I saw no signs of a security system, no cameras, no sensors, nothing. I whispered, "inside" into my microphone.

"Clear."

"Clear."

"Clear." That's what I wanted to hear.

I began my search. I didn't want to be in the home longer than ten minutes, tops. I moved quickly, my first priority to locate Isabel if she was there.

She wasn't. The house wasn't very big. It didn't take long—maybe five minutes—to do a quick perusal of the entire home, including the small basement, and see that no one was there. I went through a second time, a little slower. I don't know what I was expecting, but the house was much neater than I'd imagined. There were two bedrooms—a master and what appeared to be a guest bedroom. The master had a stack of porn DVDs on a nightstand, but all in factory cases—nothing homemade. The guest bedroom didn't look like anyone was staying there—the closets and the drawers were empty. Back in the living room, I noticed marijuana paraphernalia and a mirror with what appeared to be cocaine residue, but I don't guess that was very remarkable. There was a small desk with a laptop, but no notebooks or ledgers. I took photos of all of this on my cell phone as I went.

"Ten minutes, boss," Kenny's voice came over the headset.

"Roger. Just finishing up. There's nothing here."

I hadn't touched anything, so there was nothing to replace or turn off.

I retraced my steps and, one minute later, the house was locked back up, and I was standing by the gate. "I'm out," I said. "Am I clear to cross the street?"

"Go," Kenny said.

* * * *

"Nothing," I said. It was four o'clock, and we were back in the conference room at the office. Kenny had downloaded the photos from my cell phone, and we were all looking at them on the large monitor.

"They keep the place pretty clean," Doc said.

"That's what I thought, too," I said. "The place looked like a model home."

"Except for the bong and the mirror," Toni said.

"True. Except for that."

"Other than those things, you didn't see any drugs?" Richard asked.

"I didn't really look too hard," I said. "I looked inside drawers, but I was looking for something that would have connected the place to Isabel. I didn't go sifting through everything looking for drugs. I checked upstairs for an attic—none I could see. I checked for a basement, and there was a little one, but it was basically empty—just some boxes. Mostly, I checked all the rooms looking for Isabel. Like I said, nothing. I checked closets for clothes that might have belonged to Isabel. There was an empty bedroom, but the closet and the dresser inside it were empty as well. It's possible that Isabel might have stayed there, but she's certainly gone now, and there's nothing left behind."

"We have to remember that she didn't start off with much," Toni said. "Apparently, just a backpack and the clothes on her back."

"That's true," I said. "She was packing light."

It was quiet for a few seconds while we considered our options.

"I want to say that you all did really well today," I said, after a moment when nothing else was coming to mind. "I felt like the op was secure—no problems."

"Sorry for scaring you," Toni said.

I smiled. "That's okay. Better safe than sorry. Probably only cost me two years off the back side."

She smiled.

"I guess we can look at the bright side," Richard said. "Even in finding nothing, we discover something. Since the house had a guest bedroom, it's possible Isabel spent some time here when she first went missing. That could turn out to be a pretty valuable piece of information."

I nodded. "True enough. We'll get another crack at it tomorrow. Tomorrow morning at eleven, I want to go into the house over on Brooklyn. It's going to be tougher—more occupants, less certainty as to schedule. We'll have to be nimble and stay on our toes."

Chapter 17

I FIGURED THAT if Isabel was at any of the NSSB houses, odds favored the boys' house on Brooklyn Avenue. Paola said that they moved Isabel out of the girls' house, and I'd searched the big house yesterday. So my money was on the boys' house. Unless these guys kept more than the three houses we knew about, in which case, all bets were off. I was anxious to get inside and have a look around.

We hadn't had time to study the boys' house from outside other than briefly during our vehicle surveillance operation two days ago. Despite that, our entry plan was the same as yesterday at the big house—watch the house for a few hours, try to pick a time when it looked like everyone was gone, and then do a quick in-and-out. Hopefully, on the out part I'd be bringing Isabel with me. The big problem today was, unlike the big house, we didn't know who lived at this one, so watching the people who left didn't necessarily tell us much about who was still inside. And we had no sense of the rhythm of the house. With the big house, by contrast, we could tell that Martin left with Crystal every day around noon or twelve thirty, and they didn't return until later in the afternoon. Here, we didn't know anything. That increased the pucker factor several degrees.

Toni and I pulled up and parked on Sixty-Second Street, perhaps seventy-five yards from the target. We had a clear view of the house across the corner of Cowen Park—a little extension of the much larger

Ravenna Park.

At twelve thirty, the white BMW rolled up and parked behind a black Chevy Impala. Crystal and Martin got out and went directly inside. Five minutes later, a maroon Ford Expedition with chrome wheels and darkened windows also pulled up. DeMichael Hollins got out and also went inside. Shortly thereafter, a third car—a silver Acura—pulled up as well. Two men got out and joined the others inside.

"Crap," Toni said. "We're getting the exact opposite of what we wanted. Instead of everybody being gone, it looks like everybody's here. Looks like they're having a convention."

I nodded. "Maybe. We'll wait," I said. "Let's just see what they're going to do. Maybe they're just meeting here. I imagine they eat lunch, same as everyone else."

Kenny was our northern scout today. He was parked three blocks north on Brooklyn, near the intersection with Sixty-Fifth. Doc was parked a couple of blocks south, near Ravenna Boulevard. While Toni kept watch on the house, I studied the map and pondered the approaches. Just as the unknown number of occupants increased the risk at this house compared to the big house, so, too did the physical layout of the streets around the home. The big house on Fortieth basically had two ways in and out—one from the north and one from the south. It was possible to station Doc and Kenny several blocks away because anyone approaching had no choice—they had to take either the northern or the southern approach path. Stationed that far from the home, the scouts would be able to give ample warning if they spotted one of the known suspect vehicles returning.

This home, unfortunately, had multiple approach paths. We didn't have enough troops to cover them all. In order to effectively screen all possible approach paths, I'd have had to bring Kenny and Doc in so close—less than a block north and south—that any warning they provided would come only a few seconds before the car pulled up to the curb in front of the house. So, instead, I did the next best thing. I picked the most likely routes and opted to station the two scouts far enough away that a warning from them would actually come early enough to be useful. And in the event that someone returned to the home by one of the routes that this tactic left uncovered, it would be up to Toni to sing out. I'd have only a few seconds to get out, but it was the best we could do.

"They're leaving. Vehicles exiting to the south," Toni said into her radio.

I quickly set the map down and picked up the binoculars. Martin and Crystal, along with two other men, got in the BMW and drove off to the south. DeMichael Hollins followed them in his Expedition, along with the silver Acura—now with three men. Only the black Impala remained.

"Roger," Doc called back. Toni quickly gave a description of the vehicles to Doc.

"They're in sight," Doc called. "They're all turning westbound on Ravenna Boulevard."

"I-5?" Toni said.

"Could be," I said. "Let's watch for a few minutes. Let's just see if we can spot any movement from inside."

"And make sure one of these guys who just left didn't forget something," she added.

"That, too."

Two minutes later, the door opened and two men came out. The looked around and then walked to the black Impala. They got in and drove off.

"Another one," Toni said into the radio. "Black Impala, southbound."

A minute later, Doc said, "Got it. Turned west on Ravenna—just like all the others."

Five minutes later, we hadn't seen anything else.

"Think they went to lunch?" Toni asked.

I looked at my watch. One thirty. "Could be," I said. "Time's about right for these guys. How's the signal analyzer?" I asked.

Kenny had instructed Toni how to operate his Wolfhound cell phone detector. She pointed the device toward the house. "It doesn't look like there are any signals coming from the immediate area."

"Good. Kenny," I said into my radio. "How we looking?"

"Clear," he answered.

"Doc?"

"Clear," he said. "They all exited the area to the west."

"Roger that. I'm going in."

Toni looked at me. "Be careful," she said.

I smiled. "Of course." I leaned over and kissed her lightly on the cheek. "Keep an eye out in case someone sneaks back in."

She nodded.

* * * *

I knocked and rang the doorbell. I counted to thirty while straining to hear the sound of movement inside. I heard nothing. When I reached thirty, I did it again. Still no answer, so after another thirty seconds or so, I decided to get started.

"Seems like nobody's home," I whispered into my radio. "I'm going on around back." I walked to the side of the house—the side gate was open. I checked for dogs, found none, and started walking toward the rear of the home.

The home was big—much larger than the one on Fortieth. *Great*, I thought. *That much tougher to search.* There were two windows on the side of the house—both locked, along with an access door, also locked. I kept going and reached the corner of the house. I looked into the backyard. There were more windows, and a patio facing the backyard. I had two choices. I could either pick the lock on the side access door, or I could risk exposure to someone in a neighboring yard and try the windows and the door in the back. I walked back and had another look at the lock on the access door and decided to go in there. The door fit poorly enough that I was able to slip my knife between the door and the strike plate and wiggle the latch open—I didn't even have to pick the lock.

I found myself looking into what appeared to be a home office. There were two old desks—each with a computer. There were two doors to what appeared to be closets on the opposite wall. A large filing cabinet sat in a corner. There was a telephone on each desk. Was this ground zero for the NSSB business operations? Maybe.

I strained to listen before I left the room. From somewhere in the house, a television was playing. It effectively masked any other noise I might have been able to pick up. That was bad because I couldn't hear if anyone else was home. Then again, it was good, too, because it also meant that it would be that much harder for anyone who was home to hear me. I walked on in and closed the door behind me.

"I'm in," I said quietly into my headset. I slid a window back to where it was closed but not locked. If I needed to get out in a hurry, I'd be able to do it here.

"Clear," Toni said.

"Clear," from Kenny.

"Clear," Doc said. *Good.*

I had a tiny inspection mirror—one of those little round mirrors mounted on a handle. I used it to peek around the corner before actually stepping out. Satisfied it was clear, I carefully made my way out of the office and down the hall. When I reached the end, I mirrored around the corner into the family room. It was empty. I stepped out and did a quick scan. A large flat-screen TV sat at my end of the room. A dining area, separated from the kitchen by a low counter, was located at the other. In the middle was a sliding glass door to the backyard. I walked over and unlocked this door and tested it. It slid silently, so I closed it but left it unlocked as a secondary escape route. The stairway upstairs was located next to the dining room.

The plan we worked out was for me to spend no more than five minutes on the main floor followed by five minutes upstairs, and then two more in the basement. I needed to be in and out in under twelve minutes.

Satisfied that no one was in the family room, I searched the remainder of the main floor. In addition to the family room/dining room, kitchen, and office, which I'd already seen, there was a living room and a guest bedroom that, judging from the mess inside, was clearly being used. In fact, in stark contrast to the squared-away appearance of the big house on Fortieth, this place was a pit. It looked like a frat house. The place reeked of marijuana—an ashtray held the remains of half a dozen joints, and a glass bong sitting nearby was still full of smoke. Must have been an appetizer before lunch. Beer bottles and half-full ashtrays littered the tables.

CDs and DVDs were strewn everywhere. Magazines were tossed here and there. Judging by the covers, it appeared as though the most popular subject was sports, followed closely by pornography. I quietly made my way around the main floor, taking a number of pictures on my cell phone as I went.

When I was finished with the main floor, I went upstairs. I didn't think anyone was home, but still, I tried to step on the sides of the treads closest to the walls in an effort to minimize squeaking. There were six bedrooms upstairs, three on either side of a long hallway. My intent was to first, do a quick blitz and make sure I was the only one up here. After that, I would work my way down the hall and inspect each room more carefully as I went. It was unlikely that I'd see any of Isabel's personal property here, but I did hope to locate some ID-type things—mailing addresses, magazine labels, package labels, that sort of thing. In fact, I saw quite a bit and photographed all of it. A bedroom at the far end of the hall had been turned into a photography studio. It had a camera mounted on a tripod with a couple of photographic lights, complete with umbrellas. I took more pictures with my phone. I had just finished and stepped back into the hallway when suddenly, my radio crackled to life.

"Danny—the black Impala just pulled up!" Toni said urgently. "You gotta get out now!"

Shit! They must have used one of the uncovered side roads. I immediately started back down the hallway to the stairs. The hallway was long—this was going to take a few seconds. I hurried, but I didn't run, fearing that even if someone was standing on the porch outside, they might be able to hear someone my size running down the upstairs hallway.

I reached the stairs and started down.

"They're at the porch," Toni said. "Get out."

"I'm moving," I whispered back.

Five seconds later, I reached the bottom of the stairs—just as the front door started to open. My total warning had been maybe twenty seconds.

I considered my options and decided to escape through the family room back door. I took a step toward the door when it suddenly dawned on me that this door was directly in the line of sight of anyone coming through the front door. I'd be seen immediately. Worse, the office where I'd entered was on the opposite side of the room—I'd again be in their line of sight. I was cut off from both of my escape routes. Dumb!

I was fast approaching a dangerous situation—out of answers and out of ideas. This was bad. I looked around quickly and noticed a door at the back of the kitchen—apparently a pantry. Any port in a storm. I headed for the pantry door, hoping that behind it wasn't just a stack of shelves, but instead would be a space at least deep enough that I could step inside. Maybe I could figure out a better answer there. Failing that, things were about to get physical.

* * * *

I lucked out. The pantry was maybe five feet square—not huge, but big enough for me. I stepped inside and pulled the door most of the way shut behind me, leaving just a little crack to look through. I was just in time because I hadn't even taken a breath when I caught a quick glimpse of two men as they walked past my narrow field of view into the family room. I heard the sound of a set of keys landing on the kitchen counter.

"Why'd he send us back, anyway?" one of the men said. "Don't need to be here no twenty-four hours a day. This is bullshit, yo."

"Yeah, you think so? Why didn't you just tell him, then?"

"Fuck that," the first man said.

"That's right. That's what I thought you was gonna say."

There was silence for a few seconds, and then the first man said, "I can see his face when I tell him that."

Both men laughed, and then I heard the unmistakable sound of a lighter flicking. Back to the bong, it appeared.

"'Sides," the second man said, trying to talk and hold in the smoke from a bong hit. He blew out the smoke and then continued, "he said they'd bring us something."

"Probably some cold, soggy shit," the first man said with disgust. "Let me have that."

While the two of them proceeded to get stoned, I tried to take stock of my situation. The pantry had a very pungent odor that I recognized at once. I pulled out my Surefire pocket light and shielded it with my hand so that the light couldn't be seen through the crack in the door. I pressed the button with my thumb and scanned the tight pantry. As I'd suspected. The shelves didn't contain the items found in a normal kitchen pantry. There were probably a half-dozen cases of Heineken beer in familiar green bottles and another half-dozen cases of Pepsi. But the real intriguing item—the one I smelled—was the marijuana. There were ten kilo bricks—more than twenty pounds—probably worth close to $40,000. The bricks were wrapped in plastic, yet the pot inside was so aromatic that the smell emanated through anyway. I wanted to take a picture, but, unfortunately, there was no way my cell phone would take a decent photo in the darkness. Even though there was a light switch, I dared not turn it on.

It suddenly dawned on me that I hadn't noticed any weed on the table in the family room. If these two clowns ran out, they'd probably have to come to the pantry and get some more. What a surprise they'd get when they opened the door and saw me standing there, smiling at 'em. I might not even have to pull my .45—if they were stoned, the shock alone would probably do them in.

But comical as this dilemma was, it was bound to get serious fast if other people started returning to the house. Then I'd really be up shit creek. I needed to get moving.

I reached for my cell phone. Time to call in the cavalry.

Chapter 18

I WAITED. I could almost hear an imaginary clock ticking while the two men in the family room continued to banter as they passed the bong back and forth between them.

"I need a Heinie. You want one?"

"Yeah."

I couldn't see the man approach, but I heard him when his footsteps left the carpeted family room and stepped onto the tiled area in the kitchen. He walked over to the refrigerator.

"Yo!" he called out. "Last two."

"Go 'head and get another six-pack out the pantry and throw it in," the man in the family room called back. Uh-oh. That quick, I was out of time.

I reached down and silently drew my sidearm. When kitchen-man opened the door in about two seconds, the element of surprise would be all mine—at least for a few moments. I needed to capitalize on it. I made a quick plan. I would scream and burst out into the kitchen the moment the door opened. I'd shove kitchen-man back toward the family room with my left hand while covering both him and family room–man at the same time with my gun hand. Hopefully, I'd have them both covered before either of them had a chance to draw a weapon.

I heard the *clinks* as kitchen-man set the bottles on the counter. My weapon was raised—I was ready to go. But the door didn't open. Instead, I heard two *phfft* sounds as he removed the tops.

"You want a glass?" he said.

"No."

Now he turned to the pantry. I heard a footstep as he approached and then another when, suddenly, the doorbell rang.

"Check it out," family room–man said. "I got your back."

Kitchen-man's footsteps receded as he moved to answer the door. Through the crack, I saw family room–man move into the kitchen, where he had a clear view of the front door. His right hand held a large-caliber revolver. "Who's there?" he whispered loudly.

"Damn," kitchen-man said. "It's some fine-looking bitch, that's for damn sure."

"Lemme see," family room–man said. He holstered his weapon and left my field of view as he made his way to the front door.

My opening. I swung the pantry door open and silently crept to the end of the kitchen. I pulled out my mirror and looked around the corner. I could see one man looking out the window from one side of the door and the other man looking from the other side. The doorbell rang again.

"I'll get it," family room–man said.

I watched from behind as he opened the door.

Toni stood there, smiling one of her mega-watt dazzling smile. "Hi, there!" She'd tied her blouse up, exposing her midriff. She'd also unbuttoned the top couple of buttons, partly exposing jaw-dropping cleavage framed by the edges of a black lace bra. The blouse had short sleeves, and her full-sleeve tattoo on her left arm was on full display.

The sudden appearance of Toni, combined with his impaired mental facilities, was too much for family room–man. He was completely incapable of getting a word out. In all honesty, it wasn't really fair. I don't think very many men would have been composed enough to respond quickly when faced with a full-on frontal assault by Toni—forget the effects of the weed. I know I'd have been tongue-tied—and I don't get stoned.

Seeing his partner's slack-jawed expression, kitchen-man grabbed the door and opened it wider, so he too could see.

"Whoa," he said, when he saw Toni standing before him.

"Hi!" Toni said, again cheerfully when she saw him. "How are you guys? I'm out today with the Petition to Normalize Marijuana laws in the state of Washington. I wonder if you two might have time for a couple of questions."

I almost burst out laughing. From my vantage point, I couldn't tell if the men were looking at Toni's eyes or her chest, but it didn't matter. They were goners. If Toni had asked them for their weapons, their money—anything—they'd have probably turned it over.

I stepped out from behind the kitchen wall. Toni, looking over the shoulders of the two men, saw me. For the barest moment, her eyes showed surprise, maybe even alarm.

I blew her a silent kiss and stepped across the hallway to the other side of the room.

* * * *

Five minutes later, we drove away. "Oh my God, you're completely insane," Toni said, smiling and shaking her head slowly. "Blowing kisses to me while those two guys were standing right there."

I smiled. "I waited to leave until I heard them close the door—until I knew you were out of there. And if you're talking about them maybe seeing me? Forget it. No friggin' way they were going to turn around. They had a much better view facing your direction, believe me. Besides, how was I supposed to know those idiots were going to pop back home so fast in the first place? And by a side street we didn't have covered? I ended up spending fifteen minutes in a dark closet that reeked of marijuana listening to those clowns get stoned." I paused for a second. "Good thinking on the diversion, by the way."

She smiled. "Sorry it took so long. I had to do a little prep work with the wardrobe."

"No shit," I chuckled. "That dude opened the door and saw you standing there with your shirt the way it was. He didn't know what to think. Poor bastard went rigid—I thought he was gonna have a seizure. You were fuckin' hot!"

"*I* know what he was thinking," she said, nodding her head and smiling.

"Well, who could blame him? Damn. Him and his buddy, too." I paused. "Anyway, thanks. Thanks for bailing me out."

She smiled. "What are friends for, right?" She leaned over and kissed me. "You're pretty hot, yourself, you know."

I smiled. "It's the uniform, isn't it?"

She sat back upright and looked at me. "Well, now that you mention it, I think it is."

I smiled. I was a lucky man, no doubt about it.

* * * *

We were on our way back to the office. I'd already radioed Doc and Kenny to let them know what had happened. They were headed back to the office as well. Toni selected a pop station on her radio dial, and Katy Perry sang "Wide Awake." Toni tapped her fingers on the steering wheel to the beat of the song. "So what'd you find while you were inside wandering around pretending to be Sherlock Holmes, anyways?" she asked.

"No sign of Isabel, I can say that," I said. Toni drove under the freeway on Fiftieth and then turned south onto the on-ramp. "The house is big. It looked kind of like a frat house—even more so because of the pot and the porn. Other than that, nothing very remarkable." I paused. "Well," I said, "there was one interesting thing. There were like six bedrooms upstairs and one down. One of the upstairs rooms was set up with lights and a camera on a tripod. Like a permanent porn studio."

"Perverts," she said.

"I started taking pictures of everything, but I wasn't all the way through when they got home. I finished the main floor, and then I checked the upstairs for occupants—there weren't any."

Toni merged onto the freeway. "Was there a basement? Were you able to check that out?"

"I don't think there is one because I didn't see a basement door when I checked the main floor." We drove south on I-5 without speaking for several minutes. The freeway arced gracefully more than one hundred feet in the air as it crossed over Lake Union.

"Hey," Toni said suddenly. "You remembered that your dad's taking us to Daniel's Broiler on Friday for your birthday, right?"

I nodded. "Yep. I remember." Friday, June 15—the big three-oh. Danny Logan turns thirty. Can't believe I made it. When I was a boy, I always thought that if I ever turned thirty, I'd be old as dirt. Back then, thirty was a l-o-n-n-g way off. Then, I graduated from high school, joined the army, and almost immediately I was in the war. Thirty was a lot closer, but I tried not to think about getting old then. I suppose I didn't want to jinx myself. Now that I was safe and sound and two days away from the milestone, I actually felt pretty good—not old at all. I was healthy—probably the best shape of my life, actually. My parents were healthy. Business was good—a little slow at the moment, but good. I had good friends. And best of all, I was with a great woman—someone so far beyond what I'd ever imagined that I could hardly believe it. I smiled as we drove, the tires thumping over the expansion joints on the freeway. All these years, I'd been dreading this birthday, and now it looked like I'd been worrying for nothing. My thirties might not be so bad after all.

* * * *

Richard joined Toni and me in my office when we got back. Doc was in Kenny's office, the two of them huddled over the computer screen. "So," Richard said, "Doc says you made it out by the hair of your chinny-chin-chin." His blue eyes seemed to twinkle when he smiled.

I nodded. "I did. Thanks to Toni, here." I leaned back in my chair. "There I was," I said, dramatically, "trapped by fate in the drug-laden storage cave of some of the world's most dangerous criminals—vicious, ruthless guys. Time was running short; options—well, let's just say there weren't any and leave it at that. The bad guys sensed my presence. They were big. They were bad. They were mean. And, above all, they were well armed. They were on the hunt, and they were out for blood."

Toni shook her head. "Oh my God," she said. "You are so full of shit. They were two idiots so stoned they could barely stand up."

"Ignore that," I said to Richard. "Just as my clever hiding place was about to be compromised, just at that darkest of moments, what do I hear?"

"Ding-dong?" Toni said.

"Exactly. Ding-friggin-dong. Salvation. Salvation in the form of a stunning, dark-haired maiden who shows up and saves the day."

"Oh, puh-leeze," she said. "He sent me a text message that said 'HELP!' in all caps with an exclamation point."

Richard laughed. "From the closet he did that?"

Toni nodded.

"To be fair, that's not all the message said."

"Oh, that's true," she said. "It said 'HELP! Need diversion.'"

"See? That's right," I said. "'Need diversion.' I was thinking tactically. I didn't want to have to go to guns with these stoners. Not when a simple little distraction was all that was needed."

"So, naturally, you called Toni."

"Duh," I said. "Do you know a better distraction?" I smiled at Toni. She stuck her tongue out at me.

"Point made," he said.

"Damn straight," I said. "Quick thinking in the line of fire, if you ask me."

I heard the bell ring on the office front door. A minute later, Kenny walked into my office. "Kelli's here to see you," he said to Toni.

"Okay," she said. "Would you do me a favor and bring her on back to the conference room? Please? We'll be right out." Kenny left.

"So what happens now?" Richard said after Kenny went to get Kelli.

"We still don't know where Isabel is," I said. "The police won't step in now and raid the NSSBs to find her."

"Not with the evidence you have so far," Richard said. "They're worried about this pesky little document—it's called—it's called—oh yeah! It's called the constitution. Among other things, it deals with the concept of unreasonable search and seizure—that sort of thing."

"Yeah, well, anyway, they're not doing anything. I get the impression that we'd practically need to get a photo of Isabel holding a current newspaper or something like that in order for the police to go in and rescue her. That's if we could even locate her."

"Which leaves us precisely where?" Richard said.

"Compared to ten days ago?" I asked. "A little smarter. Maybe with a little more evidence than we had when we took this case. But, I'm afraid, probably no closer to finding Isabel."

"Any idea how much longer you're going to keep looking?"

"That's a real good question," I said. "I talked with Ferguson and Sons this morning. They're ready for us to get started."

"So?"

I squirmed in my chair. "I hate to say it, but we need to start pulling in some money. We're supposed to start the Ferguson job next Monday. I think we're pretty quickly getting to the point where we're going to have to drop this case and hope that the police can find Isabel. I can't afford to pay everyone if I'm not bringing in any revenue."

He nodded. "You don't need to explain it to me," he said. "I sat in your chair for twenty-five years. I know all about payroll and overhead."

"It sucks, too," I said. "We're close—I can feel it. But we just don't have quite enough information yet. We lack the key to get the police all fired up."

"The smoking gun," Toni said.

Richard nodded again. "It can be hard to come by," he said.

"Too bad we can't get someone from the inside to talk to us," Toni said. "Shed a little light. We probably learned more from talking to Paola than from anything else."

"For sure," I said. "But at least as of earlier in the week, she wasn't willing to say more than what she's already told us."

"I know," Toni said. "Maybe we should ask Nancy if there's been any improvement."

"Wait a second! I got it!" I said. "You can go undercover for us. You saw today—those guys practically swooned over you. You can get us all the information we need."

Toni looked at me, saw that I was joking, and then smiled. Her hands were folded in front of her. She slowly extended her middle finger.

I smiled, but I couldn't resist yanking her chain a bit more. "C'mon," I said. "Just to gather information. I wouldn't want you actually going on any dates or anything like that. I'm not a pervert, after all."

"I don't know about that," Toni said. "Besides—I'm a little too old for these guys, anyway."

I shook my head. "I don't think so," I said. "The two clowns today sure didn't think so."

She smiled. "That's sweet. But it's bullshit. I'd stand right out."

"Well, that's for damn sure," I said. "Just kidding, anyway. Besides, I'm the old one here—did you forget?"

She smiled. "That's true. You're almost over the hill."

"I know," I said. "But anyway, I guess I'll have to think about our next actions some more tonight, and we'll pick it back up at our staff meeting in the morning."

"Sounds like a plan," Richard said. "I'm going to take off early tonight. Maria and I have a dinner date." Richard and Maria have been married nearly fifty years. In this way—as in many others—he is my hero. He started to leave, and we followed him out. We entered the conference room to talk to Kelli, but it was empty.

"Hey, Kenny!" I called out. "Where's Kelli?"

"She's in the conference room," he yelled back.

"I don't see her," I said to Toni.

"Me neither," she said.

Kenny walked into the room. "She's right—" He stopped when he saw the empty room. "Well, she was right here, only a few minutes ago. I brought her back here, just like you said."

"Maybe she got tired of waiting," I said.

"What? After three minutes?" Toni asked.

"More like five," Kenny said.

"Okay, five then," Toni said.

"She left." We turned and saw Doc walking up the hallway. "She walked out a minute ago," he said to Toni. "She asked me to tell you she'd call you later."

I shrugged. "There you go," I said. "At least one mystery is solved."

Chapter 19

THURSDAY MORNING MEANS intervals—full-speed sprints up the side of a hill followed by slow jogs back down for recovery. In theory, the recovery time gives your heart rate a little time to fall back. The thing is, you repeat the intervals over and over and each time, your heart rate recovers a little less. By the last one, you're dragging. Intervals are supposed to be good for you—to strengthen and increase your aerobic capacity by pushing the envelope. All I can say is that if you do them right—you're going to feel it. This morning, I definitely felt it. I made it into the office at 7:45 a.m. for our staff meeting, and my quads were still throbbing.

I put my stuff down in my office, checked voicemails and e-mails, and then walked into the conference room at eight o'clock on the dot. Everyone was already there, waiting. Promptness is a virtue that we like to emphasize.

"Good morning, folks," I said.

Everyone looked wide-awake and eager to go. Probably none of them ran eight miles this morning. "Let's get right into the main topic. I've decided to suspend the company's active search for Isabel Delgado."

Everyone looked at me with puzzled expressions. I hadn't explained this decision to anyone—even Toni. Last night, as usual, she had stayed at her apartment, and we hadn't had a chance to talk about it.

"It's unfortunate, but the reality is, we have a paying job that can start on Monday at Ferguson and Sons. They're expecting us. The job is too big to let go and, frankly, too important for our firm. As much as I hate to pull back from any job—especially in a case like Isabel's, we don't have any choice. So—starting Monday, the focus around here will be with Ferguson."

"Kelli's going to be upset," Toni said. "I'll have to call her and tell her."

"I understand," I said. "Tell her this: say, 'Danny's had to reassign everyone to a job that pays in order for us to continue to exist as a company. But he's decided that he's not going to take a paycheck for a while, and he himself is going to continue to hunt for Isabel.'"

Toni looked at me. "What—you mean in your free time?"

I shook my head. "No. I mean full-time. I talked to the people at Ferguson, and I told them that you would be managing their job, that I was still tied up with the last job—Isabel. They were cool with that."

"Wait a minute—," she started to say.

"What? You don't think you're ready?" I asked.

"It's not that, it's—," she said.

"You don't want to be in charge of Kenny and Doc?"

"Shut up," she said. "You know it's not—."

"Oh—you need me to hold your hand?"

She gave me a look. "Okay. Fuck you. I'll do it."

I smiled. "I knew you'd see it my way."

She flipped me the bird from across the table.

"Still leaves us today, though, right?" Doc said.

"And the weekend?" Kenny added.

I smiled and nodded. "That's right. And if you guys are willing to put in the hours, there's still a fair amount of work we can do."

Toni's phone chimed—indicating she'd just received a text message. She pulled it out of her purse and read the message. A serious look formed on her face. She stood up. "I need to step outside and make a call," she said. "I'll be right back."

I watched her walk out. I wondered what that was all about.

"Anyway," I continued, "there are still things we can do today and over the weekend if need be. First off—Kenny, I took a shitload of pictures in the boys' house. They're all on my cell phone." I slid it over to him. "I'd like you to pull them off and have a look. Enhance them if they need it. Take another look at the pics from the first house, too. Then, when you're ready, let's all sit back down here and go through them."

"Got it," he said.

"I didn't see anything that looked like it might have belonged to Isabel, but who knows? I was moving fast, and it's very possible I could have missed something."

He nodded.

"Doc—where are you with the reports on the property titles and the DMV info for Nancy?" I asked.

"They're done. I finished yesterday. I've got full ownership reports on everything. Names and addresses."

"Good. Hopefully, they'll be useful when it comes time to convince Nancy that they need to raid each of the three houses and do a full search for Isabel."

Richard said, "So what we really need is a circle that links the houses, the vehicles, and the bad guys together on the one hand, and then, another connection that links Isabel to the same circle. That might give Nancy the ammunition she needs to be able to get her warrants."

"She won't move without warrants?" Doc said.

"Not unless she knows for certain that someone is in immediate danger," Richard said. "That, she couldn't ignore. Short of that, she'll rely on a warrant. Her bosses would insist on it."

Doc nodded. "We don't have much," he said. "What about more surveillance?"

I thought about this for a few seconds. "It might come to that, but for now, let's hold off. Let's have another hard look at what we already have first. Maybe there's an angle we've missed."

Toni walked back into the room. She looked at me, and I could tell at once that something was wrong.

"What is it?" I asked. "What's the matter?"

"Kelli's gone," she said.

"Gone? What do you mean?"

"That was my mom. Kelli was gone this morning when she got up. Mom said she left a note. It said 'I'll be gone for a couple of days—I'm going to look for Isabel.'"

PART 3

Chapter 20

IT WAS QUIET for a few seconds as the words sunk in.

"Son of a bitch!" I said, looking down at the table and shaking my head slowly. I looked up at Toni. "It's my fault. She was in here yesterday, right?"

Toni nodded.

"She sat right here in the conference room yesterday afternoon and overheard me moaning and groaning in my office about having to pull off this case because of money. That's why she was gone when we came out."

"Or perhaps it was the discussion about Toni going undercover to aid in the hunt for Isabel," Richard said. "She may have decided that that was a good idea."

"Damn!" I swore again.

I looked back at Toni.

"I'm sorry, Toni." She had a look on her face I'd never seen before—a mixture of fear and anger. I could only hope that the anger wasn't directed at me. Yet, as I watched her, her expression quickly gave way to a look of steely resolve.

She shook her head. "It's not your fault," she said after a few seconds. "It's nobody's fault." She paused and then added, "Well, maybe it's Kelli's fault. This is a world-class dumbass thing for her to do. She didn't like what she overheard, so she got pissed and decided to go do it herself."

She paused and then added, "She's a little hothead. Always has been."

"Well, I don't know about that, but I do know that now we're going to have to go find her before *she* gets herself in any trouble," I said.

Toni nodded.

I looked at her. "We will find her. You know that, right?"

Toni thought for a second, then she nodded. "I know."

"It's what we do, right?"

She nodded again. "Right."

"Good." I thought for a second and then said, "How's your mom?"

Toni pursed her lips, then looked up at the ceiling. She said nothing. I could tell she was trying hard to keep her emotions in check. She can be hard as a diamond in tough situations, but she's always had a soft spot for her mom—and for her little sister. When her father died sixteen years ago, Toni appointed herself as the family's designated protector. She takes her job seriously. She fought hard and brought her emotions under control, and then she looked back at me. "Mom sounded alright. Worried, but okay."

"She's home, right?"

Toni nodded.

"Why don't we drive up and talk to her as soon as we're through here?"

Toni nodded again. "Good."

I smiled at her. "We'll find Kelli," I said, trying hard to be reassuring.

She smiled back. "I know."

I nodded, and then I turned to the others. "Alright guys, seems as though Kelli's just changed our agenda for us."

"Quite a trump card," Richard said.

"You got that right," I said, leaning back in my chair. "So, let's think. Kelli's searching for Isabel. We're searching for Isabel. And now, we're searching for Kelli."

"What's Kelli's likely strategy?" Richard asked. "If we can figure out how she intends to go about looking for Isabel, maybe we can put ourselves on her path and find her that way."

"It would be better to find her before she gets there," I said.

"I agree," Richard said. "The two of them together—that might complicate things."

"Sounds like she might try going undercover," Doc said. "If that's what she heard you guys talking about."

Confident as I was that we could find her, the notion of Kelli going undercover was still pretty frightening. That meant that she could soon be rubbing shoulders with some pretty nasty folks—people like Donnie Martin and Crystal Wallace. I didn't know Kelli that well, but she *is* Toni's sister—she's bound to be pretty tough. She'd certainly need to be if she was going to play the undercover game with these people.

"That's exactly what she'll try and do," Toni said suddenly.

I looked at her. "How? How will she go about it? How will she go under? She doesn't have any of our information—names, addresses, cars—that kind of stuff."

Toni shrugged. "She doesn't need it," she said. "That's not the way she'd go about it, anyway. She doesn't have a clue about investigative work."

"Then what?"

"She's just going to follow Isabel's tracks."

I thought for a second. "You mean the mall?"

Toni nodded. "Exactly. She's going fishing, and she's making herself the bait."

* * * *

The Jeep's tires thumped as we crossed the expansion joints on the I-5 bridge over Lake Union. Toni and I were headed northbound, on our way up to Lynnwood to talk to her mom. From there, we were going to start our search for Kelli at the Alderwood Mall.

"Do you think we should just go straight to the mall?" Toni asked.

I changed lanes to avoid a slow-moving delivery truck. "Your choice,"

I said. "But remember, we don't even have a decent picture of Kelli with us. That picture of her with Isabel is probably not good enough. We wouldn't have anything to show around."

"That's right," Toni said, nodding slowly. "We need to go to mom's first. I can use her PC to print off a couple of photos to take with us."

"Remember to send one to Kenny, too," I said.

She nodded. "Right."

Before we left, I thought about a strategy and decided that it would probably be best to just keep working on the Isabel-hunt plans we'd mapped out before Kelli went missing. In other words, I had Kenny download the photos of the inside of the boys' house off my phone and put them with the photos of the big house. While we were gone, he'd enhance and study them, looking for any kind of clues that might show up.

I called Nancy as we drove and let her know what was happening.

"The Lynnwood PD might be willing to take a missing person report—but then again, maybe not," Nancy said. "Kelli's an adult. She's free to come and go as she chooses, you know."

"Understood."

"Without any indication that she's in imminent danger—especially since she left a note saying she was leaving of her own free will—the police might not even take a report at all."

"I know," I said.

"One thing I can do," she added, "I know a couple of detectives up there. If you'd like, I can put in a call—ask them to take special care of this."

"That would be fantastic," I said. "We'd definitely appreciate it."

"I'd really like to be able to do something more about Kelli, but you know I can't, right?"

"I know," I said. "I didn't expect anything. Just putting in a good word for us would be fantastic. Mostly, though, I just wanted to keep you posted on the status of our investigation. This definitely adds a new dimension."

"It sure does," Nancy said. "Do you have a picture?"

"We're on our way to get one now."

"Good. Send me a copy when you get it. We can at least keep our eyes open."

"Thanks, Nancy."

I hung up and drove for a few minutes, going over the possibilities. Then I turned to Toni. She was staring straight ahead, completely lost in thought.

"Let me ask you a question," I said.

She turned to me. "Go ahead."

"You're thinking Kelli's going to try to get herself picked up by Crystal and Donnie Martin, right?"

"Yep."

"I don't know Kelli all that well. How capable is she? How tough is she? Is she like a momma's girl?"

She gave a quick laugh. "The opposite," Toni said. "She has a nasty temper. She's been in two or three fights at school—fistfights. She actually got suspended from school twice last year. The second time, Mom had to go talk the principal into letting her go back to school."

I smiled. "Guess it runs in the family," I said quietly.

"What's that?" she said.

"No offense, but she sounds a little like you."

"I figured you'd say that," she said. She pushed her hair back off her face—a somewhat futile effort considering the wind whipping around inside the drafty Jeep. "But I suppose that's right. We're a lot alike."

"She sounds like she can take care of herself, though," I said. "That's good."

"Put it to you this way. There were several times when she was growing up that we—either me or Mom or sometimes both—had to go bail Kelli out of trouble. But never because anyone was picking on her, or taking advantage of her, or anything like that. I think everyone knew better than to do that."

I smiled. "Like I said—sounds like someone else I know." I reached over and took her hand.

* * * *

Julia Blair is a very striking woman, make no mistake about it—classically beautiful in a foreign-movie-star kind of way. It's impossible to miss the connection between her and Toni. Both are on the tall side; both have thick, dark hair; both are trim with amazing figures. Julia is forty-eight years old—manages a restaurant not far from the house. She has quite a story. She'd been a stay-at-home mom until her husband—Toni and Kelli's father—died in an automobile accident in 1996. Julia hadn't worked since Toni'd been born eleven years prior to that, but with the death of her husband, she had no choice. She got a job as a waitress in a nearby restaurant. The owners were impressed by her work ethic and the way she took care of her two girls at the same time. They'd been tolerant and flexible when it came to Julia's schedule. Now, twelve years later, Julia's in the process of buying out those same owners (who have retired and moved to Florida, leaving Julia as general manager of the place). The Blair women—Julia, Toni, and Kelli—none of them sit back and watch life go by. They jump right in.

"I'm confident that we'll find her," I said to Julia as we sat in her living room. Toni was in the study (used to be her old bedroom before she got her own apartment) printing off a couple of photos. "It's what we do, and we're good at it."

Julia had a very concerned look in her eyes. She nodded. "Tell me truthfully," she said, "are the people she's trying to locate—are they dangerous people?"

I looked at her for a moment, and then I nodded. "They are," I said. "I won't lie to you. That's the bad news. The good news, though, is that if Kelli's doing what we think she is, then she's got some time before she's in any real danger—maybe a week or two. We'll find her long before that."

She nodded. "Do you think I should I call the police?"

"Yes—but Toni and I have a friend in the Seattle Police Department who knows some people up here. She's going to put in a good word for us. We should have better instructions—who to call, that sort of thing—by later this afternoon."

She nodded. "Good. Thank you, Danny."

I smiled. "I'm just sorry you're having to go through this," I said. "I know how hard it is to sit back and worry about someone when you don't have any decent information about what's going on." Actually, I was very familiar with the feeling—just having gone through a similar situation when Toni'd been abducted three months ago. Basically, it sucked. "But remember, Kelli's a bright, resourceful girl. And Toni tells me she's tough."

Julia smiled. "That she is."

"She'll be okay," I said, just as Toni walked into the living room. "Got 'em?" I asked.

She showed me three photos that she'd printed. "Perfect," I said. "Just what we need. Did you remember to send one to Kenny?"

She gave me the "raised eyebrow" look.

"Sorry," I said, holding up my hand. "Just thought I'd double-check."

"I sent them to him and to Nancy and to me and you, too. We're good," she said. She turned to Julia. "Mom, we're going to run on up to the mall and start looking. We'll call you when we hear from the police about the missing person report. If we can give them the report, we will. But we'll let you know one way or another."

Julia nodded. Toni walked over to her, and they hugged. While they were embracing, Julia looked over Toni's shoulder and said, "Find her, Danny."

I reached for her hand and gave it a squeeze. "Don't worry," I said as I nodded. "We will."

Chapter 21

IT HAD BEEN sunny earlier in the morning, but now the clouds were rolling in. Soon it would begin to rain. I have friends in other states that were in the middle of heat waves, but here it was in the mid-sixties. I don't envy them.

I was driving north on Thirty-Sixth Avenue toward the Alderwood Mall. The mall is almost exactly one mile from Julia's house, so it wouldn't take long.

"Your mom going to be okay?" I asked.

Toni nodded. "I think so. She's pretty tough."

"She's an impressive lady," I said. "It's pretty easy to see where you and Kelli get your gumption."

She smiled. "Yeah," she said. "I suppose."

A few seconds later, I said, "Why do you suppose Kelli didn't drive?"

Toni shrugged. "Because she hoped to get picked up," she answered. "She didn't want her truck sitting vulnerable-like in the mall's parking lot for a couple of days while she was gone." She paused. "She loves her truck. She'd rather walk a mile than have it broken into."

A few minutes later, I pulled into the mall's main entrance off 184th Street.

The entrance was about a hundred yards long, then it forked left and right. "Which way?" I asked. "Got any ideas?"

Toni leaned forward and looked left, then right. "Let's just drive around the whole place first."

I turned left to circle the mall clockwise. "Where do kids hang out at malls?" I asked.

She shrugged. "I don't know," she said, as she scanned the stores. "It's been a while for me. Maybe the food court?"

That made sense. "Where's the food court at this place?" I asked.

"I don't know that either. We'll probably need to park and find a directory. But let's keep going around once before we stop."

The mall is good-sized for northwest Washington, which probably means it's average size for most other places. The perimeter road is square-shaped, maybe one-quarter mile in each direction. We entered at the top of the square—due north.

At the bottom of the square, we passed a movie theater and a couple of stand-alone restaurants. The sign read "Terraces."

"This might be it," I said. "There sure are a lot of kids around here. But I don't see any kind of food court."

"It's summertime. There's going to be lots of kids at the movie theater. But if we're looking for the food court, it's not going to be outside," Toni said. "It'll be inside, out of the weather. Let's just finish the circle, and then we'll go inside at the main entrance and look for a directory."

"What makes you think the movie theater isn't where Kelli would have gone?"

"Think about it," she said. "Kelli's following Isabel, right?" Before I could answer, she continued. "Isabel was looking for something—or someone. That's why she came here. Isabel got picked up on or just right after her birthday—May seventh. School was still in session then. So—"

"So there wouldn't have been any kids at the movie theater except for at night."

"Right," she said. "And even then, it would have been pretty light on a weekday night."

"And May seventh was—"

"A Monday. A school day and a school night. I think that it would have been relatively quiet at the theater then, and relatively busier inside at the food court."

I thought about this for a few seconds. "Well, I wouldn't want to stake my life on that theory, but it's better than anything I've got."

"So let's keep going," she said. "If it's not busy inside, we'll come back out here."

I finished driving the perimeter and found a parking space no more than a couple hundred yards away from the main entrance. We hiked on inside a few seconds before the rain started falling. Just inside was a large directory. I scanned it and located the food court.

"I was right," I said. "It's in the back in the place called the Terraces."

"Inside," Toni said.

"Leave the Jeep and walk there?" I asked.

"Yeah." We had started walking toward the mall's main entrance when Toni said, "Wait a second." I turned to her, but she was already walking toward a group of girls. I followed.

"Hi," she said. "Can I ask you guys a question?"

They nodded.

"We're new to the area, and we're supposed to meet my little sister here. But she didn't say where. Do you girls have any idea where kids— about your age—would hang out?"

"Probably the food court," one of the girls said. "There's lots of kids there."

Toni smiled. "Thanks."

She turned to me. "Sounds like we're on the right track," she said.

* * * *

We walked down the main corridor, hung a right at Macy's, and then turned left to reach the Terraces Food Court. It was a very large, open area, with ceilings probably thirty feet tall. A long double row of skylights allowed natural daylight to flood the huge area. It was about as close to being an outdoor area as you could get and still make it work in the rainy Northwest. Two-dozen food vendors occupied spaces that ringed the perimeter of the court. There must have been a couple hundred tables in the center.

Impressive as that was, though, the most impressive thing by far were the number of people. It was twelve thirty—lunchtime. It was as if every middle school and high school in the northern King County area had decided to hold class in the food court, and school had just let out for lunch. It was a huge party. There were hundreds of kids: kids talking, kids laughing, kids eating, kids standing around. There were at least a half-dozen security guards, stationed at strategic points around the area. They seemed to simply watch the action around them. Perhaps they were under orders to leave the kids alone as long as the kids behaved themselves—which they all seemed to be doing. It was a happy, peaceful, end-of-the-school-year party. And maybe, somewhere, Kelli was in there.

"Wow," I said.

Toni nodded. "We'd probably best split up," she said.

"Are we just looking? Or are we talking?" I asked.

"I think both now," she said. "Use Kelli's photo if you want, but let's not show any photos of Crystal yet. Let's do them one at a time."

I pulled out my phone and organized my pictures. I had several photos now of people connected to this case, starting, of course, with the picture of Isabel that we'd taken from her bedroom. Now, I also had a good close-up of Kelli that Toni'd e-mailed me a few minutes earlier. I also had a decent close-up of Crystal and another one of Donnie Martin and DeMichael Hollins—all taken during our stakeout at the big house.

"Okay. Let's do it," I said. "I'll take this side here on the east. Plan on meeting back here in half an hour?"

"Good."

I headed for the first security guard I saw. He was a tall guy, leaning against a post and whistling.

"Hi, there," I said. I introduced myself and showed the guy my license. "My partner and I are looking for a missing person—this girl here." I held up my phone and showed him Kelli's picture. "In case you notice us and wonder what the hell we're doing, we're going to be showing this picture around and asking some of the kids here if they've seen this girl."

He nodded. "That's cool," he said. "Let me have a closer look at the picture." I handed the phone to him, and he studied the photo for a minute. Then he shook his head. "Sorry, I don't recognize her." He handed it back.

"How about this one," I said. I scrolled to the picture of Crystal. I figured Toni hadn't been talking about the security guard when she said not to show any pictures of Crystal yet.

He smiled. "I've seen her," he said almost immediately. "She's pretty hard to forget, isn't she? Comes in here and shops from time to time."

I had a hunch. "How about this one?" I said. I scrolled to a picture of Isabel.

He scowled, trying to concentrate. "Let me have a closer look." I handed him my phone again. "I think I may have seen her here," he said. "She looks familiar. But not recently. It's been a while—maybe a month or two. I noticed the two of them in here together." He handed it back.

I nodded. "Thanks," I said.

"But you're just looking for the first one?" he asked.

"Yeah. The other two are her friends. I figure if we can find our subject, great. But if we can't find her, maybe we can find her friends. Maybe they can help us."

"Makes sense," he said. "Sorry I couldn't help. But feel free to go ahead and ask around."

I spent the remainder of my thirty minutes going from one group of kids to another, talking, showing Kelli's picture. When I explained that I was looking for my partner's little sister, and that no, she wasn't in any trouble, most of the kids were pretty helpful. Unfortunately, most people didn't remember seeing her. A few people said they might have seen her—but they weren't sure—it could have been someone who looked like her. One young guy said he definitely saw her—said she was his buddy's sister and that they were going to get married. Then again, he reeked of alcohol, so I discounted his answer.

As my half hour came to an end, I returned to our starting point and waited for Toni.

* * * *

"How'd you do?" I asked, when Toni walked up.

"Crash and burn," she said. "Nothing. Some people think they saw her, but no one was totally certain. How about you?"

"I met her fiancé," I said.

"What?" She looked at me like I'd lost my mind.

I explained about the drunken teenager. "Except for that, my experience was about the same as yours. So what's our next step—switch to looking for Crystal? The guard over there recognized her. Said she shops here."

She nodded. "Kids are going to think we're nutty doing a second walkthrough asking about a different girl, but I don't care. Let's do it. I'm pretty sure Kelli's not here—at least not inside."

"I don't think she's here, either. I looked around pretty closely." I glanced around. "When I get to the back there, I'll go outside," I said. "I think the theater must be out those doors. I'll go check out that area."

"So half an hour again?" she said.

"That should be enough," I said. "Let's do it."

This time, I'd only been at it for about fifteen minutes when I got lucky with our first lead.

"Yeah, I seen her," a teenaged boy said enthusiastically. "She's fuckin' hot, dude. She was wearing these tight jeans."

"Oh! I remember her," his buddy said. "The one in the red sweater-thing."

"Yeah," the first boy said.

"When was this?" I asked.

"A half hour ago."

"No, dude. It was more like an hour ago," said his buddy. "We just got here."

"Here? In the food court?" I asked.

"Yeah. When I saw her, she was talking to another chick—a redhead who hangs out here all the time."

"Oh, yeah," his buddy said. "Gigantic tits. I remember her, too. She was wearing a yellow shirt that said *Google* on it."

The first boy nodded. "Yeah, that's right."

"Whereabouts?" I asked. "Where was she?"

"She was right over there," he said, pointing toward the door. "One of those tables by the door."

I looked around but could see no one wearing a yellow T-shirt.

"You guys don't know her, do you?" I asked.

They shook their heads. "We don't know either of them. We just saw them today."

With a little prodding, they were able to provide a little better physical description. I wrote it down in my notepad before calling Toni on her cell.

"I've got a lead," I said.

"I saw you talking to those two boys."

"Yeah, they said they saw Crystal here an hour ago."

"No Kelli?"

"No, they didn't recognize Kelli. But they said Crystal was wearing a red sweater over dark blue jeans. Also, she was either here with or meeting with a red-haired girl, also in blue jeans. The redhead was wearing a yellow shirt that said *Google* on it."

"No shit? I just saw that girl!" Toni said.

"Where?"

"She was heading out of the food court, back toward the main entrance."

"Meet me back at the top. I'll be right there."

Chapter 22

"SHE'S MEDIUM HEIGHT and build," Toni said as we hustled back up the main corridor. "Between the yellow T-shirt and her red hair, you can't miss her."

We made our way past a half-dozen stores, walking very quickly and pausing just long enough to take a quick look inside the shops. I scanned inside the stores on one side of the corridor; Toni scanned the stores on the other. No luck. Two minutes later, we reached a junction with another corridor and stopped.

I looked both ways, hoping to spot the girl. Still no luck. "We have to split up," I said. "No telling which way she went." I pointed north. "You work up that direction. Look inside the stores on one side until you reach Nordstrom. Then turn around and work back down the other side." I pointed to the east. "I'm going to go this way and do the same thing until I get to Sears. Then I'll turn around and come back. We'll meet back here."

"Got it," she said, as she turned and took off.

The mall was busy, but not packed, so I was able to make good time. I peered into each store as I passed it—my head in "swivel mode, up and locked" as we used to say in the army. I passed bath stores, lotion stores, clothing boutiques—even a store that lets you build your own teddy bears—but I saw no red-headed girl in a yellow T-shirt. A couple minutes later I reached the Sears and turned around to work my way back down the other side of the row. And there she was, coming out of a Cromwell's Bath Shop store with a shopping bag under her arm.

She turned and began walking back toward the spot where Toni and I'd split up. I waited until she was about thirty feet away to be sure I wouldn't be heard, then I grabbed my phone and called Toni.

"I've got her," I said.

"Where?"

"I was at Sears, and she was coming out of a bath store. She's walking back toward you now. Where are you?"

"I just finished my area, and I'm starting to walk your way. Hold on—I see her now. I see you, too."

"Just let her go past, then I'll join you," I said.

"Okay." We both hung up.

Except the red-haired girl didn't go past Toni. Instead, before she got that far, she turned and walked into Macy's. I picked up the pace and made it to the Macy's entrance a couple of seconds later. I looked in and was able to spot her. She didn't seem to suspect anyone was following her—she wasn't looking around, stopping, starting, changing directions, that sort of thing.

"You see her?" Toni asked when she reached me, a few seconds later.

"Yeah," I said. "She's right over there. C'mon, let's go."

We started following her again. A couple seconds later, Ms. Red Hair turned left, still unaware that she was being followed. She continued straight ahead and walked right out the Macy's side door.

We were only twenty-five feet or so behind her, and we hurried to the door.

"Hold up," I said, just before we were about to open the doors to go outside. "She's stopping."

We watched as Ms. Red Hair walked over to a low wall away from the sidewalk. The rain had stopped, and the girl sat down. She reached into her purse and pulled out a pack of cigarettes.

"Looks like she just needed a smoke," I said. I watched for a second more, and then I said, "Let's go talk to her."

* * * *

We walked outside and headed straight for Ms. Red Hair. We were almost there before she even noticed us approaching.

"Hi, there," I said.

She looked up at me but didn't say anything. Instead, she took a drag from her cigarette.

"I wonder if you can help us out?"

She looked at me with a belligerent look and exhaled—blowing a big cloud of smoke in my direction. This kind of pissed me off, but hey—I'm a professional. I don't get rattled by this shit.

"Okay," I said. "Let me ask you this. How much does Crystal pay you when you call her up and tell her there's a fresh teenaged runaway for her to come pick up and, oh—basically enslave—in her prostitution racket?"

Ms. Red Hair's expression changed from belligerence to concern almost immediately. Even Toni glanced at me, surprised. I winked at her, from the side that Ms. Red Hair couldn't see.

I turned back to the girl. "You know that makes you guilty of being a pimp in the eyes of the state of Washington, don't you?" I said. I think this may have been true, at least in a thin sense, anyway. "That's a Class B felony." I turned to Toni. "Is that five or ten?"

"Ten years," she said. "And a $20,000 fine."

"I don't know what you're talking about," Red Hair said. She tried to sound tough, but I got the distinct impression that she wasn't as tough as she was trying to appear. "Are you guys cops?"

"Nope," I said. "We're private investigators. But we've got lots of friends who are cops. I'm sure our buddies at the Lynnwood Police Department can figure out if what you're doing is something you can go to jail for. We can call them out here and turn this over to them."

"Fuck off," the girl said. "What do you want from me, anyway?"

"Tell you what," I said, "Let's start over. I'm Danny. This is Toni.

You are—?"

"Megan."

"Megan," I said. "Good. We'll leave everything on a first-name basis for the moment. Let me tell you, Megan, before we even get started—we're not interested in seeing you get in trouble. But we need some information, and you're going to give it to us; otherwise, we're calling the cops, and you can explain things to them. Understood?"

She glared at me. "What kind of information?"

"We're here this afternoon looking for a girl. We think she's been through here probably today." I pulled out my phone, opened up a picture of Kelli, and handed it to her. "Does she look familiar?"

Megan looked at the photo and then handed the phone back to me. She shrugged. "Maybe," she said.

"Ahh—not good enough, Megan. You're stonewalling. Here's what we do when you stonewall." I turned to Toni and said, "Toni, make the call. Lynnwood police."

Toni pulled out her phone and started dialing.

"Wait," Megan said. Toni paused.

"Okay," she said.

I turned back to her.

"I saw her."

"When?" I asked.

"Earlier today. Probably around eleven."

"Where was she? Do you know where she is now?"

She lowered her head. "She went with Crystal."

Hadn't taken Kelli long at all. She'd been gone what—six hours? And she'd already infiltrated the gang.

"From the start," I said. "Tell us what happened."

She shifted her feet. "I saw her sitting outside the food court this morning. So I started talking to her. She said she ran away because her stepfather was giving her shit."

"Then what happened?"

"I told her I knew someone who helped runaways. I told her I'd call her if she wanted."

"That's Crystal Wallace?" I asked.

"Crystal, yeah," she said. "I don't know her last name."

"So you called Crystal, then?"

"Yeah."

"Then what happened?"

"It usually takes Crystal about an hour to get here. She came and talked to me for a minute, and then she went outside and started talking to the girl. Then they left."

"Are you sure they left together?"

"Yeah. I saw them leave together."

"Here's another picture," I said. I opened up a picture of Isabel and handed the phone back to Megan. "Ever see her? It would have been a month or so back."

Megan studied the picture. "Yeah. I called Crystal for her, too. Then she and Crystal came in shopping together."

"So—back to my first question. How much money does Crystal give you for the lead?"

She looked back down. "A hundred dollars," she said.

I nodded. "A hundred dollars. Do you know what happens to these girls?"

She looked at me and then shook her head. "No."

"You don't? Really?" I asked.

She shook her head again.

"You don't know that these girls are almost all turned into prostitutes by Crystal and her people? That they advertise them on Backpage.com? That they're basically held captive—sometimes for years? That they're made to have sex with three-four-five men a night, seven days a week? You didn't know any of that?" Despite my best efforts to remain perfectly calm, my voice probably made it pretty clear how upset I was getting.

Megan's eyes were moist with tears. She shook her head. "I didn't know."

I stared at her for a minute and then asked, "Do you have a driver's license?"

"I thought you said that it was just first names?" she said.

"I said 'for the moment.' That moment's over. And here's the way it is now. You're going to give me your driver's license so I can copy down everything on it. Also, you're going to give me your cell phone number. I'm not going to do anything with any of this information—like I said, we're not interested in seeing you go to prison."

"Then why do you want it?"

"Two reasons. First off, there might be a question pops up that I need answered. If that happens, I'm going to call you on your cell phone, and you're going to need to answer truthfully. Second, you may be called to testify. If that happens, you'll need to do so truthfully."

"I don't want to testify," Megan said. "I don't want to be involved at all."

I smiled. "Oops. Too late. You're already involved. You're making money off of prostitution. You don't have many options here. Remember. Ten years. Twenty grand."

She looked at me, then nodded. "Okay."

She dug through her purse and then handed me her driver's license. I took a picture of it using my phone. She also gave her cell phone number. I typed typed it into my phone and, just for kicks, tried her cell phone. It worked. When I was done, I turned to her.

"And I lied. There's one other thing you have to do, Megan."

"What?"

"I don't believe you when you say you don't know what happens to these girls. Or put it this way. If you really don't know, then it's because you don't want to know. But you have eyes. You're not stupid. So here's the last thing for you to do. When you leave the mall today? If you ever come back, it better be to go shopping. If she or I ever see you in this mall hanging around girls again, then we're turning over all this stuff to the Lynnwood cops. You'll be in jail so fast you won't believe it. And you'll stay there for a long damned time."

"One other thing," Toni said. "You'd better not try to get in touch with Crystal and warn her about us. We'll be pulling all her phone records—cell phone and home phone. We'll trace down every caller, and we'll know if you called after today. There'd better not be any calls from you. Got it?"

She nodded.

"You do your part," I said, "Just go home. Stay home. We'll not turn you over to the Lynnwood police. You go on living your life. That's a hell of a lot better deal than these other girls have."

She nodded.

"Now get out of here."

She hopped up and double-timed it for the parking lot.

Chapter 23

AS SOON AS we got into the Jeep for the trip back to Seattle, I called Doc and asked him to run over to the Bryant Neighborhood Park parking lot and keep an eye on the house on Fortieth.

"Call me if you see these guys—whether or not you see them with Kelli."

"Got it, dude," he said.

Next, I dialed Annie Hooper's number. She answered on the third ring. I explained to her about Kelli deciding to go undercover and how she'd apparently hooked up with Crystal at the mall.

"You need to get her out, fast," Annie said. Her voice left no room for uncertainty. "You have a very short period—maybe forty-eight hours or so, during which they'll try to wine and dine her—try to impress her and get her comfortable. Most likely, they won't touch her in this period. But after that, they'll start in on her. She'll be given drugs. She'll be pressured—heavily—to have sex with one or more of the gang members. Jeez," she added, "talk about a silly thing to do. She stepped right into the middle of a real shitstorm."

Annie was talking to us through the Jeep's speakerphone. I could see out of the corner of my eye that Toni was tense as she listened. I suppose that's understandable.

"That's the way we see it, too," I said. "Today's Thursday. We figure that we need to get her out by Saturday—Sunday at the latest."

"Agreed," Annie said.

"Along those lines, our goal is pretty simple," I said. "Rather than go in ourselves guns blazing, we'd prefer to get Nancy Stewart to do it. They don't have the same kind of issues that civilians do when it comes to going in with guns. But we're having some problems."

"What kind of problems?"

"Nancy needs solid probable cause before she can get a warrant. The good news is that we think we have the gang's locations and their vehicles all identified," I said. "We've spent a fair amount of time on surveillance, and we've learned quite a bit. When the time comes, it will be a whole lot easier to mobilize and move against them. But the bad news is that this information doesn't mean much unless we have some proof that these guys are somehow involved with Isabel. We need to be able to link them somehow. Unfortunately, so far we haven't found Isabel—no sign of her. And because we don't have any clue as to where she is, or even if the North Side Street Boyz are involved with her disappearance for that matter, Nancy can't get the warrants that would allow her to arrest them or even to search the houses. The best we have regarding Isabel now is the fact that the person who answered the ad for Isabel was employed by NSSB."

"But from what you just said, you *know* Kelli's with Crystal," Annie said. "You have an eyewitness. And to some degree, that corroborates the story you heard about Isabel."

"True. But Kelli is over eighteen—she's an adult. She can go where she wants and hang out with whomever she wants. The fact that she's going along willingly—at least so far—makes it so that Nancy can't go after her. No crime's been committed."

She thought about this for a second. "That's tough, then. What are you going to do?"

"Don't get me wrong," I said. "When you said that we know Kelli's with Crystal, you're right. And we know where Crystal is—pretty much, anyway. If it comes down to it, we're not going to wait for the Seattle

Police Department to go in and get her out of there, to hell with the legal concerns. We definitely have the ability to do that on our own. That said, for obvious legal reasons, we'd rather have SPD do it. Which brings me to the real purpose of my call."

"What's that?"

"I was hoping that we might be able to speak to Paola again. When we talked to her last week, she seemed like she had more information—maybe a lot more—that she was not willing to share. Most of the good information we've been able to put together has come from our interview with Paola. We're wondering if she can help us some more. Has she softened up at all? Do you think she might be able to add anything now?"

The tires hummed softly on the pavement while Annie thought. "I don't know," she said after several seconds had passed. "She's been making good progress over the past week. I don't know if that means she'd be willing to talk. And I also don't know whether she has anything else she can offer, even if she were willing to talk to you guys. That said, my inclination is that she'd probably be a lot more willing to do it now than she was a week ago. Would you like me to ask her if she'd be willing to sit down with you?"

"That would be fantastic," I said.

"Let me call you right back," she said.

Five minutes later the phone rang.

"She'll do it. Can you be here at four? She has a meeting with a counselor until then," Annie said.

"Great."

"We don't usually give our addresses out, but I don't think you two are a security risk."

"We appreciate that." She gave us the address—it was in Fremont, right on the way.

* * * *

Before I drove into the neighborhood of Paola's Angel House, I thought the streets near Ravenna Park where the NSSB houses were located were narrow. Fact is, they were boulevards compared to the streets in Paola's neighborhood. "Streets" is actually kind—goat paths might be more accurate. I resisted the urge to turn myself sideways as I squeezed the Jeep through impossibly narrow spaces on the way to Paola's house. No way could two cars ever pass side by side there. If I'd encountered a car from the opposite direction, one of us would have had to swerve into a parking space and wait for the other car to pass before proceeding. And if the skinny roadways weren't bad enough, the streets were lined on both sides with tall trees that canopied completely over the roads. The effect was very much like driving through a narrow tunnel. If a person was prone to claustrophobia, he'd be in trouble. Fortunately, I didn't see any other traffic once we pulled into the general area—the neighborhood was quiet and peaceful.

I turned onto Paola's street, and shortly afterward Toni said, "There it is." She always finds addresses first. She pointed to a house two doors up on the right. "I see the number on the mailbox." I lucked out and found an empty spot on the curb only two houses away. We hopped out and began walking back to the house. "It looks just like all the other houses," she said. "You can't tell from the outside that it's a home for girls."

This assessment changed a little as we turned up the walkway to the house and went through the front entry gate. The home's security features became more apparent. The windows were all covered with decorative wrought-iron bars painted white to match the house's trim. It looked pretty, but it was secure—no one was getting through a window unless they had a blowtorch or a chain hooked up to a truck. As we drew closer, I noticed small, unobtrusive video cameras mounted up high, under the eaves. I counted five in the front of the house alone. "Smile," I said.

I pushed the buzzer just outside the wrought-iron work that enclosed the front porch and protected the front door.

"Hello? Can I help you?" A girl's voice.

"Hi," I said. "Danny Logan and Toni Blair here to meet with Annie Hooper."

"Okay. Hold your IDs up to the camera there in front of you," she said. We each did as she said. Shortly thereafter, the gate made a loud *click.* "Come on in. Someone will meet you at the door." We did as she instructed. The gate swung closed behind us and latched shut.

"Great," I said. "Now we're in jail."

The front door opened, and Annie Hooper greeted us.

"Hey, guys," she said. "Come on in."

She held the door for us.

"Very impressive, Annie," I said. "Looks very secure."

"Thanks," Annie said. "We take precautions. Occasionally, these girls' pimps try to get them back. If they come around here, we want to be ready."

"I'll bet you have the police on speed dial," I said.

"Yeah, it usually takes them just a couple of minutes to respond when we make a call."

"And the fortifications and the cameras buy you that time."

"That's right. Come on back. Paola's in the family room, I think."

We followed her through the living room, past the kitchen and into a family room located at the rear of the home. Three girls were sitting around a coffee table—Paola was one of them. I hardly recognized her.

Without the layers of makeup and the poofed-up hair, she looked like she was about twelve years old. She wore white gym shorts and a light blue Nickelback T-shirt. Her long, dark hair was back in a ponytail. It had only been a week, but she looked fuller—as if she'd been eating better.

"She looks good," I said quietly to Annie.

"We were lucky with her," Annie said. "So many of the girls who we get are addicted to something—usually to meth. It sometimes takes a whole year to get them straightened out. Paola wasn't addicted."

"Good news," I said.

Annie beckoned to Paola, who jumped up and walked over.

"Hi, Paola," Toni said, reaching to shake her hands. "You look really good."

"Thank you," Paola said. I imagine that a compliment coming from someone who looked like Toni probably carried some weight.

"They treating you alright here?" I asked.

Paola smiled. "Yeah," she said. "It's really good." She seemed happy.

"Paola," Annie said, "Like I mentioned, Danny and Toni would like to ask you a couple more questions. They're looking for two girls now— one of them's Toni's little sister."

Paola nodded. "Okay," she said. "I'll help you if I can."

Annie led us all over to the dining room, where we took seats around the table.

"Paola," Toni said, "we're really happy to see that you're doing well."

"Thanks," Paola said, smiling. "I like it here. Everyone's nice."

"Good. Look," Toni said, "we're not going to take up too much of your time. You know that we've been looking for Isabel Delgado. I think I told you that she's a good friend of my sister, Kelli."

Paola nodded.

"We took the information you gave us last week, and we went to work. We found that NSSB seems to have three houses around Ravenna Park. Does that seem right to you?"

Paola nodded. "The house where the girls live and the house where the boys live. Plus Donnie and Crystal's house," she said.

"We've been able to study the houses, but we still haven't found anything about Isabel. We heard what you said about Isabel being taken out of the girls' house and maybe sold to the guy in Las Vegas, but we can't figure out where Donnie would take her and keep her until then. We don't think it's at either Donnie's own house or at the boys' house. What do you think?"

"If he still has her," she said, "she's at the boys' house. The basement."

"The basement?" I asked. "The boys' house has a basement?"

She nodded. "It's where they have all their parties," she said.

Toni looked at me. When I was inside, I hadn't noticed a doorway to a basement, although admittedly, I hadn't had much time to look around before the two guys who were returning home early had interrupted me.

"If you're in the boys' house," I said, "where would the entry to the basement be?"

"They have a little office in the back of the house," Paola said. "There's a door in there that goes downstairs."

That's right. There were two doors in the office. I had thought both were closet doors.

"If someone was down there, could you hear them upstairs?" I asked.

"No. They put this stuff all over down there so they can play their music really loud. You can stand outside or upstairs even, and you can't hear anything that's going on in the basement."

"What's down there?" I asked.

"There's like a room with a sofa and a TV. And there's two other rooms—bedrooms. And a bathroom."

"How could they keep someone down there? Do the bedrooms lock up?"

She nodded. "Both of them."

"So if you were locked in a bedroom, there's no way you could get out or even be heard?" I asked.

She shook her head.

"And you think this is where they'd put Isabel?" Toni asked.

She nodded. "It's where they put you if you got in trouble," she said. "They called it the hole."

Jesus Christ. If Isabel was there, I had to get her out. And I damned sure couldn't allow Kelli to be sent there. "Let me ask you something else," I said. "Do they do drugs over at the boys' house?"

She laughed. "All day," she said.

"Did you ever notice where they kept their drugs? Say, their marijuana?"

Toni and Annie both looked at me, wondering why I'd ask that.

"Yeah," Paola said. "They kept weed in the kitchen closet, and they kept blow and crystal in the basement."

"You saw it?" I asked.

She laughed. "Yeah."

* * * *

We stayed and talked for another forty-five minutes. Paola was completely candid, although the remainder of our conversation failed to yield anything else as useful as the revelation that the NSSB had their own private dungeon located beneath the boys' house. Still, the talk was very helpful. Now that she was starting to see just a glimmer of how her life had been stolen by these thugs, Paola seemed almost eager to turn against them. She agreed that she'd be willing to sign a statement about everything she'd said if needed. We were very grateful. We thanked her and Annie and headed for the Jeep.

I said good-bye and then tapped in Nancy Stewart's number. It was 5:15 p.m., but I knew she'd still be working.

"Vice and High Risk Victims, Lieutenant Stewart," she said when she answered the phone.

"Nancy," I said, "it's Danny and Toni."

"Hey guys," she said. "Come up with anything interesting?"

"We did," I said. "Two things, actually. First, we just came from talking to Annie Hooper and Paola Morales."

"How's she doing?" Nancy asked "Did she have anything new to add?"

"She's doing really great and yes, she helped us out. A lot. We think we may have discovered where Donnie Martin is holding Isabel."

"Really?" she said. "Where would that be?"

"Apparently, he has a secure room in the basement of the house on Brooklyn across from Ravenna Park."

"A secure room? Paola told you that?"

"Yeah. Apparently, she knows it well. She says it's where the gang has its parties. She says it's been soundproofed, and from above you can't hear anything that goes on down there. Basically, unless you know it's there, you wouldn't be aware of it."

"That's interesting," Nancy said.

"That's not all. According to Paola, there are two bedrooms down there, both lockable from the outside. Essentially, they're jail cells."

Nancy thought about this for a few seconds. Then she said, "And Paola thinks that that's where Isabel would be held?"

"That was her immediate response when we asked," I said.

"Interesting," Nancy said again. "What about Kelli?" she asked. "What does this have to do with her?"

"Nothing—and everything," I said. "Let me explain. As you and Tyrone explained to us, we figure that Kelli will have a small amount of time in which Crystal and Martin and maybe the others will try to schmooze her. You know—buy her clothes, treat her nice, win over her loyalty. Then they'll ramp things up and start in with the drugs and forced sex. But with Kelli, there's a twist. Never mind the fact that she's older, smarter, and stronger than any of these other girls. The big thing is she already knows what's up, and at the same time they're playing a game with her, *she's* also playing a game with *them*. But it's a dangerous game because when they move into phase two and try to get her to use drugs or have sex with one of the gang members, she's going to tell them to stick it where the sun don't shine, and then there's going to be trouble. And that's the kind of trouble she's not prepared for. If we don't get Kelli out before then, she's probably going to get beat up and tossed into one of these dungeon bedrooms until she comes around. No telling what type of abuse will be piled on while she's there. So right now, the dungeon may only be about Isabel. But within a few days, it'll likely be about both girls."

It was quiet for a second, and then Nancy said, "And so your plan is to have us go ahead now and take down the whole operation in hopes that we get both Isabel and Kelli out?"

"Nancy," I said, "first off, I think Isabel's there now. I think she's being held until she either comes around or literally gets sold to another pimp in Las Vegas. And I think Kelli's next. We know she's with Crystal. And with regards to Kelli, I don't have any choice. She's basically family. I will not stand by and allow Kelli Blair to be subjected to these guys' torture. She's young and dumb, and she got herself in a bad position, but I can't leave her there. I'd prefer for you guys to go in and bust them, but if you won't move in, I'll have to go in and get her myself. There won't be any other choice for me."

"Hmm," Nancy said. She thought for a second and then said, "Well, give me something. Give me anything I can use as probable cause—something other than you think Isabel is being held there. I need something solid. Give that to me, and I'll go downstairs right now and set it up. The problem, as I see it, is that we still don't have anything solid against these guys."

"How about the fact that there's large quantities of marijuana sitting in kilo bricks on a shelf in the kitchen pantry? Or that there's cocaine and crystal meth somewhere downstairs?"

"Paola told you this?" Nancy said.

"Yes," I said. This was most of the way truthful. She told me what and where, but I filled in the blanks concerning how much based on personal observation.

"She'll talk to a judge?"

"She volunteered," I said.

"Might work," she said. "I'll go to the judge and see what happens."

* * * *

It's exactly 1.29 miles from Angel House where Paola was to the intersection of Highway 99 and Forty-Sixth Avenue. It took us thirty minutes to get there. We got on Highway 99 at Forty-Sixth Avenue and headed south. Traffic was heavy but, fortunately for us, it could have been worse. We could have been on 99 headed north. Compared to the cars on that side that were completely stopped, our stop-and-go motion seemed damn speedy. Ten minutes later, we crossed the ship canal, and five minutes after that, I got off on Dexter Avenue—about a half mile from my apartment. We were home two minutes later. In total—forty-seven minutes to cover 3.4 miles. You gotta love life in the big city.

Just as we were walking in the front door, my phone rang. Caller ID: Nancy Stewart.

"What'd you find?" I asked.

"We got it," she said, sounding as if she barely believed it herself.

"Really?"

"Absolutely. I told the judge about Isabel being a minor and that she's missing and believed to be held there. I told him about how the NSSB gang is known to be involved in child prostitution. I told him about the dope. I think that pushed him over the edge. He called Annie Hooper, and we had a conference call with him and Annie and Paola. He asked Paola questions, and she gave him straight answers. After he hung up, he told me he was going to issue a no-knock warrant."

"Really?"

"Yeah. Paola also told him they have a lot of weapons there."

"She did?" I hadn't seen any except the sidearms the two men wore.

"Yeah. She said the weapons are kept in the basement. After we ended the conference call, the judge said he was afraid that with that much dope around, the NSSB guys might decide not to go quietly. He said they could arm themselves while stalling the cops at the front door. Paola was a very convincing witness."

I looked at Toni. She was smiling.

"That's outstanding," I said. "When do we move?"

"Well," Nancy said, "that's the problem. We can't move until tomorrow around noon."

"Why?" I asked. I didn't want Isabel or Kelli to be with these guys even one more minute.

"I don't know if it's SWAT or what it is," she said. "I think it's probably just too late in the day. I do know we have to bring in our narcotics and gang units. My captain made a couple of calls—but he just called me back and said it's going to be tomorrow. So that means . . ."

"That means it's going to be tomorrow," I said. "I spent almost eight years in the military. I know how it works."

"Good. Why don't you two come on in to my office at ten tomorrow morning. We're setting up a planning meeting then. We can use your information."

"We'll be there," I said.

I put in a quick call to Doc. He'd been in the parking lot for a couple of hours with no sign of Donnie Martin, Crystal, or Kelli.

* * * *

Toni called her mom and explained what was going on while I started working on dinner. Actually, first I worked on pouring us each an African Amber from my growler. The jug was starting to feel a little light—I could see another trip to the Mac & Jack's Brewery in Redmond for a refill in my near future.

While Toni was on the phone, I went out onto the balcony. Outside on a mid-June night in Seattle at 6:15 p.m. and it was still broad daylight. I pulled up a chair and watched the boats on the lake while I slowly sipped my beer. It had been a long day, starting with our hunt at the mall. I'd have liked to have found Kelli today and gotten her home safe and sound, but the reality was, her plan was working—I hoped she was being wined and dined by Donnie Martin right now. Unfortunately, I was pretty sure she hadn't stopped to consider that the chances of her (the new girl) being exposed to Isabel (the misbehaving girl) were slim to none. At this moment, Kelli was one of the girls Martin was trying to impress. He'd have no reason to show her the dungeon—might scare her before he could get his hooks in her. He needed her to see a good life so that he could guide her willingly into prostitution. I shuddered and took a long draw on my beer.

Anyway, I was sure that Kelli hadn't thought that far ahead. For her plan to work, she'd have to go deeper undercover than she'd probably considered—certainly deeper than she'd be willing to go. She'd have to get deep enough inside to be allowed access to inside secrets in the same manner Paola had been. But there was only one way to get in that deep, and Paola had paid dearly for the privilege—it cost her four years on the street.

All this said, I felt pretty comfortable that Kelli was okay through tonight—it didn't seem to be Martin's MO to start pressuring new girls on the first night. He seemed to have more of a drawn-out game plan. Hopefully, he'd stick to it. Tomorrow, before it progressed any further, we'd bust his ass and get back both girls.

A few minutes later, Toni joined me just as the phone rang. Caller ID: Doc.

"Doc," I said. As soon as I said it, Toni froze.

"She's here. They all just drove up—Martin, Crystal, and Kelli."

Toni watched me carefully. "Hold on, Doc," I said. "I'm going to switch you over to speaker." I tapped the little menu button on my cell phone.

"You there?" I asked.

"Yeah."

"Doc," Toni said, "does she look okay?"

"Yeah. They're inside now. She looked fine. They were all laughing and smiling."

"Good," I said. "That's a bit of a relief."

"Danny," Doc said. "My car is the only one in the parking lot here. I'm a little conspicuous. I think I gotta bail or I'm going to run the risk of getting made."

"Go home," Toni said.

I looked at her. "Do you want to go over and pick up coverage?" I asked. "We can swing by and pick up the Winnebago."

Toni shook her head. "The motor home's already been there for a couple of days. They might make that, as well," she paused. "I hate to say it, but I'm comfortable that Kelli will be fine tonight. I actually think our risk is lower if Doc leaves than if he or we stay on for surveillance. Tomorrow morning, we're going to bust them all anyway."

"We can pick up coverage tomorrow morning," I said. "Doc, why don't you swing by and pick up the white van. You watch the Fortieth street house starting at nine or so. I don't think those guys get moving much before that. Have Kenny take the green van and do the same thing on the girls' house. We'll have you guys stay there right through the raid on the boys' house."

"Got it," he said. "See you tomorrow."

I turned to Toni. "That work for you?"

She nodded. "It's the best we can do. Of course, I'd like to bust her out of there tonight. But if we did that, we might not ever get Isabel." She was quiet for a second. "We're okay waiting."

"I think you're right. How's your mom?" I asked.

She smiled. "She's good. She cheered me up."

I smiled. "*She* cheered *you* up? I thought *you* were supposed to be the one cheering *her* up."

Toni set her beer down. "Yeah, really. But I feel responsible for Kelli being where she is."

"That's silly," I said. "You're not responsible. It's like you said in the office this morning—if anyone's responsible, Kelli is."

She nodded. "I know. That's what Mom said, too. Still."

"If it all goes according to plan," I said, "Kelli's probably going to get something like the royal treatment tonight. Wined and dined. Good meal. No pressure. Crystal's probably already talking about taking her clothes shopping in the morning. Then, *pow!* Before anything else happens, we bust them, and she comes home."

Toni nodded. "From your lips," she said. She held up her beer, and we clinked glasses.

"Damn straight."

Hold on, Kelli, I thought to myself. *We're coming.*

Chapter 24

THE NEXT MORNING at ten o'clock sharp, we walked out of the elevator and into the tenth floor lobby of the Seattle Criminal Justice Center. Mickey Cole and Javier Martinez were already there, talking to each other while they waited for Nancy. When we stepped out, Mickey saw me. He nodded. "Hey, guys," he said.

We walked over. "Good morning."

"How are you two this fine morning?" he asked. "All ready to go?"

I nodded. "You bet." I looked the two of them over. Instead of the grubby jeans and T-shirts they'd been wearing when we met two days ago, today they were both dressed in tactical clothing, right down to black boots. "You know, you didn't have to get all dressed up for us," I said.

Mickey smiled. "No shit," he said. "So much for casual Fridays, right?"

I gave him another look over. "Looks pretty tight to me," I said. "Reminds me of the old days."

"You guys wore this kind of stuff in Iraq?" Mickey asked.

I nodded. "Yeah, pretty much," I said. "Different color, but same kind of gear. Course we'd have about forty pounds of shit strapped onto our belt and vest, but same basic idea."

"Cool," he said. "One of these days, I want to take you to lunch. I've got a bunch of questions about your time in the service—," he paused and looked at me seriously, "—that is, if you don't mind talking about it."

"I don't mind," I said. "I don't usually bring it up, but if someone has questions, I don't mind answering."

"That'd be great," he said.

"Why—you thinking about joining up?"

He laughed. "Who knows, right, Javi?" Both men laughed.

"That's right," Javier said. "Depends on how the contract talks between the union and the city go. Right now, they're still a long way apart. We may need another job."

"They'd probably be happy to have you," I said. "How you boys feel about low pay and the desert?"

"No mold, no mildew," Mickey said. "Sounds cool."

I laughed. "Cool is one thing it ain't," I said. "Think warm, maybe hot. Think—dry."

"Hot and dry are good," Mickey said. "We'll see. Meanwhile . . ."

"Shifting gears—," Javier said. The two partners were so comfortable with each other, they could finish each other's sentences.

"Shifting gears," Mickey continued, "we haven't been sitting on our asses over the past couple of days. We were able to dig up some more information on Donnie Martin and NSSB." He paused. "You know, this fucker's a little scary." He paused again, "Oops," he said, turning to Toni. "Pardon my language."

Toni smiled. "No problem. This guy here—" that would be me, "—talks like that all the time."

"What makes you say he's a little scary?" I asked.

At that moment, Nancy Stewart walked out of a door marked Authorized Personnel Only. She held the door open and said, "Good morning, everyone. You guys ready?"

Mickey turned back to me. "I'll go over it when we're all together," he said.

* * * *

We followed Nancy back to a large conference room. Tyrone Allison was already there, along with another man whom I recognized. Captain Gary Radovich headed up the Seattle SWAT unit. He was medium height and solid in build, probably in his mid-fifties. His prematurely silver-white hair was cut in a tight military-buzz style. He saw us enter and immediately stood up. We'd accompanied his team on a SWAT raid on the apartment of a suspected drug cartel member last August. I'm not sure he remembered me, but most people tend to remember Toni. He smiled. "I remember you two from last year," he said. *Wow. Better memory than I thought.*

"Captain Radovich," Toni said, "It's good to see you. I didn't know you'd be leading this raid today."

"It's Toni Blair, right?"

She nodded, smiling. "You remembered."

"Of course," he said. He turned to me. "And you are . . . ?"

"Danny Logan," Toni said, filling in his blanks. There. I was right about his memory, after all.

"That's right," he said. "Good to see you two again. And to address your point, Ms. Blair, yes, I am heading up the operation today."

"Wonderful," Toni said.

Two other men walked into the conference room. Radovich nodded toward them. "Let me introduce these two mean-looking guys," he said. "Dave Bryant and Lonnie Charles from the narcotics unit. Apologies for their generally unpleasant demeanor. They have to deal with crackheads, tweekers, and various other druggies all day long, and it tends to make them cranky."

"Very funny," Bryant said.

The men said their hellos and took their seats.

"Let's get going, then," Nancy said. "I'm going to provide a little background for everyone and then Gary, I think you've got an operation all planned out?"

He nodded. "I do," he said.

"Good. So what we've got is a house on the western edge of Ravenna Park." She used a projector to flash an aerial photo of the boys' house up on the screen. She walked the group through the history of our investigation, including a description of Donnie Martin and DeMichael Hollins.

"I can add a little about Donnie Martin," Mickey said. "Since we talked to Danny here a couple of days ago, we've been doing a little digging." He turned to Javier and nodded.

"Donnie Martin, as Nancy just explained, is a twenty-two-year-old career criminal. He's already spent six years of his life locked up in one institution or another, starting when he was eleven years old. He served two different stints at the Green Hill School in Chehalis. And, in case you're unfamiliar with it, Green Hill is not known for being a college prep school. Martin's no petty thief—he's a violent young man. He's been arrested twice for assault—once when he was sixteen. The second time was two years ago, when he was twenty. He beat another gang member nearly to death with a baseball bat, but the case got dropped when the victim refused to testify—said he tripped going down a flight of stairs. All the other witnesses suddenly developed amnesia and recanted."

"I can add to that as well," I said. "In the course of our investigation, we interviewed a friend of Donnie's family, Reverend Arthur Jenkins. Reverend Art's the pastor of the Twenty-Third Street Baptist Church over in the Central District—the area where Donnie Martin and DeMichael Hollins grew up. He knows the boys well—in fact, he presided over Donnie's aunt's funeral a year ago. He told me that when he tried to talk some sense into Donnie then, Donnie just laughed and wouldn't have any of it. According to Reverend Art, the word is that Donnie Martin said no way he was going to end up in Walla Walla—he'd rather go out shooting."

"Great," Gary said, sarcastically. "Your basic nutcase. I'll make sure my men are briefed. Thanks for the heads-up."

I nodded.

"Okay," he said. "Back to our raid. What do we know about the house?"

"Not too much," Nancy said. She turned to me. "Danny, you guys staked this house out, right?"

"Not this one," I said. "The NSSB gang has a total of three houses that we're aware of. We staked out one of the other ones. But we do have some familiarity with this house." I squirmed a little as I said this. The police were unaware of my clandestine recon mission the day before yesterday.

"Inside layout?" Radovich asked. "That's what would really be helpful."

"A little," I said.

Nancy looked at me curiously for a few seconds. She cocked her head slightly and gave me a look that was equal parts skeptical and suspicious.

Oh, what fun. When I'd made my little recon excursion into the house, I hadn't thought that the information I'd gathered would become vital to the success of a police raid. Now, if I held back information in order to protect myself from a possible B&E charge, I might possibly be endangering the lives of Radovich's SWAT team members. I made a quick no-brainer decision. "Look," I said. "You're going to have guys putting their lives on the line in a couple of hours, so I'm not going to hold out on you. I've been in that house. Don't ask how."

Gary and Nancy both looked at me. Then Radovich shook his head and said, "I don't care how. Tell me what you know."

Whew! I stepped over to a whiteboard and grabbed a marker. I sketched a rough outline of the floor plan as I described it. "The house has three floors—main floor, upstairs, and basement—except when I was in it, I didn't know about the basement. The main floor has a big porch and a front door with a sidelight window. You can definitely see outside onto the porch from inside the house." I drew clever little sight lines to illustrate my point. "Be careful. The front door opens up onto a living room and formal dining room area. There's also a back door that opens up onto a family room. If the blinds are open, you can definitely see into the backyard from the family room." I drew more squiggly little lines. "Again, be careful. The kitchen is also in the back near this area. And then there's another door on the north side of the house that enters into an office area, here."

"Any bedrooms on the main floor?"

"Yeah, what looks to be a guest bedroom."

He nodded. "Upstairs layout?"

I drew a separate box and started sketching. "Stairway at one end, here, and then a long hallway with three bedrooms on either side. The last bedroom in the back of the house is set up as kind of a bedroom photography studio."

He took notes. "Basement?"

"Yeah. Like I said, I didn't even know about it when I was there. But apparently, there's a basement with an entry in the office down here on the main floor." I pointed to it.

Nancy looked at me for a moment, then she looked down at her notes for a few seconds. "The judge talked to our witness—a juvenile female— last night," she said. "Our witness told her that the gang keeps marijuana in the kitchen pantry and that they keep cocaine, methamphetamine, and weapons downstairs in the basement. Also—and this is very important— she said there are two bedrooms in the basement that lock from the outside; they're essentially jail cells. We have reason to believe that a missing juvenile—Isabel Delgado—may be held in one of these basement bedrooms. Although the judge gave us our warrant specifically for illegal drugs, the warrant allows us to search those bedrooms—for drugs—and to make sure our officers are safe. If you happen to discover a young girl being held against her will while you're in there, well, let's just go ahead and bring her out, too."

Radovich nodded. "Agreed," he said.

"Any idea what we're talking about in terms of dope?" Bryant asked.

"I think there's at least ten kilos in the kitchen pantry," I said, pointing to the closet I'd sketched in the back of the kitchen. "I think it's in one-kilo bricks. I don't know anything about the blow or the crystal."

He stared at me for a minute. I didn't know what to make of his dark, beady eyes. Maybe he just didn't like me. "You seem to have pretty good information," he said.

I smiled. "I do," I said. I didn't elaborate.

"How about the guns?" Radovich asked. "Do we know anything about their weapons?"

Nancy turned to me. "Well?" she asked.

I shook my head. "No, sorry. I don't know anything about their weapons."

"How about lookouts?" Radovich asked.

"The couple times we've driven past, we haven't seen any," I said.

"So," Radovich said, "if we're going to the trouble of searching the house for drugs, and if we happen to find some, we're going to want to arrest someone. Preferably the ringleader—this Donnie Martin character. How do we know he'll even be at this house? As I understand it, he and his girlfriend—," he referred to his notes before continuing, "Patricia Denise 'Crystal' Wallace—don't even live there."

"True," I said, nodding. "But every day we've watched, Martin and Crystal Wallace leave their house about a mile away and drive over to this house at noon or a little after. We think they hold some sort of staff meeting—maybe to divvy up the previous night's earnings. But we'll know for sure whether he's there or not by whether we see his car—a white BMW."

"And we don't need to worry about these other two houses?" He pointed to photos of the big house and the girls' house.

I shook my head. "Lucky for us, they have their daily staff meeting at our target house. There probably won't be anyone at all at the big house, and most likely it will be just the girls at the other house."

"We're going to watch both of them while we're raiding the house on Brooklyn, anyway," Nancy said. "Or actually, Danny's going to have a man watching each house so that we can concentrate all our guys on the raid. Our warrant includes them, as well—just without the no-knock part. We'll hit them after we're all done with the target."

Radovich nodded. "Makes sense. So here's our basic plan, then. He spent the next twenty minutes going through a simple but very detailed assault plan that seemed to me to leave nothing to chance.

"Anything else anyone wants to add?" he asked.

"Yeah," Mickey said. "Remember to be careful with Martin. He's dangerous."

Radovich nodded. "So are we." He looked up at the clock in the back of the room. "It's eleven o'clock now. We'll meet at the rally point at noon. I'll need a couple of minutes there to go over the plan with all the men. At 12:15 p.m. we'll move to our assault positions. Then, when everyone's ready, we'll go. Questions?"

There were none. The meeting broke up, and we started to leave.

"Hey, Logan."

I turned around.

Gary Radovich approached. "I just wanted to say, I appreciate you coming clean in there. My main goal is to make sure that I go home with the same number of guys I started with."

I nodded. "Been there, Captain. I get it. Just remember: these guys are going to be either in the back of the house—the family room—or the basement. The living room's not set up for more than four people."

"Got it," he said. "Thanks."

Nancy walked up and said, "I appreciate it, too. Still, when this is all over, we need to have a little talk," she said. "Seriously."

I nodded. *You bet. Right after we pull Isabel and Kelli out, I'm all yours.*

* * * *

Since I often drive the Jeep with its hard top removed, I'd had a locking steel box welded into the floor of the cargo compartment for security purposes. Both Toni and I are almost always armed. For me, it's a carryover from my military days. Toni learned from me. On the few occasions when I needed to take my weapon off—like when I visit police headquarters, for example—I lock it up in the steel box. But today, the moment we were out of there—even as we stood there in the police garage—we "gunned" up. To not have done so would have been unthinkable. Imagine. "Excuse me, Mr. Armed Bad Guy. Would you hold up a second while I run to my car and get my sidearm?"

Although we were dressed plainclothes-style in blue jeans and shirts, we'd chosen to wear our tactical belts and holsters today—the kind that strap down around the thigh. In the unlikely event that we found ourselves in a gunfight during the raid, I wanted to be ready. Along those lines, I also went ahead and pulled out the two dark blue bulletproof vests we'd brought along. These, I tossed into the backseat of the Jeep for easy access later.

"You ready?" I asked Toni.

She nodded.

"You nervous?"

"Yeah," she said. "Mostly because of Kelli."

"Don't worry," I said. "We'll have her out of there before lunchtime's over."

Chapter 25

OUR RALLY POINT was the parking lot on the north side of the football field at Roosevelt High School, about three-fourths of a mile north of the boys' house on Brooklyn. Because we had a little extra time, we went to a drive-through at a Starbucks on the way. Toni ordered a latte, and I ordered my usual trenta-size green tea. We jumped back on the road, and we were still fifteen minutes early to the parking lot. By 11:55 a.m., though, the lot was crowded with police vehicles including a SWAT truck, no fewer than twelve patrol cars, a half-dozen unmarked cars—even an ambulance with EMTs. Altogether, there were almost fifty police officers present. Clearly, taking down a gang headquarters where the occupants were known to be armed and dangerous was something SPD was taking seriously. This was probably a good thing. Also, it made the thought of having to go in and rescue the girls on our own seem a little overwhelming. I'm glad we were able to get SPD to do the heavy lifting.

At noon, everyone assembled around an easel near the steps at the side of the SWAT truck. Nancy started us off by pointing to a map on a flip chart mounted on the easel. "Here's how things are laying out," she said. "We've got search warrants for three houses including our primary target, which is this house here at 6147 Brooklyn Avenue. The target house warrant is a no-knock. At this time, we've got people watching all three houses, just so we can keep tabs on everything. Just for your background, these places have been identified as houses used by the North Side Street Boyz gang—the subject of our raid. Our intel tells us there's a daily meeting about this time at the target house on Brooklyn where the gang members get together. In fact, right now as we speak, Donnie Martin, leader of the gang, is at the target house for the meeting. Nancy paused and flipped a chart to a page with blowups of the surveillance photographs we'd taken. "He's a BMA, aged twenty-two. Approximately six feet and weighing a hundred and sixty-five. He drives a white BMW 750i, with Washington tags: 375-WAK. Our surveillance team says it's parked in front of the house right now."

"Martin rarely travels without his two lieutenants—DeMichael Hollins and Crystal Wallace." She flipped the chart and showed photos of the two. She read off their descriptions as well.

"Now, we will continue surveillance on the other two NSSB houses while we raid the target. After we hit the target house, we'll release SWAT, and then we'll raid the other two, starting with the house on Nineteenth. We don't believe that there are gang members at either of the other two houses at the present time. If that changes, our surveillance people will let us know." She looked at me, and I nodded. The surveillance people she referred to consisted of Doc at the big house and Kenny at the girls' house. She continued, "At the target house, we're going to detain everyone inside and, if the narcotics guys locate the drugs we expect to find, we'll go ahead and arrest them all." She looked around. "Questions so far?"

There were none.

She smiled and continued. "You may have noticed all the guys in the black tactical clothes," she said, sweeping her arm toward the SWAT truck. "Because of the gang presence and the nature of the men we're after, the actual entry and clearing of the target house will be handled by SWAT. Let me introduce Captain Gary Radovich."

"Thanks, Nancy," Radovich said. "Okay, we have a pretty simple plan." Radovich gave a detailed description of his plan to the assembled police officers. I glanced around and noticed everyone taking notes.

"Now listen up, because this is important. We have word that these are potentially very bad guys—potentially heavily armed. The word is that Donnie Martin's said he won't go back to prison—he intends to shoot it out. We need to shock and awe these guys so fast and hard that they don't have the chance to limber up any heavy firepower they might possess. After we're safely in and secure, I want Team Two to quickly clear the main floor. While this is happening, I want you three guys from Team Three in the office to secure the entry to the basement. No one goes in—no one goes out. Including you. Don't go downstairs. Just secure the door. After we're clear on the main floor, then I want six guys to clear upstairs. When that's done, we'll clear the basement."

He went quickly through the rest of the briefing. When he finished, he asked for questions—again there were none.

"Okay then, let's get everyone in position. On my command, we'll close the streets and move everyone into final assault position. Then, again on my command, we'll execute. Everyone be safe. Let's go."

* * * *

Radovich planned to park the SWAT command vehicle on the corner of Sixty-Second and Brooklyn. He'd have an oblique view of the front of the house from there but, unless an occupant came out the front door and walked to the sidewalk and looked north, he'd be reasonably hidden from their view. "You guys can just follow us in," Nancy said. "We'll be at the CP. As long as you stay with us up on Sixty-Second, you'll be good." She looked us over. "Nice stuff," she added. "I like your vests."

"Thanks. I hope we won't need them today."

"Absolutely," she said.

Because of the one-way streets, we had to drive west on Sixty-Sixth for a block to Roosevelt and then south until we hit Sixty-Fifth. Then we turned north for a block back to Brooklyn before turning south again. The area around Ravenna Park is a nice suburban neighborhood. The streets are a little skinny and lined with large shady trees. The homes themselves are quite grand, built in the first half of the last century. Most feature large porches with several steps leading up to wide entryways. Hell, the homes are so nice that the porches might even be called verandas. I'm sure no one around suspected that their neighbors in the tan two-story were running a large prostitution ring right in the middle of the neighborhood. Oh well. They were about to find out.

* * * *

We parked right behind Nancy and Tyrone on Sixty-Second and joined them at the CP in front of the SWAT truck.

When everyone was assembled, Radovich reached for the microphone on his radio and said, "Okay, folks, the CP is up. Let's have the entry teams into pre-position," he ordered. I watched as a large unmarked van rolled past us from the north and stopped in the road two houses above the target. Ten heavily armed SWAT team members in full black tactical gear, including Kevlar helmets, hopped out. At the same time, another van did the same thing but coming from the opposite direction. Three men emerged from that one. From our briefing, I knew that a third van was also being positioned in the alley with four more men.

"One's ready," Gary's radio crackled to life.

"Three's ready." That was the team in back.

"Two's ready." That was the north team.

"Surveillance one?" Radovich said. He had a plainclothes officer in the park with binoculars on the front of the house.

"The front of the house is clear," the voice on the radio said. "There's no one outside and no one appearing even to be looking outside."

"Surveillance two?" He had another man in the alley behind the house.

"There's no one in the backyard. The drapes are drawn—should be able to walk right up."

"Excellent," Radovich said to himself. He keyed his microphone. "Close the roads," he ordered.

Seconds later, I saw a patrol car block Brooklyn about a quarter mile south. Although I couldn't see, I knew that Brooklyn was also being closed on the north, along with Sixty-First Street to the west. All vehicle access points were now sealed off.

"Okay. Entry teams, into assault position." The ten-man team on the north moved single file down the street while, at the same time, the three-man team from the south came forward in similar fashion. When they reached their respective edges of the property, all three members of the south team went to the side yard south of the home. The north team split—three men going into the side yard on the north side.

The remaining seven men on the north team ducked down past the living room windows and silently approached the front door on the porch. Once there, they moved quickly into their pre-assigned assault positions—two men holding shotguns aimed directly at the door locks, one man between them holding a heavy steel battering ram. The four men who would enter first crouched single file behind the man with the battering ram.

When Radovich saw that the entry team was in position, he said, "Time is now 12:17. Entry team commander—you have the command."

The man in the front of the entry line immediately started a count we heard over the radio—"one, two, three," and then he pointed at the door at the same time he said, "Go!" into his radio microphone.

The two shotguns exploded simultaneously, sending breaching slugs into the locks and leaving gaping holes where a split second before a deadbolt and a door handle had been. Almost immediately afterward, the man wielding the battering ram swung it with such force that the front door was blown back on its hinges. The next man in line tossed a flashbang grenade into the home that exploded with a brilliant flash of light and a loud *bang!*

The noise hadn't even quieted when the first SWAT members charged through the door yelling, "Police!" and "Hands up!"

* * * *

"Move in!" Radovich said to the officers in the squad cars. "Go! Go! Go!" He waved them forward as the cars shot past him one by one before screeching to a halt a couple of seconds later in front of the house. The patrol officers immediately jumped out of their vehicles, weapons drawn, and took up defensive positions behind their cars.

The CP was nearly forty yards from the front door, and we obviously couldn't see what was happening, but we were still able to hear the men yelling inside the house, "Hands up! Don't move!" A neighbor in an adjoining house opened his front door and stepped out onto the porch to see what the commotion was about.

"Go back in your house, sir!" one of the patrol officers barked. The man looked around, trying to make sense of what he was seeing. Then he scurried back inside and shut the door.

Shortly afterward, a voice I recognized as belonging to the entry commander said over the radio, "Main floor's clear! Starting upstairs." Then he said, "We've got eight in custody. We're going to start bringing them out now. You guys ready?"

"Ready," Radovich said. He ordered the patrol officers to move forward out of their defensive positions and prepare to start handling suspects.

We watched as the SWAT team began marching out the gang members who'd been captured in the raid. The young men walked outside, hands held high, squinting against the bright daylight. I couldn't see from this distance, but if they'd been acting true to form, most were undoubtedly stoned. Once outside, they were immediately lined up against a planter wall by the patrol officers, frisked, handcuffed, and made to sit down.

Three minutes later, the entry commander again spoke over the radio. "Upstairs is clear!"

"Good," Radovich said. "Two down, one to go."

Less than three minutes afterward, the radio sprang to life. "House is clear! We're Code 4. Bring up the medics and the ambulance. We've got a girl in bad shape down in the basement."

Uh-oh. Radovich called the EMTs and the ambulance and sent them in. Then he turned to us. "That's our cue. Let's go," he said. We hustled over to the house just as the EMTs were entering. They carried a collapsible gurney with them.

I looked at the gang members seated against the planter wall, and then I turned to Toni. She was staring at the front door, obviously worried about the girl inside. My skin went cold when I realized that I hadn't stopped to consider that it might possibly be Kelli who was injured. Obviously, Toni had already thought of that.

But as I looked around, I became certain that this was not the case. "It's not her," I said to Toni.

"You don't know that," she said, continuing to stare at the front door.

"Yeah, I do. Look at these mutts here."

She glanced at the men seated against the wall.

"So?"

"He's not here," I said.

"What's that?" Nancy asked. She'd been listening to us.

"Donnie Martin isn't here," I said.

"Isn't that his car?" she asked, pointing to the white BMW beside us.

I nodded. "Yeah, it is. But he's not here."

Nancy turned to Radovich. "Anyone else inside?" she asked.

Radovich spoke into his radio, then turned to her. "This is it," he said. "All present and accounted for."

I motioned Nancy and Radovich away from the detainees so we wouldn't be overheard.

"We've got a problem," I said. "Donnie Martin isn't here. Neither is Crystal Wallace. Neither is DeMichael Hollins. And neither is Toni's sister Kelli." I looked over at Toni. "I'm pretty certain the girl they bring out isn't going to be Kelli Blair."

I continued. "But Martin's going to find out about this bust pretty quick. And when he does, we don't know how he's going to react, but it probably won't be good. You better make sure you collect up all the cell phones from these guys. We need to find him and bust him pretty damn quick." I looked up to make sure Toni wasn't listening. "And there's no telling what he'll do if he suspects Kelli Blair is somehow involved."

"There's nothing to make him start thinking that, is there?" Nancy asked.

I thought for a minute. Then, slowly, shook my head. "I don't think so," I said. "Unless she talks, and there's no reason for her to do that. But still, trying to match wits with a lunatic is a dangerous game."

"He's right," Tyrone said, "this guy's a wacko. He might start lashing out just because she coincidentally shows up the day before the raid."

"Like I said," I repeated. "We need to find Donnie Martin. And hopefully Kelli."

"Okay. Got any ideas where we should start?"

"Toni," I called out. She turned to look at me. "Do you remember what kind of car DeMichael Hollins drives?"

"Dark red Ford Expedition. Maroon, maybe." I looked around, but I already knew the answer. There was no dark red Ford Expedition there.

"There's your answer," I said. "Martin and Crystal and probably Kelli came over here, and then they all loaded up in DeMichael Hollins's Expedition and took off. That's what we need to be looking for. You should have all the details in the surveillance report I gave you."

"I've got it," Nancy said, pulling a vehicle report we'd given her from a file. "Ty, call it in, will you? It's a 2009 Ford Expedition, maroon in color, Washington tags: 585-UWW."

"Got it," Tyrone said.

* * * *

I wouldn't say that I had a bad feeling about things, but I was definitely starting to get a little uneasy. I suppose we should have known there was no guarantee that Martin and Crystal and Kelli would be at the house, but with his car parked there, it had seemed a reasonable expectation. I suppose that just because Martin went to the boys' house at the same time every day that we had him under surveillance didn't mean he was guaranteed to be there today. Still, we'd hoped to end this right now.

Five minutes later, they brought the victim up. Toni had been staring at the door, but when the men and the gurney started to come out, she turned away and buried her face in my shoulder, unable to watch. Toni is tough as they come, but I guess the thought of her sister being rolled out on a stretcher was maybe a little too hard to take. I watched for both of us. Two SWAT officers assisted two EMTs—one on each corner—as they carried the girl out on the gurney. The EMTs had already started an IV, and a fifth person carried the IV bag. I strained to see who the victim was. At first, I couldn't see her face—she was blocked by the guys—but judging by the way one arm was sort of halfway flopped off the gurney, it sure looked like she was unconscious. Then, I caught a glimpse of her. Her small face was bruised and swollen, but I recognized her. I looked down at Toni.

"It's okay, Toni," I said. "It's not Kelli."

"No?" She turned to look.

"No," I said. "It's Isabel. And I hate to say it, but she doesn't look too good."

Chapter 26

AS SOON AS they were out the front door, the EMTs extended the wheels on the gurney and started to roll it to the waiting ambulance. The EMT walked alongside, trying to hang Isabel's IV bag on a stand mounted to the moving gurney. Toni walked quickly in their direction after I identified Isabel. I followed.

The EMT noticed Toni walk up and guessed correctly that she was about to be questioned. "Relative?" she asked as she worked.

Toni shook her head. "Investigator. And friend."

"What's her name?"

"Isabel Delgado," Toni said. "What happened to her?"

"The poor girl's been beaten—probably with a club of some sort and maybe a belt, judging from the looks of it. She's lucky she's alive."

"Is she conscious?" Toni asked.

The EMT shook her head. "Not really. She's kind of in and out of it. I think she's been drugged—no telling with what—we can't determine that here. I think her arm's broken there," she pointed. "And she's had internal injuries, too, that much I can say for sure. She's been bleeding vaginally. She's got blood all over her legs." I looked at the sheet that covered Isabel from the waist down, but I couldn't see any blood.

"Will she be alright?" Toni asked.

The EMT held a finger up to her lips, indicating that Toni should be careful about asking such questions in the event Isabel could hear what was going on. Then she shrugged her shoulders and opened her hands up in the universal "who knows" signal. But, apparently for Isabel's benefit in the event she *was* able to hear, she said, "Of course she will. Do you hear that, Isabel?" to the motionless girl. "You're going to be fine. You just hang in there for us—we're going to take good care of you. And you're going to be fine."

Toni cringed. "Where are you going to take her?" she asked.

"We need to get her straight to the university medical center ER," the EMT said quietly. "If she's still bleeding internally, that has to be stopped right away." She turned to the other EMT. "Ready," she said. Together, they rolled the gurney up to the back of the ambulance. Then, when they pushed forward on the gurney, the legs folded up and tucked under as the gurney slid inside. The third team member had already entered and was waiting at the head of the gurney.

"Hello, Isabel," he called out animatedly. "We're taking you to the hospital now. We're going to take good care of you, and you'll be just fine." He immediately started a transfusion as the two EMTs outside slammed the doors shut and sprinted for the doors. They fired up the ambulance's diesel engine and pulled away. A second later, the siren blasted to life across what had been a peaceful neighborhood up until about twenty minutes ago.

Toni stood and watched the ambulance drive away. I walked up close behind her and put my hand on her shoulder. Together, we watched the ambulance drive up the street.

"You alright?" I asked.

She nodded. I leaned around her so that I could see her face. She was biting her lip, and tears were streaming down her face. "Jesus Christ," she said. "Did you see her? These guys are animals, Danny," she said. "And Kelli's still out there."

I watched the ambulance round the corner onto Sixty-Fifth Street. I didn't say it, but I was thinking, *Better out there than in the back of that thing.*

* * * *

"The house is all yours," Gary Radovich said to Dave Bryant. "Ready to be searched. Pretty sure we didn't miss any bad guys." He had a sly grin. "You should be alright."

"Oh, thanks a whole hell of a lot," Bryant said.

Radovich laughed. "Happy to be of service," he said. The SWAT officers were all out of the house now and on their way to the SWAT truck at the CP. "We're going to head out. We've got three more of these scheduled today down south."

"Thanks, Gary," Nancy said. "You guys were total pros, as always. We've got two more houses to take down."

"We aim to please," Radovich said. He turned to Toni and me. "Sorry we didn't find your sister here," he said to Toni. "But judging by the condition of the other girl, maybe that's a good thing."

Toni nodded. "Thanks," she said.

"You ought to have enough to charge these guys, though—right, Nancy?"

"Absolutely," she said. "At this point, even if the search doesn't turn up any dope, these idiots are all going to jail," Nancy said, pointing to the men sitting against the wall. "If nothing else, we'll charge them with assault, and I think we can charge them with trafficking, as well."

"You don't need to worry about finding dope," one of the SWAT team members who'd been in the house said as he walked to the truck. "It's like a pharmacy in there."

"Yeah," his partner said, "the kitchen pantry has about twenty-five pounds of high-grade pot inside."

"You should be able to stick them with some sort of firearms charge, too," the first officer said. "There's a regular arsenal in the basement. And, from the looks of it, several of the guns down there aren't exactly what you'd call legal—some of 'em even look like they're full auto."

"And some of the shotguns are sawed off," the other officer said.

"Jackpot," Dave Bryant said, smiling. "So we've got 'em for

possession, possession with intent to distribute, trafficking, ag assault, ag battery, firearms violations—and maybe more. Who knows? Not their lucky day." He turned to his crew. "Let's go, boys," he said. He led his eight-man team inside to begin the long task of thoroughly searching the house.

"I want to go inside, too," Nancy said. "Have a look around. But we only have a minute. I want to roll to the house on Nineteenth—," she looked at me, "I think you guys call it the 'girls' house.' Then we'll swing on up and hit the house on Fortieth—the 'big' house. Also, hopefully, I'll be able to talk to Isabel at the hospital later this afternoon. I'm hoping she can give us information on Donnie Martin, DeMichael Hollins, and Crystal Wallace. Even if she can't, though, based on everything that's going on around here, I'm sure I can get arrest warrants for the three of them. Ty—why don't you call the office and get that started."

"Got it," Ty said.

"Meanwhile," Nancy said, "maybe Kelli will find out about this bust some way and just decide to walk away now. She'll figure out that Isabel was rescued. And with Isabel safe, there's no reason for her to hang around with Donnie Martin anymore."

"*If* she finds out about the bust and *if* she's allowed to simply leave," I said. "Neither of those is automatic—at least not right away."

She thought about this. "Where else would they be?"

"My guess is if they find out about the bust, they'll either run past the house on Fortieth—it's Donnie Martin's residence—or else they may hightail it to the neighborhood where they're originally from."

"Central District?"

I nodded. "Yeah. They might figure that they need to lay low. Someone over there would probably take them in."

"They wouldn't take Kelli there, would they?"

I shook my head. "I can't see why they would. They'd probably just jettison her when they find out what's happened." I didn't want to consider the fact that in the event they decided they didn't want any witnesses, things could go badly for Kelli. The thought made me shudder.

Nancy nodded, thinking. Then she said, "That makes sense. I'll tell Ty to alert the East Precinct. We can get—." Suddenly, my cell phone rang, interrupting her. Caller ID: Doc.

"What's up?" I said.

"They just pulled up," Doc said. I turned and whispered to Nancy. "Donnie Martin just drove up to the house on Fortieth."

Everyone turned to me and froze.

"Who all is there?" I asked Doc.

"Martin, Hollins, Crystal, and Kelli."

"Outstanding."

"What?" Nancy said.

"Donnie Martin and DeMichael Hollins plus Crystal Wallace and Kelli."

"Dude," Doc said. "They're moving shopping bags."

"They're what?"

"They're moving shopping bags," he said.

I turned to Nancy. "They've been shopping."

"Do they seem nervous or alarmed?" I asked Doc.

"No. They're just standing around talking, shooting the shit."

I turned to Nancy. "They don't even seem to know there's been a raid here. We need to move fast before they put in a phone call and figure it out."

She nodded. "Got it."

"Good work, dude," I said to Doc. "We'll be right there. If Donnie Martin leaves before we get there, follow 'em. But we'll be there in under ten minutes." I hung up.

Nancy put two fingers in her mouth and gave a surprisingly loud whistle. "I need everyone who's scheduled to take part in the next takedown to assemble here, now!" She shouted. "We have new information. If you're not involved in the search or the transport of those guys, we need you over here real quick," she yelled out to the officers.

"Ty! Call in and get these guys some more backup to help process this gang."

"Right!" Ty said.

Nancy assembled her troops. There were twelve officers in six patrol cars. She pointed to three patrol teams. "We'll all head out of here north on Brooklyn."

"We're in the park," one of the officers said. "Shall we just shoot through?"

"Absolutely," Nancy said. "You all use the park if you're blocked. We'll all shoot across Sixty-Fifth together. We'll go in Code 3 until we get to Thirty-Fifth but after Thirty-Fifth, lights only. This is important—I want no sirens east of Thirty-Fifth. Everybody understand?"

The nine men and three women nodded.

"Good. We'll make two groups." She pointed to three patrol officer teams. "You, you, and you—approach from the south. Tyrone and I will lead you guys in. Our group will turn on Thirty-Fifth, go down the street and around the block so we can come up on Fortieth from the south. Last guy in, seal off the street. You, you, and you—," she pointed to the other three patrol teams, "you approach from the north. Come in off Sixty-Fifth and turn right on Fortieth—straight shot in. Last guy in, seal the street off. You guys coming in from the north—you have a shorter way to go, so don't come around the corner until you see me pulling up. The subject house is only three or four houses from the corner." She turned to me. "Is that right, Danny?"

"That's it," I said.

She turned back to the officers. "I don't want you getting there ahead of us. We have confirmation that Donnie Martin, DeMichael Hollins, and Crystal Wallace are there, along with another female who is not part of the investigation. And all of you—remember—assume that they're armed and dangerous. Be careful. Any questions?"

There were none.

"Let's go," she said. We all sprinted toward our cars.

Chapter 27

NANCY AND TYRONE gave the patrol officers a few seconds to
make it back to their cars and get going. Then, the two of them jumped
into her silver Crown Vic and burned rubber pulling out—she drove. She
hadn't made it clear where she wanted us. Since we were civilians, most
likely she wanted us in the back, safely out of harm's way. But then again,
she hadn't actually said anything. Since we were parked right behind her, I
took off as soon as she left and fell in right on her bumper. I never liked
being in the back.

The patrol car that had been blocking traffic onto Brooklyn from
the north had already swung out across Sixty-Fifth and stopped, blocking
traffic for us. Nancy took advantage of this as she switched on her lights
and siren and rounded the corner onto Sixty-Fifth. "Hold on," I yelled
to Toni as we blew around the corner behind her. Six more patrol cars
followed, right behind us, all with lights flashing and sirens on. Talk about
an adrenaline rush! I hadn't been "Code 3" since my earliest CID training
days. Part of the curriculum was serving six months as an MP—for me,
this meant at Fort Lewis near Tacoma. Occasionally, we'd been involved
with a chase—usually of a soldier who'd had a little too much fun at one
of the local drinking establishments. The MPs on gate detail take a dim
view of soldiers who crash through without clearance.

As we hustled eastbound, I noticed that Northeast Sixty-Fifth Street gradually changed character from almost pure residential where we started to almost pure commercial by the time we crossed Twenty-Fifth Avenue Northeast. We picked up speed. Ten blocks later, we slowed again as we reached Thirty-Fifth. It had taken about two minutes to cover the mile between Brooklyn and Thirty-Fifth. As we reached the intersection, I hit the speed dial on my cell phone for Doc. I put it on speakerphone and when he answered, I said, "How we looking?"

"They're all still inside," he said.

"Good. We're only a few blocks away now."

"I know. I can hear you. You guys gonna turn them sirens off?"

At that moment, Nancy turned her siren off, and everyone else followed suit. I smiled. "How's that for service?" I asked, as we made the turn southbound on Thirty-Fifth.

"Cool. See you in a minute."

I watched in the rearview mirror as three patrol cars followed us onto Thirty-Fifth while the other three went straight through the intersection.

"You ready to go get Kelli?" I asked Toni.

She nodded. I saw her hand gripping the door, tightly.

I reached over and put my hand on her shoulder. "She'll be fine, Toni. Those guys don't even know we're coming. They won't know what hit 'em."

She nodded. "I hope so. I'll be glad when it's over."

I glanced at her. I don't think she gets scared—or at least, not to the point where it incapacitates her. I've seen her in action plenty of times. Focused? Yep. Pissed off? Sometimes. Scared? Never. That said, having her little sister in a threatening position was clearly getting to her.

"It'll be over soon," I said. "Just a few minutes now."

Our group reached Sixty-Second Avenue and turned east off of Thirty-Fifth Street. Suddenly, the street narrowed considerably, and we had to slow down to no more than twenty miles per hour. After our high-speed run, it seemed like the minute-long drive down the five blocks to Fortieth Street took forever.

Just as we turned onto Fortieth, my phone rang. Caller ID: Doc. I hit the button to answer the call on the speaker.

"They're coming out!" Doc called.

Oh, shit. Nancy was already around the corner, heading north toward the house, no more than 150 yards away from them. I needed to warn her. I pulled up behind her and started flashing my lights like crazy. I didn't want to honk my horn, figuring that that would alert Donnie Martin. Unfortunately, while I was trying to flag down Nancy, she and Tyrone were looking for the house—she wasn't looking in the rearview mirror. I didn't have her number on speed dial, but it wouldn't have mattered anyway. Five seconds later, she drove right up to the house and stopped in the middle of the road. I pulled up and stopped not far behind her.

From my vantage point behind her, I saw Donnie Martin walking from the front door of the house, following Kelli and Crystal. DeMichael Hollins was already in the maroon Expedition, waiting for the others. At the same time I saw him, Martin looked up and saw Nancy and Tyrone drive up and stop in the middle of the street with their red-and-blue flashing lights turned on. He didn't hesitate.

Martin reached behind his back and pulled out a handgun—looked like a full-size Glock. Without pausing, he opened fire.

Martin's first shot blew out the side window in the Crown Vic right behind Nancy. She reacted instinctively and put the big car back in gear and floored it. Just as she started moving forward, Martin fired again. This time, he blew out the driver's side window right beside her face. Immediately, the big car veered off the road and plowed into a tree with a *bang! Holy shit!* The hood sprung and the airbags deployed. There was no movement from the car—I couldn't tell if Nancy and Tyrone had been hit or were simply dazed. From the corner of my eye, I could see the patrol cars at the top of the street just round the corner from Sixty-Fifth, unaware yet that Nancy was under fire.

Martin began walking toward the car. He started to raise his handgun. He was moving in to finish them off. Instinct kicked in.

"Hey!" I yelled, as I opened the door and started to get out.

This surprised him for a moment. He'd apparently been focusing on

Nancy so much that he hadn't even noticed me behind her, or maybe the Jeep had thrown him off. "Toni, get down!" I yelled. Her door flew open, and she dove out the right side as I finished getting out on my side. I now became Martin's more immediate threat, so he turned to face me. We were probably one hundred feet or so apart, so I wasn't too worried that he'd be able to hit me from that distance. Which, I suppose, is the reason I was so surprised when one second later, he opened fire on me, and the driver's side mirror on the Jeep blew up. Damn! That was a lot closer than I'd expected. I heard the sound of the gunshot a split second later.

The gunshot apparently roused Nancy as well. Her door must have been jammed, and she chose that moment to start kicking on it from inside in order to get free. Unfortunately, Martin heard her, too. He started to turn back to her, back to his original mission. Behind him, I could see the squad cars screeching to a halt. Now the officers inside saw what was happening.

"Hey," I yelled again. I had my .45 drawn at the low ready. "Donnie Martin!" I yelled. "Drop your weapon! Do it now!"

He looked at Nancy; then, without turning his body, he looked sideways at me. He smiled. Guess he figured I couldn't hit him, either. Then, still looking at me, he started to raise his gun at Nancy. She was less than twenty feet away from him—he could hardly miss.

Suddenly, without consciously thinking about it, I made a quick decision. The outside world seemed to recede. Everything switched to slow motion. My arms came up automatically and once again, all my training kicked in. As my arms came up, my right thumb pushed the safety lever off. I took one deep breath and then held it in as I completed the movement. My eyes instantly found the front sight as I raised it to Donnie Martin's head. With all my concentration, I focused on the front sight. Steady. Squeeze. *BOOM!* The round fired. I didn't need to look.

Chapter 28

AS THE SOUND of the shot died away, things started happening fast. All twelve uniformed officers converged on the scene, guns drawn. I'd already holstered my weapon—I did it automatically after the threat was over. Besides, it's generally a bad idea to have a gun in hand in the vicinity of police officers—especially if they're already jumpy.

Some of the officers headed for Donnie Martin, his lifeless body sprawled faceup on the pavement. Others headed for the red Expedition.

"Get on the ground!" They had their weapons drawn and pointed at DeMichael Hollins, Crystal, and Kelli. "Out of the car!" they yelled at Hollins.

For his part, Hollins seemed like he was completely stunned at the turn of events. One second, he's going on a shopping trip. The next second, a police car pulls up, his best friend pulls a gun and opens fire and is in turn killed right in front of his eyes, not six feet away. And now, the police were all over, guns pointed at *him,* ordering him out of the car.

"Show me your hands!" an officer standing right outside the driver's door yelled. The officer's weapon was pointed at Hollins's left ear, probably forty-eight inches away.

Hollins apparently hadn't gone to the same "they'll never take me alive" school that Donnie Martin had attended. He did what he was told and raised his hands as the officer opened the door. Strong hands grabbed him and yanked him out of the truck onto the ground. I watched as he landed on the street beside the truck where Crystal and Kelli were already sprawled out. All were quickly handcuffed.

"Damn," Toni said as she ran around the Jeep to my side. "Are you alright?"

I nodded. "Look. Fucker broke my mirror," I said.

"He hit the windshield, too," Toni said.

"No shit?" I only remembered hearing one shot. I looked at the windshield and sure enough, a clean bullet hole right in the middle.

"I think there might have actually been three shots."

"Really?"

"You guys alright?"

I turned and saw Doc running up to us. He'd been in the surveillance van in the parking lot of the park.

"We're good," Toni said. "Did you see Kelli?" she asked.

"Yeah. She's alright," Doc said. "I was watching her."

"Thank God," Toni said.

"She was standing about ten feet away from Martin," Doc said.

Toni nodded. "I think he was gonna kill Nancy," she said.

"I think so, too," I said. Hearing Nancy's name caused me to snap back to reality. "Damn. I've got to go see if she's alright."

I ran toward her car. It was already surrounded by four police officers. I could see blood on the inside of the car as I approached. Both side windows on Nancy's side—the driver's side—had been completely blown out. The officers were so busy trying to get Nancy out that they didn't notice me when I walked up and stood behind. One of the men tried to open Nancy's door, but it was hopelessly jammed shut. "We're going to have to get her out from the passenger side," he said. He turned to Nancy. "How you doing, Lieutenant?" he asked. "You alright?"

"I'm fine," Nancy said, still a little dazed. "I'm alright." She looked down at the blood on her hands. "This blood isn't mine. There's nothing wrong with me. Check Ty. He's been hit."

I looked through the blown-out back window at Ty. He was bleeding from a head wound. The blood had gotten all over the airbag. When he heard Nancy, though, he turned to her.

"Glass," he said, a little dazed himself. "I'm not hit. The bullet hit the mirror. I got cut by the glass."

"Thank God," she said.

* * * *

The officers helped Ty and Nancy out of the smashed-up car. When Nancy walked around the back of the vehicle, she noticed Kelli, still on the ground in handcuffs alongside DeMichael Hollins and Crystal Wallace.

"Let this one go!" Nancy said, pointing to Kelli. "She's not involved."

Kelli was quickly released and helped up by the officers. She immediately ran into Toni's arms.

"I'm so sorry," she said, crying as they embraced.

"I know," Toni said. She started crying as well. "It's okay, Kell. You're alright now."

"I just wanted to find Isabel so badly, and I thought you guys were going to stop looking."

"Don't worry," Toni said. "We've got Isabel. She's at the hospital. And you're okay now. Everything's going to be fine." She held her sister tightly.

"Is Izzy okay?" Kelli asked.

"I don't know," Toni said honestly. "She's not in good shape."

"Can we go see her?"

Toni nodded. "Yeah." The hug went on for several more seconds before Toni broke it off. "But right now," Toni said, "before we do anything else, you better go sit your butt down in the Jeep and call Mom and tell her you're okay. She's worried to death about you. Here—use my phone."

Kelli nodded, crying again. "Thanks," she said. "I love you."

"Me, too," Toni said. "Watch out for the glass," she called out.

Toni turned and looked at me and smiled as her sister walked away.

"Thanks, Danny," she said.

I leaned over and kissed her lightly. I shook my head as I smiled back. "You know you don't have to thank me," I said.

* * * *

Within a few minutes, it seemed like every police car in Seattle was on the scene. They parked in the street, they parked in the parking lot at the park by our surveillance van, some even parked in the park itself. Fortieth Street was closed top and bottom. One of the officers used about a hundred yards of yellow crime scene tape to cordon off the area. Next came the news helicopters followed by the news trucks. They parked in the parking lot at the park, extended their microwave masts, and immediately started "live, on the scene" coverage of the aftermath. "Police gun battle near Ravenna Park leaves one dead."

Not long afterward, the ME team showed up and, after much photographing and measuring, removed the body. I, along with all of the other officers who were witnesses, was questioned preliminarily about what happened. Our versions were all recorded. My sidearm was confiscated—this pissed me off, but I knew it was going to happen. They promised I'd get it back at the end of the investigation.

More photographs were taken and more measurements were made. Sketches were made of the entire scene.

"One hundred thirteen feet," I overhead one officer say to another, shaking his head as he rolled up his tape. "That's incredible. No fuckin' way I could ever make that shot."

"Me neither," the other man said.

When they were done giving initial statements, the paramedics wanted to load both Nancy and Ty into an ambulance for transport to the emergency room, but Nancy pulled rank and insisted that they ride in the back of a squad car instead. The car had just begun to pull away when it stopped suddenly. A back door opened, and Nancy got out. She walked over to me.

"I'm not sure I did it—things have been pretty confusing—but I wanted to be sure I said thank you. Thank you for literally saving our lives." She reached out and shook my hand. "Tyrone feels the same way, but he's still a little woozy to be walking around."

I smiled. "Don't even think about it," I said. "I'm glad I was there."

"So am I. You know, I already owe Dwayne for saving my life, and now I owe you, too. My debts are beginning to pile up."

I laughed. "No worries. You don't owe me anything. We're good."

"We are, aren't we. We're good." She nodded and smiled. Then she became serious. "But I am still interested to hear from you how you managed to find your way inside the house on Brooklyn." I must have had a deer-in-the-headlights look, which caused her to smile again. "Off the record."

I nodded, relieved. "You're on."

She turned to leave, then turned back suddenly. "What hospital did they take Isabel to?" she asked.

"University Medical Center," Toni answered.

Nancy nodded. "Good. Then that'll work for us, too."

* * * *

They wanted me down at police headquarters for more thorough questioning. And since it turns out that Donnie Martin *had* fired three shots at me and his third shot went through the Jeep's radiator, I had to ride in the surveillance van with Doc, Toni, and Kelli back to the office. On the way, I put in a call to my lawyer, J. David O'Farrell. David's an old family friend and one of the best criminal defense lawyers in Seattle. I pay him a small monthly retainer, which enables me to call him at moments like these when I need help. He said he'd meet me at the office and drive me downtown to talk to the DA.

The ride to the office took thirty minutes, giving me a chance to reflect. Several of the officers had come up to me and shook my hand. "Good job." "Way to go." "Nice shot." I was okay with accepting this in the way of thanks for maybe saving Nancy's and Tyrone's lives. But when one of them commented, "The bastard got what he deserved," this made me a little uncomfortable. I didn't necessarily look at it that way.

For me, anyway, taking someone's life is not something you can do and not be affected by—even if the guy *is* shooting at you. I know some of the guys in my unit in Iraq were different. They could kill someone, then go have a beer like nothing happened. I'm not one of those guys— never have been. At times, killing someone might be necessary (if he's trying to kill you) and it might be the right thing to do (again, if he's trying to kill you), but it's not something to throw a party over. I don't know if it's the way I was raised or just the way I'm put together, but I believe God created all life—even scumbags like Donnie Martin. I've had to kill people in war and now, for the first time, as a civilian. I hope God doesn't hold this against me. I think He's alright with it—after all, He gives almost all living creatures the ability to defend themselves. Still, it weighed heavily on my mind. I was lost in thought and didn't have much to say on the ride back to the office.

Chapter 29

"THEN I YELLED at him to drop his weapon," I said. I was at the Seattle Criminal Justice building, almost two hours into explaining to a group of three police captains plus Harold Ohlmer and Denise Free from the King County DA's office exactly what had happened, starting with our initial efforts to locate Isabel and culminating with the shooting.

"And you had your gun out at the time?" Police Captain Scott Cristello asked.

"I did," I answered. "I was at low ready."

"Safety?"

"Safety was on," I said.

He nodded.

"Then?" Harold asked.

"He didn't do it—he didn't drop his weapon. He did turn and look at me. But then, while he was still looking at me, he started to raise his pistol in the direction of Lieutenant Stewart and Detective Allison. He was already in the street—only twenty feet or so from their car. He'd already fired at them at least twice in addition to the shots he'd fired at me. I thought there was a very high probability that he was going to turn back to them, take aim, and open fire. I'm certain he would have hit them this time since their car was stopped and so close. So after he refused to drop his weapon and instead, started raising it to fire at the officers, I fired a single round at him."

"Before you fired, were you able to see Lieutenant Stewart and Detective Allison?" Ohlmer asked.

I thought for a second, and then I nodded and gestured with my hand. "Yes. They were in front of me, a little off to my right."

"Did you wonder why they weren't returning fire?"

I tried to remember back. "I wondered if Lieutenant Stewart had been hit. I didn't know if that's why she drove into the tree. I saw them sitting in the vehicle, and I saw that they weren't moving or firing back. But it happened fast. It was all over in a matter of just a few seconds."

He nodded.

"And you believed Martin could hit them from his distance?"

I nodded. "Absolutely. Like I said, he was twenty—maybe twenty-five feet away. That's a pretty easy shot. He'd just fired a shot at me from more than one hundred feet, and he blew out the mirror on my Jeep, two feet from where I was standing. That was a hard shot, and he damn near hit me, so I figured the man had good gun control. From twenty feet, he'd have most probably been deadly."

It was quiet for several seconds as they flipped through their notes, trying to tie off any loose ends. Finally, David said, "We've been at this for nearly two hours now, and the questions are starting to get a little repetitive. Do you folks have any further questions of Mr. Logan?"

"Yeah," Captain Cristello said. "Where the hell'd you learn to shoot like that?"

I smiled. "U.S. Army."

He nodded. "Good."

"Alright, then," Ohlmer said. He turned and looked at his associate.

"Denise? Do you have anything else?"

She shook her head. "I don't. I think we've got everything covered."

"Okay then," Ohlmer said. "Let me wrap things up. Based on what I've heard, there seems to be little question that the shooting was justifiable. There seem to be about nine witnesses—police officers—who corroborate your testimony. Accordingly, based on what we know now, I can say that, pending the results of our final report, the district attorney's office will neither be referring this matter to a grand jury, nor will we be filing charges on our own. When the complete investigation is wrapped up, we'll make our decision formal. Until then, do us all a favor and please keep this conversation confidential."

I nodded. I never expected to be charged for anything, but it was still a relief to hear it from Harold.

"Thank you, Harold," David said. "Are we free to go, then?"

"You are," he said.

"Thanks," I said.

"Thank you," he said. "And Danny," he said, turning to look at me. "Thank you."

"Abso-fucking-lutely, thank you," Cristello said. "I'm pretty certain it's safe to say that if you hadn't been where you were, we'd probably have two dead officers on our hands. The department owes you for this."

I smiled. "No problem," I said. I shook hands with each of them, and David and I left.

****

As we began to walk down the hallway to the lobby, I felt a hand on my shoulder. I turned and saw that it was Cristello.

"You okay, Danny?" he asked. "Is it alright if I call you Danny?"

I nodded. "Yeah," I said. "And, yeah, I'm okay. Thanks for asking, though."

He nodded. "Just checking. I know it can be rough when you have to shoot someone."

I looked at him carefully. "You?" I asked.

"Yeah, 2004. Kid with a gun. Messed me up for a couple of months. But we've got some good people you can talk to if you need it. I sure as hell did."

"Thanks," I said. "I appreciate it. Give me a card, Captain. If it gets to a point where I think I need to, I'll give you a call and get a number."

"Good deal," he said. He handed me a business card.

"You take care of yourself," he said. Then he turned around and walked the other way.

"I'm proud of you, son," David said as we watched Cristello leave. "You did a good thing today. You're a fine young man." He thought for a second, and then he chuckled and added. "If all my clients were like you, I'd probably be out of a job."

* * * *

We reached the fifth floor lobby and found several police officers, including Dwayne and Gus, waiting to meet me. Dwayne shook my hand.

"Well done, Danny," he said. "Good job."

I nodded. "Thanks."

"I know you, and I know you're going to go all humble on us here, but you made a damn tough shot under very difficult circumstances and in so doing, you almost certainly saved the lives of two friends of mine. So thank you."

"That goes for me, too," Gus said.

"Me, too." Said another officer. The other officers present all agreed.

I smiled and nodded. "Thanks," I said.

"We talked it over," Gus continued. "We decided that in a show of appreciation, we're going to go ahead and waive one of the lunches you owe us."

I smiled. "Gee, really?" I said. "That's touching."

"Well, hold on," he added, "before you get all blubbery on us, the lunch we're waiving—it's got to be one of the ones where it was your turn to pick. Not one of those where we get to pick," he looked at Dwayne. "Isn't that right."

Dwayne nodded. "That's it."

I chuckled. "Thanks a lot, guys," I said. "I know how hard that must have been for you two. I'll be sure and let Nancy know the depth of your gratitude."

"You bet," Gus said, nodding.

"By the way," Dwayne said, "there's a shitload of reporters downstairs. Unless you guys feel like holding a press conference, you might want to follow us. We know a secret way of getting out of here."

I looked at David, and he nodded. I turned back to Dwayne. "By all means," I said, "lead on."

When we were safely on our way, I closed my eyes and took a deep breath. Isabel was almost forgotten in the events of the past couple of hours; thoughts of her small, frail body being carried out on a stretcher having been pushed to the back of my mind. Now that things were at least a little back under control, I found myself thinking about her. I needed to get to the hospital. Toni was there waiting for me. I was suddenly very eager to see her and find out how Isabel was doing.

Chapter 30

DAVID DROVE ME back to my office, where I picked up the surveillance van. Toni'd had my Jeep towed to the dealership earlier in the afternoon. Apparently, they didn't have all the replacement parts, so it wouldn't be ready until next Monday or Tuesday. By the time I reached the University Medical Center at Montlake and Pacific, it was already past six. I called Toni on her cell and found out where they were. I hustled over to the surgery waiting room.

When I entered the room, I saw Toni sitting with Doc, Kelli, Julia, and Mary Webber. Toni got up and walked over to me as soon as she saw me. She hugged me tightly. I took a deep breath, smelling her hair and her makeup. For a moment, I felt like I was home, like I was safe, like the shitty events of the day weren't a part of me any longer.

"You alright?" she asked, pushing me back and holding me by my arms, studying me closely.

I nodded. "Yeah, I suppose. It's been a tough one."

She nodded. "Did it go okay with the police?"

"Yeah. Remember Harold Ohlmer?"

"The DA? Tall, silver-haired guy?"

"Yep." I explained how the interview had gone and how Harold had said that the DA wouldn't refer the case to the grand jury.

"Bastards better not," Toni said.

I smiled. "How's Isabel?"

Toni glanced toward the nurses' station. "She's out of surgery, but she's still in the recovery room. She had a partially ruptured spleen that was causing internal bleeding. She has some sort of infection and some sort of immune system reaction—they call it sepsis. Oh, and she also had a broken arm."

"Jeez," I said. "Anything else?"

She shrugged. "I don't know. They seem pretty close-lipped around here."

"She's not conscious yet? No one's talked to her?"

Toni shook her head. "I don't know. None of us have been able to talk to her. But I don't know if she's awake yet or not. They won't let us back to see her."

I made sure that Mary couldn't hear, and then I asked, "Is she going to be okay?"

Toni looked at me, and I saw tears start to form in her eyes. "They don't know," she said. "From what they said, sepsis is really dangerous. She's bad, Danny."

I felt like a huge weight had just hit me in the chest, and it wasn't just because I hated to see Toni hurting. Fact is, I'd never even stopped to consider that after we rescued Isabel from Donnie Martin that she still might not be out of the woods. I guess I'd assumed that she would be okay physically, aside from being beat up while she was held captive. The notion that she might have been beaten nearly to death was a blow.

I looked over at Mary. Her hands were clutched tightly around a tissue. She stared at the ground, not looking around, not saying anything. Kelli sat on one side of her, with Julia on the other, holding her hand. From time to time, one or the other spoke to her. Mary nodded, but didn't speak. "How's Mary holding up?" I asked.

"She's in shock," Toni said.

Understandable. "How about Kelli?"

"She's good. She's trying to be strong for Mary. You know," she said, "I told her that you volunteered to keep looking for Isabel, even without pay. She didn't need to go out and try to be a hero."

I shrugged. "Don't be too hard on her. She took action. She did what she thought she needed to do."

"She could've gotten herself killed."

I smiled. "She didn't. She's safe. Isabel's rescued. Soon, Isabel will be better. Trust me."

Toni looked at me for a moment, and then she smiled. "I do," she said. "I do trust you."

I nodded. "Good. You better." I hugged her again. While I was holding her, I looked over to the group. "I think I'd better go talk to them," I said.

Toni nodded. I walked over. Julia smiled at me when she saw me. When Kelli noticed me, she got up and walked over to meet me. She stopped when she was a couple of feet away. "Danny," she said. "I'm so sorry." Tears filled her eyes.

I looked at her for a moment, and then I smiled. "Come here," I said. She rushed over to me and we hugged.

"I was so afraid for Isabel," she said. "I didn't know what would happen to her if you guys stopped looking."

"It's alright," I said. "For the record, we weren't quite ready to give it up. We had a pretty good idea where Isabel had to be, but we needed more evidence to get the police involved. We were frustrated, but we weren't done. But then when you went out on your own undercover investigation, well then we didn't have a choice. We had to stay in then—all the way in."

"I'm sorry," she said again.

I smiled. "It's alright. Really. Hunting for you allowed us to uncover another few leads that made it so that we could bring the police in. So I guess I'd have to say that you made a difference." I paused, and then I added, "But if you want to become a private investigator—a real one—then come and talk to Toni and me first. We'll help you out. Meanwhile, no more playing Nancy Drew on your own. Got it?"

She nodded.

"Good. Now we just have to say our prayers for Isabel."

She nodded again. "I've already started," she said.

* * * *

Twenty minutes later, we were all still seated in the waiting room, hoping to hear something, anything, from Isabel's doctors. Suddenly, Kelli's eyes opened wide. "Oh, shit," she said, quietly. "What's he doing here?"

I turned and saw Tracey Webber enter the waiting room. Like the last time I'd seen him, he was wearing dark blue uniform pants and a light blue, short-sleeved uniform shirt—untucked and greasy. His face was red—he looked like he might be drunk. *Great.* He stood at the entrance, looking for someone—Mary, I suppose. He didn't look happy.

I glanced over and saw that Toni'd seen him, too. She immediately jumped up and walked toward him. *Uh-oh.* She had a look in her eye. This could end badly.

"What are you doing here, asshole?" Toni demanded as she crossed the room. As I'd feared, she decided to skip the niceties. The nurse on duty took one look at the developing situation and immediately reached for her phone.

Tracey, as seemed to be his habit, was a little slow to catch on. His eyes scanned the room, pausing momentarily when he saw Kelli and me.

"I'm here because my stepdaughter's in the hospital," he said. "They said she was here." His eyes continued to search the room. "Where's my wife?"

"It's thanks to you that Isabel's here in the first place, ass-bag," Toni said. She now stood right in front of him.

"What?" he said, his head spinning back to look at her. "What'd you say?" he demanded.

"Tracey, go home."

His head popped up and his eyes locked on Mary.

"What?"

"Go home, Tracey," Mary said again as she walked toward him.

"What the hell's going on around here, Mary? Why are all these people here?"

She didn't answer. The silence lingered for a few seconds, and then Tracey, apparently tired of waiting, said, "Fuck that," his anger rising. "I drove all the way down here from Lynnwood. I'll go home when I'm good and goddamn ready."

Doc stood up at the same time I started walking toward Tracey.

"Hey," I called out. "Big guy."

He turned and looked at me. "You know, I didn't like it the last time you called me that, Mr. Private Investigator. And I don't like it now. What do you want?"

"Sorry about that," I said, smiling. "I'm not trying to piss you off." I was nearly to him now. I stopped and leaned toward him and spoke quietly. "If you want to know the truth, I'm actually trying to save you."

"Save me? From what?" he asked, derisively.

"I'm trying to save a big guy like you from getting his ass kicked in public by a woman maybe half your size." I nodded toward Toni. She was about an eighth of a second away from going nuclear and dropping this asshole, right there in the waiting room. As it was, I halfway expected to see a Doc Marten come flying through the air any second, aimed right at his nose. "She's really pissed."

"Fuck that," he said. "Why's everyone so pissed at me, anyway? What'd I do?"

"Really?" I said. He'd have been better off following Mary's advice and leaving. Now I was getting pissed, too. "You're going to stand there and say 'what'd I do' when your stepdaughter is inside there, fighting for her life?" I said. "You're a real piece of work."

"Fuck you, buddy," he said. "I don't care what you think."

"I'm sure you don't," I said. "But when all's said and done, everyone knows you're the reason Isabel's lying in there on a hospital bed. Turns out, big strong guy like you—you've got a thing for little girls, right?" Uh-oh. Now I felt myself getting into the windup. This sensation usually signals my last chance to exercise restraint and control in emotional situations like these.

Fuck that. I was pissed.

So was he. His eyes were filled with anger now. Good.

"And Isabel was right there, right? Every night when you got home, right? You're one sick bastard, big guy." We stood staring at each other, each hating the other. I was aware that he was two inches taller than I was and maybe fifty pounds heavier. *Too bad.* That wasn't going to help him. I spoke, more quietly this time. "I'm hoping you get busted soon, for your own good. Because if you don't, you're going to need to watch out for me. I know all about you. And I will never forget about this. Never. Meanwhile, do yourself a favor—maybe your last one. Take a hike. No one wants to see your sorry ass around here now. And you're damn sure not getting anywhere near Isabel."

How about that? I was proud of my self-control.

"Is that right?" he said, puffing himself up even further. "Who's going to stop me? You?" He nodded toward Toni. "Her?"

"They won't need to."

Everyone turned and looked at the new voice. Nancy Stewart had just walked out of the swinging doors that led to the recovery room. Tyrone Allison and two uniformed officers flanked her. Tyrone had a big white bandage taped to his scalp. At the same time, three hospital security guards rounded the corner and entered the room from the main entrance. "Tracey Allen Webber," Nancy said, walking up to us. "My name is Lieutenant Nancy Stewart, Seattle Police Department Vice and High Risk Victims Unit." She held up her badge. "I'm placing you under arrest for second-degree rape, statutory rape, child endangerment—and whatever else I can think of to charge you with."

Tracey looked at her, stunned. "What?" he said. "That's bullshit."

"Nope," she said, "It's real. Why don't you go ahead and turn around and put your hands on the wall."

He stared at her but didn't move.

"Now!" she said, using her command voice.

This time, he complied.

"Read him his rights, Ty," she said, as she patted him down and put handcuffs on him. When Ty was through, she turned Tracey around.

"This is bullshit," he said again. "I never touched her."

"We've been talking to her for the past forty-five minutes," Nancy said. "She's a very sick girl, but she managed to tell us everything. Every sordid detail—right down to your so-called birthday present and her decision to run."

Mary let out a sob. "You bastard!" she screamed.

"She's lying," Tracey said. "She's sixteen years old. She's full of stories."

"Really?" Nancy walked right up to him. Nancy is maybe five four, and Webber is six four or so. Nancy stopped just far enough away so that she could look up at him. "You listen to me, you ignorant piece of human excrement," she said. "That girl ran away from you—her stepfather— because you repeatedly raped her. You were supposed to be someone she could trust. Instead, you violated her in the worst way possible. So she ran. And she ended up with people who were at least as bad as you— maybe even worse, if that's possible. When she refused to put herself on the street and sell her body for them, they beat her up. Donnie Martin beat her with a hose. He kicked her in the stomach over and over until she lost consciousness. He kicked her so hard, he ruptured her spleen." She paused. She was steaming mad. "And he kicked her so hard that she lost the baby she was carrying."

Oh my God. I glanced over at Mary. Her eyes were squeezed tightly shut. Everyone else's eyes, mine included, were wide open, stunned. The entire room was frozen.

"That's right," Nancy continued. "Little Isabel—all ninety-eight pounds of her—was almost three months pregnant. And for the last week, since Donnie Martin almost beat her to death, she's been carrying a dead fetus in her body. And you know what that means, right?"

He looked at her with a dull expression.

"That means that we have a DNA source, asshole. We're going to match up the DNA from the fetus to a sample that you're going to give us. And what do you think we're going to find? What do you think it's going to tell us about who the father of that baby was? And since Isabel was three months pregnant yet only turned sixteen last month, it means she was underage at conception. Face it, buddy. You need to pack your bags. You're going on a little trip."

He stared at her for a moment more, and then he dropped his eyes. Julia put her arm around Mary as she sobbed openly while Tracey was led away.

PART 4

Chapter 31

MY MOM AND dad saw the news coverage that evening, and before we'd even left the hospital, my phone started ringing. They were worried about me—I had to work hard to convince my mom that I was alright. In the end, we agreed to move my birthday dinner to the following week. I needed a little downtime. I'm lucky. I have people who care—always have. I thought about this in contrast to poor Isabel. Obviously, not everyone's as fortunate as I've been.

Toni stayed with me at my apartment that night after we left the hospital. We didn't do much of anything—mostly just talked a little, drank a few beers, listened to music, and watched the boats out on the lake. Except for talking about our concern for Isabel, the other events of the day never even came up. But the quiet, the relaxation were just what I needed as I came to grips with the shooting of Donnie Martin. She stayed with me that night and held me tight, all night long.

The next day, Saturday, June 16, was my birthday. Right after my run, we packed the Jeep and hit the road early. We took the Edmonds-Kingston ferry and then shot across Highway 3 until it ran into US 101. We turned north and drove all the way around past Port Angeles. We found a quiet spot on the north shore of Lake Crescent in the Olympic National Park, where I set us up a little camp. We fixed lunch, and then I played guitar and fished the rest of the day. Toni kicked back and read a book until she got tired of that, and then she came and sat by me and watched me catch the same three little trout over and over.

We didn't say much—just relaxed. We were content to simply listen to the sounds of nature on the lake, punctuated by the occasional *whizzz* of my spinning reel.

Talk about therapeutic. I can't imagine a better way to celebrate turning thirty.

By Sunday morning, thanks to the combination of Toni's quiet nurturing and the majestic setting, most of the damage to my soul was healed. Donnie Martin's shooting was safely tucked away in its proper place—sad, but necessary. Our thoughts and prayers were for Isabel. We packed up and hit the road after lunch and made it home by five.

Then, she left.

Not permanently, but she left. She went back to her apartment, and I went home to mine. After spending the past sixty hours with her, there was only one word to describe things around my place without her.

Empty.

* * * *

"Good morning, everyone," I said Monday at eight o'clock. "Hope you all had a great weekend."

We were assembled in the conference room for our staff meeting. Toni sat in her customary spot—at the opposite end of the table. She was completely dazzling this morning. She wore a long, pleated bright-yellow skirt with a royal blue sleeveless top that showed her tattoos in their full glory. Her four-inch heels made her almost as tall as me. She wore a deep-blue eye shadow that complemented her sparkling eyes. On each ear were three stud earrings—she didn't wear any nose piercings today (sometimes she does). She was simply stunning. She could stop an Amtrak train today.

"Very nice weekend, indeed," Richard said. "Maria and I took the ferry to Bainbridge. We had a pleasant Saturday afternoon on Main Street. What about you two?"

"We spent Saturday at Lake Crescent," I said.

"I watched Danny fish," Toni said.

"Sounds enjoyable," Richard said. I couldn't tell if he was serious or a touch sarcastic.

Toni cocked her head and thought for a second. "Actually, it was."

Cool.

"We stayed home and kicked back," Doc said.

I nodded. "Good deal. Where's Kenny?" I asked. His customary chair across from Doc was empty.

"I'm here," Kenny said, smiling, as he entered the conference room. He was carrying a pink box. "Sorry I'm late. I stopped off at Top Pot and got some donuts."

Toni beamed. "Kenny!" she said, "Top Pot! What a nice thing to do. Did you get apple fritters?"

Kenny stopped, and the smile left his face. "I—I—," I thought he was going to say, "I forgot," when he suddenly smiled again. "Of course I did," he said. "Gotcha!"

I don't eat donuts, which is fine since Toni can eat enough for both of us. She loves apple fritters. She works out at the gym or at the Krav Maga studio three or four nights a week to maintain her conditioning and her figure. She waited eagerly as Kenny went to his seat and set the box on the table.

He reached to open the box when Toni suddenly said, "I'll get it." She shot out her hand and slid the box in front of her.

"Well, you don't have to be pushy about it," Kenny said, giving in.

Toni smiled as she unlatched the box and flipped the lid open, and then all hell broke loose.

Toni screamed and pushed back from the table so fast that her chair fell over backward when she stood up. She knocked her teacup over, and it spilled on the table and dripped onto the floor. I was sitting at the other end of the conference table and couldn't see what was happening, so I jumped up as well. I could feel the adrenalin surging through my body. I moved to the side so that I could see over the lid into the box of donuts.

At that moment, an enormous, black, hairy tarantula stepped gracefully across the top of an apple fritter to the edge of the box and stopped. It waved an arm in Toni's direction as it looked for a place to take another step.

"Oh my God!" Toni said. Her eyes were wide open—she had a look of abject horror on her pale face as she stared at the spider. She tried to retreat further from the table, but her chair was blocking her way.

"What the—?" I started to say, when Kenny suddenly burst out laughing.

I looked at him, then at the spider, then back at him.

Toni glanced quickly at Kenny, then looked back at the spider, which was still in the same position, waving at her, apparently unable to figure out how to get down from the top of the box to the table.

"Did you—?" Toni sputtered.

Kenny laughed hysterically, nodding his head up and down. "I got you!" he managed to say, tears starting to run down his face.

"You got me?" she asked, incredulously. "You got me? You put a spider in the donuts?"

Kenny was still nodding. "I did," he managed to say, stopping his laughing long enough to answer. "Still want an apple fritter?" He started laughing uncontrollably again. He was barely able to stand.

I looked over at Doc. He was doing his best not to laugh, but he looked like he was about to blow any second. Even Richard was chuckling to himself.

I relaxed and shook my head and started to laugh.

"You little bastard," Toni said, regaining her senses, the start of a smile on her face.

"I got you," Kenny said.

Toni kept a wary eye on the spider, but she nodded. "Okay," she said, nodding slowly. "You win. This one."

"What do you mean 'this one'?" Kenny said. "I owed you. Now we're even."

Toni looked at him. "You think?"

"Yeah, we're even."

She smiled a wicked, nasty smile that probably should have scared him. "You're right," she said, with false sweetness. "We are even." She looked up at him. "And you don't have anything to worry about."

"Uh-oh for you, dude," Doc said to Kenny. "I told you she'd be pissed—payback's a bitch."

I smiled. "What are you going to do with that thing now?" I asked.

Doc reached over and placed his hand flat in front of the spider. The tarantula, looking like he'd been standing on a curb waiting for a taxi, immediately stepped aboard.

"Eeww!" Toni said.

"Guess he's tired of donuts," Doc said. He looked at Kenny. "You still got the cage in your office?"

"Great," I said. "Let's get this crap cleaned up, and we'll try this again at 8:15."

* * * *

Fifteen minutes later, the spider was safely back in his cage in Doc's office. Turns out he belonged to one of Pri's nephews. Doc had been babysitting when Kenny came over and was inspired by the possibilities. He actually paid fifty dollars to *rent* the spider.

We reassembled back in the conference room, where Toni had cleaned everything up.

"That was fun," I said, smiling, after we were all seated.

"Oh, bucket loads," Toni said. "Good prank." Kenny wore a smug smile, satisfied with himself.

"We all done with the fun and games? Okay. Moving on to business," I said. As soon as I had everyone's attention, I started. "First off, I checked this morning before I came in. No news on Isabel. She's still listed in critical condition in ICU."

"Do they know what the problem is?" Kenny asked.

"They say her miscarriage led to an infection. Her body reacted badly to the infection, and it triggered a condition called sepsis. Sepsis is apparently very serious."

Doc said, "Pri says that with sepsis, it might take a week or maybe more before they'll even know for sure if she can pull through. Even then, she could be hospitalized for maybe a month."

"Well, say your prayers for her," I said. "Isabel's been through too much as it is."

We spent the rest of the meeting outlining our duties and roles in the upcoming Ferguson and Sons surveillance job. The retainer check had arrived in the mail over the weekend—just in time to keep me from having to dip into the reserves. We were scheduled to begin installing hidden cameras later that evening. It would be nice to have things back to normal.

* * * *

After the meeting, I called Toni into my office. I closed the door when she came in.

"Uh-oh," she said, smiling, as we sat down. "Am I getting fired?"

"Nope," I said. "I wanted to talk to you alone."

"What? You didn't get your fill of me over the weekend?" she asked.

I smiled and shook my head. "No. How 'bout you? You sick of me yet?"

"You kidding? I can barely stand you."

I smiled. "You look really pretty today."

She smiled. "Thank you," she said. She paused and then said, "Just today?"

"Let me rephrase. You look beautiful. Every day."

"Why, thank you."

I continued. "Yesterday, when I got home, I had the chance to do some thinking," I said.

"In addition to all the other thinking you did over the weekend," Toni said.

"Will you stop and let me finish?"

"Sorry."

I looked at her. "I was with you all weekend long and an hour after you'd left, I found myself missing you."

"Go figure," she said.

"Exactly. So I started asking myself 'what's up with that?' See, whenever I've been with someone in the past, and I knew that they'd be leaving soon—well, that was pretty much a good thing. A relief. I'm a pretty private guy, and I like my space. Now, though, with you—I'm to the point where just knowing you're going to be leaving—like yesterday afternoon—well, it really sucks. And you actually leaving—like last night—well, that's even worse. I don't like it."

She smiled. "So you're saying you like me?"

"No," I said. I stood up and walked over to her. "I'm saying it took us five years to get together. Silly me. But it's only taken me three months to realize that I've fallen in love with you. I'm flat crazy about you, Toni. And I think I'm getting more that way every day. That's it."

She smiled and stood up. "So you're saying—"

"I love you, Toni."

She looked at me, and her eyes started to moisten. Then she smiled. "Me, too," she said, quietly. "I love you, too, Danny Logan."

I stepped forward and took her in my arms. We hugged for a solid minute, saying nothing. Then I pushed back just far enough to kiss her softly.

"Wait," I said after a few seconds. "I'm not done. I wanted to give you a present."

"A present?" she said, sniffling, "This is good. Presents are good."

I turned and picked up a small box on my desk. I handed it to her.

"Whoa. What's this?" she asked, looking at me warily.

"Open it and find out."

She fiddled with the lid, got it off, and then pulled out a shiny gold key. She held it up, knowing immediately what it was.

"When you're over at my place," I said, "I don't want to have to suddenly start worrying anymore about you leaving to go home. I want you to already be home. Us—together."

She looked at me. "Are you sure you're ready for that?" she asked.

I nodded. "I am definitely ready. I want you to move in with me. I want us to be together."

She was quiet for several seconds. Then she said, "I've been thinking about this, too. Maybe you'd better sit back down."

Oh, shit. That didn't sound good. Could I have misjudged this thing really badly? I took a seat.

"Here's the deal," she said. "Call me old-fashioned, but I don't want to live together, at least not for real, unless we're married. And—before you get alarmed," she said, "this is not a ploy to get you to propose." She smiled. "Believe me, we're not ready to get married. Maybe sometime in the future, but not today."

I hadn't even thought about marriage. Well, that's not entirely true. I'd thought about it a little. Then, I had started feeling overwhelmed, so I'd come up with a brilliant solution–I decided not to think about it anymore. And now, maybe Toni was right. As usual. Maybe it was still be too early. Things were already moving fast between us. Maybe moving in together now would be too fast.

"Besides–I like my independence," she continued. "I'm not saying I don't enjoy my time with you—I love it, actually, but I don't know if I'm ready to totally give my independence up yet. Obviously, I'm not seeing anyone else. But I don't want to screw this up between us, you know?"

I nodded.

"So," she said, "I have a counterproposal for you."

"What's that?"

"I'll keep your key," she said. "And I'll put it on my ring. But I'm not going to move in with you. At least not formally. I'm going to keep my apartment. That way, I can always tell myself that we don't live together. At least technically, anyway. Case anyone asks, you live on Lake Union—I live in Fremont. If you piss me off—just in case—then I'll still have somewhere to go. Separate."

I started to talk, but she cut me off.

"But I will start moving some things over. This afternoon. And I will start staying with you at your place. At least some of the time. How's that?"

I was sitting down, and still, my head was spinning. The first thing I felt was immense relief—relief that she wasn't flat-out turning me down like I'd started to think. And on the heels of that relief, I felt elation. My heart soared. Toni Blair was going to start moving in with me. I smiled. "I can live with that," I said. Part-time Toni is better than no Toni at all.

She smiled back at me. "Deal, then."

We both stood up and stepped toward each other. I took her in my arms and held her tightly. "Besides," she said, "the view at your apartment's a lot better than the view at mine."

She was looking over my shoulder, out the window. "The lake *is* nice," I said.

She smiled and leaned back so that she could kiss me. "I'm not talking about the lake, you big dope. I'm talking about you."

Epilogue

Sunday, August 19, 2012
10:45 a.m.

THE CONGREGATION AT the Twenty-Third Street Baptist Church spoke quietly to each other as they waited for the sermon to begin. They fanned themselves with hymnals and church bulletins in an effort to keep cool. The church's ancient air conditioner was working hard, but it was questionable as to whether the air conditioner actually conditioned the air or had given up at some point and simply acted as a large, somewhat noisy fan. But even if it didn't work well, it was worth a try, since even at the early hour, it was already in the low eighties outside. The people crowded inside needed all the help they could get.

A tall, thin, distinguished-looking black man approached the lectern. He wore a simple black Geneva gown over a blue long-sleeved shirt with a black tie. He was a handsome man, middle-aged with tinges of gray beginning to show in his short hair. Already, his face glistened with sweat. When he stepped up and gripped the lectern, the church became quiet except for the rumble of the air conditioner and the ruffle of the handheld fans. "Thank you all for coming together on this fine Sunday morning," Reverend Arthur Jenkins said as he looked out across his congregation.

"You all know why we're here today." His deep baritone voice, though not raised, reached into the furthest recesses of the old church. "There's an ugliness in our community—a sin that is an abomination in the eyes of the Lord. Right here, not one-quarter mile from the doors of this blessed church, there are young boys growing up without moms, growing up without dads, growing up without the guidance and moral structure that any small child needs to mature into a righteous man in the eyes of the Almighty. Some of these people are known to have committed some of the most heinous, the most brutal, the most depraved crimes imaginable. Brothers and sisters, these men are literally stealing innocent young children from our community and placing them in servitude to the depraved lust of grown men. They're taking these innocent children, enslaving them, plying them with drugs, and turning them out onto the street as prostitutes for their own financial benefit." Reverend Art's voice began to rise now. "They use these children up, they chew them up, and when they're finished with them, why, they toss them out just like day-old trash. No second thoughts." He looked around at the members of his congregation. "And just what do you suppose happens then? What happens to a fifteen-year-old girl who's been made to be a prostitute for four years—who's been made to have sexual relations with *thousands* of men in that period of time? What happens to that girl then?"

He paused. "Brothers and sisters, I want to tell you all a story this morning. It's a story about a girl named Isabel Delgado who went through this very experience. When the men—men from right here in this area—when those who held her decided it was time for her to go sell her body for them—well, she didn't go along. No. She revolted. God gave her the strength to say, 'No, I will not!'" His voice thundered across the church. He paused for several seconds, and then he continued, "Now you must understand, brothers and sisters, that Isabel was sixteen when this happened to her—she was older than the children these men normally like to work with. Yes, even though Isabel may have been small of stature, she was tall in self-conviction. Isabel had courage. She told these men no. So they decided to teach her a lesson. These degenerate men took turns raping her. When they'd had their fill, they started in on beating her. They beat her half to death with a hose. They hit her so hard that they broke her arm. But that wasn't enough, no! Then, they kicked her. The animals!" He was nearly yelling now. "These animals kicked that girl so hard they ruptured her spleen. They kicked her so hard that they killed the child that she was carrying from a previous rape! Sixteen years old and they beat her so bad, she had a miscarriage! When they were finished, when they'd had enough, they locked her in a basement and decided that since she still wouldn't agree to do what they wanted, they'd just go ahead and sell her. Sell her! Brothers and sisters, I thought slavery been dead and gone for 150 years!"

He took a breath as he looked from person to person. "I'm going to ask you some hard questions, and I'm not asking for a show of hands because some of you would be embarrassed. Just look in your heart instead. How many of you know somebody who's involved in this sordid business? Some of these men are from around here. You know that. How many of you have received any money from these immoral, degenerate men? If you have, I want you to seek forgiveness from the Lord almighty. I tell you right here and now, brothers and sisters, you will not pass through to eternal salvation with this stain on your souls. No, sir. You will not! You need to choose sides and take a stand and, brothers and sisters, if you're involved in this, you need to do it fast. You can trust me on this—you do not want to suddenly meet your maker with this item unresolved. You need to take a stand."

"Amen," said several people in the congregation, nodding their heads in agreement.

Reverend Art took a drink from a water glass on the lectern before he continued. "Like I said before, some of these immoral, degenerate men participating in this abominable activity are from right around here. You all knew these boys when they were kids." He looked from face to face. "Some of you know them now. If *any* of you know any of these men, now that you understand what they're doing, there's no reason for you not to come forth and seek to stop it. Talk to them! Tell them to stop their sinning! Tell them they must turn to God. It's up to you, my brothers and sisters! You need to take a stand!"

"Amen!" The audience was more enthusiastic now.

"For those of you with young children, you need to know that they are at risk! You need to gather those young children to you and nurture them and love them and protect them from these degenerates. There are monsters out there, and they are after your children! Don't let them slide down the slippery slope of sexual enslavement—either as a slave or as a slave master. You need to take a stand!"

"Amen!" the members of the congregation stood and roared their agreement.

Reverend Art allowed the people to retake their seats. "That's what this is about," he said, more conversationally now. "It's about taking a stand. Taking a stand and making a difference in the life of a young child." It grew quiet for a few seconds.

"What about Isabel?" a congregation member suddenly called out.

Reverend Art looked at the woman. "What about Isabel Delgado?" he said. "What became of the girl who was so horribly abused?"

At that moment, the congregation gasped as Kelli Blair pushed a wheelchair carrying her friend Isabel Delgado from around the curtain behind the lectern. She pushed her to the center of the church, just in front of the altar. Kelli placed her hand on Isabel's shoulder and then leaned forward and whispered into her ear.

Isabel sat up straight and smiled and waved shyly at her mother, who was seated in the front row of the congregation.

"Despite the horror that this girl had to endure," Reverend Art said, "Isabel is one of the lucky ones. She fought back. And after a long battle, she's winning."

Kelli helped Isabel slowly rise to her feet.

The congregation collectively gasped and then rose to their feet and started clapping. From the second row, Danny Logan reached over and took his partner, Toni Blair's hand. Both had tears in their eyes. Danny turned to her. "She made it," he said.

Toni nodded. "Thanks to you," she said.

Logan pursed his lips and shook his head. "Thanks to Kelli. Thanks to us." He paused. "Mostly, thanks to God and thanks to Isabel herself. She's a fighter."

When the congregation calmed, and everyone retook their seats, Reverend Art continued. "God has sent us Isabel to show us the resiliency of the human spirit—," Reverend Art's voice boomed, "and the courage of the human heart." He paused. "And now," he looked around, "now it's in your hands. It's up to you to take up her cause. Take a stand, brothers and sisters! Take a stand for Isabel and for all God's children just like her."

* * * *

Author's Notes

I'm a storyteller, and I don't think it's my role to "preach from the pages." That said, I'd be lying if I said I didn't have an agenda with *Isabel's Run*. My goal from the start was to spin a Danny Logan story that was entertaining and, at the same time, would shed light on the national tragedy that is the exploitation—enslavement, really—of underage children in the sex trades right here in this country. The FBI estimates that there are more than 100,000 American children currently being victimized in this horrible manner. Average age when they start: eleven years old. It's enough to make you cry. In my opinion, not nearly enough is being said or done about it.

In the words of Reverend Art, I urge you to take a stand. Have a look at the website for the National Center for Missing and Exploited Children at www.missingkids.com or the FBI Innocence Lost Task Force website at http://www.fbi.gov/about-us/investigate/vc_majorthefts/cac/innocencelost/.

Acknowledgments

Isabel's Run required a great deal of research and specialized information, which I was fortunate to obtain through the efforts of the following people I'd like to acknowledge:

To Dr. John Kremer, for helping to keep my presentation of medical topics accurate.

To Gabe Robinson, for helping to identify and bring out the real story hidden in the jumble of words that was my original effort.

To Brynn Warriner and Carrie Wicks, for helping me take what I (mistakenly) hoped was a finished manuscript to a manuscript that is now really finished—a humbling but necessary experience. Brynn and Carrie both work in Seattle; they also provided sound advice and assistance on specifics of the novel's Seattle setting.

To Ellen Johnson, Casey Jacobs, Dennis Doppe, and Jennifer Norton for reading early versions of *Isabel's Run* and providing valuable feedback.

Finally, as always, to my wife, Michelle, for her constant support in this and all my other endeavors.

About the Author

M.D. Grayson is the author of the Danny Logan mystery series including (so far) *Angel Dance*, *No Way to Die*, and new *Isabel's Run*. He lives on an island near Seattle with his wife Michele and their three German shepherds.

Before becoming a full-time writer, Mr. Grayson worked in the construction industry, as an accountant for six l-o-n-g weeks (square peg/round hole), and as a piano player on the Las Vegas strip. When he's not writing, he loves zooming about on two wheels, bicycles and motorcycles alike. In addition, he's a pilot, a boater, and an accomplished musician—always ready for a jam session!

Connect Online:

Blog: http://www.mdgrayson.com
Twitter: http://twitter.com/md_grayson
Facebook: http://facebook.com/mdgraysonauthorpage

Also by M.D. Grayson:

In the Danny Logan series debut, beautiful Seattle business heiress Gina Fiore has vanished without a trace. Desperate for help, her family turns to Danny Logan, Gina's former boyfriend, to find her and bring her home safely. Logan is a fifth-generation Seattle native who owns Logan Private Investigations. Along with his associates Antoinette "Toni" Blair, Kenny Hale, and Joaquin Kiahtel, he accepts the case and begins the hunt for Gina.

Logan and his team dig for clues and soon find that they're not the only ones looking for Gina. The Tijuana-Mendez drug cartel is keenly interested in her whereabouts, as is the Calabria crime family from Chicago. The race is on to locate Gina—the stakes could not be higher. In order to prevail, Logan's going to need all the skill and luck he can gather, and he's going to need to confront the unresolved feelings he still has for Gina—feelings that might just get him killed!

Why would renowned mathematician Thomas Rasmussen drive to Discovery Park at six-thirty on a dark, rainy morning, put a .357 magnum to his head and pull the trigger? The police say the evidence is conclusive - it was definitely a suicide. But that made no sense to his wife, Katherine. Thomas had everything to live for. So she did what people in Seattle do when they need help on matters such as these. She turned to Danny Logan and Logan Private Investigations for answers.

Logan, along with his associates Antoinette "Toni" Blair, Joaquin "Doc" Kiahtel, and Kenny Hale roll into action, determined to find out what really happened. Did Thomas die by his own hand? Or was he murdered? Either way: why? The answer to these questions would only be found at the end of a trail full of lies, conflicting evidence, and extreme danger. But one thing was certain: alone in a car in a dark parking lot in the rain is No Way to Die